Praise for the *Tempest Blades: The Root of Hope*

"An explosion of action, world building, hope, and intro-
spection, Ricardo's Tempest Blade series is a non-stop
rollercoaster ride as the characters battle otherworldly
creatures, and their own insecurities. This series has everything a modern fantasy fan will enjoy: gods, monsters,
magic, spaceships, high powered heroes, and sentient
swords. All with an anime twist."
Alan Bailey, *If This Goes On* podcast

"*The Root of Hope* is an astounding tale of love, hope, re-
venge, and belief. The sacrifices made by the characters
makes the story all the richer. The Tempest Blades is a series
unlike any other."
Jodie Crump, Witty and Sarcastic Bookclub

Other Books by Ricardo Victoria

Tempest Blades Series:
The Withered King
The Curse Titans
The Magick of Chaos
The Root of Hope

Other Titles:
Green New Worlds: A Quick Guide to Sustainability through Science Fiction and Fantasy
(as Ricardo Victoria-Uribe).
Co-authored with Martha Elba González-Alcarez.

Diseño emocional aplicado.
Una guía para proyectos de diseño
Ricardo Victoria-Uribe & Marco Antonio García-Albarrán

TEMPEST BLADES
THE ROOT OF HOPE

By
Ricardo Victoria

Shadow Dragon Press

ISBN: 978-1-951122-93-5 (paperback)
ISBN: 978-1-951122-94-2 (ebook)
LCCN: 2024933271
Copyright © 2024 by Ricardo Victoria

Cover Illustration: Salvador Velázquez
Logo Design: Cecilia Manzanares & Salvador Velázquez
Cover Design: Ricardo Victoria & Salvador Velázquez

Shadow Dragon Press
9 Mockingbird Hill Rd
Tijeras, New Mexico 87059
www.shadowdragonpress.com
info@shadowdragonpress.com

Follow Ricardo at: https://ricardovictoriau.com/

Content Notice: There is a scene in the book that relates to miscarriage. There are discussions of PTSD and the repercussions of this ailment. Also, there is a lot of violence against a demon, but he totally deserves it.

THE FIGARO MARK III

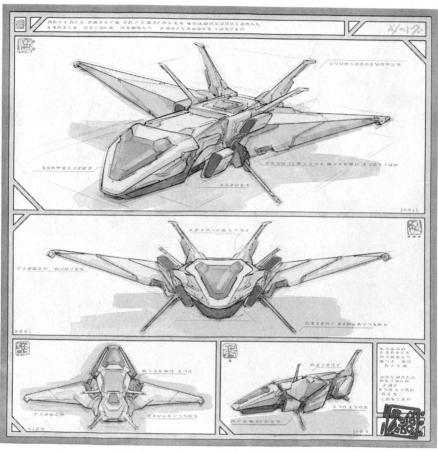

Acknowledgments

To everyone that made this journey with me.
To those that helped with it.
To those that left it before its time.

Timeline

The Heroic Age (from 180 years ago to current time) Year 1820 After Death of the Dragons (ADoD) to Present

1820: The magick field regenerates. Powerful Magi are born. The Society of Wanderers is created. Yokoyawa (Yoko) is born in the Samoharo Hegemony.

1844: Fraog finds the Silver Horn and takes it to the Humbagoo Forest deep into the Mistlands to stop a reopening of the Gates containing the Wyldhunt. Siddhartha (Sid) is born in the Samoharo Hegemony.

1850: Fraog meets Hikaru the Demonhunter.

1852: Fraog meets and marries the Freefolk Dawnstar, the last of the Wind Tribe

1855: Izia is born in Skarabear.

1856: Fionn is born.

1861: The remaining members of the Wind Tribe of the Freefolk are chased away from their ancestral lands by the Silver Fangs. Fraog dies, Dawnstar settles her family in Skarabear with the help of Hikaru.

1863: Ywain is found as a baby, later to be adopted by CastleMartell. It's later found that he was born a Gifted. Hikaru trains Fionn and Izia.

1866: Hikaru disappears during a Demonhunter mission.

1868: The Blood Horde attacks Ionis. The Great War begins.

1872: A scouting cell of the Blood Horde attacks Skarabear. Fionn finds and reclaims Black Fang and kills every member of the scouting party. King CastleMartell of Emerald Island plans the counterattack of the Blood Horde. The dreadnoughts start their construction at the behest of the newly formed Free Alliance between the Emerald Island and Portis.

1873: Fionn joins CastleMartell's army by killing a succubus. Izia joins the army a few weeks later. They are placed under Byron's command.

1874: Byron is corrupted by the Golden King's treasures, using his soul as avatar.

1875: The Great War hits its apogee. The Twelve Swords are created. Joshua destroys the last weapon stored in Carpadocci.

1879: Fionn and Ywain destroy the Onyx Orb. Fionn becomes Gifted.

1880: Signature of the Free Alliance Charter in Sandtown, including most of the city states of the Ionis continent and part of the Freefolk tribes. Fionn marries Izia, travels the continent.

1887: Ywain finds Byron's treachery. They fight and Ywain is presumed dead. The Secret Rebellion begins.

1888: King CastleMartell falls ill, Byron is ready to take the throne.

1889: Byron kills most of the Twelve Swords. Izia sacrifices herself to save Fionn and separate Byron's soul from his body. Fionn sleeps for a century.

1959: The Foundation is created.

1969 Harland is born.

1955: Korbyworld is built in the Coyoli Archipelago. The Dark Father secretly returns.

1979: Gaby is born.

1980: Alex is born.

1981: Kasumi is born.

1984: Sam is born.

1989: Harland's finds Fionn. Fionn finds and adopt Sam after the death of her parents.

1992: Gaby becomes Gifted and escapes the Sisters of Mercy.

1994: Sid is banished, starts building the Figaro.

1995: Alex becomes Gifted, first major demonic incursion takes place in ages.

2003: The A.I. Wanderer is developed by Esai, Alex's friend.

2005: The Withered King adventure takes place.

2007: The Cursed Titans adventure takes place.

2009: The Magick of Chaos adventure takes place. Kasumi becomes Gifted.

2010: The War in the South Ends, several small adventures take place. Joshua joins Hildebrandtia.

2011: The Root of Hope adventure begins.

Prologue
A World before Worlds

ONE NIGHT, AFTER A LONG trek through the lands of grass, blue flowers, and snow, our group stopped. Of the original tribes that began the trek after Noc, the elder that forged our alliance, was kidnapped by the First Demon, only a few remain with us. These lands were considered sacred and dangerous, for they were filled with ruins of ancient tall people, the same people I keep seeing as kaa'mani—ghosts as the human female, the Seer, called them. She and the other human leader, a male from Old Earth, decided to leave most of their group behind for safety, including their kindred, as they were small and rambunctious. The Prophet, a samoharo, came mostly alone, save for a couple of followers with him, carrying his large, black curved sword that sung to the stars. His metal birds that screamed into the air a distant image in my mind. And with me, only Yahel—my secret heartmate—and my childhood friend Marfel came with me. The elders were fearful that this newfound power of creating miracles was a bad omen, despite assurances by the Stranger that they were a blessing from the Mother of Warmth Water.

The four of us, the Prophet, the male human, the Seer, and myself, gathered around a fire away from the main camp. The male human wished to talk in secret about fears and concerns that shouldn't be shared with the volunteers.

As soon as we were warm enough, the human male asked us: Have you ever seen the creature we are tracking? Or their kind? Are there songs and tales about where it came from?

To this the Prophet, who rested on his side with his head

on his hand, said nothing, remaining in sad silence. I have heard songs about their mother world becoming dust in the dark.

To this, I said I knew nothing, for before the migration from our mother world through the gates made of light, I was a simple eldara that weaved baskets from reeds.

To this, the Seer replied that the same creature had been behind the destruction of Old Earth. And that the weapon it had used on their mother world, at the time when they were helping and protecting refugees as they entered their star ark, unleashed an invisible miasma, which she called radiation, and had given them a lethal disease that she called cancer. Because of that none of them would see their kindred grow. The human male explained their days were short now and that was why they had volunteered for the mission, as they knew there would be no return.

To this, I shook in fear, for a creature that powerful would crush this simple reed weaver. And then I recalled the stories and songs from the elders, telling us when our mother star became a dark eye surrounded by a ring of fire and the world became slow. I wondered if the creature had been the curse that changed our mother star into the corpse of fire.

And I cried in fear.

It was then that the Stranger spoke.

As in days before, their voice came first. It sounded both deep and forceful as the human male, and kind and sweet as the human female.

Then came the feathers of light that dissipated as soon as we touched them.

And from the darkness, with glowing eyes, came the Stranger. The being that brought us here from our mother worlds, that chose us for this quest. The one that blessed me with the change and the miracles. The one that looked like me.

The one that the humans called The Trickster, for they spoke of things to be, things to come, things to guess.

They were as mighty as the samoharo Prophet, who silently nodded their way, as if they were old friends, old relatives.

They seemed as indomitable as the human Seer that welcomed them with open arms for she was always friendly with the Stranger. And as indomitable as the human male that regarded them with suspicion.

Of me, a simple changeling girl, they only said that the freefolk—the name they gifted the eldara with—after me would be powerful. Maybe they would be powerful weavers of reeds.

The Stranger took a seat among us and sighed. Their visage shifted to match the human female Seer, but also shared eldara features, for we were genderless shapeshifters of grey skin and large colorful eyes. The Stranger smiled at me as if they could read my thoughts. They said that two of her own, her kindred, shaped after humans and eldara, would join us soon as our quest was near its end, as we were closer to the Tree that shone in the night with the light of the stars. Also we would need their help.

The Seer asked if that aid was related to the dreams of doom she suffered.

To this the Stranger said no word.

The human male asked his questions once more, for he had seen the creature before leaving their mother world, the last of his kind to leave Old Earth and come into the Great Ark that brought humans to this new mother world. He called the Stranger a Trickster, who played rousing songs. But his words were not filled with anger, but with fear, sadness, and piety. He asked for wisdom and comfort, to know he hadn't lost his mind, for the creature belonged to the ancient songs and tales of Old Earth and seeing it face to face had shattered his heart and broken their bodies.

To this, the Stranger sighed and acquiesced, acknowledging that from now on their name would be the Trickster, for it was penance for their many transgressions, of which they said nothing more.

The Trickster blew a sweet wind on the fire, and it changed its color, to match the rainbow, and inside it, images formed that matched their words.

They talked of a time before time had a meaning, before the humans sung their first words, before the samoharo chased their first star, before we swam the first wave. Of a World before Worlds, when the World of the Spirit, the World of the Thoughts, and the World of the Stuff were one, and only the ancient tall people lived there. They were what humans, and samoharo, and eldara called Gods.

It was a world where reality was made after thought and the miracles were made by all. A world where Kaan'a had went to sleep the sleep that dreamt the universe, and the Tree they had planted grew in blessings. In this world there was a brilliant ancient, tall person who cast a dark shadow in his wake. He led a group of inquiring minds who searched for the answers to the questions we all ask during the nights: who we are, where we came from, why we can choose. These questions had been raised to Kaan'a but they remained asleep and refused to answer, their voice saying only that the universe was and it was the fate of the ancient tall people to assign a value of things to existence.

But the brightest one rebelled, for he considered it ill-suited. Not enough. He sought more knowledge and tried to convince his siblings to aid him. The sibling of the paths refused, the sibling of the sword refused, the sibling of the undying fire remained silent, the sibling of the scythe left, and the sibling of the trumpet accepted, at first.

But when the sibling of the trumpet realized the folly in the plan of the brightest one, they advised against it. Kaan'a in punishment, erased the minds of all the siblings, but the brightest one was stronger than the deliverance.

The brightest one and his followers, thousands by now, built a Great Machine, that allowed them to peek beyond the veil of Kaan'a's dream, beyond the birth of universe. And what they saw brought them madness, for beyond the veil there was a dark void, where beings of incoherence that were begotten even before Kaan'a were trapped. And the brightest knew that they were at the beginning and the end of all things, only the Universe itself keeping them at bay in dreams.

And the brightest one knew insanity, for he and his followers began a war against his siblings, against the First Heaven, against Kaan'a themselves.

Thus, the Universe restored the minds and memories of the siblings and gifted them with knowledge. They awakened the ancient Aditis, machines from before time to use as weapons of protection.

But the brightest one had awakened his own Aditi, and to battle they went.

The conflict was terrible, for things died before being born, for things never were after long existence. Stars became dark eyes and dark eyes ate everything.

But as happens with siblings playing on the shore of the sea, a truce came to be, for one of the creatures threatened to escape. To this the siblings begged Kaan'a for forgiveness and help—and the Universe replied with a second birth. A new dream.

The World of Spirit, the World of Thought, and the World of Matter became separate from each other, three realms only tied together as three sticks, by a terrible tempest born of the friction between the three of them. And in the center of the three realms there was a mother world with a single star and a single moon with rings around it. There would reside the ancient tall people made flesh, punished to be mortals, their godly powers contained, forced to teach others that would be born in this new realm how to contact and dwell in the other two.

Above and below the three, two more worlds were created.

Above, a Last Heaven for the surviving Gods to reside and repair the Universe, as most were forbidden to enter the three realms aside dreams and nightmares, aside voices in the air and miracles unseen, for they took no part in the conflict.

Below, a world with no light, of brimstone and sulphur, thousands of layers deep, each layer a labyrinth designed to contain the worst of the rebels and those that would listen to them, but even more important, to contain the beings from before time, of incoherence, from reaching the Universe ever again.

All of these new realms connected by the Tree that symbolized hope and whose fruits were our very own souls. Its seeds, carried in a bag by the soul of an ancient hero dreamt by the Universe, would create new mother worlds where new living beings would evolve, for they were the answer against the beings of incoherence.

The brightest sibling, now the dark one with ruby eyes, became judge and jailer of all the new and old beings that would rise against their siblings again.

Of the other three siblings, one was sent to prophesize, one to guard, and the trumpet one, twin sister to the brightest one, to redeem herself by inspiring and teaching the old and new beings, aided by their kin, the ancient people.

One of the scythe became the gatekeeper between the Spirit and the Matter Worlds. For the friction there was the strongest once souls tried to travel between Worlds, creating a Tempest.

With time the ancient people grew small and passed away but were barred from entering the World of Spirit and the Last Heaven, until their transgressions were repaired tenfold. They became kaa'mani: Ghosts in their own world.

The siblings were gods themselves and truly tried to take better care of this new Universe dreamt by Kaan'a. However, a creature of incoherence briefly slipped through the cracks of its original prison during the war and corrupted a third of the rebels, for it had seen and tasted reality, and reality was painful. It swore to escape one day and destroy that reality, one mother world, one star at a time if needed, so there were no surviving seeds of the Tree. A day would come that the creature of incoherence would destroy the Tree itself and then reach Kaan'a in their sleep to murder them and end all things. So its own siblings could exist in a painless nothingness.

The Trickster became silent after this. She had adopted a form more like the human Seer or mine. We realized she was the sibling of the trumpet.

The Prophet only acknowledged, for he claimed that in his veins the blood of the sibling of the paths ran, and his mother world had been destroyed by followers of the creature. And the humans connected the destruction of Old Earth with the myths of their past, having witnessed the creature firsthand.

They were the ones that bestowed it the name of the First Demon.

But the Trickster called it Abaddon, the first destroyer.

And when Abaddon became one with the World of Matter he sought to capture Noc, the mortal that knew where the Tree was located, for Abaddon had destroyed many worlds and was closer to his goal. And Noc, while he looked human, and had lived among humans, was the last living ancient people. The Trickster called him Akeleth, the Messengers.

And then the Trickster stood up, revealing her form as Goddess, cracking the world, and said to the winds with many voices as one, that echoed into the air as trumpets: This has been agreed, as is above is below and my words are blessed by the Universe.

For the Blood of the Prophet runs among his children, the samoharo, travelers among the stars, making them blood of my blood, they are fit to fight Abaddon with fist and a sword made of Night Sky.

For the blood of Kaan'a and the stars runs in this simple girl, weaver of reeds, of the humble eldara of a lonely world, making her from now own weaver of reality. And she and those who follow her in her change, are fit to fight Abaddon with mind and a gemstone made of Life and Soul.

Then the Trickster looked at the human couple with sadness and said: For the blood of the akeleth shall run in the veins of all who follow you after this. For both are dying after saving their tribe. And I say, he is to be reborn now with the Gift, to be fit to fight Abaddon with heart and light made steel in his hands. And she is to be reborn to become Yaha, which means The Light of Hope.

The Prophet kneeled before the Trickster and cut his thumb, drawing blood and the drops of blood glowed like stars. He swore: My people will honor thy covenant, defending and guiding our younger allies in this quest. And its glow will resonate on every samoharo that joins the Covenant.

I knelt in pain as my body changed to be able to absorb the power of the stars. I saw for the first time the webs that made reality, matter, spirit, thought, and I saw I could weave them. But the pain was such that I screamed. Then two soft arms wrapped around me, for the Seer took me in her arms to share my pain in her already pained body, and we became soul and matter sisters. For my body began its slow change to become like hers, in almost all aspects but my large, colorful eyes, and her mind became similar to mine for she shared the sight of the web of reality. From then on Freefolk and Human were siblings, and I swore to teach both to weave reality.

The human male tried to kneel but instead collapsed as his ill body failed. Lighting struck him as the Trickster ordered one of the kaa'mani to merge with his dying body. He then rose as the first Gifted, embodiment of the elements of nature, lightning coming from his eyes. He swore that those of his kin that gave their lives for others will become one with the elements. And the Prophet said that of the Gifted, those that rode the storm, would be known from then on as Iskandar.

The Trickster whispered words into the ears of the Seer. Words that I heard but will never repeat. And the Seer's heart became filled with fear, determination, and hope in equal measures—for those words were of the future.

The Trickster's final words of that night still ring true today: For your three species have raised by their own will among the countless stars and shall achieve what we were unable to. For the Samoharo are mighty, the Freefolk are powerful, and the Humans are Indomitable. Together the three are Unstoppable. We the Akeleth, leave Reality in your hands.

As the two Moons appeared in the sky, the Round and the Long, portents of fate, the Trickster left, flying away in the shape of a bird the humans called 'raven.' And they hugged each other in tears, for their personal fate had been cast.

With the truth of our mission revealed, our hearts grew heavy. We remained silent, deep in our thoughts, for a truth had been unveiled and truth is always a difficult present to accept. Yet inside my heart I sensed our resolves grow firm, for while the creature was one made of multiple nightmares, our journey had become one of survival.

Excerpt taken from the remains of the
'Grimoire of Asherah'.
Part of the Ravenstone book collection.
Loaned to the Foundation for study by the
Freefolk Librarian Stealth Drakglass.
Translated to Core by Harland Rickman,
Professor Vivienne Ortiga, and
Hon. Samantha Ambers-Estel

Chapter 1
Of Victories and Defeats

*"It's not the journey that matters,
it's with whom you shared it."*
Belfrost's Open Concert Hall
Hildebrantia's Tour restart concert, sold out.

"ANXIOUS?" JOSHUA ASKED GABY AS his hands trembled.

Gaby stood in the wings, shaking her hands to get rid of the nerves, waiting for the signal. Her outfit was black leather pants with black leather boots, a blue crop-top with a sheer fabric covered in rhinestones below the neck. Over that, a silver jacket. Both wrists were covered with bracelets, including her silver heartmate engagement bracelet with dragonwolf and the pearl. It had been inspired by the one from her mental battle with the tovainar Gavito months ago, but in real life the engagement bracelet was tighter than she'd expected for some unforeseen reason. But there was nothing to be done for it now as she was about to take to her battlefield: an open-air concert.

A part of her—the Izia part, as Gaby now had access to all the memories and emotions of her previous life—was anxious about not being on the actual battlefield, which was kilometers away, deep in the Jagged Mountains. There her friends, her family, were about to do the craziest thing: launch a direct attack on the last base of the Golden King. But everyone was to play a role and hers was to offer a distraction, thanks to the concert being broadcast from Belfrost to the entire region via the recently repaired communications network. Given that her battlebard enhancing qualities traveled through the broadcast, in a way she would be participating, inspiring her found family and increasing their abilities.

Gaby's second reason was that it was almost certain that *he* would be watching the concert from the base. Not the Golden King, but one of his advisors, her own father. This was another reason she had opted out of the mission. It would be too personal for her, and beating the crap out of her man could prove distracting. It was already a risky plan, and they all knew it.

There was a third reason why everyone had voted for her to remain behind. She looked down at her belly and rubbed it with her right hand, smiling. It was a whole new sensation. From now on, but especially the next few months, she would have to be more careful when it came to the heroic side of her life. Which was also the reason Hildebrandtia had added a new member, making it now a five-person band instead of four. Of course, the new band member also moonlighted as her personal bodyguard in case someone tried something during the concert. Which had made her nervous, but not as much as it affected the new guitarist.

"Not as much as you, apparently," Gaby replied with her crooked smile.

"It's my first concert as a new member of Hildebrandtia. I never played in public," Joshua admitted, as a small flame threatened to set fire to his instrument. "Not a fan of being in the spotlight."

"You get used to it," Gaby replied, as she put the fire out. The smoke from the short-lived flame was faintly acrid, but not so much so to be bitter. It was just there. "Although, to be fair, what the others are about to do is less nerve-wracking."

The stagehand tapped her shoulder; everything was ready to begin. Her Hildebrantia's bandmates were already on stage, waiting for her entrance. She took to the stage, microphone in her left hand and her right raised, waving to the audience to greet them and pump their energy. A couple of minutes into the concert, the rest of the poorly named Band of the Greywolf would be taking to their own stage.

"Hello, Belfrost!" Gaby yelled into the microphone. "Thank you for the warm welcome! We have exciting news, although if you follow gossip news you already know. So, without further ado let's give our new and very nervous guitarist, Joshua, an even warmer welcome! He can take the heat!"

Joshua entered the stage, playing a riff on the guitar and took his place to Gaby's right. No one could deny that Gaby knew how to work a crowd. She was in her element.

"Are you ready to rock?" Gaby yelled to the cheerful reply of the attendees. She smiled as she placed the mic on the stand. "I can't hear you! Are you ready to rock?"

"Yes!" the audience replied in unison.

Gaby began to sign the lyrics of a new song from a new album entitled "Subconscious Serendipity."

It was her stage, it was her band, and it was her song.

Let's see what tomorrow will bring.
Time to make a choice.
If the world weighs you down, you
Raise your voice!
For every time they tell you to close your mouth.
For every time, that they want to count you out,
Keep fighting!

† † †

Alex knocked on the door of the fortress once more. By now, the concert must have started. He could feel in his bones as his comms played Gaby's song. He couldn't avoid tapping the snow-covered ground to the beats from the band's drummer, Scud. He smiled. Because for the first time in... ever, no one had complained about his plan. On the contrary, all took it and expanded upon it and even left the craziest aspect of it intact, which was based around the idea that there was no point in infiltrating a fortress when they were expecting you. What the enemy doesn't expect is a guy, wearing a blatantly fake moustache, nose, glasses, and a delivery service cap, holding a pizza box in one hand while knocking on the door.

"Hey!" Alex yelled. "This pizza is getting cold and I'm not gonna pay for it when I arrived before the thirty minutes' warranty. Which was not easy given that your address is a lonely gloomy fortress in the middle of a mountain range! Are you going to receive it or not? I don't get paid enough for this shit!"

"You technically don't get paid to deliver pizza," Sid's voice whispered in his ears.

"Yeah, but they don't know that," Alex said with a smile. "Frigg it, is everyone in position?"

"Yes," Sam replied behind him.

"Then I'm gonna knock down that door," Alex replied, placing the pizza on the ground. "What a waste of good pizza."

But the doors to the castle opened on their own. Alex shrugged, and walked through the threshold as he hit his arm bracers together to summon his tactical gear. A vest he had designed years ago, plus protection for legs, grew over his regular clothes like creeping vines that melded together into a solid form. Blue energy lines ran across seams, powering the gear. He touched a gem on one of his bracers which glowed for a second, summoning to his hand his Tempest Blade, Yaha, which he placed in the sheath on the back of his vest. This new version worked in a similar fashion to samoharo battle armor. It had taken all of the Foundation's technical resources to develop two suits of armor, one for him and one for Sam. They needed it given that they were the crux of the plan.

As Alex stepped into the front yard, he heard the cocking of guns and the firing of bullets. His irises glowed with the familiar golden hue as he extended his hands in front of him, and all the bullets stopped in mid-air. He closed his hands and the bullets dropped to the ground with a clatter.

"My turn," Alex said. On his left wrist a bracelet with a bow charm began to glow. Circles rapidly orbited around it, materializing a golden bow engraved with runes emitting blue light. When Forge had given him back the bracelet after defeating Shemazay, it hadn't been a token of friendship. The freefolk weaponsmith had placed on it a new bow that would allow Alex to shoot energy arrows without risking his health or depleting his Gift again.

As the guards ran to take better shooting positions, Alex released energy arrows in quick succession, taking out four guards that fell to the ground with loud thuds from the battlements. He was taking aim at a couple of guards to his left when from his right he heard an explosion. A bullet the size of a melon had been fired his way.

Before Alex could react, the bullet crashed against an invisible shield that flickered with spastic purple hexagons. The air was filled with the smell of bubblegum as the sound of heels clacking on the ground echoed around the walls. A red headed woman in boots, a wagging fox tail, and a black dress—like the one she had created for her magickal duel against the fallen god Shemazay but made from the same nanomaterial as Alex' gear—entered the yard. She wore a crystal pendant that rested against her chest, hooked on a silver dragon claw. The pendant emitted a lilac light that matched the light running through the seams of her dress.

"Watch your six, hon," Sam said as she stood next to one of her heartmates.

"I thought you were watching my six," Alex said. Guards kept coming, seemingly from every door, guns blazing, bullets bouncing against the Bubble shield, Sam's True Spell that she could cast with a thought.

"That's no excuse to not notice the cannon shooting at you," Sam said. "What am I gonna tell Kasumi if something happens to you?"

"Good point, she *would* probably kill me," Alex said with a nod. "How's the gear?"

"A bit tight," Sam replied as she summoned a white and crystal quarterstaff from one of her bracers. "Needs some adjustments. But I'm not planning to jump around like you will. The advantage of being the magick caster. And speaking of magick users, look!"

From the main door, a group of robed figures—members of the human exclusive cult known as the Brotherhood of Gadol arrived—carrying their grimoires.

"How long do we have to keep this? I mean, stalling," Alex asked.

"Just a few more seconds," Sam replied as she closed her eyes. Alex knew she was using a tracking spell to find out where Kasumi was, as Sam had placed enchantments on them to always know where they were. She was worried that the physical combat members of their throuple would get into trouble. Alex liked that, it saved time on this kind of thing. Sam opened her eyes. "She's in. Now, there you go."

"Finally, some fun." Alex smiled as he collapsed the bow, summoned Yaha, which disappeared from the back sheath and materialized in his right hand.

"Be careful, hon," Sam said as the shield opened to allow Alex to jump at the guards, using Yaha to deflect the bullets and cut down their weapons.

Alex and Sam made quick work of the guards. Both worked in silent coordination, the result of the absolute trust they had in each other coupled with having survived way too many battles by their age. If Kasumi were with them, the fight would've been over faster, but she had her own mission alongside Yokoyawa, and thus Sam and Alex were trying to keep as many enemy resources tied up as possible.

"How cute!" Sam grinned as the cultists read from their grimoires, carrying out their hasty rituals to summon their spells, their familiars, and sick them on her and Alex.

"Don't mock them," Alex said. "Freefolk have natural affinity to magick, we don't."

"I'm not mocking them for that," Sam said as a goblinoid familiar went for her throat. She gave it a heavy hit from her quarterstaff. "I'm mocking them because they think they can summon something to actually hurt us."

"What? You want them to summon a dragon? They are a bit dead."

"That might not be an issue, y'know?"

"Let's talk about that *after* we finish here and are at home with Kasumi. Last thing we need is a zombie dragon flying around."

"Spoilsport."

"You notice the irony of me pushing pause on your plan, right?"

Sam only shook her head and chuckled, as Alex and her kept dealing with their attackers. It had worked, though. They had attracted the attention of what felt like all the guards and magick wielding cultists, making short work of them. As they did so, a series of vines grew all over the place, covering the walls, breaking windows, filling crevices. Outside the castle, Vivi was using her magick to create her signature plant spells. It had been a case of the student becoming the teacher as with Sam's help Vivi had unlocked her True Spell and was making good use of it. When you have the future DragonQueen and fixer of magick on your side, becoming the second freefolk to use the alternative way to cast magick was easier.

Above Vivi, the Figaro drew the attention of the turrets while the massive speakers installed on it for this mission broadcast Gaby's concert, and with it, the empowering effects of the battlebard music.

††††

Heroes think they are so clever with their little schemes, brave words, and defiant actions. They are reactive by nature, avenging, righting perceived wrongs. And sooner or later they believe in being proactive, like now. Yet, even that is predictable, we knew they were going to come for us sooner rather than later. You understand that, right? Otherwise, why would you have thought of giving the Mask to such a useless, unworthy vessel as Robbet Dewart? Oh yes, because the mask is nothing but a symbol. It is the void beneath it that matters. The void that is already inside you. The mask will transform him into a godly avatar. And if he pulls his weight, he might get lucky before being erased from existence. Regardless, we have won. For it was their silly ethos, their misguided actions under the banner of a goddess known for her half-truths that had finally released us. You understand that right?

"Right," Girolamo muttered under his breath, holding a golden mask resembling that of the Golden King. He watched the three screens in the room next to the throne room where the Golden King, his master, held court. Not that he had attended any of said reunions himself, for Girolamo had always been busy with some private errand or another from the King. Dealing with the Brotherhood of Gadol cultists or politicians that had joined their war against the Free Alliance was the job of Dewart, his partner of decades. And when someone broke the King's trust, or failed in some unforgivable way, or simply became a hindrance, well, dealing with them was the job of the man smiling at his right. A man that at first brush looked to be young—deceptively so, even—but on closer inspection turned out to be older than anyone in the room, for his short blond hair and pearly smile, decked out in pure dramatic blacks, hid the identity of the oldest serial killer in Theia.

Disposing of those that annoyed the Golden King was Deacon Mabuse's job. And Girolamo had to give it to him, the *man* enjoyed his job.

Girolamo turned his attention to the screen to his left where his estranged daughter, Gabriella, and the traitor, Joshua, were performing their concert in Belfrost. A crude distraction, as crude as the disguise of that pauper pest that had always pranced around his prized daughter. If Girolamo hated anyone, it was Alex. Fionn got some begrudging respect from him, but Alex had thwarted his plan at Kyôkatô by putting his other master down. And Girolamo hadn't forgotten the punch that Alex threw at his face one day when he had visited Gabriella at her flat, when they were kids entering the university. No one in his life had dared before put a hand on him, and the pauper pest had done it, warning him to stay away from his own daughter.

But Girolamo was calm enough, was controlled enough to realize that even as annoying as the 'Godkiller' was, the real threat was elsewhere. The other screens showed the Figaro flying around, and the guards running towards the front yard to give a warm welcome to the pauper pest. Yet unseen, Girolamo knew that his daughter's brand-new husband and father-to-be was the real threat. Thus, he suspected that Fionn the Greywolf was already in the building.

"Kill the prisoners that are still alive at Mabuse's laboratory," Girolamo ordered to the guards. "In fact, better destroy the laboratory. We don't need witnesses nor evidence of his experiments."

Then he turned to Mabuse. "I expect you have all you need for your red fern and your other tools of trade that are going to be used in the next months."

"Of course, sir," Mabuse said with a bright laugh. "I even posted some of them ahead after Edamame's tragic demise."

"Why are you giving orders?" Dewart asked. "You knew this was going to happen and didn't care to tell me? I'm the right hand of the Golden King!"

"Anyone with two fingers of forehead could have predicted this, Robbet," Girolamo replied coolly. "After Mon Caern, it was the next logical step. The Greywolf proved that he and a handful of followers could make our army bleed."

"Including your own daughter! You never reined her in!" Dewart snapped, his face flushing red beneath the well-trimmed beard.

"Your point being?" Girolamo raised an expectant brow. The golden mask became hot in his hand, and a subtle vibration could be heard by those of the right disposition, such as Girolamo himself, or Mabuse.

"Why are you giving orders?" Dewart interjected, his voice filled with anger. "This is not what was promised to me. I should be the one in charge. I was to be one taking over the new Alliance!"

"You may well be the right hand of our liege," Girolamo said with an increasingly hollow smile at Dewart, leaning into his personal space and taking full advantage of their height difference. "I am his left hand. That said, you are correct, our liege hasn't fulfilled his promise to you. But we will make that right, Deacon Mabuse."

Mabuse pulled out an onyx knife, which he twirled on his hands, before handing it to Girolamo.

"Wha... what are you doing?" Dewart stuttered as he took a step back. But it was too late.

"You, my friend," Girolamo whispered as he plunged the blade into Dewart's heart and forced a second Golden Mask onto his face, "will at last get payment for your ambition. To experience the power you craved for so long. Because for the next minutes, perhaps an hour if you are lucky to last that long, you will *be* the Golden King—or rather his puppet— while the good Deacon and I enact the actual plan."

"So wise of you, sir," the deacon said, his voice ringing oddly hollow behind the mask. "Wishes do come true!"

Both men left the room as Dewart collapsed, the Mask melting over his flesh to become a perfect golden mirror, with only two slits for the eyes. Said eyes, morphed from the human likeness they held until mere moments ago, now resembled two perfect black gems that absorbed every mote of light. The pool of blood that had poured from Dewart's chest wound, transformed itself into a vermillion robe.

† † †

You see, and follow me here. Every tovainar they killed had a shard of me. When they killed them, that shard was absorbed by the void beneath the mask. Byron understood that, the Golden Child. No offense, but I expected him to become my new body. However, you have proved an excellent replacement to him, and to the traitor. I believe you comprehend that. Now you are set for bigger things. Because the tovainar were shards, the screws that kept the halves together. The halves are the important thing. And the traitor, the Godkiller, and their pets, did us the biggest favor: they released the essence trapped in the half that was my sibling, the Creeping Chaos. You see, my dear sibling had found the way to get us back to being one. But he got desperate, went native. A whisper here, a suggestion there, through you of course, set him to the path where his death was our biggest triumph. For you see, a reality in life is that defeats can be victories if you know how to play your hand. While so-called heroes blind themselves to the actual truth: all their victories, all their actions aided our goal to free the shards and the two essences so they can merge and I, Abaddon, the First Demon, become one once more. Their victories amount to nothing but a resounding defeat. That truth will crush their hope. Now you understand. Good.

"I do understand," Girolamo replied, as he placed over his face the real Golden Mask while Mabuse looked on with delight. One of the biggest secrets housed in the castle wasn't the location of the Golden King, nor the experiments that Deacon Mabuse carried out on the prisoners. Robbet Dewart's deception wouldn't amount to even a footnote. No. It was that Girolamo and Mabuse were hiding that the Golden King's real avatar, and Girolamo himself, were one and the same.

"Let them keep going with their mission," Girolamo said as his voice changed, deepened. "It will keep them distracted from our actual plan."

He and Mabuse descended a staircase that would lead them to an ancient chapel deep in the innards of the mountain, far from prying eyes.

† † †

Inside a dark tunnel, a secret corridor that in previous times served as the castle's escape route in case of a siege, Kasumi and Yokoyawa moved swiftly and silently. While that was easy with Kasumi's demonhunter gear, it was still surprising to witness a two-meter tall samoharo wearing nanoarmor made of orichalcum. Both wore glow-in-the-dark gloves, for they were only using hand signals to communicate. Kasumi's hearing aids emitted a frequency that would have alerted the guards so sign language was a better option. As a bonus, this allowed Kasumi to rest from the cacophony echoing through the caves.

Yoko pointed towards a grate a few meters in front of them, then signaled.

"That's the entrance to the section of the castle with higher energy use, the laboratory."

"Prisoners might be there, still trapped," she signed.

Kasumi and Yoko reached the grate. The long corridor was empty, the only sign of the experiments were the bodies of two unfortunate solarian knights, twenty titanfighters, and almost fifty civilians: mutilated, mutated, *butchered*. Their broken bodies chained to the wall, strapped to tables, with their skulls opened, emptied. The telltale signs on the remains let Kasumi know that their brains had been removed while alive and conscious. She and Yoko had arrived too late for these people.

"Maybe we can still find other survivors," Yoko signed. But her irises were already glowing. Yoko knew what would come next, and he moved behind her and back to the first corridor.

In an uncontrolled outburst of anger Kasumi let go of her Gift. While she had been able to harness the Gift for the increased physical aspects it conferred, the primary and secondary manifestations of the Gift were still a problem for her. This added to the anger she felt at the senseless deaths of the prisoners because she felt the lingering influence of the Gift's previous owner.

"Ahhhhhh!" The shout that escaped Kasumi as she released the energy buildup in her body was almost more felt than heard. Every water pipe in the castle exploded, flooding the place. Before the rushing water even had time to settle, it flash-froze. Kasumi dropped and Yokoyawa ran to her, kneeling at her side. There was a shudder that rained dirt and pebbles onto them, and the ceiling began to collapse. Yoko used his body to block the falling rock and keep Kasumi safe. As the dust cleared sunlight filled the corridor followed by the sounds of Hildebrantia's music coming from the Figaro flying above. Looking past Yoko's bulk, Kasumi could see that the corridor had become a large, icy tunnel in which their breath fogged heavily.

"I'm sorry," Kasumi whispered to Yoko. "This was not part of the plan."

"It's all right," Yoko signed back, then shrugged. "You have given me a chance to snowboard. I will go ahead, while you catch your breath."

Yokoyawa ripped a heavy door from its hinges with a metallic whine and used it to propel himself towards the cells, sword in hand. He hoped that there were still prisoners alive to free. He hoped the early signs of the kind of experiments conducted in this place were just a gruesome oddity. Hopefully.

†††

The vines around the castle grew like weeds, invading every nook and cranny as the Figaro made another run. The ship evaded the turret fire, getting as close as possible to the ground without risking a direct shot. As it did so a shadow dropped from the Figaro as it lifted once more to take into the air.

The shadow fell on one of the vines and ran to reach the shadows of the corridors that led to the innards of the ancient castle. He had memorized the layout before the mission, hoping that the new occupants hadn't made renovations since they'd been squatting there.

"The interior design of this place is rubbish," Fionn muttered as he shed the cloak that had camouflaged his arrival. He was wearing the first tactical gear that Alex had designed and built for him. He liked the nanoarmor and had grown quite fond of the equipment his former student had created. It was every bit as comfortable as his tried-and-true leather jacket had been. Peeking around a corner, he saw a guard chatting on the radio about mobilizing forces to defend the castle while Gaby's song echoed all over the place. With a swift movement, Fionn closed the distance between himself and the guard and broke his neck, catching the limp body that dropped like a sack of potatoes and lowering the corpse to the ground. He took the radio and moved to the next corridor, evading the cameras as much as he could. If everything went according to plan, this war would be over before it became a large-scale conflict. It all rested on him killing the Golden King.

Simple.

†††

"The fatal flaw of mortals is to delude themselves with hope, do you understand? Hope is nothing more than a mere illusion created by their feeble minds to allow themselves comfort from the vagaries of a random, careless, cold universe. And they fool themselves because, deep down, they acknowledge this truth. They destroyed their original home worlds long before I even thought to whisper into their ears. And they will destroy this one as well. Hope is but a mirage. Even Power is not real—not in the truest sense—but it is sturdier than the flimsy hope. Power is a basic tenet of the universe. Power makes stars burn and destroy themselves. Mortals turn to power when their hope fails. But you do understand that, don't you? I know you do. Otherwise, you would have sacrificed your wife, your only daughter, for the sake of power. When you summoned me in that ritual to activate my dormant Golden Mask, you never hesitated to slaughter your personal assistant as an offering—his soul still screams inside me—nor to give me your wife's life-force and covering it with a 'car accident.' You wanted power, and you are about to achieve it at last, eternal power to shape this flawed universe unto us. Hope will dissipate and with it, life."

Inside the chapel, a ritual had begun. Around Girolamo, in their designated spot on the circle engraved into the stone surface, trapped by strange magicks, the chosen ones of the Brotherhood of Gadol stood. Each held in their hands the charred, bloodied, dusty remains of the heads and hearts of Byron, Edamame, Gavito, and the Creeping Chaos. When they were destroyed by Fionn, Gaby, Sam and Alex, what they thought were ashes flying into the air, was nothing but a spell to bring the rotting remains here for their final purpose.

The chosen ones stood, their eyes darted from one side to another, unable to utter a word or to think about what would happen next because their minds were on fire. Their mental agony lasted little time, for Deacon Mabuse slit their throats one by one, with such ferocity that he almost ripped their heads off as a metallic scent filled the air and their mouths. Once he slashed each waiting throat, he opened the gash with wrenching force, pouring the blood of the sacrifice into the heads and hearts, dissolving them and making the blood drip from them, thicker, oily, and ichorish. By the time the Deacon reached the last volunteer, the eyes of the latter blinked fast, mumbling, struggling to move, to escape their slow-moving fate.

But no one escaped Deacon Mabuse, for if Fionn had become the mentor of heroes, the Deacon was the mentor of killers. And the First Demon's very first student.

† † †

Reaching the room without being noticed had been tricky, but not impossible due to the ruckus Alex and Sam were causing in the front yard. Or Kasumi and Yokoyawa for that matter, making their way to the prisoners' cells. Then again, Fionn had run many secret infiltration operations during the Great War. Many ended in eliminating rival leaders from the Horde, weakening it slowly. It was not something Fionn had ever been proud of. It was probably the only thing he and Sid could share and bond over with a few beers as lubricant to their otherwise somewhat factious friendship.

Fionn had managed to slip through the corridors in silence, taking down cultist and guards alike with decisive action. While Alex had proposed the overall plan, Fionn had made a few last-minute adjustments before dropping into the castle, adjustments that only Sid, Harland, and Vivi were privy to. He didn't want Sam to see him plowing his way through and leaving a trail of corpses. She knew of his past. But knowing and witnessing were different things. He did find it ironic, though, that not that long ago, as Justicar, he had been tasked to track the kind of people that were doing what he was doing right now. And only one had escaped him, a fabled serial killer that a few knew as the Deacon.

In scant minutes, Fionn passed through a door at the end of a large corridor to stand in front of a throne made of dark spiky bones. Behind it was a window filled with darkness. It did not look out upon the courtyards below but allowed a viewer to catch a glimpse of the dark void of the Infinity Pits, where the only light came from the fire pits that pocked the surface. Sitting on the throne, in his vermillion robes and mask of gold, the second asurian deity avatar to inflict pain in Theia: the Golden King.

The whole scene would have made another person confused, dizzy—even paranoid, for witnessing the madness that were the Pits would affect anyone within an inch of their sanity. But Fionn merely shook his head to clear his mind. He had seen that place before, and it hadn't been when he'd been lying unconscious after facing Byron at Ravenstone. He had been in that place, or at least the surface level.

This was the secret that not even Gaby knew, the secret not even Fionn was sure he didn't dream as a nightmare: When he died the first time, he had been sent to the Infinity Pits. Momentarily. But it was enough. It was something he had no desire to experience again.

For years after getting the Gift in the Light Explosion, Fionn had a recurring nightmare, one that felt more like a repressed memory with how it invaded his mind. During the time that it took the Gift to rebuild his body from scratch, his soul had been forced to spend what felt like an eternity trapped on the surface of the Pits. There he'd been judged by the Devil, forced to endure test after test of his character, his soul taken from him, then released after passing each test. Even at the end of the ordeal, the Trickster Goddess had to fight the Devil for Fionn's soul.

The result had been constant nightmares. His only way out had been to climb up on a tree root that glowed with green sparks in the dark. The light had guided him during the tests, until he eventually woke up in his body. Bandaged and in a cart, his body regenerated at an astonishing pace, as Izia and Ywain cared for him as he was ferried back to Saint Lucy. Everything had been a blur. His body had been wracked with mind-numbing agony that would have killed anyone else. His healing factor rebuilt every muscular fiber, every layer of fat and skin, every vein and artery, from the bones outwards. Once his body had been rebuilt, the healing factor cured his eyes from blindness, regenerating his retinas and corneas, his irises. By the time he could breathe without feeling like his lungs were on fire, his teeth had regrown as well as his hair. Even some of his scars reappeared. After three months of agony, he was as good as new, physically. But mentally, the nightmares never left. He suspected that they never would.

Gaby knew he had them but what he had never told her is that for him, it was not a nightmare, but a repressed memory. Even today he wondered about the nature of the visions, and why he had survived that ordeal.

But the whole experience had insulated his mind and soul from the devastating effects of the Pits.

He closed the door before anyone else reached the place. He would deal with this all on his own.

"Let's get done with this, shall we?" Fionn said.

† † †

All of what is going to happen from now on, Girolamo, it was your choice. And I thank you, for you willingly chose to become my new body, my new soul, my tether into the universe. I will try to make your absorption into my being painless. But I am a Demon, so of course you can't trust my word. And there is no escape, hope or help for you, avoid us the indignity of surprise. It is beneath us. But you knew that, deep down. Be glad.

"I see that Dewart will at last be of some real use," Mabuse said, as his lips curved into a wicked smile.

Girolamo became immobile, his muscles frozen, as he stood in the middle of the circular diagram. The blood from the ritual sacrifices filled every crevice, every crack, and channel of the diagram, all leading to the center of the diagram. As Girolamo stood there, the blood flowed over his feet and legs in thick waves and began to enter his body through every pore. It flowed under his skin with uncanny ripples and his face melted, features disintegrating and sliding away, leaving behind nothing but a void in the shape of a human head.

"My lord?" Mabuse asked.

"The False King will keep the Greywolf busy while we finish business here. The Golden Mask will control my hastily made clone to oppose that interloper. Regardless of who wins and who dies in that battle, the victory shall remain mine. My loyal Deacon Mabuse, my favorite demon, gets the orionians here. I'm certain they will love to have found their ancient enemy and get payback from almost being eradicated. And destroy the gestating new avatar of the Trickster Goddess, regenerating somewhere in the Mistlands. Do it discreetly, don't spoil those lands, let's give their inhabitants the illusion of sanctuary. Then their screams will be all the more delicious when we arrive."

† † †

The Golden King spoke in a language Fionn didn't recognize, although the intent of the words were crystal clear after the Golden King's first attack. Fionn felt a bone crushing pressure on his body, pushing him inwards, trying to smash him into a ball of flesh and blood. The Golden King had unleashed a gravitational wave the moment he had extended his hands forward.

Fionn stood his ground, summoning all the power of the Gift at his disposal. And, as he found out in that moment, it was more than he had expected.

"Enough!" Fionn yelled as he pushed against the waves, breaking the spell. His healing factor mended his aching bones instantaneously.

No more words were exchanged. It was a battle of wills

more than one of brawn.

In the background there was banging on the door that ceased when the door became covered in frost. Over that was the music coming from the castle's hijacked speakers, Gaby's voice filling the air with words that made their blood sing. Fionn took them all in and ran towards the Golden King. The swirling reflection on the Golden King's mask distorted space-time in the room. At one point, the room twisted enough unto itself that Fionn was running on the ceiling, but he was now an unstoppable force. The closer he got, the brighter Black Fang glowed, ready to deliver the final strike.

The Golden King multiplied his arms and horns grew from his forehead. He delivered what seemed like thousands of punches per second at Fionn, who managed to evade some but received the brunt of the others. Only his healing factor pushed to the max kept him alive.

The maddening vision in the window began to whisper and swirl, forcing Fionn to close his eyes for a second, muttering "This is not real, this is not real."

As he did that, his own body began to glow green as well and for the first time in a century, the unbearable pain of having his body on fire returned.

† † †

"And the Greywolf? The Goldenhart? The traitor?" Deacon Mabuse asked.

"I will deal with them in due time," Abaddon replied, for he had ceased being Girolamo Dewart as soon as the ritual had ended. "Time itself is meaningless when you have eternity at your hands."

The Deacon admired his liege. After a wait of millennia, plotting how to reunite all his pieces into a single body once more, the First Demon, the scourge of Theia and source of incursions, plagues and calamities, the destroyer of worlds across the universe was back. And it was due to the admirable efforts of those mortals that believed themselves to be heroes. That brought a smile of delicious irony to the Deacon's lips.

The Deacon turned to the injured members of Brotherhood of Gadol that had arrived at the catacomb. The Deacon closed the door and looked at a screen showing the Greywolf at last defeating the 'Golden King.'

The members of the Brotherhood stood in shock at the carnage of their companions, their blood drying over what was left of their carcasses.

"Indeed, what is time when you have eternity at your hands?" the Deacon whispered as he began his task, knife in hand. The bloodcurdling screams of his followers were muffled by the thick walls of the catacomb and the transmission of the concert, which in a way, had been a success.

† † †

Alex broke the door with a punch into which he had put all his strength. It helped that it had been frozen—Kasumi's doing, he knew—and had become weak and brittle in the cold. Sam stood guard behind him, but all the soldiers had died or fled. Most likely the former. As the door thumped to the ground Yoko slid up on the frozen floor atop an iron door, and Kasumi seemed to skate along effortlessly behind him on the frozen floor.

"What in the Pits..." Alex muttered as the four of them entered the room. The walls were twisted like those swirly licorice candies he hated but Kasumi loved. Every surface in the room, or what was left of it, had been crystalized by an extreme release of energy, and the entire room emitted a smell that had hints of Sulphur and petrichor, competing against each other. The wall at the back of the room was simply gone, as was the throne. In the middle of it all was Fionn. He was on his knees, bleeding from every pore, his clothes and armor torn and tattered. Black Fang was still gripped in his left hand. He breathed heavily, sucking in deep, ragged breaths as if his lungs were struggling to relearn how to function. In front of him lay the body of the Golden King, head several meters away, the mask melted over a caved face.

"Dad!" Sam exclaimed as she ran towards Fionn.

Alex placed a hand over Fionn's shoulder but had to pull it back. He stopped Sam.

"Careful, Sam, his body is quite literally scalding."

Kasumi approached Fionn and placed her hands on his back, using her Gift to decrease his temperature.

"What happened, Dad? Are you okay?" Sam asked, kneeling in front of him.

Fionn smiled at her, from eyes that were surrounded by dried blood and through sweat damp strands of hair. His breath was still ragged and short. It seemed that his Gift had burned out trying to keep him alive during the fight. The same way Alex had burnt through his years ago.

"When you told me," he said, his voice a raspy whisper, "that your and Alex's fight against the Creeping Chaos had been the most harrowing experience in your lives..." He paused to suck in more breath, "I never expected it to be the nicest way to describe it."

Fionn turned to Alex, his strength slowly returning. "Now I'm even more proud of what you two did in that fight. And with Shemazay. This was the fight of my life."

"It seems that it is over," Yokoyawa said as he examined the remains of the Golden King. Only the melted mask remained from the head. He had been yearning to have another shot at a godly avatar after his loss against Shemazay. It wasn't a matter of pride, but rather of testing something he had rediscovered within himself, in the right conditions. "It would have been over sooner if someone hadn't closed the door."

"The important thing," Fionn said as Sam and Alex helped him to stand up, "is that it's over."

"What now?" Kasumi asked Fionn.

"I'm going to retire," Fionn said.

"Not fair," Alex quipped half serious, half joking as he helped the man that had been his mentor. "It means that I'm stuck with that awful nickname of Godkiller."

"I'm not planning to challenge another god, godly avatar, or their ilk just to free you from that. You earned it," Fionn laughed, which made him wince. "If anything, Sam should get to use it, too."

"Leave me out of that silly discussion please," Sam interjected as they left the room. Yokoyawa stared at the remains of the mask a bit longer. There was something that bothered him, and probably would for days. But he couldn't quite pinpoint what it was.

Maybe it was the whole retirement thing. In this line of work, mentors, no one really got to retire. Not without consequences.

Chapter 2
A Year from Hell

SAM LOOKED AROUND AS SHE stood in front of a cosplay stall. *I expected something larger.* The comic and toy convention was taking place in the empty conference rooms of the Star Mall's third floor. It was convenient because the food court was only a few floors down and the other stores benefited from the passerby attendees.

"What do you think?" Alex asked Sam, as both were examining a petite costume displayed in the stall. Technically, they had been invited to the convention, which Sam found uncomfortable. Alex was like a fish in his pond, happily swimming around browsing comics and staring at action figures he knew he shouldn't buy now that he, Sam, and Kasumi lived together, and space was tight.

"It's too small for me," Sam replied without looking.

As they stood there a young boy holding a comic with Alex on the cover approached and tentatively held it up for Alex to sign. Despite his enthusiasm for the toys, Alex said he hated signing autographs. He didn't feel like he'd done something worth the attention, a point on which Sam disagreed and he agreed to disagree. But in this moment, he took the comic and signed it before returning it to the boy who went away with a smile.

"No, I meant for Kasumi," Alex said.

Kasumi, current Champion of the Chivalry Games seemed to thrive on the attention of autograph seekers. Sam glanced over to where Kasumi stood and who was again being asked for her autograph, this time by two preteen boys to sign autographs of her cover in "Combat Illustrated." It didn't help that the two hormonal boys were staring at the revealing outfit Sam's and Alex's girlfriend was currently wearing. She was dressed in a white and blue short shiny dress with a short hemline, blue gloves and knee-high white boots, and two dazzling fairy wings attached to her back via a clever harness that tucked up between her shoulder blades. Her face had been glammed up by Sam with glitter makeup. Kasumi was cosplaying as a reimagined version of the "Snow Princess" tale and later cartoon, which she loved and had used to teach Alex first and Sam later, both Kuni and Sign language. Kasumi had gotten into cosplay after serving as her impromptu illusion assistant during the fight to stop Shemazay. Now, it seemed that every other step they took in the exhibition room she was being stopped for autographs or photos; and she graciously agreed each time. Except, unfortunately, for one lecherous guy who tried to grope a feel and she injured his hand. Most likely broken bones, from the look on his face. When the guy complained, the murderous looks of Alex and Sam had sent him running.

"I don't picture Fionn being retired, nor being a stay home dad," Alex said, changing the subject so fast it nearly gave Sam whiplash. "I'm sure they'll travel with Gaby on her tours all the time. Who do you think he'll leave in charge?" Alex asked as he pointed out another costume.

Sam had been looking at costumes and props for the illusion show she wanted to create. Now that she found herself with more free time, no day job, and an eager assistant, she needed to stay busy. Even Gaby had promised to connect Sam with her agent and maybe incorporate the illusions into her new next tour, after the baby was born. While magick, actual magick was a well-known quantity in Theia, humans for some reason—maybe because they had difficulties using real magick, or maybe because of ancient traditions from the Dawn Age—loved illusion shows. Freefolk were more sanguine about them, because for them magick was a more spiritual thing.

"That's not what I asked you," Sam replied, slightly annoyed. That particular topic was a sore spot. The freefolk elders were pushing hard for her to become the next DragonQueen, after saving her whole species' ability to cast magick. But she refused each time because she knew that accepting would make her beholden to those old geezers. And frankly, she wasn't keen to do that. She finally had a stable relationship with the two people she loved the most in all the universe, and being the next DragonQueen didn't fit into that. Now, taking over for her dad as head of the tribe was a different matter, though even that would be complicated if she tied the knot with the dummy next to her and the beautiful icy fairy a few meters away, signing autographs. "I asked you if that costume fits her as my assistant for the illusion show."

Alex examined once more the costume. It was a red and blue catsuit with LED lighted lines to give the appearance of a cybernetic body. It was matched with a corn blue short wig. It would make Kasumi look like a mechanical doll.

"Fits her, but do you think she'll agree?"

Both felt a tap on their shoulders and turned around. Kasumi pointed at her hearing aids, which meant she had turned them off. The place was incredibly noisy, so it made sense if she wanted to avoid a migraine. Both Sam and Alex changed to sign language to keep talking.

"What are you two doing?" Kasumi signed, smiling at both. She had the look of someone happily head over her heels in love with her two interlocutors.

"Helping you choose your next cosplay-slash-illusion assistant costume?" Sam replied. Her signing was slower as she was still getting the hang of it. It was difficult because if she forgot for a second what she was trying to say, she might accidentally cast a spell. Last time she had frozen Kasumi in time for almost a day and then set on fire the blinds in their home.

"Cosplay or for more personal play?" Kasumi signaled as she raised an eyebrow.

"Both?" Sam and Alex looked at each other, then replied with beaming smiles. "Both is good."

"You two together are way too kinky for me." Kasumi shook her head as her face turned red.

"You don't like that?" Alex asked.

"I do, but you make me blush. And it is two against one."

"And I thought you liked that," Sam signed with a mischievous grin.

"I will wear that if you buy it," Kasumi signed to Alex.

"Is this your way to tell me to get a job?" Alex replied.

Kasumi nodded.

"Well..." Alex turned towards the vendor and said, "Yeah, that one. The whole thing with accessories."

As Alex purchased the costume, Kasumi turned to Sam. "Where did he get the money?" she signed.

"He sold his first short story collection," Sam replied, pride radiating in her smile. "Including audio rights to be aired at the urban legends podcast he is addicted to."

"Why didn't you tell me?" Kasumi signed so fast that Sam had trouble following her hands. "That's why you were invited here?"

"Ha! I wish," Alex interjected. "I'm lucky that I got invited to submit a script for consideration for a comic that Salvador Drakaralov will be drawing in autumn." His hands seemed to mirror his mood as he added, "Along with a dozen other writers."

"Where do I know that name from?" Kasumi asked.

"Y'know, the former Solarian Knight turned artist that made Hildebrantia's first album cover."

"That's not bad," Kasumi said. Then she hugged Alex, kissing him and covering his face with glitter. "I'm proud of you, *kareshi.*"

"I didn't tell you before," Sam added, "because I wasn't supposed to know until today, but I was the one who signed for the package with the printed copies. At least bed hair here had the decency to dedicate it to his 'two loves of his life.'" Sam laughed and gave a playful nudge to Alex.

"And we were invited for the same reason you spent most of the conference outside,' Sam continued. "Signing copies of your interview after winning the Chivalry Games."

"Sorry about that." Kasumi bowed in form of apology.

"It's okay," Sam mouthed as she tenderly lifted Kasumi's face so she could read her lips. "I guess it is an unfortunate side of what we have been doing." Sam put her forehead on Kasumi's and they rubbed their noses together, a freefolk loving gesture. "As long as it keeps me far away from the Freefolk Elder Council."

"Still trying to get you to apply to the DragonQueen spot?" Kasumi asked, turning on her aids. As much as the excess noise bothered her, the topic was too complex for Sam's poor sign language. "You know you can do the job."

"I can, but I don't want to," Sam said, her voice quiet. "I don't need the elders telling me what I can and can't do in my private life, up to and including them vetting my heartmates. I'm happy with the ones I chose."

"Good, because I think my warranty just expired and the

product has been damaged, so no take-backsies," Alex interjected, lifting the left sleeve of his t-shirt, showing the yellow bandage Sam had made from her own t-shirt years ago to stop a deep gash from bleeding. Alex had it cleaned and sewn it into an armband he now wore for luck. Sam could still see the fading scar below. In retrospect, Alex's left arm had always gotten the worst of the injuries, which explained why his wrist was so stiff and why he had kept doing physical therapy. Gift-enhanced healing or not, the injuries piled up. Not everyone was like her dad.

"I wouldn't change you, bed hair," Sam replied tussling his head. "Now what's on the rest of the shopping list?"

"Alex?" Kasumi asked, noticing that he was staring at a lightbulb above one of the stalls.

"Did that light flicker?" Alex asked.

"Yeah, so what? It's a bulb," Sam said. "Bulbs like that flicker all the time, that is why they are being phased out to more reliable and less polluting LED lightning."

"No. Those are sensor bulbs; they are not supposed to flicker unless something is making an incursion," Alex explained.

"The alarm didn't go off," Kasumi added, as she took a deep breath. As an exceptional demonhunter, Kasumi had always been able to sense the ebbs and flows of the spirit world. Now that she had the Gift, she had become the primary alarm for when an incursion occurred—which had become less and less frequent since Fionn killed the Golden King. But they still happened. "But something feels wrong. Really wrong."

"I think we better check," Sam said, then she turned to Kasumi. "Just in case, get everyone to evacuate the place."

"Why me, *kanojo*?" Kasumi said, annoyed.

"Because people will listen to the Chivalry Games Champion and won't argue out of fear of angering you."

"And here I was thinking it was because your costume doesn't look too comfortable for a fight," Alex added.

"That, too," Sam replied.

"We will discuss about that later at home," Kasumi replied, daggers in her eyes, and turned to inform the authorities.

"We are in *trouble*," Alex whispered to Sam.

"Incursion or Kasumi's anger?" Sam replied. "Both are terrible sights to behold."

† † †

Despite having a comic convention on the third floor, the Star Mall was as empty as it usually was. The mall had a reputation for being haunted by fey, the result of a piece of the Tempest having bled into a deserted video rental store many years ago. Also, many people were probably going to the festivities where Prince Arthur would give his first speech after succeeding his grandmother and was only days from becoming king.

Alex and Sam descended the stairs and split up to examine both sides of the first level. Alex kept eyeing the tables of the food court below. There was an eerie sensation coming from there, and the ringing inside his ears began at the same time the alarms blasted. Ruefully, Alex said, "*Now* they sound."

On the floor below he saw a dark knight, followed by a pair of incursions that looked like zombified mastiffs. The dark armor-clad knight created a strange sensation in the air, not unlike a vacuum, a void of sorts. Despite his size, he made no sound. In fact, he seemed to glide over the floor. It was no wonder, then, that the alarms were delayed. A guard came out from a nearby store and raised his weapon towards the dark knight. The knight raised one fist and it turned into a cannon's barrel, charging to unleash a blast.

Alex barely had time to react and tried to reach the guard, but a shockwave knocked him backwards, slamming him against the wall with enough force to punch the air from his lungs. Sharp pain stabbed his left arm.

Not again, Alex thought as his head cleared from the impact. *I'm barely recovering full mobility in that wrist.*

When he looked up, what he saw made him regret such petty concern.

The space where the guard had been standing had been rendered a strange clump of deformed, decaying matter. It resembled necrotic tissue. "Ouch!" Alex looked at his own arm. The bracer had taken the brunt of the attack and had cracked. The skin below and around had turned black as if he had suffered from severe frostbite. Crackling arcs of electricity surged from his arm as his Gift tried to heal the injury, which to Alex's surprise was still working.

The poor guard hadn't been as lucky. He'd been fused with the wall, like the troopers Alex had encountered when he went inside the Bestial Core Engine room. What had been the man's arms wiggled pathetically in the air. The sight sent made Alex's blood. He summoned Yaha from his wristband and jumped to the floor below. He used the momentum of the jump to pierce the head of one of the incursions then rolled to cushion the fall.

"Enough!" Alex shouted at the dark knight. But he only got inhuman laughter in reply and more blasts aimed at him, which Alex dodged this time with ease. Those blasts transformed the walls behind Alex into pulsating necrotic matter that emitted the same glow as the circlets used to create more incursions.

"You should have waited for me," Sam scolded him, as she floated down through a spell. Her hair and irises glowed lilac, her fox tail wagging.

More incursions appeared from the pulsating blotches.

"I got carried away," Alex muttered. "The main target is that guy."

"You mean the big scary guy in heavy armor with cannons for arms? I would have never guessed that," Sam said, wry. As she levitated next to Alex she cast offensive spells at the many incursions: Daggers of lilac energy pierced one, and blades made of wind gusts sliced another.

Alex ran towards the dark knight, who stood there, as if examining Alex's reactions. Two incursions jumped in front of Alex and snarled. Alex pivoted towards a table in the food court. He jumped and slid over the table, grabbed the condiments bottles, flipped the table with a kick to use it as a barrier, and squished the bottles, aiming the squirt of ketchup and mustard towards the eyes of the two incursions chasing him. They were blinded momentarily by the sauces smelling of vinegar.

"Really? Mustard and Ketchup?" Sam asked as Alex beheaded the blinded incursions.

"It worked, didn't it?" Alex replied as he stabbed their hearts. His left arm gave a sharp twinge of pain that caused Alex to wince, but at least he still had a functional arm. He turned around as the knight was about to shoot another blast at the pet store, full of puppies and kitties. "Aw, c'mon, we already know you're the bad guy!"

Before the blast could impact the store, three light circles engulfed it, leaving behind a circular hole.

Alex turned and gave a thumbs up at Sam who had cast

a teleportation spell to get the animals out of harm's way. "You won't shoot those again," Alex said, and dashed at the dark knight, Yaha in hand. The black knight was fully focused on Alex, which was the idea.

Kasumi appeared out of nowhere above the knight, still in her cosplay costume, having summoned the Breaker, which cut through the cannons mounted in the knight's arms like warm butter. Cannon and arms alike clattered to the linoleum floor. The dark knight stared blankly at what remained of his arms. He mustered some words in a language Alex couldn't translate, but he knew they were bad news as three new incursions came from the mutated sections of the mall, as if they were some kind of organic dimensional punchers. The incursions this time were like the ones that had attacked Alex the day he got the Gift: Stalkers.

Kakkakkakkak.

The familiar nightmarish sound made Alex hesitate for a second, which would have been trouble, if it weren't for Sam and Kasumi who got rid of all the three incursions with ease. However, that was all it took for the dark knight to disappear amidst the confusion.

"Are you okay, hon?" Sam approached Alex, as her body returned to normal, the fox tail disintegrating in an explosion of light. "You got distracted for a moment there."

"Sorry, just bad memories from when I got the Gift," Alex said with a heavy sigh.

"Oh, those were the ones that, you know..." Sam pointed to Alex's left side, where he still bore the stabbing marks that destroyed his liver and put him at the edge of death, with in turn allowed Mekiri to bestow the Gift upon him.

"Yeah, won't happen again," Alex promised, inwardly berating himself all the while. It was past time he pulled his own weight, instead of always being dependent on Sam or Kasumi. He approached to examine the detached arms and black armor before they disappeared. The material was matte and absorbed all the light. Even Yaha was slightly strained from it. But Breaker—no surprise—had been able to cut them with ease. Looking at the clumps of mutated matter around them, and his own injured skin, Alex's mind raced through a series of scientific facts, trying to correlate a plausible theory. The only reason he could come up with was that only extreme temperatures or energy outputs hurt this kind of material. Which would explain why the Breaker could cut it, as the Tempest Blade was able to reach particularly low temperatures. He wished to salvage a sample for further study, but the remains were already dissolving, for without an energy core or a puncher translating the matter from one realm to another, it couldn't stop degenerating into dust. And yet, the clumps of mutated matter remained. He looked at his left arm and found his skin had returned to normal, having healed from the blast. The bones still hurt though. He had been lucky, but there was someone that hadn't. Alex looked at the poor guard transformed into a clump of matter stuck to the wall, still moving its limbs in a zombie-like manner, and he felt a pang in his heart.

"We need to see if we can save that man," Alex pointed where the man had been standing.

"I'm not sure I have the knowledge to do it," Sam said sadly. "We need to inform the Justicars of what happened here, so they can close the area for safety's sake."

"I had hoped that after killing the Golden King that these kinds of things would stop," Alex muttered. "But, I guess there will always be incursions."

A cellphone ringtone broke their conversation. It was the ringtone Kasumi had assigned to Harland when she was his bodyguard. But Alex knew he would never call her on a free day, not unless there was an emergency.

"Sammy, Alex, I just got a call!" Kasumi ran towards them, phone in hand. "It's Gaby. It's bad."

† † †

"What happened?" Alex asked the doctor outside Gaby's room. She had been entering something into a tablet. He could see Kasumi through the window who had gone in to check on Gaby. Joshua stood guard over Gaby, unmoving, like a statue.

"An allergic reaction to a plant we haven't seen before," the doctor said.

"What sort of plant? Where?" Alex asked.

"We are still unable to identify it. As to where, she came into contact with it while walking in a park earlier today. Her friend," the doctor motioned at Joshua in the room, "was with her and brought her directly here otherwise she might have died.

"What happened to her?" Alex asked.

"A severe immunological reaction that we have not been

able to determine the exact nature of."

"And the baby?" Sam asked.

The doctor only responded with a silent shake of her head.

Alex hugged Sam as she began to cry, as his blood was boiling from the news. *That plant bypassed the Gift?* Alex mused, as he looked through the window of the room.

A nurse entered to check on Gaby's vitals.

"Mr. Estel," the doctor continued, "is at the coroner's office as he is the next of kin. Mr. Rickman is with him. We wouldn't bother him with that right now, but there are certain regulations to follow, considering we are dealing with an unknown agent that can even affect... your peculiar physiology. We might have to declare a sanitary crisis if that plant is all over the city. It's technically against regulations," the doctor added with a lingering, meaningful pause before continuing, "but all of you can enter and see her. I'm sure she could use all your love and support."

The lights flickered. The whole building shook as an explosion of light, followed by a shockwave, hit the hospital. Pieces of the roof began to fall. Then a whole side of the building collapsed, leaving it without a wall, exposed to the outside. Through the window, Alex saw Joshua leap over Gaby and shield her with his body even as Kasumi protected the nurse. Sam cast her bubble spell to keep almost all patients and staff protected on the side of the building that was not collapsing. However, the doctor that had been speaking with them slipped, scrabbled for purchase, and fell from the gaping hole in the side of the building.

"Not on my watch," Alex muttered, his Gift activating. He jumped after her, keeping his arms next to his body to offer the least resistance and catch up with the doctor.

The doctor screamed as she fell. Alex reached her and pulled her into his embrace. She grabbed him tightly around the neck as he tried a trick he hadn't used in years. As both approached the ground, their speed, instead of reaching terminal velocity, slowed down. Alex was pulling the electromagnetic field from the planet itself to stop the fall, as he had done at Mercia University the night before he met Fionn and Harland.

He sucessfully slowed the fall but couldn't stop it completely. Alex hit the ground hard, cushioning the doctor with his body as the air left his lungs with a wheeze. It took him a moment to recover, for his head to stop spinning.

Finally, Alex asked, "Are you okay, doc?"

Her eyes closed and she was almost hyperventilating. She opened them and looked around. "We're alive. How?"

"Magick trick?" Alex offered a tentative smile.

"Oh, right," the doctor replied, as she seemingly remembered with whom she was talking. "Thank you."

"No worries," Alex said as they stood on slightly wobbling legs. He still felt the impact, and hers was probably from a near heart attack. They were both covered in dirt, grit, and grime of unknown origin. The whole place was chaos as medics and nurses swarmed whatever survived of the building to check on their remaining patients. "But you'd better get checked in case you have injuries."

"The patients come first," the doctor insisted as she joined a nurse pushing a gurney with a badly injured patient.

Alex tried to activate his comms, but there was only static. He pressed the button to try a new frequency.

"Kasumi, Sam, are you okay up there?"

"We're fine," Sam replied. "All of us. Can't say the same for the rest of the hospital. Have you seen my dad? Harland?"

"It's chaos down here, but I'll look for them," Alex said as he eyed the corridor with the half-broken sign saying 'Coroner.' When Alex reached the end of corridor, he found Fionn covered in dust and healing wounds, no doubt from having taken the brunt of the explosion. The corridor ended in a chasm, and a few meters below, there was a crater, the size of a whole borough. The nearby Haida River that formed as the sea passed the bay threatened to flood everything, if it hadn't been for a group of Freefolk passerby that were casting magick spells to keep it contained. A quarter of the city had evaporated in a flash of light, leaving scorched ground and red ferns. As Alex approached the other two men, it dawned on him. The hospital, if you crossed straight through the park that used to be there, overlooked the castle. The seat of the crown.

Aw, crap, Alex thought.

"The castle was there. With all the remaining Castle-Martell, the Solarian Knights," Harland said, barely acknowledging his presence, his phone ringing over and over. "If Doncelles is still alive, he might be at the Alliance Parliament."

Fionn remained eerily silent.

"A quarter of the city just evaporated. The river is only being held back by magick," Alex said. He put a hand on Fionn's shoulder and could see that his mentor had been crying. Alex grabbed Harland's phone to silence the ringer. He noticed the incoming messages, and that the man had just lost his childhood friends. It was Doncelles, the First Thain, begging Harland to reach the Parliament as soon as possible.

Aw, crap, Alex thought for a second time.

"Harland, aren't you one of the senior signees of the re-formed Alliance?"

"Yes," Harland replied, his fugue state broken by the question. Alex gave him his phone back and the small man saw the messages. Color drained from his face.

"Kasumi, we need to take Harland to the Parliament, right now," Alex said through the comms. "Sam and Joshua, we need to evacuate Gaby and Fionn from here. It's gonna get ugly."

Alex was doing something he didn't like, probably fueled by the adrenaline. He was taking charge.

"On my way down," Kasumi replied. "Can I change first? I don't think Snow Princess costume is a helpful look. I'll grab some scrubs."

"What are you doing, Alex?" Fionn muttered under his breath, not breaking eyesight with the razed ground.

"You need to go to Gaby," Alex replied with his poor attempt at a soothing voice. "I will take it from here." He paused then added, "If you don't mind."

Fionn barely nodded in acknowledgement.

"Why do you want Kasumi to take me to the Parliament?" Harland asked. It was clear he wasn't connecting the dots yet due to the shock.

"Because right now," Alex said, trying to sound like he knew what was going on, "you might very well be the only senior member that knows how to keep the Alliance from collapsing. You will have to convince them of that. That's why Doncelles wants you there. He might hate your guts, but respects you."

"He is right," Fionn added. "Whoever did this, will pay."

"They will," Alex replied. "I will make sure of that. Take care of Gaby, please. Leave the rest to me."

† † †

Alex and Kasumi lost track of how long the debate, the political tug-of-war had endured. What had started as a nice break, a trip to an amusing activity, had soured pretty quickly, eventually becoming a nightmare. They took turns sleeping in an alcove, looking over the Parliament forum, always keeping an eye on Harland, who—as the proceedings advanced—was becoming perhaps the most important person in the Alliance.

It had been chaos at first, everyone wondering what to do when the future head of the Alliance had been killed in an explosion. What many hadn't expected, until Doncelles of all people brought it up, was that in the Alliance's constitution there was a provision, updated after the events at Kyôkatô, to keep the leadership from being an inherited position after the last CastleMartell had passed away. The next leader would be elected from the pool of representatives to initiate a transitional period then making it a fully elected position. Of course, with all the chaos, organizing elections would have been complicated. Alex had fallen asleep halfway through the proceedings and Kasumi had to explain to him where the situation stood. There had been a lot of horse trading among the groups, but the growing consensus—surprisingly, formed by Doncelles—was to elect someone that was neutral, had a decent track record dealing the same with the Freefolk, the Samoharo, the Kuni and the Ionis' city states, someone who had a good knowledge of the ground level issues and was aware of the incoming threats. And above all, had always vied for the well-being of the Alliance. Which, as Alex had suspected in a brief moment of inspiration, described only one person.

A few voting rounds later Harland had become interim president of the Free Alliance. There was a delay as ownership of the Foundation had to be addressed. Sid was ultimately selected, which raised a few concerns among the samoharo representatives because Sid remained a banished samoharo. Eventually Sid was allowed to become the head of the Foundation as everyone agreed that they needed Harland to get the Alliance through this emergency.

The next morning Alex and Kasumi watched from a nearby rooftop, tracking every single movement below as Harland's bodyguard, as Harland took the oath as the new leader of the Alliance.

"I, Harland Rickman, pledge to uphold the values of the

Alliance and fulfill my duties as emergency president until the crisis is over..."

Harland continued, his left hand on the Book of the Alliance's Foundation, held by Doncelles. Among the sea of people, he seemed a small man. This was in part due to his condition. But he also looked haggard, weighed down by the events. But he remained steady in spite of it all, his words both a rock upon which to support the Alliance and a balm to soothe everyone's fears, as he took the oath, surrounded by representatives and reporters alike.

Alex recalled something Harland had told him, when he had bought Alex a birthday cake and tried to cheer him up after he'd been disqualified from the Games:

I had this vision of me talking with the Trickster Goddess, and she told me that it was the size of our heart and the strength of our will, what you decide to do with your life is what defines who we are. For even the humblest person can create great change and be the hero we need. She called me a 'human that walks tall alongside true titans, unflinchingly.'

Alex reflected upon that memory. If he didn't know better, he could swear that Mekiri was talking in the past, about this very moment. For Harland seemed a giant taking on the daunting task of keeping the Alliance together after what had been a heavy blow into its foundations.

In that moment Alex decided he would help Harland keep Saint Lucy—what was left of it, anyway—safe. The Alliance too. He would take charge to allow Gaby and Fionn to mourn and heal. To allow Sam to oversee the needs of the tribe in front of the Freefolk elders, to let Sid take charge of the Foundation, without any of them having to worry about a second attack.

"What are you thinking about?" Kasumi asked him.

"Of how much I admire Harland," Alex said. "And how to help him."

Under any other circumstance, Saint Lucy would have fallen into crisis and criminals would have taken the opportunity to fill the power vacuum. After that, the rest of the Alliance would have crumbled. But to their credit, the Alliance stayed put, with Doncelles, the Freefolk and the Kuni propping up Harland's impromptu leadership role to keep things from collapsing.

After the ceremony, as Harland focused on his new role, Alex took to the streets to make sure the criminal elements didn't try anything. Most malefactors knew better than to take their chances with a pissed off Greywolf. Some turned out to have a strange sense of honor and came together to help the citizens of the city. But a few couldn't resist the lure that the partially destroyed city, saved by grace of the ancient wards engraved in their foundational stones that absorbed part of the explosion, offered them for wealth or power. Those found out the hard way that it was the 'Godkiller' who now kept the city safe.

Alex already had a reputation as a vigilante from before the Chivalry Games. Things were simpler then. Now, that reputation wasn't even close to what Alex could do to someone taking advantage of the tragedy.

If only things had stopped there.

† † †

Kasumi was worried. She usually took things in stride, but the past several days unnerved her. Her and everyone else, at this point. She and Alex had been tracking a couple of murderers, cannibals, based on what Culph had shown them. Saint Lucy had been relatively quiet crime-wise in the three months after the explosion, until these murders began. The scenes were grisly, which had made her suspect incursions. But it had been the few surviving witness descriptions of the events—already unreliable—that amped the unsettling factor: two humanoid demons led by three men, as if they were a boisterous tourist group, snatching and eating people from every borough left standing. The few witnesses left alive had described the demons as human-looking, wearing clothes stained with dry blood. Perhaps their most striking features were the mouthful of sharp fangs instead of teeth, the black pitch eyes, and their stilted, unnatural gait.

The only good side, if that was possible, was that the trail had been easy to follow for a demonhunter and a vigilante. Finding the group, and stopping them while saving the next victim, who ran to call the Justicars, had been relatively quick and uneventful.

It was what happened when Alex confronted the demons that had Kasumi worried. Not just for the mental and physical health of her boyfriend, but also for the people that would encounter him during one of his bad moods which had become more frequent.

She could tell he wasn't acting like himself, as he always

avoided her eyes.

Sammy needs to be back here soon, Kasumi thought, as the noise of breaking bones and crushed trashcans echoed through the back alley. *I could use her help.*

"So, you two work for the guy that did this. That hurt my friend?" Alex said out of the blue, shocking Kasumi with the severity in his voice. It was more a growl than coherent words.

Since when has he been suspecting that incursions had to do something with what happened to Gaby? Kasumi thought. *And why didn't he tell me his suspicions?*

"What of it? We are of the One Hundred and Eight under Abaddon. You are just human." They no doubt had hunted and eaten so many humans in recent days that they expected these two to be easy prey, despite how oddly calm one of them seemed. The other, to them, smelled of unbridled rage.

"Like I care," Alex muttered, his irises glowing under the goggles. He called Yaha to his hand and the sword materialized instantly. Even the sword sang with anger, practically vibrating in a way easily understood outside of its handler.

"Alex..." Kasumi tried to calm him, but his body was expelling so much energy that her hand went numb after a discharge.

"Stay back," Alex called to her. "Please. This won't be pretty."

Alex bellowed at the top of his lungs like a bull as he charged the two demons. Startled by the speed and ferocity of Alex's attack, their arms rapidly shifted into weapons.

It didn't help them. Alex reached the demon on the right and landed a knee strike with such force its face caved in with a wet crunch, followed by the wall behind it as the demon's head struck it. The demon was stuck there. The second demon lashed out at Alex, but Alex turned and grabbed its arm with one hand, crushing it. Then he yanked the arm down to the point of ripping it off and as the demon collapsed to the ground in a bloody heap. Alex cut its head with a swift movement and enough force to cleave the concrete. He then stabbed the demon's heart, to dissolve it.

"Impossible," the demon with the caved in face mumbled as it witnessed the speed at which its comrade was dispatched by a mere human. With no small effort, it pulled itself from the cratered wall and attempted to jump on Kasumi, only to find itself pinned to the wall again, Yaha impaling its chest, below its core. If the demon moved, the glowing sword would destroy the core and it would be dead. The demon tried in vain to pull Yaha from its chest, only to receive an electric discharge so strong that Kasumi had to close her eyes and the place shook as if lightning had struck, leaving the air smelling of ozone.

Alex hardly acknowledged the demon as he activated his bow and shot three arrows at the now escaping cultists that had been guiding the demons and kneecapped each one of the three. Alex stalked toward them.

"You two, stay here, if you move the next thing I will blow up will be your heads," Alex said to them, seething. "You, on the other hand," he grabbed one and dragged him back to where the demon was pinned, "will tell me who summoned these creatures, who blew half the city, who created the red fern.

"I... I won't say anything. I swear for my lord."

"You'd better swear to me!" Alex screamed at his face, while punching the man so hard in the stomach, that blood erupted from his mouth.

The demon licked his lips at the smell of blood.

"Oh no, you won't feast on them," Alex said. "They are mine. I might, and that's the keyword, allow you to return to your dimension on your own if you answer the questions I made to this asshole."

"You don't frighten me, human," the demon replied. "You might have killed my companion; you might be torturing this human. But you don't have the stomach for—Argggh!"

Alex ripped its left hand off.

"You were saying? The moment you manifest here, you have to create a body. One that has to feel to interact with the world." Alex's lips twisted into some mockery of a vicious grin. "And how did that feel?"

"You're crazy!"

"You hurt my best friend. You haven't seen how crazy I can get."

"Abaddon and the Deacon will have you for this."

Alex leaned in close to the demon's face. "Good. Tell them that the Godkiller will add their heads to his count."

That's when Kasumi knew something was wrong. Alex hated that moniker, to the point he would never use it willingly.

"Alex, please, you have to calm down," Kasumi said.

"Yes, please do calm down," the demon said, mocking. "Listen to your girlfriend, Alex, like a good boy."

Alex responded by ripping off the other arm with inhuman force. His Gift seemed to be burning at the maximum.

The cultist tried to slither away, but Alex stomped down on his arm, snapping it with a crack that echoed down the alleyway and made Kasumi feel sick.

She knew Alex had his temper. She had heard Gaby's and Sid's accounts of the day he got the Gift and how he had dealt with the cultist that had created an incursion that had killed several teenagers. Sid had described it as stomach churning, keeping it light on details, save for making the point that at the time, Alex hadn't been in total control, but rather the being that had fused with him to bestow him the Gift. But this time was unlike then.

This time he was in total control of his actions, even in spite of his clear exhaustion.

Kasumi had no interest in the lives of members from the Brotherhood of Gadol that kept aiding demons and incursions. She also knew Alex had killed before, in battle. But never in cold blood. She could understand the rage. She was feeling it as Shemazay's whispers still echoed in the background of her subconscious. But she wasn't going to let Alex become a murderer.

With a swift movement beheaded the demon with Breaker, its body slumping over Yaha and destroying the core. It dissolved like fog on a sunny day.

Alex avoided her gaze and snatched the cultist by the throat, heedless of his own rampage. "Fine by me. You'll just have to serve before you pass out from the beating I put on you."

"No, he won't," Kasumi said, and struck a pressure point strike to make Alex's arm go limp and numb, releasing the man. "It is one thing to kill in a fight, but this is cold blooded torture and murder. Let the Justicars deal with them."

"Thank you," the cultist said.

"Don't thank me, asshole," Kasumi replied, and promptly relieved him of consciousness with another pressure point strike.

"I get why you did it," Alex said to Kasumi as he pulled Yaha from the wall. His voice was uncannily calm. "But I don't appreciate it. I think you better go back to Samantha."

"When *I* am the one asking you for restraint," Kasumi

said, "you know things have escalated too far. Let us help you to go back to how things were before all this happened."

"I don't need help with that, Kasumi," Alex insisted with that same eerie calm as he turned away. "I only need help to track the Deacon and Abaddon. So, either you help me, or you go home."

† † †

"And he left you there?" Sam asked Kasumi. She had just returned from Ravenstone, to find Kasumi distraught and rattled to her core. Sam had never seen Kasumi like this—not even when she was bleeding out and almost dying before getting the Gift. She handed her girlfriend a cup of steaming chamomile tea.

"I should have gone after him," Kasumi said, her eyes welling up. "To keep him from doing something stupid."

"He already did," Sam said matter-of-factly, placing an empty pill bottle on the counter. They were in Gaby's old apartment which she had left for them after she moved out of the city. "He hasn't renewed his prescription. Has he been sleeping?"

"No," came the reply, full of self-reproach.

"That tracks."

"I'm sorry," Kasumi cried. "I should have kept better care of him, instead of tagging along on his vigilante rounds."

"It's not your fault. He's an adult that knows he has a medical issue that needs to be kept in check," Sam soothed her, taking hold of her hands. Slowly, she brushed the pads of her thumbs along Kasumi's knuckles. "We're already altered. For what happened to the city, and for what happened to Gaby. I mean, the fact that you went with him and stopped him from doing something he would regret, that *was* taking care of him."

"It was odd," Kasumi said. "The first few weeks he was acting fine. But the more he visited the site of the explosion, in search of clues, the angrier he grew. Not at me, of course, here was all sweet and calm as usual. But outside, that was another matter."

"Did he hurt you?"

"No, of course not," Kasumi replied. "Even after I numbed his arm, he walked away, very calm, never so much as raising his voice. It was almost as if he wanted me to leave him alone. He didn't want me to see him like that. Gaby and

Sid told me what happened in the Straits. I fear he is regressing to that."

"But he became angrier after visiting the site of the explosion?" Sam asked, raising an eyebrow. "And you never went there?"

"No, I usually waited on the sidewalk in case the seals that are keeping the river from flooding the place fail and I needed to freeze everything. Easier to do from the outside."

That dunderhead, Sam thought. "Did you notice something weird or strange in the place?" she asked, starting to get an idea of what was going on with their boyfriend.

"It gives me a bad vibe, which makes sense with all the deaths there. And it smells weird. But I never paid much attention. We didn't spend much time there, maybe half an hour at the longest," Kasumi explained, and as she did so, her eyes widened in realization. "I should have used an ofuda to check how clean the place is."

"Happens to the best of us," Sam said. "And the thing is, he's going through one of his lows in his cycle, which is made worse since he's not taking his meds and the withdrawal symptoms are already bad in a regular brain. In one with the Gift, there is no frame of reference. He is doing the same thing he did during the Games, pushing himself far too hard. That's left him open to get worse by whatever the place is emitting. We don't know what caused the explosion but I'm guessing those red ferns are involved."

"I saw a few of them there, but Alex never got close to them," Kasumi added. "Should we go after him?"

"Yes, but we will need someone to actually knock some sense into him," Sam said as she grabbed her phone.

"I could do it," Kasumi offered. "You know I can beat him."

"Oh, I know, hon. That's plan B," Sam smiled at her girlfriend. "But if he hurts you, he will never forgive himself and that would only make things worse. We need someone that has gone through something similar."

"He's a dummy," Kasumi said with a smile as she wiped her tears.

"But he's *our* dummy. And he has been there to help us, it's time for us to help him. Keep him from hurting himself again." Sam lifted her index finger, then placed the phone on the counter and pressed the speaker button. "Hi, Dad. I know you and Gaby are working things out, but we need your help. It's an emergency."

"What happened?" Fionn said.

"It's Alex," Kasumi replied. "Kyôkatô all over again."

They could hear Gaby saying something in the background.

"I will be there as fast as I can," Fionn promised.

† † †

To say that it was difficult for Sam to track Alex would be erroneous. She knew exactly where he would be: at the sidewalk overlooking the site of the explosion. The runes on the magick seals that kept the river from flooding the whole district were glowing, under the stormy night.

"You scared Kasumi," Sam scolded Alex as she stood next to him. She was wearing regular clothes, rather than combat ones. "She didn't deserve that."

"I know," Alex said, sadness clinging to his voice. "Wasn't my intention. Did I hurt someone? Her?"

"You hurt some cultists and definitively mauled a few demons. You didn't hurt her." She paused for a moment then added, "But you should apologize to her for being an ass."

"I will after I finish this." Alex jumped onto the rail. He looked at Sam with a weak smile. "Maybe you two are better without me. I know I suck."

"Stop with the self-pity party," Sam admonished. "You are in one of your lows, you don't suck. But you need to come with me, with us, so we can help you."

"I'm not sure I'm worth the help." Alex jumped off and onto the scorched ground below.

Kasumi and Fionn had stayed back to allow Sam to talk with Alex so he wouldn't feel pressured. They now approached her as Alex ran towards the center of ground zero, avoiding the red ferns.

"He has been like this for weeks. He is obsessively looking for clues of who did this, who created the plant that hurt Gaby. I get the why. But he barely sleeps, and is becoming irascible," Sam said.

"Yesterday," Kasumi added, "I had to stop him from torturing some cultists, before Agent Culph arrived to take them away. I don't want to even mention what he did to two of those demons that have appeared lately." She wasn't wearing her combat outfit and looked small compared to the taller Estel. Sam took her hand.

"Has he taken his meds?"

"No," Sam said.

"The doctor that prescribed them died in the explosion," Kasumi said. "Also, the supply of the drug has been hard to get. It's not easy to get antidepressants for a Gifted since our brain chemistry is different from a regular person."

"See that? The miasma?" Sam pointed at ground zero.

"Yes," Fionn said. "It's a residual from all the negative energy unleashed after the explosion. And it's affecting him harder than it would do to any of you because he *is* off his meds."

"What can we do?" Kasumi asked. "How bad is it?"

"Not the first time that I have seen this happen." Fionn smiled at her. "I fell prey to that a couple of times and Izia had to smack some sense into me. The Great War left many places like this and it took a century to clean them. I'm not surprised that no one noticed before now with all that's going on, so not your fault. That said, we need to purify this place. But first, I'll get him out of there. Don't worry, I'll bring back your boyfriend."

"Thank you, Dad," Sam sighed in relief.

"I know of a demonhunter cleansing ritual," Kasumi offered. "I have never done it before. And the area to cleanse is so large."

"There is always a first time," Fionn said, and he jumped onto the rail.

"I'll help, tell me what to do," Sam offered.

"Can you summon rain?" Kasumi mused. "That would be faster if we literally bless the water."

"With this weather, it should be piece of cake," Sam said.

"I hope this works," Kasumi whispered.

† † †

"Cloudy night," Fionn said as he approached Alex at a casual stroll.

"I'm busy," Alex said.

"What are you doing, Alex?"

"Trying to find who did this. Because I keep getting the same answer: the Deacon and Abaddon, two of the so called One Hundred and Eight. Well, one hundred, after yesterday. I ran into a few more of them. And I can't seem to decipher what that does mean."

The mention of the Deacon took Fionn back for a moment. The Deacon had been an infamous serial killer he had tracked but never caught during Fionn's heyday as Justicar. He even suspected the man had become some sort of 'mentor' to other killers, like the infamous Dr. Cessaire Murder on Canvas case, and his secret sponsor Alastor Ray. But Fionn had never been able to prove the connection and by then his relationship with Culph had become hostile. That case triggered his PTSD and sent him into a downward spiral, one that ultimately made him a hermit until Harland asked him to track Professor Hunt after Byron had kidnapped him. The second name, Abaddon, was one that Fionn didn't recognize, but his instincts screamed that it was bad news. If it was true, then getting Alex back to a level keel was paramount.

"Maybe you can't because you're exhausted. You've been doing this for three months nonstop." Fionn placed a hand on Alex's shoulder but received a shock. "Sam told me you haven't take your meds."

"They block my creative thinking, make me less aware." His hollow tone made it clear that not even he believed that.

"You of all people know that's not true. That's not how your meds work. They are meant to keep your brain chemistry regulated. Right now, it's not, even less if you haven't taken a break."

"Can't take a break. I need to find who did this to Gaby, since you're not doing it!"

"You were the one to tell me to take care of her. That's what I have been doing. Taking care of my wife. And I was mourning, too, you know?" Fionn reminded him gently.

"Good for you."

He didn't mean that, he didn't mean that, Fionn repeated to himself to keep from punching Alex in the face.

"Alex, you are spinning out of control. You need to rest. You even managed to scare Kasumi, of all people. She faced a titan without special abilities. She doesn't get rattled. And yet, you did it. You need to learn some restraint."

"Funny that from everyone, *you* are the one asking me for restraint."

Fionn raised an eyebrow. "What's that supposed to mean?"

"I know your history, the 'one-man army thing.' Your past is filled with a trail of broken bodies." Alex stood up, facing Fionn. There was a hint of anger in his voice.

"Seriously, Alex, there's a strange miasma here, one that

is affecting you even more harshly because you're not taking your meds. You can't keep doing this. Let's go home. Samantha and Kasumi are freaking out about your current state."

Alex raised his voice as thunder stroke the clouds above. "Are you saying I can't do this because I'm crazy?"

"That's not what I said." Fionn remained calm, but this time he was doing mental calculations on how to stop Alex without hurting him. The storm that Fionn had sensed inside Alex the first time they met was raging, which was the very scenario Fionn had feared all these years. "We're worried about your mental health being altered by whatever is polluting this place."

"Stop saying that I'm crazy!" Alex exclaimed. "I am not! I'm just a bit unwell. Maybe this whole conversation is because you think I'm not good enough to step up?"

"Again, I didn't say that you are crazy. As for the second, if you are asking that then you know the answer already." Fionn replied, showing his open, empty hands.

"Fine. It will prove to you that I'm not crazy. The old-fashioned way," Alex said, and summoned Yaha to his hand. The sword materialized, but this time Fionn noticed it looked like a regular sword. It was as if the sword itself was trying to stop Alex before he hurt himself.

"Put Yaha down," Fionn instructed with a calm voice.

"We knew that one day, it would come to this for us," Alex said. "All students challenge their teachers."

"The last one didn't fare well," Fionn replied. "You are in no condition to do this. Put Yaha down."

"I am not like the last one. And I will prove it."

Alex leapt at Fionn with Yaha in hand, forcing Fionn to unsheathe Black Fang.

As the clash began it started to rain. Neither of them had time to notice how the black, scorched earth changed to a more natural brown where the drops fell.

Yaha and Black Fang didn't transform into Tempest Blades. They were subdued, almost unwilling to engage, not emitting even a faint glow. Both swordsmen traded a swift succession of blows and parries, neither of the blades scoring a hit. Seeing as he wasn't getting anywhere, Alex added kicks to keep Fionn off balance.

I have to give it to him, Fionn thought. *He has improved a lot since I trained him at Skarabear. He is aggressive, but with a plan in mind. Impressive, honestly, considering his exhaus-*

tion and state of mind.

Alex's aggression didn't abate, prodding Fionn's impervious defense for blind spots. But while Alex had improved in his overall swordsmanship, Fionn had spent the past years modifying his combat towards a total defense stance. One could wonder why someone with healing factor would prefer a defensive stance, but Fionn still felt every injury, and the healing process wasn't entirely painless.

Riposte, parry, deflection, slash, kick. Alex tried every combination on Fionn till he managed to push Black Fang to the side, opening Fionn's defense. But instead of slashing, Alex went for a kick that pushed Fionn backwards.

For someone bent on beating me, he certainly is avoiding lethal blows, Fionn thought. He needs the outlet to get it all out of his system.

Fionn rolled back and got into position for a second barrage of attacks. He walked backwards with each blow, ceding more ground to Alex. The rain continued to fall.

Alex made for a spin attack, the kind both knew were fancy but functionally useless. This time Fionn used that to push Yaha aside, grabbing the hand holding it and twisting it, allowing him to punch Alex in the face.

Alex threw his head back enough to roll with the blow, but not enough to avoid a bloody nose. With his left hand, he wiped the blow and approached Fionn with relentless attacks.

I'm proud of him. He is good, even as tired as he is. Fionn smiled. But I'm better.

Putting his duel with Byron aside, Fionn hadn't had an opponent that pushed his skills to the limit. Gaby was certainly more than capable to beat him, and had done it before, but theirs were sparring sessions, aimed at working out how to improve, and always ended in other types of 'concessions.' This was different. It was a proper fight. Even if Alex was somehow managing to contain himself from whatever was making him attack his mentor, it didn't mean that the blows weren't dangerous. Fionn found himself relishing the duel. It brought back memories of training with Ywain, who could get quite intense in their fights.

Same tree, different branch.

Alex tried broader slashes, forcing Fionn to open his defense enough for the former to return the favor to the latter and deliver a haymaker to the face. Fionn heard the crushing bones of his nose under Alex's fist. Fionn fell to the ground as Alex approached.

That was unexpected, he didn't pull that punch. So I won't.

Fionn kicked Alex in the solar plexus, making him expel all the air in his lungs. Dizzy, Alex shambled for a few seconds until he recovered his breath, dropping Yaha for a moment. Then delivered a flying kick towards Fionn, who was getting up. Fionn fell back once more and rolled to his left to avoid a stomping kick. Jumping to his feet, Fionn threw a punch with his right hand, which Alex deflected with his forearm. They traded kicks and punches in quick succession, most of them being blocked, a few hitting ribs, abdomens, or faces. Alex threw a second haymaker, but Fionn managed to grab his arm in time to torque at the hip and throw him over the shoulder.

He several meters away. Alex stood once more and cleaned the blood still running from his nose. Fionn did the same, then, biting his lip, broke his nose again to fix it in the right place and allow it to heal faster. Breathing with more ease, both saw their respective blades lying a few meters away and darted after them. Fionn grabbed Black Fang in time to block the incoming attack.

There is no way Alex moved so fast, unless he already learned to call Yaha to his hand.

Both began a second furious barrage of attacks that ended with both blades blocking each other. Both threw a punch towards each other's face, and both fists intercepted each other.

The force of the clash sent them flying backwards, with each of them hitting the ground hard. But whereas Fionn had his healing factor to rely on, Alex had his stubbornness. They ran to each other to clash swords once more.

The third time, Alex changed approach. Instead of going for fast attacks, he delivered more powerful, focused, bone rattling blows.

This was how he beat Shemazay, Fionn mused as he gritted his teeth. That last blow was painful. It is a good plan.

Fionn braced himself for another blow with Yaha. What he didn't expect and caught him by surprise, was that Alex instead swept his legs.

Fionn fell to the ground flat on his back, as Alex kicked him again in the sword holding hand, forcing him to let go of

Black Fang. Alex raised Yaha to deliver a thrust with the sword, as Fionn readied to block it barehanded.

But the thrust never came.

Exhausted, Alex finally threw Yaha to the side and let his arms hang limply at his sides as small drops of water descended upon them. It wasn't a heavy, belly-washing rain, but a light and steady drizzle. Kasumi's ritual had worked.

Fionn sighed and considered Alex, finding unexpected tranquility in the moment. He rolled to his side and stood up.

"I'm sorry," Alex whispered, kneeling before Fionn, realizing what he had been close to doing, exhausted as the restlessness of the past three months at last caught up with him. Fionn extended a hand to him. "I'm not doing well inside my head. Sam, Kasumi! I'm so sorry for scaring you! I know I suck!"

"You don't suck," Fionn replied with a smile as he helped Alex to stand up. "You spent the past three months taking care of the city nonstop and trying to find out who caused this mess, so Gaby and I could take some personal time. You took it upon yourself to be the leader, and helped Harland as much as you could. We all know your meds have become hard to get, that you are not taking them anymore to save them for an emergency. But caring for your mental health *is* the emergency. You're not crazy, just relapsed and exhausted. That left you open to be manipulated by whatever miasma is polluting this place. Even Yaha knew that because it still worked with you, but not at full capacity. Part of being a leader is remembering the lesson that you of all people should know all too well: don't push yourself that far, and remember to ask for help."

"I know, I just..." Alex sighed. "I thought I could do it, but never considered the miasma affecting me because running out of my antidepressants."

"You did it well for as long as was humanly possible. As for the other thing, it happens to the best of us."

"Did it happen to you?"

"More times I want to admit, luckily for me Izia was a great shaman and knew how to fix it."

"I need help."

"I know," Fionn said as he hugged Alex. He didn't need someone berating him, he needed compassion. It had taken Fionn quite some time to understand Alex's condition, not being aware that his own PTSD wasn't that different. He even had a long talk on the way there with Yokoyawa to understand how to approach Alex. He wondered if eventually pushing Alex into a leadership role was a good idea. But Fionn's faith in Alex remained steady. "That's why I'm here for you, little brother. Let it all out."

"I don't want to be like this again," Alex cried as Sam and Kasumi jumped into the now cleansed ground and ran towards him at a full sprint. "Something is broken inside me."

"We will find a way to help you get through this until we can get more of your meds. The same way you helped me and Gaby by taking care of everything when we needed the time to heal," Fionn offered. He let go of Alex and guided him towards Sam's and Kasumi's open arms.

"I'm so sorry, Sam, I thought I was better," Alex sobbed, finally letting his guard down. "I'm sorry, Kasumi, for disappointing you, for scaring you. Did I hurt you?"

"You didn't disappoint me," Kasumi said. "And you only hurt my feelings a bit. But I forgive you."

"Wait ... You aren't disappointed? You expected me to fail?" Alex replied, taken a bit aback.

"No offense, hon," Sam added. "But you have this bad habit of pushing yourself too hard, to the detriment of your well being. And when you do that, you tend to forget your treatment or even getting enough rest. I hoped that you wouldn't, but I'm not surprised."

"Please don't take it the wrong way, Alex," Kasumi said. "We love you very much, as you are, but we do want you to get better. You have to be more responsible from now on with your health. We can help you, but you also have to help yourself."

"I'm sorry," Alex replied, humbled. "You are right. I will be more disciplined from now on. Let's go home."

Fionn knelt and to the surprise of everyone, lifted Yaha without rejection.

"I could eat something," Fionn said. "Let's get you home. And tomorrow I will check with the Foundation to get your prescription refilled. Yoko is on his way too, for a therapy session. We will get you through this—"

"People of Theia!" a booming voice interrupted Fionn. It came from the sky, as the image of a humanoid demon, wearing a robe to cover its flayed body appeared in the sky.

"What the hell is that?" Kasumi asked.

"An astroprojection into real world?" Sam mused.

"That's a high-level spell."

"And who the hell is that guy? Why does he look familiar?" Alex asked.

"You know me as the Creeping Chaos, the Golden King," the image said, almost as if it was answering Alex's question. "You might have heard of these names. But they don't matter anymore. There is only one name: Abaddon. I am the First Demon. I am your *reckoning*. Your time is up. Your heroes won't save you. It will be painfully slow for you, but in the end won't be mercy or surrender. Only oblivion."

Alex noticed how Fionn clenched his fists till his knuckles were white. It wasn't the threat making him seethe. Or at least, not just the threat. It was something else. Alex leaned on Sam.

"Is it me or are his eyes way too familiar?" Kasumi whispered to Sam and Alex.

"It's not just you," Sam said, somber. "Dad noticed it, too. This Abaddon is mocking them specifically."

"The alternative is even worse," Alex muttered as he glanced towards where the morgue room of the hospital should have been. Sam tightened her grasp on his hand.

For Abaddon's eyes were one blue and one green. The exact tone and color of Gaby and Fionn's respectively. The implications were dire in the best case, disturbing in the worst. A vibrant red light exploded on the horizon. All at once, locations all over Theia began to suffer from multiple planar incursions. The Pits were infesting Theia with some sort of dimensional cancer, trapping many inside the incursion zones, killing even more, and sending the world into the end of the days.

Those mocking green and blue eyes were the last thing many saw before closing their own.

Chapter 3
Weight of the World

IF THERE WAS SOMETHING HARLAND hated about his new job, and there were several things—like bureaucracy amidst a planetary crisis—it was watching the news. It has been almost a year since the explosion that had put him in power and the planet was by now peppered with quarantine zones, regions where the Pits had manifested in reality, warping all inside them, unleashing incursions all over the continents. These incursions were led by the 'one hundred and eight generals of the Inferno,' which was what survivors reported the demons called them. Which tracked with the lore from each region. If Harland had known that the star fall he had witnessed after Gaby had destroyed the Crown of the Dead were those demon generals, as many legends and prophecies warned, he would have asked the samoharo to blast them with nova bombs before they entered the atmosphere. Well, less than one hundred and eight now, if the Band of the Greywolf kept whittling them down after grueling fights. Either way the result was the same, the planet was slowly becoming a corrupted, entropic mess, infested with a cancerous rot.

The poor souls trapped in those zones were either encased in stone or changed into horrible creatures that begged for mercy. And leading all of this was an entity that called himself Abaddon, the First Demon reborn. To make matters worse, Sam hadn't been able to contact Mekiri's divine form, nor Joshua to locate his patron Ben Erra, which meant that two gods—The Trickster Goddess and the Devil, the Judge and Jailer of evil—who were supposed to be on their side, were gone, maybe forever. Had they been destroyed by this Abaddon?

With half the planet bisected by walls of pit fire, communication with the Samoharo hegemony had become erratic. Harland was keeping the Alliance, or what was left of it, together by sheer force of will. He was worried and beyond exhausted.

Makes you wonder how Alex, Sid and Yoko are dealing with not hearing anything from their families in the South.

There was only one news station that was still operational, so Harland had to hear his least favorite news person, Mr. Funktastic.

Carolina, she's professional. I can take the hits from her. But Funktastic? His comments are unprofessional and only cause more tensions. If only he could be a bit more balanced in his opinions, Harland thought, as a migraine began. He reached for the pill bottle out of habit, but then he remembered that medicine supply chains were the first thing to collapse and the few raw materials available were being used to manufacture the most essential pharmaceuticals. And, by his own orders, distributed to the emergency health systems in the refugee camps. Both human medics and freefolk healers were reaching their breaking point, and the samoharo weren't returning his calls. As if she had read his mind, Amy, his assistant from the Foundation gave him a soothing gummy that the freefolk healers had advised as alternative.

Harland took the gummy from Amy's hand and the transmission began its countdown to start.

At least I have this. Alex must have run out of his antidepressants by now and the ones he needs are harder to make. And Gaby... Harland stopped his train of thought. The intimate tragedy that befell the Estel-Galfano family was still a raw nerve that made his heart ache. The transmission began, providing merciful distraction.

"I am Carolina Buenrostro."

"And I'm Mr. Funktastic, for Aethernet News."

"Earlier today, a group of refugees protested during a meeting between interim Alliance leader Harland Rickman and elders of the Freefolk Fire tribe, to ask them to take in more human evacuees from the quarantine zones. The elders agreed on condition that the humans abided by the tribe's rules, especially when it came to starting fires to keep the cold at bay. The Freefolk have lodged complaints that humans are using their sacred trees as fuel rather than asking the Freefolk magi to aid them. While the Alliance and the Freefolk managed to reach an agreement, the protest erupted and disturbed the meeting. The protesters were demanding that the Alliance do more to help people reach the World's Scar, the last place of refuge for many. Mr. Rickman explained that the Alliance and the Foundation were doing all they could but were severely short staffed. As we know, the first casualties in the massive waves of incursions were Alliance titanfighters that were not prepared to deal with this crisis," Carolina explained.

"He looks exhausted," Mr. Funktastic added. "Makes you wonder what the Samoharo and the Band of the Greywolf are doing. I'll tell you: nothing of worth!"

"While the samoharo claim to have evacuated the Straits and south Kuni inhabitants, there is no proof as communications have been interrupted. The Band of the Greywolf did make several appearances to reinforce Mr. Rickman's claims," Carolina continued with her report.

"Some caravans reported the famed Figaro airship kept flying incursions away from them, while two surviving Solarian Knights led them through the gravitational alteration near Manfeld," Mr. Funktastic added. He was a well-known fan of the Figaro and had raised several times that more ships like that should be built—and fast—to save more people from the growing pit-infected zones. That had prompted Harland to instruct the Alliance to rebuild the remaining dreadnought from the Great War. Meanwhile, the Figaro and the X-23 were doing all the heavy lifting. Sid and Scud were probably sleeping less than three hours per day, running on cacao and adrenaline.

We need more pilots, Harland thought. The only other two certified pilots were either busy running the Alliance or running into infested zones to rescue people.

"Today the city of Darrington fell to the incursion wave and became an infested zone, as the surviving titanfighters, veterans Bev Johnson, Simon Belerofont, and their fellow titanfighter, and former runway model Jean Aramis, were the last ones to keep the few survivors alive. Our exclusive footage shows ash falling, as demonic incursions were about to kill the titanfighters when the signature energy arrow of freefolk adoptee and hero of the titan crisis, Alejandro León destroyed several incursions. Aided by current—or would it be former Chivalry Games champion?—demonhunter Kasumi Shimizu, and Joshua, another Games competitor. The so-called 'Godkiller' managed to save the titanfighters and take them and several hundred citizens of Darrington to a refugee camp."

"What was left of them," Mr. Funktastic added, his voice dripping in sarcasm. "I have it on good authority that Alejandro León has not had treatment in many months. How advisable is to have a guy nicknamed the 'Godkiller' without his meds? No wonder Darrington fell."

Harland scowled. Darrington fell because the city state leaders were too slow to evacuate. And the distance to cover, even with Sam's teleportation spell, which she could only cast a few times a week, plus the lack of capable fighters meant that Alex, like the rest of the Band was working with no sleep, barely eating and holding on by a thread. And yet the kid, as Harland liked to call him, never complained, just went on to the next mission. And the next one, ad nauseum.

"Remind me to punch Mr. Funktastic in the face for that comment," Harland said blandly.

"I won't boss," Amy said, faintly wry. "You need to keep a certain image. I, on the other hand, don't. I'll punch him for you. And I'm sure a queue will form to take turns."

"As that took place," Carolina continued, "Lady Galfano-Estel visited another refugee camp near the ruins of Saint Lucy, aided by her assistant Vivienne Ortiga, former freefolk magick instructor. They distributed medicines, food packages, and counseled survivors. Lady Galfano-Estel even offered an impromptu concert to lift the spirits of the camp."

"No one cares about her music," Mr. Funktastic said. "She should go and grieve in private."

"Vivi won't like that," Amy said, holding Harland's hand so he wouldn't break the screen. "And while I'm sure milady won't care about that comment, I'm also sure her husband is another matter. We might have to send Funktastic into witness protection."

"This just in," Carolina said, both to redirect and clearly irritated by her co-host. Gaby's personal tragedy was well known, and many considered her child the first casualty of this apocalypse. "Fionn Estel, the Greywolf, just destroyed one of the one hundred and eight reported demonic generals, a few minutes ago, outside the ruins of Portis. What made this feat even more impressive is that we have received reports, footage, and personal accounts by evacuees, that the Greywolf battled this incursion of gigantic proportions, across the continent. There are unconfirmed reports that the Greywolf sprouted wings and punched the incursion through a mountain. One of the reporters following the caravan caught up with the Greywolf outside Portis and asked him about the situation. The Greywolf, still carrying the demon's head in his hand, only replied that the self- proclaimed First Demon, Abaddon, would be next. The Greywolf then ran towards another incursion. This brings the Band of the Greywolf's tally of defeated demonic generals to one hundred destroyed, fifty alone by the Greywolf himself. If I didn't know better that sound mythical."

Mr. Funktastic gulped, and that brought a smile to Harland's face.

"Insulting the wife and friends of the person that did that might have been a mistake," Carolina said with a coy smile. "This is all the news for now. This was a production of Broadcasters United."

Amy turned off the screen. "You need to go to sleep, boss, you can't do your job and help others if you're too exhausted to function," she said.

Relenting, Harland said, "I think you're right."

Seeing his friends carrying the weight of the world on their shoulders—while being insulted daily on the news, with no complaints—rekindled the tiny spark of hope Harland often forgot he still had.

If they can keep doing it despite being punched on a daily basis, so can I. So can we all.

† † †

"This is depressing," Alex said to no one as he looked at the three lousy antidepressant pills left in his bottle.

To say that the surrounding landscape had seen better days would be an understatement. It was gray. The sky was under a perennial twilight. The land only needed one strong wind to start a dustbowl, the trees were dead and fossilized. The few signs of life remaining in what should have been a green valley was a pathetic stream and the fortress still hosting a sizable town population. They were survivors of the first wave of incursions that the First Demon had unleashed months ago after E-day, the explosion that had obliterated most of Saint Lucy. Most survivors, those that had managed to evade the incursions or avoid being fossilized into the new reality had been evacuated either south to the Samoharo Hegemony—like Alex's parents had been—or north into Freefolk territory past the natural defense that was the World's Scar. Of course, that only included the Core Regions. Alex wondered how the people in the Grasslands or in the Wasteland were faring, the same way he wondered why these last stragglers remained in what was soon to be a dead land.

"It's their home. They'll try to remain here as long as possible," Sam told him from her trike, as if she had been reading his mind. Since that day at the crater, Alex had become more closed, keeping himself in check. In part, this was to avoid another incident, because his antidepressants having almost run out created the side effect of making his reactions slower than usual. And the voices in his head were back, telling him how much he sucked. He'd been asking Yokoyawa for more therapy sessions and he felt guilty about that. Yoko's time could have been better used to help others in worse situations. The Foundation's resources were all spread thin at the moment, trying to rescue as many people and creatures as possible that were fleeing from the encroaching ruin. It had been only the insightfulness of Sam, inherited from her adoptive dad, and the recent calmness of Kasumi, that had helped him to keep his worst enemy, his own mind, more or less under control. Without them, Alex knew he would have fallen quite deep. Deeper than he already had, even after hitting a new low. And while it was not exactly the best nor healthiest option, to depend that way on his partners, it would have to do for the time being.

Alex gave Sam a weak smile as both turned off the trikes. Joshua soon joined them after making a lap to look for potential problems.

"I get that," Alex replied. "But I'm not sure how long that will keep motivating them. Even the fauna left this place months ago."

"As long as they have their alchemic terraforming to coax as much as they can from the ground, they will stay."

"Alex is right," Joshua added after turning off his trike. "Time ran out. There are no incursions yet on this plateau, but I saw a few mutated corpses coming this way."

"And those always precede the big ones," Alex sighed.

"Hon." Sam placed a hand on his shoulder. "I know how

much this whole situation gets to you. And we love that quality of your heart. But two things: don't let it get you down, and remember that we're here with you. You are not going to lose another settlement. Just let me do the talking."

"It will be fine, Alex." Joshua offered a sympathetic smile.

"Famous last words," Alex said.

† † †

"I appreciate and I'm honored that the three of you came to check on us," Marshall said. "But as you can see, we are doing fine."

Alex observed from the battlements at the land inside the walls. While the population of the town was smaller than previously reported—a bout of maroon fever had claimed many lives—the land was thriving. To a point. The people here had developed a nano-chemical procedure that bordered on alchemic transmutation at the atomic level to terraform the ground and make it fertile. Whereas the stream had become dryer, deep drilling into phreatic mantles provided water. It was enough to keep them growing their own vegetables. But a second round of the fever would doom this population. Since the Decay began to rot the planet in splotches, the fever had spread like an ancient plague.

I guess it's a good thing the Gift makes us immune to the fever, Alex thought as he recalled Kasumi telling him how she'd gotten the illness as a little child. She had survived but the illness had taken away most of her hearing. *I miss Kasumi.*

"Your people are not safe here, Marshall," Sam continued. "The fever took a huge toll in lives."

"And there are a few incursions in close proximity to you," Joshua added.

"My outriders didn't see anything," Marshall said as one of the outriders, a tall, muscular woman, handed him a recurve bow. "And even if that were true, these bows that combine your magick with our alchemy are all the weapons we need."

Sam grabbed the bow and examined it, before passing it to Alex, who took it to the other side of the battlement to examine it.

"He doesn't talk much, does he?" Marshall whispered, to no avail, for Alex could hear him perfectly. "I expected the

Godkiller to be more... outspoken."

How I hate that stupid nickname, Alex thought as he pulled the string. The quality of the bow was undeniable, sturdy, and powerful. Probably better than the bows he had designed years ago. His examination was interrupted when he saw something shambling in the distance, through a group of dead trees.

"He has taken a vow of silence out of respect for the fallen," Sam explained with a forced smile, and accepted the bow back from Alex.

"It's a nice weapon, and I'm sure your alchemic arrows are quite effective," Alex said. "But I'm breaking my vow momentarily to tell you that they won't work against the bigger incursions. It will work with the small one coming this way though. As long as it's not part of a swarm."

"Small one?" Marshall questioned as he took out a pair of binoculars and examined the landscape, then passed them to the outrider, who whistled to call two more archers.

In the distance there was a half-rotten humanoid body shambling its way towards the fortress. Probably a poor victim that didn't get fossilized, but rather half-eaten, half-possessed, judging by the torn jaw barely containing the tentacles protruding from its mouth, or the scorpion tails—plural—sprouting from its back like overgrown kudzu vines. Inside that formerly human body, there was an incursion, a literal demon from hell puppeteering the corpse, looking for more energy to drain. It was another reason Harland had dispatched them there: the alchemic process used by this town to survive emitted enough energy to attract incursions. Also, the process could prove vital to an eventual planetary recovery effort, once they, which meant the band of the Greywolf, found a way to deal with the First Demon, who was more interested in slowly consuming the world than in an outright confrontation for now. As if Alex or any of them needed the extra pressure.

The outriders released a volley of arrows that swiftly crossed the distance and transformed the corpse into a pincushion.

"As I said," Marshall said. "We have everything under control. Look, Samantha, I respect you people for all the efforts you have made to help others during these testing times, but I can't avoid that your boss or your father only want to take us as refugees for our knowledge. The Mistlands are not particularly suited to grow crops and hunting to feed all the refuges would soon create an ecological collapse on par to... this." Marshall waved his right hand in an arc to encompass all what the eye could see.

"I resent that last remark," Sam said tersely, struggling to keep her temper in check. "You are right on your assessments but for one: we care about your people first, not your procedure. We would be here even if that didn't exist."

"You, sure. But where is your father?"

Alex kept listening to the conversation while he leaned on the edge of the battlements. As years gone by, his senses, thanks to the Gift, were evolving. Becoming more powerful. Whereas he once had to wear glasses to see well beyond ten meters, now he only used them as protection from the sun or from spending too much time in front of a monitor. It was also why he was able to see that the pincushion was moving again. He traded a look with Joshua, nodding towards the horizon.

"My dad is busy, dealing with a bigger incursion east of here, closer to the Line," Sam said.

The Line was the band across the planet that was for all purposes lost, the total dominion of the First Demon; a land that warped reality, bent light, and slowly decayed everything. It was the event horizon of an entropic black hole, if such a thing could exist. But Alex was not in the mood to think of a proper metaphor. He had spotted more movement.

"Is he so busy that he can't pay us a visit? I get his deeds are legendary, but that's not how to convince us to leave out ancestral land, you freefolk of all people need to understand that."

Fionn's deeds had indeed became the stuff of legends, like that time he dragged a massive incursion, a demon as twice the size of an elephant across the Long Horn Valley and kicked it all over the continent. Or when he cut a mountain to create a pass to evacuate a town. If they were rumors about another person, not even Alex, who had stared down two actual gods in their avatar forms, would believe it. But since losing their unborn child, Gaby and Fionn tried to deal with the grief as best as they could when they were not together. Gaby composed music to lift the spirits. Fionn literally dragged demonic spirits across the continent and destroyed them with ease, as if he was some sort of mythic being. His Gift hadn't given any sign that it would stop increasing in strength. It was inhuman, even for a Gifted. Fionn was all over the core regions, taking advantage of the way Sam rewrote the rules of magick two years ago to allow herself and a few select magi, like Vivi, to use the teleportation spell more efficiently. Of course, even Sam's meddling had limits given the circumstances which surrounded it, and the spell only worked well for smaller groups, which made evacuations harder. Yet another reason the Foundation was trying to develop more flying machines to accelerate procedures. The mother of necessity and all. Harland had unearthed the other dreadnought from the Great War, but it was still months from being usable.

When Sam spoke, she raised her voice. "So, you think we're second fiddle?"

"Let's be honest. The big gun is Fionn. You are his students, and most of what you say you did, is no more than urban legends," Marshall said. "Why should I trust the safety of my people to you? How many refugee caravans have been lost so far? We have heard the news too. Your esteemed Godkiller here lost a whole city."

"He did not lose a city. Last time I checked people made it out alive thanks to my heartmates and the only two titanfighters brave enough to actually do their jobs. Want me to call Bev Johnson, so you can verify?" Sam challenged.

Alex still felt guilty for losing Darrington, having arrived late. Sure, they had been in time to save Bev Johnson and his friend Jean Aramis, who had taken it upon themselves to protect civilians in the ruins of the ash covered city. After the E-day, only two Solarian knights had survived, Chakumuy and Salvador Drakaralov. They'd been lucky enough to be off duty when the deluge happened. The rest, including Augustus Mu, had died in the explosion, taking all the armors with it. And of the rest of the titanfighters, most had run away and died scared, easy pickings due to their lack of actual combat experience. Only a few veterans such as Bev Johnson had risen to the occasion. The Kuni Empire had fared better, as the demonhunters were by far better organized than the more individualistic titanfighters—but even they were losing members fast. Unfortunately, that meant the Gifted, of which there were only five, plus a few very special allies with enough experience, had to pick up the slack. And protecting a whole continent even with teleportation spells at your beck and call was not easy. It made Fionn's prowess all the more epic.

"As for the other caravans, we weren't there. We *are* here now so that doesn't happen again. What do you even want? A show of power?" Sam continued as her irises began to glow.

"So much for a diplomacy skill check," Alex whispered.

"I prefer intimidation myself," Joshua said.

Both walked towards Sam and Alex took hold of Sam's hand, which was already releasing tiny sparkles of thaum particles, the stuff that made magick happen. In the past he would have been hot under the collar and tempted to challenge the man, but after a year from absolute hell, Alex was exhausted, sad, and more concerned about the metaphorical weight of the world on their shoulders rather than proving a point. He had found that those points tended to prove themselves, anyway, as if the universe wanted to have the last word. And who was Alex to deny the universe said pleasure?

"The pincushion corpse is up and shambling its way here, along with four friends. And judging by the scorpions' tails, they are not minor incursions."

"Class three, at least," Joshua confirmed.

The outriders and Marshall ran to the battlements and saw the small cluster of corpses walking their way. A class three incursion was enough to kill anyone below a titan-fighter level. It was the kind of incursion that had almost killed Alex the day he got the Gift. And he'd had to deal with swarms of them for the following days, without sleep or food. Five was enough to level the whole fortress, despite how ridiculous they looked as rotten corpses.

"There are five of them," Marshall muttered. "Shoot them!"

The outriders did as ordered, but not even the alchemic arrows stopped them. The lumbering tapered off into a pregnant pause, but it wasn't enough. It only delayed their march for a few minutes.

Alex crept towards the battlement as the energy rings coming from his bracelet on his left hand formed a facsimile of an atomic structure. His golden bow formed in his hand. Standing in front of the outriders, Alex let loose three energy arrows that obliterated the corpses with ease. Maybe Fionn was on an epic level, power wise, but Alex was not far behind.

"You missed two," one outrider muttered.

"He didn't," Sam said, and made a short, quick gesture that released three crystalline missiles of energy that destroyed the remaining two. A third missile went further back, and the explosion took down a sixth incursion that was hidden behind a tree. "He left them for me as a courtesy."

Alex's energy bow went back into the bracelet, and he went back to watching the farmed land.

"You got your power demonstration," Sam said to Marshall. "Now, are you willing to trust us that this land is safe?"

"How long do we have to evacuate?" Marshall asked.

"Three days, maximum," Joshua said. "Class three incursions usually travel in small clusters like that one and far ahead of larger swarms of class four and above. But not that far. And the soil is already showing signs of decay, not just erosion. Soon your water will be contaminated. Living here won't be sustainable any longer."

"If you can get your people ready with whatever vehicles you still have and taking enough for the trek to the Scar, we will go with you. And I swear," Sam added, "we will keep you all alive. As you saw, we are more than capable."

"Okay, we leave in two days," Marshall told his outriders.

What a shame, Alex thought. As small as the farmed land was inside the fortress, it was living proof of human ingenuity and a good application of permaculture. Yet maybe it had come too late for a planet that was for all intents dying. *I hope we can fix it somehow.*

† † †

As Sam, Alex, and Joshua led the caravan towards the pickup spot where Sid agreed to meet them with the Figaro, the ash rain fell once more. He noticed a small child walking with his parents. They were a bit away from the rest of the group. He did a quick scan of the area but didn't see anything.

Alex stifled a yawn and looked upwards to the cloud covered sky. He could feel in his bones that the key or keys to save the planet were tucked somewhere in the databanks of the space station only he and Sam knew was out there, disguised as what others knew as the Long Moon. He could also feel, due to the buzzing in his ears, that something was off, but there was nothing in sight.

They'd had to convince Harland to allow Sid to fly the Figaro there, not because he didn't want to, but because Harland depended on the Figaro for rescue missions. But as mentioned before, the universe had this innate need to make a point and have the last word, and soon, it would take care of convincing Harland for Alex.

The Figaro appeared on the horizon and Alex gave a sigh of relief. Then he saw that it was being chased by airships of unknown origin. Before he could fully register the threat to the Figaro, Alex felt a vibration in the ground. He turned toward where the child and his parents were walking and saw a new kind of incursion surge from the ground. It went for the small child. Alex's reaction was too slow from too many days of ceaseless activity and even less rest, but still fast enough to take the hit instead the kid. The incursion, which resembled a large lizard with sickle-like claws, brought one down on Alex. Blood washed down his back with the wound that gouged across it from hip to shoulder, and he fell face first into the rocky ground with a muffled grunt of pain.

"Alex!" Sam yelled. She immediately went to work to cast one of the largest teleportation spells anyone had ever tried.

"I got him!" Joshua replied as he activated Fury, converting the double-bladed weapon into pure fire.

"Listen, everybody," Sam ordered the caravan. "Joshua will cover you while I teleport you to Skarabear. Remain together because it's dangerous to step out of the circles."

"What about you three?" Marshall asked.

"Our ride is coming in hot. We will cover you till the spell is concluded. Keep your people safe!" Sam said as she pushed him into the teleportation circle.

"Thank you," Marshal said. He shouted, "And I'm sorry for doubting you!" as the teleportation spell sent him and the rest of the caravan to the safety of Skarabear.

Bleeding from the mouth after his fall, Alex stood up and summoned his atomic bow. His sight was too blurry to aim.

Joshua destroyed the incursion.

The Figaro approached on what seemed a collision course. Or a quick pick up, as the enemy airships were quickly approaching.

Should have taken one of my pills, Alex thought before Joshua lifted him over his shoulder. Joshua picked up an exhausted Sam and ran towards the Figaro as Alex finally gave into to his exhaustion and passed out.

Chapter 4
Defiance in the Sky

"Again," Fionn said to Kasumi.

Kasumi took a deep breath and tried to focus on her Gift. The core inside her activated, but it still had too much pent up 'emotion,' so to speak, and as Kasumi's irises glowed with a white-blueish light, a wave of cold air hit Fionn, leaving him covered in frost.

"Apologies, *sensei,*" Kasumi said, bowing her heard towards Fionn as he shook off the frost.

Fionn smiled. The word *sensei* reminded him of when he trained under his own sensei and adoptive second mother, the demonhunter Hikaru. It also reminded him that he would have to visit her again, for after decades searching for her, he'd finally found her as the oracle of the Storm Temple, the oracle that had provided Kasumi with Breaker.

Fionn had taken Kasumi under his wing as mentee, as he had done before with Alex, Gaby, and Sam. She had asked him to teach her how to control her Gift, which still had the propensity to explode in the worst moments, deep-freezing everything in the immediate vicinity. Despite her training as a demonhunter, which should have given her the basics to control the Gift, she still lacked the finesse the others had. Her advantage was that her integration, aside from the occasional emotional outburst, had gone smoothly and progressed to a stage not far from the others in less than two years. But Fionn knew the real reason she had asked him for lessons was that she wanted to learn the special technique to focus her inner power into a ranged energy attack. "A fireball attack like the arcades," Alex had called it, to differentiate it from the thunder strike he had used when killing the Creeping Chaos and Ywain decades before him.

Kasumi had suggested *Kaminariken*, a combination of two words from Kuni that roughly translated into 'fist of the thunder and lightning.'

The kanjis used to write it could also be translated as 'Fist of the Gods.' All had agreed to the suggestion, after seeing a demonstration by Fionn.

Fionn had learned how to do the kaminariken with his bare hands and had destroyed a tovainar at close range. After the past months, as he and Gaby worked on their grief, he had found training Kasumi in learning how to control her Gift to later learn the kaminariken technique unexpectedly soothing.

He and Kasumi were training in the courtyard at the former headquarters of the Foundation, the old mansion that Harland's father had acquired decades ago. It now stood empty, a hollowed-out husk of its former self. Harland had moved the Foundation to Skarabear after the Chivalry games and he had moved the leaders of the Alliance there, too, after the initial incidents as it was far from the incursion zones.

Gaby was off to the side doing her own training, freefolk therapeutic meditation under Vivi's guidance—even though Vivi had left a day ago to join Sid on a mission. Gaby had gotten the gist of what she had to do. The loss of their child had made her reluctant to fight. Her Tempest Blade rested inside the gauntlet on her left wrist. But as many an artist would understand, Gaby had found an outlet for her pain in her music and had gotten back to writing a new album, even though nobody knew when Hildebrandtia would have another chance to play in public.

Fionn looked at Gaby meditating and then back at Kasumi. He laughed.

"Don't worry," Fionn said. "You're way ahead considering that not long ago you got the Gift. Which might be the problem; there might be some residue from its previous owner. We will leave it for now and return to practice later in the afternoon."

"And what we will do meanwhile?" Kasumi asked.

"I suggest you take a break, get some food. Me? I'm gonna use the Foundation's thermal bath," Fionn said. He'd been waiting for months to have a day off between missions to take that restorative bath.

† † †

"Can I ask you something, Kasumi?" Gaby asked, breaking out from her mediation pose on a large concrete planter. "I love Fionn, but even as observant as he can be, some things need a less warrior-esque approach. And my question might help you and I find out why your Gift activates in such an explosive manner."

"Sure. You can ask me anything," Kasumi said, taking a seat next to Gaby.

"After these years of knowing you, you have always seemed to be an extrovert: assertive, dominant. But I have noticed that when you are with Sam or Alex you become quieter, relaxed, and almost submissive, perhaps? I was curious because despite being with Fionn all these years and you know, a previous life, I'm still new to how things work with a freefolk throuple."

"And Fionn is single person focused, basically you and only you? Unlike most freefolk?"

"Vivi also only has eyes for Sid, so it is not that uncommon for them. I apologize if it is too intrusive."

"We are friends, and I told you to ask me anything. Yes, it has been a curious process, coming to terms with my sexual orientation. The Kuni are conservative in that regard. And people from the Straits are too, so Alex has been on a learning curve as well."

She paused for a moment, then continued, "Now, to answer your question. You know how—due to all we have done in these past years—people outside our quirky family-slash-tribe expect us to act in a certain way that it is unlike how we are in private? Like Alex being this daredevil god killing machine when we know he suffers from crippling anxiety along with his chronic depression? Or how Sam can come off as a bit haughty, bullish to strangers when in reality she is such a caring, tender, joking person?

"Or how Fionn is looked up as a hero when he kinda dislikes people in general after years of seeing the worst of society while working as Justicar? Or me always being labelled the rich rock star or you being the Games Champion and strongest woman in the world?" Gaby said.

"Yes. Most people, including my own blood relatives, tend to see me and expect me to act as this tough, disabled girl that has to prove constantly to the world that being deaf is not a barrier to be the best warrior. And I'm not deaf, I'm hard-of-hearing," Kasumi added, sounding annoyed.

"I bet it gets tiresome," Gaby said.

"It is," Kasumi agreed. "Interviews, predictions, being called an example for all. I don't want to be an example for anyone. I just want to be me. And I can only be me when I'm with Sam and Alex."

Gaby showcased her crooked smile. It was as she suspected. Maybe those semesters studying psychology before switching to music weren't wasted after all.

"I think that might be the issue," Gaby explained. "Your two personas, so to speak, are on opposite ends of a range, and you go from one to the other right away. Maybe your Gift is reacting to that and, given that it is connected in part to our emotions, the jump creates some unseen pressure that it's relieved in this 'explosive' manner."

Kasumi pondered Gaby's analysis for a moment.

"It makes sense," Kasumi said. "But what should I do?"

"Just choose who you want to be, and the other be damned," Gaby replied.

"Thank you, *sensei*," Kasumi said. "I want to ask you a question now: how are you doing?"

"The show must go on," Gaby said with sadness in her eyes. Changing the subject, she added, "I'm hungry. I'm going to the kitchen, wanna join me?"

"Maybe in a minute."

† † †

Kasumi was relaxing, meditating on Gaby's observations. She had just lifted her water bottle to her lips when she heard a strange noise in the air. Kasumi paused and looked up to see a squadron of airships that she had never seen before. They crossed the sky and shot at the Foundation's building, destroying most of it.

Her first reaction was to pick up Breaker, which glowed a pulsing white in response. She sprinted towards the building, as Gaby and Fionn were still inside. She could sense their presence there, in the rubble. But that vague feeling didn't tell her if they were conscious or in need of assistance, and right now, her main concern was to make sure they made it out alive.

The ships flew by once more and from them several creatures jumped. They landed, surrounding her, a group of strange alien creatures, with four arms, deep blue, slippery skin, round yellow eyes with no pupils, broad muscles and cybernetic implants all over their bodies. They began yelling at her in a language that Kasumi had never heard, even less understood.

"I don't understand what you are saying, but I'm sure it's not nice," Kasumi said, not expecting for them to understand her either. She glanced the beings around her, counting five of them in close proximity and around a dozen further ahead between her position and that of the Foundations burning building.

"Awg spdnel, garofo!" one of the aliens shouted.

"That sounded like a threat. Good luck, then," she replied.

Kasumi stood in the middle of the circle and reactivated her Gift. The temperature plummeted and froze the feet of those around her in what was no doubt the worst case of frostbite in their lives, giving her more than the usual time altered perception of a Gifted. One of the aliens charged her from behind, but Kasumi pivoted and parried that with Breaker. Two more attackers jumped on her in tandem. She deflected both attacks, grabbed the staff-like weapon of one of her opponents to keep him pinned, and swung Breaker to relieve the third one of his arms. Kasumi then spun, slashing wide with her naginata. She hit the one with staff in the belly and beheaded the first attacker.

Clearing a path, she ran towards the building, when another of the creatures blocked her path, trying to hit her with its staff, which was releasing reddish, crackling energy. Kasumi blocked the attack with Breaker, took a few steps back, pulling the alien with her, then punching it in the face so hard that something—probably its jaw—broke. Another attacker tried to hit her, with the same technique, but Kasumi simply deflected the attack and cut the alien in half.

"Oopsie," Kasumi half-joked.

The rest of the group, enraged, screamed at her, and attacked en masse. Kasumi managed to keep them at bay and cut down several of them, growing frustrated at not being able to reach her friends.

A dragonwolf howled as the rubble broke. From it, a clearly pissed off Fionn emerged. Seconds later, from what used to be a terrace, Gaby leapt at the attackers, landing next to Kasumi and cutting the four arms of one alien with a single strike of Heartguard, her still functional Tempest Blades.

"Care if I join? They ruined my lunch," Gaby quipped.

"The more the merrier," Kasumi replied, before a gust of wind killed most of the remaining alien squadron. "Although Fionn might not leave many for us."

The aliens screamed into their wrists, where some sort of communication device was grafted.

Gaby was about to reply when the ships returned, firing upon them. "As fun as this has been, we need to regroup because we can't fight flying ships from the ground."

"Any suggestions?" Kasumi asked.

"Get the car and get the pits out of here."

Fionn must have thought the same, for he raced to get his trike, turned it on and revving the engine. He drove it into the courtyard, to serve as distraction for the aliens as Gaby and Kasumi made a run for the car.

Both jumped inside, Gaby in the driver's seat, and peeled out. She aptly drove the car, evading the blasts from the ships that didn't follow Fionn, as they hit the gravel road that was the entrance for the Foundation and then onto the highway.

Kasumi looked back and her heart sank. What had been one of the main buildings of her work, a place she had grown to love, that housed many relics from around the Core regions, had been destroyed by a new enemy, seemingly only to add misery to an already tough time. It had been only fate or coincidence that the place had been empty.

"I'm gonna kill them," she said matter-of-factly, as one of the ships passed too close above the car and Kasumi cut through its hull with Breaker, like a hot knife through butter. If she had been able to cut a biomechanical wyrm in half before getting the Gift, now that she had it and was in synch with her weapon, this presented no effort whatsoever.

† † †

Gaby took a left turn and reached the road that offered a panoramic view of the great lake that used to be near to what was now the ruins of the Foundation. The shore to her left, red maple forest to her right, the distant roar of Fionn's trike racing behind them and several alien ships pursuing them. Her plan was to reach the mountains where Fionn used to have his cabin, the haunted hills of Samheil, where the multitude of caves there would offer them better cover from aerial attacks.

The issue is getting there in one piece, she thought as she evaded the blasts from the ships in her rearview mirror.

"There's something in the lake," Kasumi said, and Gaby glanced in that direction.

A shadow appeared below the surface of the water, keeping parallel with Gaby's car. One of the ships closed in on the car, its weapons warming up to shoot, when it exploded without apparent reason. The water above the shadow rose as something large was breaking its surface. Gaby expected it to be another kind of alien ship. But the shadow increased its speed, revealing the familiar grey, green and red hull of the Figaro, sporting a few more recent scorch marks. As the Figaro gained altitude, its cannons continued to fire at the alien ships, offering Gaby and Kasumi cover as they drove.

One of the pursuing ships launched a missile, forcing the Figaro to break to its left and Gaby to turn the car to the right, allowing the missile to pass between them. It hit the ground dozens of meters ahead, creating a wide and deep crater, quickly filling with water from the lake.

"I think we just ran out of road," Kasumi said nonchalantly. The Figaro turned back and kept shooting as it tried to get ahead the car, as its hatch was opening.

"Ladies," Sam called through the radio. "I hope you're ready to jump."

"I really liked this car," Gaby complained. "Can you at least pass me the umbrella in the glove compartment?"

Kasumi opened it, and handed the umbrella to Gaby, who with one hand extended it and used it to stick the pedal to the floor. She kept driving to dodge the attacks as the Figaro managed to get in front of them. The crater was approaching fast.

Both Gaby and Kasumi left their seats, jumped onto the car's hood, and waited until the Figaro's rear hatch was fully open and aligned to their car. Gaby took a deep breath to activate the core of her Gift to empower her jump. She could feel how Kasumi did the same, with slightly more control than before, but still wild enough to feel chilling waves of air around her. Gaby could see the condensation of her own breath.

"Ready?" Gaby yelled. "Now!"

As they jumped, one of the ships blasted the car from

beneath their feet, sending it careening and rolling over the roadside. Gaby landed inside the hatchway with a loud thud. When she turned around, she saw Kasumi holding on for dear life from the edge of the hatch door. Gaby grasped Kasumi's wrist and pulled her inside the ship.

"Rough landing?" Gaby asked.

"Yeah. It happens. I wish I was a bit taller," Kasumi said, getting up as the Figaro rocked and the hatch door closed. Both went towards the cockpit, trying to keep their balance as the Figaro flew around. When they entered, they saw Sid focused and exhausted, piloting the Figaro. Alex sat in the copilot seat, bare-chested and with bandages covering his back, while Vivi healed him. Yokoyawa was seated at the weapons console. Sam was taking care of the comms.

"What happened? Alex why are you bleeding from your back?" Kasumi asked, as she ran towards Alex and examined his wound. Her eyes welled up. Sam grabbed her hand and pulled her to take a seat next to her, then placing the harness over Kasumi to keep her safe from the constant rocking of the ship. Her voice became a whisper. "And where is Joshua?"

"I'm in the turret," Joshua replied through the comms.

"As for Alex, we got attacked by a new type of incursion as we were escorting a caravan. At the same time those ships—" Sam began, her explanation fronted with a soothing voice.

"Orionians," Yoko interjected with a somber tone. "And those are dartships, I believe."

"Attacked us," Sam continued. "He will be fine, or would be if he stayed still till Vivi finished healing him!"

"I'm the copilot," Alex replied through gritted teeth as Vivi reapplied the disinfectant paste and cast a new healing spell.

"The gash is dirty, deep, and infected, so I'm healing it layer by layer as I disinfect, because the healing magick doesn't always clean the wound as well," Vivi explained. "Not everyone has the healing factor that Fionn has. By the way, where is he?"

"You wouldn't believe it if I told you," replied Sid.

† † †

Fionn was annoyed. He'd been getting undressed to take a bath, on his first day off in months. His exertion wasn't physical. Since the fight against the Golden King, he rarely got physically exhausted. At most, a bit sore. Mentally? He was drained. It had been a taxing year emotionally and mentally. So, some light training and teaching for a couple of days had been a welcome change amidst a non-stop sequence of soul eroding months. At this point, taking a bath in the large spa that the old Foundation's headquarters had built for its employees seemed like paradise.

This made the whole place being bombarded by interlopers while he was wearing only his jeans and ready to ditch them for the steaming water not just rude, it was unfair, infuriating and a myriad of synonyms that Fionn had no time to ponder. Enraged, he hit the road on his trike, Black Fang in hand, chasing the interlopers who in turn were chasing his wife and youngest student. Someone would pay for ruining his day off—and for blowing up Gaby's car, as she and Kasumi barely jumped into the Figaro's cargo bay.

"They keep adding insults to the list," Fionn growled as he invoked his own Gift. In his case, invoke was the most apt word, for it felt otherworldly by now. It allowed him to do feats of prowess verging on the mythical. His irises glowed green almost constantly and his healing factor had increased tenfold. His body covered in goosebumps when his Gift activated now without concentrating. As if it was always 'on,' only increasing or decreasing the energy output as needed. It was as if his Gift wasn't a separate entity inside him anymore, rather, like he *was* the Gift. Edamame, of all people, had been right; his power had evolved in ways Fionn was only just beginning to understand.

"Your Gift has changed in way you can't even imagine," Edamame had said. Killing the avatar of the Golden King had only exacerbated that.

And now these stranger interlopers would become the perfect test subjects for this evolution.

Fionn wasn't sure this idea would work or not. For weeks he had been operating on instinct when it came to these things, but he did it anyway. Fionn veered the trike towards the left edge of the road and accelerated to reach full speed. A few seconds later, one of the airships fired on him, causing the trike to go over the edge and fly into the air as the shots peppered holes clean through the frame of the bike. Fionn barely noticed. He jumped with all his strength from the trike as it reached the zenith of its arc. As the trike crashed to the water below, Fionn landed on the wing of the ship and proceeded to cut through it with Black Fang. The Tempest Blade sliced through it as if the ship was made of cardboard rather than the alien alloy that allowed for space travel. As it exploded amidst the screams of its two pilots, Fionn jumped to the next ship.

Its pilots tried to shake Fionn off by rolling to the right, to no avail. Fionn had sunk Black Fang into the ship and held on with his left hand while, with the right, he charged the kaminariken. As the ship tried to stabilize, Fionn jumped on top and unleashed the attack, leaving a gaping hole smoking through it. The ship descended towards the lake below at a rapid clip as Fionn jumped to a third ship so high and far away that it should have been impossible.

But he did it. Wearing only jeans and barefoot.

† † †

The Figaro dodged enemy fire, courtesy of Sid's finely honed piloting skills, while Alex and Yoko fired the cannons to shoot down the enemy ships. Sid glanced at the rear camera screen, and saw a man covered by a green glow taking apart ship after ship with nothing but a fangsword and his hands.

"This power escalation is getting ridiculous," Sid muttered.

Now that is something the samoharo elders would fear if they knew about him, Sid thought. Fionn was unleashing the kind of power that would make the samoharo, himself included, very, very concerned.

"What *is* he doing?" Sid mused aloud to no one in particular.

"Taking down a whole squad of—" Alex replied, wincing as the latest impact on the Figaro made his copilot seat rock violently. It re-opened the wound on his back, forcing Sam to move over and try to heal him once more.

"Orionians," Yokoyawa added again, trying to make a point. For the samoharo, the orionians were a sore spot, they had caused the destruction of the original samoharo home world. "The ancestral enemy of the samoharo species."

"—those, on his own," Alex finished as Sam placed her hands on his back and closed the wound with a spell.

"Alex, the adrenaline shot is to keep you from passing out, not for you fight again," Sam admonished him.

"We can't leave him out there," Gaby whispered to Sid.

"Of course I won't, kiddo," Sid said to Gaby with a smile, trying to reassure her. "He is just making my job a tad more difficult and dangerous because I need to get closer to the guys trying to kill us."

"You better jump towards us," Gaby said into the comms mic, hoping that Fionn had taken with earpiece with him to the shower before the attack.

Sid made several quick, stomach-churning maneuvers to dodge the dartships and get closer to Fionn's position for him to jump towards the Figaro.

"Hey!" Joshua objected, falling from his turret chair. "You are not transporting cows here!"

"Sorry," Sid said, annoyed. "But our fearless leader is not making things easy for me to pick him up without us getting hit."

"On three," Fionn replied through the comms.

Vivi opened the rear hatch from her station, as Sid got into position. Yokoyawa kept firing the cannons to provide cover.

"Three!" Fionn exclaimed as he released another kaminariken on the ship below him, the last one of the squadron, and used the explosion to reach the Figaro, barely grasping the edge of the hatch door. Joshua was already there to help him get in and pulled Fionn with enough force to launch him into the air and across the bay as the door closed.

I can't believe it, Sid thought as he reflected upon something he had noticed through the cameras but apparently no one else had: from Fionn's back, two green wings, like those of a bird but constructed of pure energy, had emerged. Briefly, but they had existed.

The only time Sid had seen something like that in real life, rather than in a codex safely kept at Calakmul Library, was when Alex managed to stop a warp train barehanded. He would have to rack his memory later to remember what the codex said, for a new squadron of dartships appeared on the radar, approaching fast.

I feel it will become a regular feature from now on.

† † †

"Want me to go outside again to help you take those down?" Fionn said without a hint of his comment being a joke.

"No, flyboy," Sid replied, then looked at Gaby, who

seemed to breathe a sigh of relief. "Your wife would kill me if I let you. Now it is my turn to deal with these cockroaches. And put on a shirt and shoes. Your musculature appears to be enhanced by an editing software and is distracting."

"What are they?" Fionn asked as he took his seat and strapped his armor vest on. He didn't have a change of clothes on the Figaro.

"They are orionians, our ancestral enemy," Yokoyawa replied, clearly annoyed.

"Yeah, you already said that. Care to expand?" Gaby replied.

"History and politics lessons can wait," Yoko replied.

"This is your captain, any non-Samoharo or without a protection spell, better turn your Gift on full, because this will be worse that those roller coasters at Korby World!"

"What are you planning to do?" Sam asked as she fastened her harness.

"A Greatest Hits maneuver list."

"Aw, crap." Alex pulled down his shaded goggles, flipped a few switches and grabbed tight the copilot joystick. "This will be a pretty bumpy ride. Fasten your harness!"

"I'll cast a holding spell," Vivi said. After Alex and Harland, she was the one that had flown with Sid the most, thus she knew what the samoharo was about to do. She whispered a cantrip in the freefolk language, and a wave of energy grew from her hands and enveloped everyone in the ship, as if they were covered by a thin film made of inexplicably of gravity. Sam stared at her, quizzically, to which Vivi mouthed: "Senior professor spell for when students shifted the gravity center of the classroom." Vivi winked, reminding her former student what a professor of the fabled Ravenstone School of magick could do.

The spell took effect just in time, for everyone could feel the gravity pull forcing them into their seats as Sid took the Figaro upwards at speed.

The Figaro's nose rose, then it made a barrel and began a quick descent towards the lake's surface. Sid pulled up at the last moment and flew a mere meter above water, straight into the incoming swarm of ships.

"Joshua, keep shooting!" Sid exclaimed through the comms. He wasn't fazed by the extreme G-forces he was creating, thanks to his samoharo body. "You better not throw up, Alex!"

"You better keep dodging them!" Joshua replied from the turret.

As the dartships flew past the Figaro shooting their energy weapons, the Figaro returned fire, successfully taking down one. Chased by the rest of the swarm, the Figaro flew towards the nearby mountain range.

"This is gonna be a tight fit, Sid," Alex mumbled.

The Figaro's right wing almost touched the ground as it banked right to enter a crack that knifed between two mountain walls. Then veered to the left to go into a cavern, narrowly avoiding the jagged stone formations that destroyed another ship. Sid maneuvered the Figaro in the narrow space, with millimeter precision in order to avoid the stalactites and stalagmites while forcing the dartships—which were smaller and, in theory, nimbler—to do the same.

However, it was not only the ship which did the job. It was the pilot's skills. And when it came to Sid, he was aiming to prove that his boast regarding being the best pilot in Theia—when he was one of the few known—was not an empty one. Sid had built every version of the Figaro from scratch, from the first one using an old samoharo asteroid mining ship, to the current Mark III, which incorporated all the hard lessons of more of a decade of testing, all the samoharo knowledge he could take with him after being banished, plus all the human ingenuity that the Foundation had provided him with, as well as the freefolk expertise in energy. Plus, more recently, the lovely addition of one or two arcanotech innovations by him, Alex, and Vivi. By now the Figaro Mark III was the best example of what the three species could build when they joined forces.

As a result of that meticulous process, Sid knew his ship better than the back of his hand. He and the Figaro were one symbiotic being. The orionian dartships chasing them through the cave were finding out the hard way that no matter how nimble they were, the Figaro was better. Two more of the dartships crashed and exploded into the walls of the cave.

"Four down, six more to go," Yoko announced.

As the Figaro emerged from the cave, Sid pulled the yoke all the way back to raise the Figaro into an incoming thunderstorm—one of the largest ever seen.

"That thunderstorm doesn't look natural, it's fueled by the ionosphere," Vivi said.

"Maybe you know how it's still watching over us," Sam replied.

"Why are we going into those storm clouds? If lightning hits us..." Kasumi began.

"They can get hit too. The Figaro is insulated, those ships might not be," Sid replied. "Besides, there are other things more dangerous than lighting in Theia's beautifully weird skies."

Sid pricked his thumb with one of his fangs, extracting a few drops of blood. These began to float as he whispered a samoharo prayer.

"Divine serpent that watched us from the start, show me the way."

The blood evaporated and Sid pushed a few buttons.

"Everyone hold on tight; this will get bumpier."

"How can it get bumpier?' Kasumi asked incredulously.

"I'm starting to consider my interrupted lunch a blessing," Gaby said.

The Figaro ascended into the clouds, followed by the orionian ships. It was almost dark, only illuminated by the electrical surges fueled by the unnatural ionosphere. The Figaro stabilized at the altitude where the clouds were thicker. The dartships opened fire on the Figaro, but Sid jerked the yoke left and right to dodge the majority of the attacks. One of the blasters hit the Figaro, shocking it.

"Everything is fine, don't worry," Sid whispered as he directed the Figaro to enter the belly of the biggest thundercloud of the cluster.

"Define 'fine,'" demanded Fionn tersely as a large dagger of ice flew past the Figaro's cockpit, too close for comfort, crashing directly into another orionian ship.

"What no one but us knows," Sid smiled, "is that at this altitude and inside these storms, there is a whole ecosystem of thunderbirds, ice daggers and other awful things. Lighting is only one concern of many." An orionian ship got close to the Figaro, to the point it could be seen from the cockpit, when a tentacle came from inside an electrified cloud and grabbed it, dragging into the cloud, where an explosion ensued. "Like that one."

"And you waited all these years to tell us this?" Fionn asked, annoyance dripping from his words.

"You never asked," Sid said simply.

"That's why you knew how to deal with the Bestial,"

Fionn prompted.

"Those four ships left are good," Joshua said over the comms.

"I'm better," Sid said as matter-of-factly. "All of you are about to see an amazing view."

"Sealing the Figaro, air pressure stable," Alex replied as he flicked another set of switches. Sid smiled. There were only four certified pilots in the whole Alliance. Alex was one of them. And his best friend and found brother, as Sid considered Alex, had endured as many test flights as Sid, which meant that by now, Alex knew exactly what Sid was planning to do and thus, what he had to do as copilot.

Sid opened a clear plastic lid and pushed a red button.

Six seconds later the kick came, and the thrusters of the Figaro fired at full power, making the dragon cores that fueled the ship *work*. The Figaro roared as it raced upwards. Once more, the Figaro reminded everyone that while the dragons of yore might be gone, they had a worthy inheritor.

If the Figaro were an organic being, it would be laughing with delight. Because by now, it was as much a part of the Band of the Greywolf as any of its occupants. It accelerated to full escape velocity, soon breaching the atmosphere and entering outer space. The Figaro raced past the Samoharo satellites that confirmed Fionn's long time suspicions about their existence and entered the ring that orbited around Theia.

Under another set of circumstances, with a more peaceful trip, the view would have been astonishing. Theia, a blue, green and brown marble with poles covered in white, floating in space, orbiting its star, Tawa Seridia. The Round Moon and the Long Moon at distant orbits, looking larger as they were closer now. And between the planet and the moons, several rings made of ice, dust, and particles of different sizes and the odd asteroid, orbiting the planet in a silent cosmological concert.

But right now, in that instant, it was mostly a blur as Sid maneuvered the Figaro across an infinite number of particles of all sizes floating around, hitting the five ships. However, the Figaro was only hit by the smallest, less dangerous ones thanks to the blood spell Sid relied upon to show him the path. The Orionian dart ships weren't as fortunate. Two giant floating, ice covered rocks crushed all four mere seconds after the Figaro wove between them.

Sid flew the Figaro towards the largest piece of ice floating around and shot four hooks into it, anchoring the ship to the ice. Sid turned off the engines and activated the stealth mode, as a second squadron of ships flew by several kilometers away.

"I will never, ever doubt your boast about being the best pilot on the planet," Fionn said, visibly dizzy.

"Solar system. And, about time," Sid said. "Tt only took you four major adventures and several minor ones to admit it." Sid relaxed into his chair. "We will hide for a short time here. It's a shame Harland isn't here to see this."

"It seems that they're looking for us," Gaby pointed out.

"Or trying to stop anyone from leaving the planet," Kasumi added, taken aback by the view. Sid noted something curious. Sam wasn't as impressed as everyone else other than Alex and Yoko, who already had seen this. If Sid didn't know better, he might think Sam had already been in outer space. His train of thought was interrupted by the blinking lights of an indicator on the console. A really, very, important indicator at that.

"Now what?" Sid said with a sigh as he sat up once more.

"Seems that we *did* get hit by something. There is a small breach on block A-7. One of the cargo lockers," Alex replied, slightly more relaxed as Vivi finished patching him up with her healing spells.

"I will close the airlocks there to keep as much oxygen as possible. This might be a problem," Sid said, concerned.

"Why?" Joshua asked, as he entered the cockpit. He looked oddly relieved and sheepish for a titan of fire. Almost as if he had thrown up in the turret.

"I don't have the equipment to go outside to fix it," Sid explained. "And we can't go back planet-side because those things are hunting us, and the breach might prove catastrophic for reentry. Also, the Figaro's radiation shield won't last long out here. Which is bad."

"Space travel has way too many variables for my taste," Fionn muttered.

"Look, this wasn't a planned outer space exploration," Sid said. "It's not like I had considered taking an orbital flight when I took my morning tea." For that matter, he hadn't anticipated dealing with orionians of all things, though it made sense that Abaddon had called on his alien minions to keep everyone on the planet as that meant no survivors this time.

Perhaps these dartships had gone rogue and decided to attack the Figaro as soon as it appeared on their radars. Or maybe the First Demon had sent them to harass the band for his own devious pleasure.

"So, now what?" Yoko asked. If someone knew what they were facing in terms of inhospitality in space, it would be his cousin. Every samoharo learned the basics of space travel theory, even if the Council had forbidden practicing them for security reasons aside a couple of designated ships no one had seen. Their policy was to keep Theia hidden from other species, to represent the planet as devoid of life and technology, taking advantage of the think ionosphere blocking everything and impeding spaceflight. Sid had broken all those rules with the Figaro.

Sam and Alex looked at each other. Then both smiled at Kasumi and she returned the smile.

Those three are planning something.

"Can you get us to the Long Moon?" Sam asked.

"What for? It is a moon. Same problem with the nearest planet," Sid replied, more curious than annoyed.

"We haven't told you something... well, Kasumi knows, of course," Alex replied.

"But you have to trust us that it was for a good reason," Sam added.

"Fine," Sid replied. "I hope we get there before being detected."

Sid pushed a couple of buttons to unhook the Figaro from the asteroid. However instead of turning on the engines, he used only the positioning thrusters on the wings to get the Figaro out of the rings, rotate and aim it towards the Long Moon, and give it enough impulse to get it moving.

"Why are you not using the engines?" Fionn asked.

"Because doing so will alert any orionians still near to Tawa Seridia. This might be slow, but given that there is no gravity here, the inertia will get us to the Long Moon with minimum effort and as stealthy as possible," Sid replied.

The Figaro approached the Long Moon slowly, the cockpit only illuminated by a few lights from the console. As the ship approached the celestial body, Sid activated the thrusters intermittently to correct course. The Long Moon was almost within reach. But it looked different from how it did while on Theia's surface. It was almost as if the rocky surface of the elongated moon was some sort of hologram.

"Okay. We're here, now what?" Sid asked.

Alex grabbed the mic as Sam opened a channel on the comms console.

"Forge, are you there? This is an emergency?" Alex said into the mic.

A few seconds of silence passed, to be broken by the sound of static and then a familiar voice. "Hey, buddy! Yeah, come in!" Forge replied. The holographic surface disappeared on a particular section as if it was a magickal mirage, revealing a large hangar bay where a mecha suit as large as the Figaro rested on a perch. Cables were everywhere. The Figaro rocked with a loud thud. And its course became locked into a predetermined flight path.

The hologram restarted.

"That's the Long Moon up close?" Kasumi asked, more intrigued than surprised. "Doesn't look like you described it to me."

"No way," Joshua said.

"That's no moon," Sid mumbled. "It's a space station."

"Akeleth space station to be exact," Alex added with a wide grin.

Chapter 5
Messages in Space

"**WHY IS STEALTH WAVING AT** us? Wasn't he at Skarabear with Harland? Did he teleport?" Sid asked as he landed the Figaro onto the landing pad in the hangar. It was perhaps the softest landing ever. The occupants descended the ship to be greeted by a stocky man, with dark brown hair, but without the elder tattoos. It looked a lot like Stealth.

"Let me introduce you to Forge," Alex said as he stepped up to Forge, who coyly waved to everyone. "Stealth's twin brother and the creator of the Tempest Blades. And my Thunderbow."

"Thank you for helping Sam and Alex." Kasumi bowed to Forge, then hugged him. His face went red as a tomato. "I was waiting to meet you for quite some time."

"The creator of the...?" Fionn asked, confused. "That includes Yaha? Does that mean that you are over several thousand years old? How is that possible?" As a kid he had heard of Stealth from his mother Dawnstar, and his grandfather Greygulch. When he met him years ago, he struck him as too young for his grandfather to have heard of him, but some freefolk magi grew old at a glacial pace. And then there was Mekiri, who was the avatar, the mortal incarnation of the Trickster Goddess. Finding out she had mortal children, or mortal to an extent, was certainly a surprise. Though by now, Fionn mused, little should be a surprise. There were many questions he wanted to ask Forge, such as how he came up with the concept of the Tempest Blades, how come the Stellar Ehécatl was considered one despite existing before.

"I don't experience time the same..." Forge began.

"It's a super long story, just leave it at that both are the children of Mekiri," Sam interjected.

"So... demigods?" Gaby asked. "Is that possible?"

"Old Earth was full of them," Forge mumbled. "The samoharo Prophet is technically my uncle-cousin..."

"Some priest at the Hegemony is gonna get an aneurysm hearing that," Sid whispered to Yoko.

"Ahem!" Alex interrupted everyone.

"Greetings!" Forge exclaimed, reading from a card. "I have heard so much of you. I'm a big fan."

"Fan?" Fionn looked at Alex and Sam. Kasumi was examining Forge with more curiosity that surprise. No wonder she might have already known about this, considering her intimate relationship with the other two.

"He is the one who came with the whole 'Band of the Greywolf,'" Sam explained, embarrassed. "He and Alex have become great friends."

"I think I need a drink," Fionn said.

"Make it two," Gaby added.

"I have something called rum," Forge offered. "Follow me!"

Fionn looked around as Forge led them into the depths of the station, explaining the place. It had been built by the akeleth a few million years ago when they manifested in real space, or real world at the start of the livable universe. It was the earliest example of arcanotech, the merger of science and magick, the stuff that Professor Hunt, Harland's father, and even Sam had been researching. Speaking of Sam, she and Alex were walking behind, whispering to Kasumi. It was to be expected, the tour was more for the new visitors than the ones that had already been there, apparently more than once.

The walls of the station, made of something called 'morphocrete,' were decorated with runes and engravings that glowed with a faint blue light and emitted something so like magickal energy, that even Fionn, never one apt for magick, despite coming from a family of powerful users, could feel it running across his body. The same light ran through lines etched on the floor and walls. In a way, the place was reminiscent of Ravenstone... or even Ravenhall. The air smelled of red oak, maple syrup and incense.

"Why didn't you tell us about this place?" Gaby asked Alex and Sam.

"Because I asked them," Forge said, with a forlorn tone. "This is the last thing we have remaining of Mother, and now that she is gone, I would hate for this place to be destroyed. Her memories are still stored in the databanks, most of them anyway."

True, Mekiri is gone, Fionn thought. His mother died. Even if she still exists in another realm, in her real form as the Trickster Goddess, or as Sam called her once, Ishtaru of the Sacred Trumpet.

Fionn changed the subject. "So, 'Band of the Greywolf,' huh?"

"It was the most popular of the options I posted in the forums?" Forge shrugged.

"Forums?" Fionn asked again. Unlike the younger members of the group, he rarely spent any time on the Aethernet.

"Aethernet social networking sites," Gaby explained. "You post a topic, and someone replies, like debating with hundreds of persons at the same time."

"That's how Alex and Joshua entered that stupid wager about capturing criminals," Sam added, unamused.

"You can use the Aethernet here?" Fionn asked.

"Yes, why?" Forged asked.

"We need to contact Harland, he doesn't know we made it," Fionn explained.

"You can use my terminal at my laboratory," Forge offered.

"We might need to make a few adjustments though," Alex said. "You know, to keep the signal masked, and we could send a coded forum message to Harland to let him know to get ready."

"He uses those things?" Fionn was surprised that everyone knew and used those networks but him.

"He is now a politician, he has to," Sam pointed out.

† † †

"Forgive the mess," Forge said, ducking under a console and extracting a handful of cables covered in clear slime. He handed them to Alex and Sid. The plan was to create connections to the Aethernet and into the holographic display, to keep the signal untraceable. "I've been busy working around some issues Alex and his friend Birm faced with some nanoarmor and the portable gauntlets where your carry your weapons now."

"Birm knew of this place before me?" Sid eyed Alex.

"No, he and Andrea knows of a friend of mine named Forge I met online."

"So, all the new equipment we used when taking on the fortress of the Golden King was your invention," Joshua asked, looking at the designs.

"Ah, no!" Forge replied, working on the holographic projector. "Those ideas are from your designers' team down there. I just aided them when they stumbled on how to keep the entropic stability of nanoarmor not made with orichalcum, like the samoharo ones, or the coherence of a portable hyper gemstone, souls and inorganic matter trapped inside within the molecular matrix, as they don't have all the knowledge yet to properly merge spells and matter at quantum level without a quantum computer of at least a thousand petabytes—or an exabyte, if you prefer—in random access memory. But I already knew that because that's how I managed to reproduce Yaha's creation procedure, as the original was more a fluke than anything."

"That sounds so simple," Joshua said, clearly confused by all the tech-jargon.

"It's easy when you get down to it, as—"

Vivi made an inquisitive sound, drawing their attention. "Sorry to interrupt your discussion on arcanotech," Vivi said as she examined a monitor, resembling an oscilloscope, with an all-black screen, except for the parallel thin lines being displayed. When a line got interrupted, after a few seconds it disappeared. A new one was created later. And this time, thousands of lines got interrupted by the second. "But what's this? And why is it going haywire?"

"Ah, that?" Forge smiled as he and Alex caused a small spark fire that Sam had to put out with a spell, as Sid shook his hand to free it from the numbness caused by the energy surge. The hologram glass tube filled with mist.

"It's a Life-Fate Monitor. It tracks the lives of all the people on Theia. You can see them in clusters or zoom in to a single one. That's how Mother used to check on you guys. Lately it has gone absolutely mad, what with so many lines disappearing."

"What happens if all disappear?" Gaby asked.

"It means all of us are dead," Forge said simply. He "I think the projector needs some percussive maintenance, Alex."

"Percussive maintenance?" Kasumi looked at Alex, raising an eyebrow.

"He means hit it until it works," Yoko explained as Alex smacked the projector console with an open palm, and an image displayed in the middle of the room. It was Harland's face, but the image was in monochrome greyish green and white.

"Apologies for the resolution," Forge said.

"We need to keep it in a basic code hidden within the static of the Aethernet to keep the signal disguised," Alex explained.

"I'm so glad you are alive," Harland said, background static taking little bites out of his voice. "Where are you?"

"The Long Moon, believe it or not," Fionn said.

"So, I was right about it being artificial?" Harland replied, excitement bringing his voice up. "I wish I could visit it."

"Yeah, arcanotech created by the akeleth," Forge interjected. "Nice to meet you Mr. Harland. I'm Forge, Stealth's twin brother. It's an honor to talk with you. Oh, and you are welcome to visit any time."

"Thank you, Forge," Harland smiled. "I'm happy to know that all of you are alive. Although, not everyone will be."

"What happened?" Gaby asked.

"Abaddon sent another message. He put a bounty on your heads. He will postpone the destruction of Theia by one year per head of the Band that's delivered to him."

"And people believe him?" Alex exclaimed, throwing his hands up. "He *is* a demon!"

"It doesn't matter, Alex, some did," Harland said. "Desperate times call for desperate measures. They make people believe anything if that might offer them a chance of survival or deny their reality. Some of the remaining city states are seriously considering the offer. The samoharo have cut all communications with the world, except the Straits."

"What about the freefolk and the refugees?" Sam asked.

"Almost all the freefolk, aside from a certain tribe, are on our side," Harland said. "Some refugees demanded I deliver you and threatened violence. Luckily Culp, and the surviving titanfighters, calmed things down a bit. But that did make several refugees leave Skarabear. Here at the Foundation, there are only the titanfighters and a handful of refugees remaining. The Kuni remain on our side, but we can't be sure for how long. If the worst comes to happen, humans will go extinct. Same for freefolk."

"So, what? Should we surrender?" Vivi said, skeptical.

"Pits no!" Harland exclaimed. "You nine are our last hope to defeat Abaddon and I will never surrender you."

"Thanks for the vote of confidence. While we come up with a plan, how can we help?" Fionn asked.

"Can you deliver a message to the samoharo?" Harland asked. "They are our only hope. I know they have the ships, Scud confirmed it. I need to tell them, to beg them, to evacuate as many human and freefolk as they can if that's their plan."

"I'm not sure what their plan will be, with the orionians dartships in the radar," Sid said, his voice full of anger and contempt. "However, I will deliver it personally. And I will make them listen."

"Thank you, now we better cut the call before either side gets tracked. I hope to meet you again in Plan B," Harland said. "See you on the other side."

The hologram dissolved in the air and the mist dissipated.

"What's plan B?" Vivi asked.

"A second site connected to Skarabear through a portal spell my mother developed," Fionn said, "to evacuate the town in case of invaders. Harland and I designated it as the Plan B location in case Skarabear wasn't safe during the conflict with the Golden King. Kasumi has seen it."

"It's in Husvika," Kasumi added. "As bodyguard of Harland, I went there to put some demonhunting seals to keep it invisible from incursions and scrying. Although not sure who would want to go there. Husvika is deep in the North Pole and the Mistlands, and the place is protected by the Elder Ice People."

"I thought they were an urban legend," Alex said.

"No," Kasumi replied, "they are real and as gruff and cold as the weather. But their weapons are durable. The crystal sai I had back home come from there."

"It's freezing cold there!" Sid exclaimed. "Why can't Harland choose a warmer place for his business partner? Samoharo hate cold."

"Ahem!" Forge interrupted as he inserted a data crystal in a slot in the holographic projector console. "Sorry to interrupt your meditations on your plans, but I also have a message to give to you."

"I feel like the past hour has been message after message. My brain is fried with this much info," Sid groaned.

"Stop complaining!" Vivi and Yoko scolded in unison.

A new hologram came to view. It was Mekiri, smiling at them.

† † †

"Hi, people! If you are watching this, it means that I'm gone. Not like you, when a mortal passes away, but for the purposes that brought you here, I'm sorry I won't be able to help. Something happened to this avatar's body, and I couldn't replace it. What happens in heaven reflects on earth and vice versa. Which means my kind is already fighting the same war as you in our own plane. I will try to summarize a large infodump worth aeons into a short message.

"Millennia ago, there were many planets teeming with life. Granted, in a universe as infinity as ours, 'many' is a relative term. When the strange elder deities trapped at the bottom of the Pits began to exert their influence to destructive ends, they found out that the way they were trapped made it impossible to sweep all of the universe in one go, thus decided to go one planet at the time. The cumulative effect would weaken the Tempest enough for them to break the trap, attack the Last Heaven and then destroy Kaan'a or the universe from the inside. They slowly corrupt the planet and its inhabitants as happened with Old Earth. If that fails, they call forth their followers, misguided species allied with him and his general, through fear, greed, or misguided hope to stave off their own destruction. Like the orionians who destroyed the solar system of Ka'ab, the samoharo home world? Freefolk were luckily ignored for their planet, Hada'waii was at the edge of Known Space. But nonetheless, the actions of Abaddon made their home star become a black hole. Thus, I brought them here. And while they don't have to destroy all worlds, Theia is the last one they need.

"By now Abaddon might have reunited all the fragments Asherah sealed in different bodies and objects, with the help of the Iskandar and the Prophet. That plan was an emergency pause to weaken him enough after millennia, trapped in Theia as long as its magickal field remained intact, so a further generation like yours could deliver the final blow. Don't feel bad if you played a hand on freeing said fragments. It was a possibility. This is the endgame.

"Abaddon will ultimately seek to destroy the planet, one way or another. Now, why hasn't Abaddon accelerated his plan when he is close to winning? My bet is his ego. You know gods are egomaniacs, and in the case of Abaddon, he went native after the Founders split and trapped him in semi-mortal forms. And given how long the three species have survived his designs, he is essentially choosing to torture you. That offers you a window of opportunity to reach the Life Tree before he does.

"Lastly, why you? I'm sure you're all asking that. It all comes down to the old adage: 'samoharo are mighty, freefolk are powerful, and humans are indomitable.' Together the three, are unstoppable. Thus, why we created the Gift. The Blood Covenant. The Magick Laws. Your three species are the ace up our sleeves. Our chosen weapons, so to speak. If you work together, you can still save the planet. If you keep the Life Tree safe, it will reverse all the damage and with luck, save those afflicted by the corrupting infection—which is why you have to find it and defend it, because Abaddon surely is searching for it.

"Take anything from the Long Moon you need for this. Thank you for everything. I will miss you."

The hologram disappeared, leaving Forge stifling silent sobs at the last sight of his mother. Sam hugged him, and Alex offered him a tissue.

"We will miss you too," Fionn said, softly.

"Fake thunder for dramatic entrances and all," Sid added with a smile.

"Thank you for everything, Mekiri," Gaby concluded.

A long silence fell upon the place, only to be broken by Forge himself. "I take it you have much to think and plan," Forge said, still maudlin. "You are free to explore the lighted up parts of the station, take a shower, eat, rest, or do what you need. I don't suggest going into the lights off sections as some of them have been rendered inoperative after millennia."

"If you have a library," Vivi replied. "I would love to give it a look."

"Of course! It's not Ravenhall, but you are welcome to use it, it's after the hydroponic gardens."

"You will love them," Sam added. "What will you do in the meantime, Forge?"

"If Lady Galfano-Estel allows me, I would be happy to try and repair her broken blade. Although I need to figure out how to turn on the foundry, the temperature needed to even dent them is quite high and it consumes a lot of energy. But it would be the same problem in the one you have down there."

"I can help," Joshua offered. "I'd like to learn how to do it myself, in case necessity demands it."

"Oh, yes! Yes! The Titan of Fire certainly can help."

Gaby unsheathed Soulkeeper, which had cracks and dents all over the blade from destroying the Crown of the Dead. She had looked into how to repair it, but no one on Theia knew how to do it, and that was before Abaddon. The only reference they had was the foundry that Izia's father had built a century ago to repair Black Fang once, but he didn't leave any notes on how to use it or how to repair a Tempest Blade.

"Here it is, my friend," Gaby offered it to Forge. "I apologize for damaging your creation. And you can call me Gaby, a friend of Alex and Sam is my friend too."

"Thank you," Forge replied.

"Well," Sam grabbed Kasumi's hand. "I, for once, really want a break. Come. We will show you the place where Mekiri taught me how to fix the whole magick concept. It's quite a trip I want to share with you, Kasumi."

"What about me?" Alex pouted.

"You need to rest so your back injury can finish healing properly, mister," Sam admonished him.

"Don't worry," Kasumi said. "You can show me around the workshops later, when you're healed."

"That's not fair," Alex mumbled. "A guy gets his back flayed like a fish by a new kind of incursion and has to miss the tour."

After Sam dragged Kasumi away, and Vivi offered to finish healing Alex's back, everyone went their way, leaving Gaby and Fionn alone. She stifled a laugh.

"What so funny?" Fionn asked her.

"Nothing," Gaby replied with her crooked smile.

"I will pretend as if I didn't hear that," Fionn scoffed.

† † †

"How are you feeling?" Gaby asked her best friend. Alex was staring at a holographic representation of Theia, with all the incursion hotspots over its surface. She couldn't avoid wondering how the regions outside the Core, the ones not in the Alliance, were faring. Often, in such situations, the focus was only on a particular region of the planet, but the consequences reverberated on a global scale.

"Left out?" Alex replied, only half-focused on the hologram.

"She means your back," Fionn said, redirecting.

"Sore," Alex explained. "Can't move my shoulders much yet, as the layers of skin and muscle are still healing. Vivi said that I was lucky the claw didn't touch my spine. Even with the Gift, that would have been hard to heal properly. But I should be fine in a few hours after the spell finishes. Not all of us have instantaneous healing."

"What can I say?" Fionn shrugged. "Never understood why the Gift manifested in me that way. What are you looking at?"

"The locations of the incursions. They match leylines cross points, that makes sense. The energy readings though, they are similar to the portal used in the incursion where I got my Gift," Alex explained. "Which means that the circlet, the whole Bestial summoning, everything, was a test for this moment."

"So that's what has been bothering you for months, hon?" Sam asked as she entered the room. She seemed more relaxed, smiling even. She hugged Alex from behind, which offered quite an image for Gaby, given the height difference between them, Sam being the tallest. "Good, because I thought I was the only one. Shemazay's betrayal gave Abaddon an opening. That's what he was trying when he said he wanted to usher the end of the days."

"Where is Kasumi?" Alex asked, relaxing his shoulders.

"Asleep," Sam replied with a wink. "She told me you should go later and wake your Snow Princess with a tender kiss. You know how she's a romantic at heart."

"We all could use a good sleep, to be fair," Alex smiled back, as his face turned red. "I will wake her up later."

Gaby turned to Fionn, who was looking at the hologram, tracking all that Alex had pointed out, too absorbed to hear anything else. He wore the same expression when he was trying to solve a puzzle or assembling one of his model kits.

"Are you mad that Alex is right?" Gaby asked him, struggling to ask the question she herself had been pondering in recent months. That everything they had done so far had only aided Abaddon, instead of stopping him. "That all we have gone through was for nothing?"

"Why would I be mad?" Fionn asked. "That somehow we freed his split parts while stopping the Creeping Chaos, the Golden King and his minions? I don't think our efforts were for nothing. If we hadn't stopped Byron and the Bestial, Saint Lucy and the Alliance would have fallen way before they knew what was happening, and he would have found a way to free his split parts anyway. If Alex hadn't stopped the Creeping Chaos and us the titans, the Kuni Empire would have been destroyed, with thousands of casualties and who knows what kind of mayhem the world would be in by now. You and maybe every Sister of Mercy might have lost her body to that tovainar. Mon Caern would be a crater, magick would have been gone for good, leaving the Freefolk defenseless. Everything we did was about protecting others. Expecting the enemy to stand there without having a countermeasure to our plans is naïve. It's not different to the plans we did in case of a scenario like this. Plus, he is missing a good chunk of his original power."

"What chunk?" Alex asked.

"Joshua's. The Beast is still in him," Gaby said. "It means that Abaddon is not at full strength, which gives us a small gap to work in our favor."

"He doesn't know where the Life Tree is," Alex muttered. "Technically, neither do we, but for us it works just as well for it to be hidden. He's stalling."

"Hence the bounty on our heads. Destroying the planet means nothing without taking the Tree," Sam added.

The exchange made Fionn smile. It was a kind smile, one of relief. To Gaby, it seemed he thought that Alex and Sam were ready. Even if some implications of that were not nice.

No one really retires in this line of work, she thought.

"It's fixed," Forge announced as he and Joshua joined them. He was carrying Soulkeeper, looking good as new. Joshua was visibly exhausted at his side but seemed content.

"I can't thank you both enough," Gaby said as she accepted the blade. "Sometimes I wonder if what we do is worth doing when people are willing to deliver our heads on a silver platter."

Gaby, for all the strength she had shown in recent months, was emotionally tired. Of the losses, of the damages. Even if Fionn and Alex's optimism wasn't misplaced, she was still hurt by the idea that people they have been helping in recent times were willing to fulfill the bounty, even if others supported the so-called Band of the Greywolf.

"In a few hours, the view from the hydroponic gardens is something you must see, I find it particularly relaxing," Forge said. "It kinda gives you a new perspective on things."

† † †

"It's beautiful," Gaby said. The nine of them were resting on an artificial hill at the hydroponic gardens from where Forge grew his food.

"Peaceful even, which is all one can ask," Yokoyawa said.

Forge had been right. The view from the viewports at the hydroponic garden with the light tuned down to simulate night, was unique: the endless sea of stars in the background, with the galaxy crossing it from one side to the other, a purple aura around it. Closer to the Long Moon, there was Tawa Seridia, the star of the system, a small but brilliant ball of fire. Then the Round Moon, further back, half eclipsed by the shadow from Theia.

And lastly, Theia itself, with its rings orbiting around it, thunderstorms visible over the green, brown, and blue surface. A lonely pebble still teeming with life despite the visible damage from the infected zones created by the incursions. The planet itself was fighting for its life, its very existence. If it managed to prevail, though, the changes to it might prove too harsh for whoever survives this nightmare. Yet the idea remained: a single, small world, trying to survive in the vast immensity of the cosmos, fighting, because there was nothing else to do or say. It did put things into perspective.

We are not doing this for those that want an easy exit. We are doing this for those that want to save the world but don't have the means to do it, for those that come after us, Gaby thought.

The nine of them drank from the poetry of the image, taking the time to reflect.

Fionn knew he had been right, even if all they did had only aided the nightmares to bring forth the dark, even if there was a bounty now over their heads, nonetheless every life saved back then was its own reward.

The first to break the silence was Alex. As usual. Gaby had been expecting that. Her best friend always cared too much about others to even bother with detractors. Their comments hurt him, but he kept going in spite of it. That was the main reason Fionn had been considering leaving him in charge after this adventure.

"I don't know about you, but I'm tired of always being on the back foot, always running to meet the monster on their own terms, hoping not to die. It's enough," Alex said.

"What do you propose?" Fionn asked, more curious than anything. He had told Gaby earlier that he would prefer it if Alex and Sam made the call.

"I know what he is thinking," Sam added. "No more running. Let's find that Tree, wait for Abaddon there, and kill him once and for all."

"I'm in," Kasumi replied as she cuddled between Alex and Sam.

"Me. too," Joshua said. "I know this is a bigger quest than any personal grudge I might hold, but I do want to beat that asshole for what he did to me, and to others."

"Saving our home, a good excuse to come out officially from retirement," Yokoyawa said, wistfully staring at the planet.

"I think that particular ship sailed long ago," Sid muttered.

"I guess I wanted to join in the adventure," Vivi sighed looking at Sid. "I'm in as well."

"It will be the end of journey, y'know?" Sid said, more as an affirmation than question.

"And what a journey it has been," Fionn murmured with a smile, staring at Gaby in the eyes. She offered a sad smile.

It was decided, then. The unspoken consensus had been agreed.

It was time to retake the planet.

† † †

"Vivi and I went over every archive in the station's database, the closest thing we have to Ravenhall, that mentioned the Life Tree," Sam explained as the holographic diagram displayed three tablets, made of unknown material. They were shaped as pentagons, but with some differences: three of their sides were perpendicular, like a square, with the other two sides closing in a peak. They were placed where their tips converged into a single point.

"The only consistent mention we found were these three tablets," Vivi continued. "It seems that the Life Tree, and the surrounding land, has been changing locations since the very first attack by Abaddon. The magick involved makes anyone unable to remember or record where it is. And that includes deities."

"If I were the Life Tree, I would do the same. I mean, considering what Shemazay tried to pull," Alex said. "These tablets seem to be for data storage."

"Yes," Sam said. "Magick of a superior order. Divine but primordial. Now, these tablets were given one to a representative of each of the Three Species. They hold the key to find the Life Tree before Abaddon."

"Let me guess," Gaby said. "No one knows where they are."

"Not exactly," Vivi replied. "We know of the location of two. The first one is in the Samoharo Hegemony, in the Calakmul Library."

"I knew that weird metallic tablet was important," Sid said. "It's stored in an exhibition. Few people can access it."

"I take it that you know someone who can?" Fionn asked.

"Of course," Sid said with a broad grin.

"The second one has been seen in a shrine at the summit of the God's Eye," Sam continued, acknowledging their banter with a faint smile.

"No one has entered the God's Eye in centuries. There is a sigil that makes access impossible. And it is close to the Line of Fire," Fionn observed. He was well acquainted with the stories around the God's Eye, the tallest volcano in the Core Regions, located on a small island near the southern coast of the Kuni Empire. Hikaru had taught him everything about it, including how the island had been the stage of the final battle between the Storm God and the original Titan of Fire more than five thousand years ago. Its conclusion was what gave birth to the volcano.

"There is a way," Kasumi said. "All the temples in the Kuni Empire are connected through magic tunnels. The closest one to the God's Eye is the Temple of Sound."

"The third tablet is the problem," Vivi lamented. "It was originally in possession of the Freefolk, but it was lost during the war with the Asurian Empire—several centuries ago—

when both realms collapsed. No one knows where it is."

Joshua raised his hand. "I know where it is, not a pretty place, in the Deseret," he said.

"Deseret?" Gaby echoed, raising an eyebrow at him.

"The original name for the Wastelands. So, it is in Meteora," Fionn said matter-of-factly.

"No," Joshua replied. "Meteora was ruled by a theocracy, they would have destroyed it. It is in the only place that actually knew its value: Carpadocci, the city where I was created as a tovainar."

"The haunted city?" Sam asked with fascination in her eyes, always the scholar interested in ancient ruins. Harland had rubbed too much of his interest in archeology and the strange off on her.

"How do we tackle this?" Yokoyawa asked. "There are logistics to solve."

"I will take the Figaro with you and get the tablet, and the asset that will retrieve it for us," Sid said to Yoko, who nodded in mute agreement. For them, or at the very least for Sid, returning at the Hegemony after having been banished, was tantamount to death. "We will also deliver Harland's message to the Council."

"That means that you are planning to serve as a distraction while the tablet is acquired by your asset. You will need an extra pilot to use the Figaro in a quick extraction for you two," Alex said. "I will do it. Also, I understand samoharo."

Sid and Alex fist bumped each other.

"Vivi and I will go with Joshua to Carpadocci," Sam said. "That tablet belonged to the freefolk, it is just that we are the ones recovering it. Plus, we will need two spell casters to teleport in and out. Can you guide us to where the tablet is?"

"I can, but be aware that city has a malevolent sentience. It will be tricky."

"How exciting!" Vivi exclaimed. When they looked askance at her, she said, "What? It's like my second adventure of this kind with you people. Of course I'm excited to take part in it."

Everyone laughed, including Vivi.

"That leaves the Temple of Sound for me, Gaby, and Kasumi," Fionn said once the good-natured laughter subsided. "But how we will get in and out without a ship or spell casters?"

"The last Aditi mecha armor won't be an option without

a pilot," Alex said.

"This keystone can hold two preprogrammed spells," Forge said, showing everyone a clear ovoid gemstone. "One to get you there, one to get you out. Once they are used, the keystone is burned out. It's the last one of its kind."

"We'd better make it count," Gaby said, handing it over to Sam after a brief inspection for her to charge it with the spells. "That settles it. Anything else?"

"We will need weapons, at least for those that don't have a Tempest Blade. Otherwise hurting Abaddon won't be easy—not that it'll be easy anyway, mind—and we need all hands on deck," Alex said.

"You are welcome to anything from the armory, and I will modify your choices so if you can insert them with a piece of the Tree's roots. That should give them enough sacred power to hurt him," Forge offered. "Won't be a Tempest Blade because it lacks a soul, and..."

"We get it," Sid interrupted him. It was well known that the samoharo found the process to create a Tempest Blade rather morbid and tragic. He would never accept one if there was one available. But this option was more palatable.

"But it will be closer to one," Forged continued, throwing dagger eyes to Sid. "Those roots have power on their own. They can also learn, copy and absorb from your Gift, your Magick, or your Covenant."

"I don't need to choose anything, I want to use Izia's staff," Sam said, then looked at her dad and Gaby. "That's, of course, if you both agree to the modification."

"Of course. It is yours now," Gaby nodded. She might have access to all of Izia's memories, but she saw herself as Gaby, not as Izia, even if the latter was now part of her. Always had been, perhaps, even if in dormancy.

"So, it is decided, then. Three tablets, three teams. Once we get them, we reconvene in the Husvika Fortress," Alex said.

"Before you go," Forge interrupted, grabbing a large case from one of the workshop tables and offered it to Gaby. "I also have something that was requested of me for you, m'lady, a present from all your family that I finished while you rested. It's something that befits a battlebard of modern times."

Gaby opened the case and from it she took out a surprisingly modern-looking guitar. It was red with transparent gold parts; it had a golden heart etched on the arm, and a strap to carry it. It fit perfectly in her hands and turned out to be already tuned. She played a chord, and it resonated across the station, although she couldn't see where it was plugged in.

"It's impact reinforced, can be carried in the gauntlets, has its own energy core and magick spells for sound amplification, and has a slot to insert one of your Tempest Blades to increase power," Forge explained. "I call it Goldenhart Special. But you can name it as you see fit."

Gaby's eyes welled up as she looked at the guitar and then to all her friends, her family, as Fionn hugged her.

"Thank you," Gaby whispered. She hugged Forge, surprising him. "Everything about it is perfect."

"I know it doesn't make up for all you have gone through in recent years," Alex said. "But it's something from all of us, to the heart of this weird little family."

"It's something you should have had earlier," Sam said. "But better late than never."

"It's amazing," Gaby said, openly weeping now. Sam and Vivi approached to hug her, while Alex took a step back and stared nervously both at the group and at the holographic display. His right foot bounced slightly, as it often did when he was nervous. The enormity of what he had proposed along with Sam finally hit him.

"This will be fun," Alex whispered, half excited, half worried. Mostly worried. Okay, completely worried. Fionn patted him on the shoulder, to reassure him with a half-smile.

"This will be soooo fun."

Chapter 6
City of the Lost

"HOME, SWEET HOME," JOSHUA MUTTERED as he led Sam and Vivi though the entrance chiseled into the rock. It led to the underground city of Carpadocci, the place where he had been born some time ago, and that would be the best answer to the question because he didn't remember anything before the previous century.

"You don't seem particularly fond of the place," Vivi observed, her voice muffled a bit from the dust mask she wore. Joshua had insisted that she and Sam wear them because of the risk of biological contamination.

"I'm not. And trust me, the city isn'tt fond of me either," Joshua said as he passed a stone statue of a female figure holding a fiddle. Vivi couldn't help but notice the forlorn look on Joshua's face, full of regret. It made her wonder if he had known the person that had posed for the statue, perhaps the only positive memory he still had of the place.

Vivi, on the other hand, as one curious about legendary cities from the ancient past, had other recollections from her studies. Carpadocci had been a mythically infamous city for the freefolk. One of the three main cities of the ancient Asurian Empire, old foes of the freefolk, who waged an intercontinental war that ended with the summoning of the Bestial, the death of Black Fang, the destruction of the Kingdom of Umo, and the eventual fall of the ancient empire. The war turned once fertile lands into a wasteland of deserts and plains where few crops could be grown. The unforeseen desolation was due to the strange science the empire used in tandem with the magick they stole from the freefolk. By the time the empire had tried to take on the Straits and the Kuni, it was too feeble and was rebuked with ease, as the Kuni were well organized, and the Straits had the aid of the samoharo in one of the few times they had decided to intervene in human-freefolk affairs.

Carpadocci, according to what Vivi had researched and the few things Joshua had mentioned as they got ready for the mission, had been a cyclopean hidden city, most of it carved out of a network of caves below a massive rock monolith. It was secluded, even though it was not far from the borders with the Kuni Empire and the Straits, and that seclusion made it perfect to be the Asurian's prime weapon research center. According to Joshua, this was where the 'The Dark Father,' one of the many identities of the Crawling Chaos, had transformed him into a prototype tovainar by forcing the Beast, a symbiont from the Infinity Pits, into his spine. Joshua had described the experience succinctly: thousands of pricks in his bones, the oppression in his chest, the blood in his mouth, the endless migraines he endured during the procedure.

He had left it at that.

The mere description of the procedure had sent shivers down Vivi's back and motivated Sam to hug their friend. While Joshua now had the Beast under control it didn't make Vivi feel less uneasy. Joshua was a good man and a staunch friend now. But even he admitted he didn't know who he was before being subjected to the experiment, or if he underwent it voluntarily or had been forced.

"Maybe I was the one who designed the procedure and I tested on myself out of hubris," he had said with a shrug. It made her wonder what he had been like before everything that made Joshua who he was today.

And like him, the city seemed to have been its own twisted experiment. But unlike him, it had never gotten an opportunity to redeem itself.

Vivi had reached the level of magus where she could perceive miasmas or the essences of a place. They are not necessarily magick in origin, but they have an effect on the magick field of the location. Vivi knew she was perceiving *something*, because Sam's walk had stiffened as soon as they had crossed the entrance and promptly summoned the nanoarmor Alex had designed for her. Even Joshua was visibly unsettled as he guided them.

Vivi examined the place. The whole place smelled of putrid humidity, the floor full of fungus and dust from degraded biological matter. Tiny, metallic scarabs scuttled away from Joshua's approaching form and the heat that rolled off him. She recognized them as mechanical, clockwork scarabs made of copper and that ate organic matter, like an insectoid bear trap. Joshua acted as a shield for Sam and Vivi, for which she was grateful.

Yet, in spite of the intended gory trip trap that were the scarabs, the builders had an eye for beauty. Maybe they weren't as wicked and corrupt as she originally had thought. Perhaps they lost their way before being corrupted by half of Abaddon. And, hidden beneath the decayed decadence of the ruins, there was the essence. It was as if it were alive, and not because of the previous inhabitants, but as if Carpadocci had a mind of its own.

Even centuries after whatever led to Carpadocci's downfall—according to Joshua it he had been the one who had caused a massive fire that had killed most of the inhabitants after he had released a plague. By its description it had sounded to Vivi as 'maroon fever.' She saw scorch marks on the wicked, and thankfully destroyed, statues consecrated to the Creeping Chaos.

Joshua stopped in front of a slab of rock with diagrams engraved on it.

"The original language is long dead," Joshua explained. "But a corrupted version is still spoken in Meteora. This is a map of the city."

"Where, then?" Sam asked. "The city is larger than I expected."

"It goes for kilometers. The good thing is you have me." Joshua gave a sardonic smile as he pointed at a faded spot on the slab. "We need to reach this place. The laboratory is in the bowels of the city, many levels below. If the tablet is here at all, it must be down there."

"How can you be so certain?" Vivi asked.

"Because that's where all the freefolk stuff robbed by the Asurians during the Old War was tucked away. Most would expect it to be in the vaults full of gold, but if you are trying to use it in your experiments, that would have been impractical."

"Gold?" Sam raised an eyebrow, and Joshua chuckled.

"Don't even think about it. It's cursed. And, probably, the vault is the only place with actual traps. Better avoid going there."

"Are you saying that the rest of the city and the laboratory don't have traps?" Vivi interjected, thinking of those scuttling scarabs.

"Not very practical to have traps on your daily commute." Joshua shrugged. "The city is already cursed; traps would have been a useless overkill."

Vivi couldn't withhold her sigh. To say that the part of her that enjoyed adventure movies of daring explorers was disappointed would have been an understatement.

"And if there *were* any traps, I can deactivate them with a spell," Sam added with a shrug.

"I don't think they would be so easy to deal with," Joshua replied, but Sam was already out of earshot.

"Sometimes I worry about her," Vivi muttered.

"Why?" Joshua asked in a low tone. "She seems to have a perfect handle on everything."

"That's why. She's always been a good student, but not on this level. And she has always been a rule breaker. She is now creating her own spells on the fly and making them work. A spell takes years to perfect. Don't get me wrong, I'm not jealous, I'm worried about how quickly she's breaking new ground. The fact that she managed to even change how I cast magick to enhance it to a level that would have taken me another four decades to achieve…"

"I guess that's what happens when you get a crash course by the entity that rules magick, and you rewrote some of the rules. But she has had good teachers. I trust her."

"I trust her, too. I'm just worried she will get in over her head one day and won't be able to get out of that. Overconfidence is the magus killer," Vivi said as a knot formed in her stomach.

† † †

Joshua led them through the city as if he'd walked the paths just yesterday. Ruins or not, muscle memory persevered. They descended to the lower levels and Vivi was once again disappointed in the lack of traps or even hazards beyond the dust their gear stirred up. Once they reached the laboratory, Joshua led them to a storage room. It was massive space, littered with the cracked and broken remains of what were once large glass tubes—large enough to hold the bodies of grown men. In the middle of the room was a cenotaph, the tip of pyramid etched with energy canals. They were pulsating with a faint red glow. Half the room's roof had collapsed, burying the rest of the lab's secrets.

"This place is too dark," Vivi complained. While freefolk had decent vision in the dark, there were limits. Joshua moved with ease, but she kept hitting rocks every other step.

"Allow me," Sam said. "Vivi, can you cast your glowing floating dandelion?"

"Sure, but it summons just a few, not enough to light this whole place," Vivi replied, as she placed her hands together and whispered a few words:

Dandeluz makeyt
Fasthlig aderd

A dozen floating lights, resembling bright yellow dandelions, came from her hands, illuminating her face. Sam approached, her irises glowing lilac, and dispersed the dandelions into the air with a swift motion of her arms. In an instant the dozen dandelions turned into thousands, illuminating the darkness of the cave as if a cloud of fireflies had descended upon it.

"See what I mean?" Vivi whispered to Joshua. Sam had taken a spell Vivi had developed for years and had managed to increase its power tenfold in a blink of an eye.

"You won't believe what I found!" Sam exclaimed with glee.

"As long as is not a cenotaph," Joshua admonished. "Leave that thing alone."

"Cursed?" Vivi asked.

"Worse," Joshua replied. "It has the original tovainar symbiont trapped there."

"Not that." Sam ignored the cenotaph and walked straight to a wall that she force-opened with a swish of her hand and a magick spell. The wall gave way to a large display case containing crystals and the five-sided tablet they were after. "I'm not that foolish to touch something I don't know in an archeological dig. I'm talking about these, next to the tablet we are looking for."

"What are those?" Joshua asked.

"The freefolk equivalent to a modern datacrystal hard drive: ancient crystals containing the instructions and powers for several spells created by Asherah herself," Vivi explained as she grabbed the tablet and examined the rest of the crystals, or, at least, the ones Sam wasn't already stuffing into a duffel bag.

"I thought you needed a special device to read them," Joshua mused as he grabbed a crystal.

"Usually, yes," Vivi replied. "But when you have years of experience—or, in her case, a massive power up—you can sense which spell is contained there. You can't cast it, but you can read it."

"Interesting, they have several spells we thought were missing, let's take these too," Sam said. "Bummer. Most are damaged, but a few—Oh, the Encantation Spilknoth is intact, and with some notations!"

"What's that for?" Vivi asked. She wasn't familiar with that spell. It wasn't even listed in the one hundred twenty lost spells list.

"Sort of a fertility spell used to allow different species to have children until they were naturally compatible, like freefolk and humans. Or to allow children from throuples to share genetic characteristics from the three parents. It helped the freefolk to obtain human's versatility to endure different climates, and humans got the potential to use magick," Sam said as she read the crystal. And it dawned on Vivi why Sam was interested in that spell, and how she knew about it. "Some of the notes explore bridging samoharo-freefolk biochemical barriers. And creating bioweapons. Now we know where felp orcs, goblins, and other creatures came from. Damn!"

"What?" Vivi asked.

"It also mentions human-demon hybrids. Sound familiar?" Sam grumbled, looking at Joshua and then to the cenotaph.

"We should leave these spells lost then," Vivi said matter-of-factly, even if it hurt her in her core to leave behind such a trove of freefolk treasures. "They are too dangerous."

"A spell to raise the dead, with sentience. That could be useful," Sam muttered.

"Samantha, did you listen to me?" Vivi raised her voice. "I know you are not my student anymore, and that Ethics of Spellcasting wasn't your best subject with me but let me remind you that necromantic spells are taboo for a reason: they violate the dignity of the deceased by overriding their consent on what happens to their bodies. Even a proxy's consent such as a family member is being debated as to whether it is ethical or not."

"But we *are* allowed to summon their spirits to talk," Sam pointed out. "Shamans do it all the time, a few even raise animals for a short time."

"Talk is one thing. Raising the dead is another. Most animals are not sentient, yet. They are not raised with their soul back." Vivi rolled her eyes. It was no secret among the faculty of Ravenstone that Sam had a strange interest in necromantic spells. Many tacked it to the loss of her biological parents. It was not uncommon among students with similar backgrounds. But most left the subject by the time they reached adulthood. Sam never had. And no other student had shown the potential she had, which was why she hadn't been allowed to take the equivalent to a doctorate study and instead had been sent to assist Professor Hunt, with the hope that Sam would develop other interests that would allow her to take the next step in her studies. While Vivi couldn't necessarily speak for the other teachers, in her case had always acted in Sam's best interests. To Vivi, she was like a younger sister, now a teammate. And while Sid kept reassuring Vivi that Sam had everything under control Vivi couldn't avoid being worried about the power levels Sam was reaching. Queen Khary hung over every freefolk magus as a cautionary tale after using a spell that stopped a war, at the cost of burning up the magick field of the whole planet for centuries, and the cost of her life.

"But if you had the consent of the soul?"

"Even then, no one has managed to put back a soul inside the original body. But even if that *were* possible, can you imagine being put back into your body, only to find it's rotten and beyond any repair by medicine or magick, eaten by worms and missing parts? And that doesn't address that you would have to find a way to carry the soul from the summoning spot to the place where the remains lie."

"Okay, and if I had the consent, found a way to ease the pain, and I could personally guide the soul to their body?"

"I see that you have given it a lot of thought," Vivi said slowly. "Except for one thing: there is no spell to make it possible. No one has created it yet. Then again, I'm sure that won't stop you. Just be sure when you do it, it's for the right reasons, for it can and will hurt a lot of people, including yourself." Vivi snatched the crystal from Sam's hand and returned it to its resting place. She hoped it would be the end of the matter, though she wondered if Sam hadn't already memorized the spell. Sam had never cheated on her exams, even if she had spent all night partying. She didn't have to, she had almost eidetic memory. Which would explain why the Trickster Goddess had chosen her for her crash course.

Joshua chose then to interrupt. "We are losing sight of our mission, ladies," Joshua said, and he grabbed the five-sided tablet. "This is what we came for. Now this is when we leave this cursed place."

† † †

An hour later, Vivi broke the silence that settled over them. "I have to say," Vivi said as she stretched her arms overhead, "that I'm a bit disappointed." The three of them had returned to the place where the slab of rock with the map of the city was located, the former center of the market-place of the city.

"What are you talking about?" Sam asked. She, for one, was quite happy that this mission had gone relatively easy and without surprises. She could only hope Alex's and Kasumi's went the same way.

"Ancient, cursed city; full of secrets?" Vivi prompted. "I was expecting, y'know, more traps, hidden treasures."

"You watch too many adventure movies," Joshua said, and shook his head. He was distracted, as if something else had drawn his attention.

"I beg your pardon?" Vivi raised an eyebrow.

Sam gestured for Joshua to quit while he was ahead. She had learned from experience that arguing with Vivi rarely had the desired outcome, unless you had a good argument to make your case. And when it came to her favorite movies...

"This city is millennia old. It was a scientific outpost. Having traps would have made work difficult. Also, while it was cursed, I banished the spirit that haunted the city a century ago. So, no more haunted place. This used to be my home, the home of many people that lived their lives like we do, not a set for a movie," Joshua said tersely.

That's a good argument, Sam conceded.

Vivi pointed at the newcomers that emerged surrounding them. "It seems to be theirs, now."

"And there's the surprise," Sam muttered.

† † †

"Who are you?" Joshua asked the people gathering around them. They couldn't be more than thirty in total. They were humanoid but had uncommon features; a few were felp orcs. Others were thin with large bulging eyes or with atrophied bat wings. A couple looked like humanoid hyenas. One tall woman with ebony hair and pale skin looked not unlike Joshua had before he had tamed the Beast, which meant she fed on energy or blood. The woman tried to hide behind the others and Joshua had to wonder how many like them were still around the world, the aftermath of an ancient conflict hiding children of their own in a cursed city.

"We... we are outcast from Meteora and Kashen," one said, haltingly. "We... we are descendants of the creatures created by the Priests. Our ancestors moved here a century ago, after the Shadow Avenger..." He stammered and stood with his arms in a defensive position before Joshua. "He destroyed the lasts of the Priests, and we heard rumors of how he had cleansed the Curse of Meteora. The city welcomed us. We have been living here in peace, hearing of your exploits, giving us hope that we, too, could find our place, until the creatures arrived. The city has been trying to protect us, but it's dying. And then we saw you with the freefolk magi and we..."

"Incursions and infection zones are near here," Vivi whispered to Sam.

"Have you come to help us, Avenger?" a small teenaged girl asked Joshua, tugging his shirt. She had snakes for hair and wore tattered but surprisingly clean clothes.

He looked at the girl. She reminded him of Aldai, his only friend back in the alleys of Meteora, the fiddler whose statue decorated the entrance of the city and whose death had set him into his current path to stop being a monster.

No, I'm not a monster. I never was, Joshua thought firmly. It had taken him time to come to terms with what he was, between the persistence of his friends and his own efforts, he refused to fall back into that trap.

He looked around at the sparse inhabitants of the city, the downtrodden descendants of the Scientist Priest of the Asurian's experiments. Subjects, like him. These people weren't monsters, either; they were beings with rights, dreams, and hopes. They had formed a community under the shelter of the presence of the city, which had seemed to have redeemed itself as well. Joshua felt a new appreciation for his hometown. While he wouldn't be able to personally save the place, he could honor its efforts. He had made the decision: no matter what, these people—his people, now—would be under his protection one way or another.

"Yes," Joshua replied to the teenaged girl and then turned to Sam. "We can't leave them here. You know this place will be infested with incursions soon."

"Who said anything about leaving them here?" Sam said, smiling at him. "What's our number one rule?"

"We never leave behind our own," Joshua said, relieved. Unlike Fionn, who had his own reasons to be warry of strangers, Sam had always jumped at the opportunity to help. She was both like and unlike her father in many ways.

"Right now, the whole planet is our own. Hence, they come with us," Sam said.

"People at Husvika will get nervous," Vivi said.

"Then they can take it up with me," Sam shrugged. "If they dare."

"Okay," Vivi replied, smiling at her former student. "I'm with you all the way, just wanted to be sure you are aware of the consequences. My job as a teacher is never done."

"I know," Sam said, then looked at Joshua. "Make sure they don't move too much; for their own safety."

The familiar circles of light from the teleportation spell appeared around all the people gathered.

"Listen!" Joshua exclaimed, and his voice echoed through the ruins of the city. "My friends here will take us all with them. Remain calm and quiet inside the summoning circles."

"Keep your hands and legs inside at all times. If you feel like you want to puke, don't worry, that's perfectly normal. It'll be a bumpy ride," Sam warned before she began to dissolve as everything exploded around them, with only scorch marks as proof that someone, at some time, had been living there.

Chapter 7
Of Mortals and Gods

DONG!

The most surprising thing about the Temple of Serene Sounds was not that it was a giant bronze bell that could easily fit a castle inside its mouth. Nor that it had been built on the face of a cliff overlooking a beach from which one could see the God's Eye on a clear day. Perhaps the most surprising thing of all was that it had remained a popular touristic spot until a scant few hours ago when incursions invaded the place and it had to be evacuated. The Kuni Empire had a marked advantage in that its demonhunters were better organized than the Alliance's titanfighters, and since they trained in temples such as this, there had been no civilian casualties. In that regard, the Kuni Empire had fared better than many other regions—save perhaps the Straits—whose inhabitants were so used to creatures creeping out of the ground with every daily earthquake that they were rarely fazed by them. They seemed to be the only neighbors the samoharo cared for as their cultures shared a few similarities.

DONG!

It also helped that when things got hairy for the demonhunters gathered there, three people teleported into the middle of the temple, to the utter confusion of about fifty incursions and locals. Noticing the situation, struggling to shake off the effects that teleportation spells have on people, the newcomers then made short work of the incursions, allowing the demonhunters to evacuate the premises. It was useful that one of the arrivals was the first Chivalry Games champion the Kuni Empire had in decades. The person that had claimed the title of the 'Strongest Human in the World' by defeating the Titan of Sound without any special ability.

DONG!

Because Kasumi, even while under the side effects of the spell, had made short work of a bit more than a third of the incursions on her own. The remaining incursions were dispatched by Gaby and Fionn.

† † †

"One would have thought that we would eventually get used to teleportation," Fionn muttered as he beheaded an incursion. His words rebounded off the walls of the bell.

"Maybe we never will," Gaby whispered, stabbing an incursion. Her words rebounded as well.

"How come she is unbothered by the spell and the noise?" Fionn asked, dodging an incursion's attack above his head.

"She is not unbothered, she loves the effect and she and Sam have practiced a lot," Gaby murmured almost directly in the ear of her husband, who chuckled in response. Then she pointed to her own ear, trying to explain to him that Kasumi had turned off her hearing aids.

"Then we should use sign language," Fionn suggested with a hand sign.

"Agreed," Gaby replied with her own sign.

"Okay, now that we have the temple for us, before incursions return, how do we open the portal, tunnel, whatsoever to the God's Eye?" Fionn signed. "Kasumi, you know more than us. Advice?"

"Wait," Kasumi signaled. She looked down at the bottom crevices of the temple and then looked up. She signed to Gaby and Fionn. "This temple, like the one my family guarded, probably has an elemental activation to access the hidden temple. It may be explained in a poem." She pointed to the walls which contained carvings of Old Kuni ideograms. "I need to find the poem among the engravings written here." She moved along the walls, reading, and raised her right thumb as she found the poem. She beckoned to Fionn and Gaby.

She read the Old Kuni and translated it as she signed.

Touch, taste, smell, hear, sight.

Many doors open

Through our senses.
But only the right words
Can open the Eye of a God
And lead to their heart.

"So, we need to speak here?" Fionn signed. "What words? With many visitors around the year every combination must have been tried and yet it didn't activate." Fionn ran his fingers along the carved poem. "What are these dots and lines under each line of the poem?"

"Musical notations," Gaby gestured with a smile.

Kasumi placed her hands over her ears and Fionn followed suit.

Gaby read the notations to memorize them. As she did so, new incursions appeared. Fionn was about to unsheathe Black Fang again, but Kasumi shook her head as she saw Gaby taking a deep breath. Her irises glowed as the incursions closed in.

And Gaby began to sol-fa.

As she went note by note, the round crevice where they were standing commenced to glow while the notes echoed one after another into the bell, decibels climbing in rapid succession. Gaby winced from the pain the sound caused and Fionn covered her ears. Within seconds, his own Gift activated as his ears began to bleed. A white light soon shone from the crevice and engulfed them as the sound waves vaporized the incursions in one fell swoop.

Fionn blinked and found himself on the shore of a lake. His ears were still ringing despite his rapid healing. He pulled his hand from Gaby's ears, and he saw Kasumi activating her hearing aids. Tall cliffs rose all around the lake and Fionn realized they were in the crater of the God's Eye.

In front of them a woman bowed a welcome to them. She was tall, with long, dark hair that covered her eyes. She wore a veil that obscured the rest of her face, and purple demonhunter armor of a style that indicated its age. No one had used shoulder fins in more than a century.

"She is the oracle that gave me Breaker," Kasumi said.

Fionn recognized his old master and surrogate mother. "Hikaru?"

"*Baka* student," the blind oracle said. "You finally made it here."

Fionn stepped up and gave her a hug. And for the first time in a year, since the hospital, he cried.

†††

"After Kasumi told me about you, I went to the Water Temple to search, but I couldn't find you," Fionn said. It was as if he was a preteen again, chattering nonstop with his mother about some new discovery he had made in the nearby forest.

"But you found my notes and messages to you. Including the ones on the use of vital energy as attack," Hikaru observed and took Fionn's hands.

Despite his healing power, there were still faint scars from using the power and Hikaru caressed them. "Yes. I polished the technique. Kasumi calls it *kaminariken*." Fionn nodded towards Kasumi, who shyly waved back.

"A good name for that technique," Hikaru acknowledged. She turned to Kasumi. "I'm happy to see that you have made good use of my friend Breaker. You honor your family, Shimizu Kasumi."

"Tha... thank you, venerable *kami*." Kasumi bowed.

"And you," Hikaru continued. "I'm glad to see you again, Izia."

"I'm Gaby," Gaby said, a bit shortly.

"My apologies," Hikaru bowed. "I'm an old lady and blind as you can see. I got confused."

"It's okay, many of Izia's friends make that mistake," Gaby allowed. "After all, we're all family now. You are the second mother of my husband. I guess I never expected to meet one of my in-laws."

"Your life is confusing. I give you that." Hikaru smiled and hugged Gaby. "Thank you for taking care of my son."

"Master," Fionn said. While Hikaru was his surrogate mother, he had always called her master. "I was expecting to reach the shores of the God's Eye Island, and then make our way here to find what we are looking for."

"*We* tweaked a bit the Temple of Serene Sounds' gate," Hikaru explained. "Time is a valuable resource to be wasted by cutting your way through the hundreds of sacred monsters guarding this place."

"Thank you. We are in search of one of the tablets that hold the location to the Life Tree," Fionn said. "We suspect Abaddon is searching for it."

"And you plan to make a last stand there," a new male voice said. They turned to see a man of short stature, dressed in an old fashioned black *kamishimo* decorated with thunder clouds, approaching the group. He had Kuni features, like Hikaru and Kasumi. In fact, there was an eerie resemblance to the former. He sported his long, black hair in a tight top knot, and had a well-trimmed goatee accompanied with a friendly smile. But perhaps the most unusual feature was that his irises glowed with gold light. "It's a plan with risks. But it would be the only way to make him come out of hiding."

"Wait a minute," Kasumi said, openly gaping at the man. "I *know* you. I've prayed to you!"

"I have seen that face before, carved in a statue at the Temple of the Seven Fortunes!" Gaby added, recalling her fight against the Titan of Earth that took place there.

"Yes, good observation," Hikaru nodded. "Although technically it's not a temple, but a shrine. Anyway, allow me to introduce you all to my father, Igarashi Narukami, the Storm God. Which makes me Igarashi Hikaru, Oracle of the Fates."

"Your father? You never told me that, and how old were you before you..." Fionn stammered. To him, Hikaru had been his second mother, the best friend of his parents. The one that taught him everything about fighting while consoling his widowed mother. Hikaru was family, not yet another deity, of which Fionn had been growing tired of. "Did my parents know?"

"Older than you, but not as old as you think. And yes, they knew," Hikaru said, gentle. "They knew I would have to leave someday to take my place as the Oracle of the Fates. But I tried to stay by you and my beloved Dawnstar's side as long as I could, my son." She looked pained even through the veil covering her eyes. "I had a promise to keep with my dear Fraog. And I tried my best."

"If you have been here all this time, why are you not helping us to fight Abaddon's forces, venerable *kami*?" Kasumi asked.

"Who says we haven't?" Hikaru countered. "We are but minor gods, spirits if you like, and the world is a big place. We simply don't have the same provinces as your friend the Trickster Goddess. But we have helped to keep the Kuni safe as long as we could. Sadly, our energies are becoming meager the longer the planet suffers."

"All the more reason to help us find the tablet," Gaby said.

"I have the tablet here," Narukami showed it before tucking it back into his yukata. "But to get it from me, you need to show me that you are ready and understand what will be asked of all of you."

"And how do you propose that we demonstrate such?" Gaby asked, annoyed. "I mean, given that stopping Byron, defeating the titans and the Creeping Chaos, as well as Shemazay and saving magick itself doesn't seem to be enough."

"Patience, for fighting the First Demon is no common feat, much less succeeding in defeating him or surviving the encounter," Narukami replied with a half-smile, trying to be polite, although thunder was heard not far from there, betraying the actual feelings of the Storm God. "One of you shall fight me while keeping the water in this cup from spilling. You win if you land a strike on my neck while doing that. I win if I manage to make the water spill. The one that challenges me has three chances. If you fail, I keep the tablet and I will send you back to the Temple of Serene Sounds."

Fionn looked at the cup in Narukami's hand and then to the Storm God. He would have a decent chance due to the difference in height and reach. "I will do it," he said. "I guess that seniority gives me that claim. Am I correct master? Kasumi? I'm a bit rusty with the rules of demonhunting schools."

"You are correct, student," Hikaru said. "Although, knowing the dunderhead you are, I bet either of them would pass the test faster than you."

"Many thanks for the encouragement, master," Fionn said, dry.

Hiraku cuffed him. "Do not sass me, my son." She then indicated for Fionn's companions to follow her. "Come with me. Gaby, Kasumi, let's see if something I taught this unruly child stuck in that stubborn head of his. Your father was less stubborn than you and he refused to acknowledge when he was injured."

Hikaru led Gaby and Kasumi to a rock formation where they took a seat, while Narukami led Fionn to the lake's shore, where the cup was filled and Narukami placed it on Fionn's head, tying it with a red string around his head and below the chin.

Narukami walked a few steps back and summoned to his hand a wooden *bokken*. It seemed to have been carved from an old oar, like the legend said the Storm God had done before encountering Yaha.

Fionn regarded the absence of another blunt weapon. "I don't see another *bokken* here and Black Fang will cut yours with ease, master," he said respectfully, his tone even. For Narukami was, in a way, his master as well. "I have no desire to harm you." There existed an invisible chain uniting masters and students across history. It was almost like an ersatz family tree.

Narukami smiled politely. "Student, you won't... even if you did so desire it. Let us begin." A subtle golden hue glowed within his eyes.

Both opponents showed to each other the hilt of their respective weapons and got into a ready stance.

Fionn began the first bout. Without much warning, he launched a series of fast slashes, aimed at Narukami's midsection, who blocked each one of them with such ease that he seemed statuesque from how little he moved. The *bokken* was hardly bothered by Balck Fang, as if it were an extension of the Storm God's will. Fionn—who, to his merit, had managed to keep all the water in the cup by keeping his spine rigid—pressed, to push Narukami back, but with blinding speed, the later gave a step to the left, hit Fionn square in the chest with enough force to crack a rib, and followed with a swift spin, to hit Fionn in the back, making him drop all the water.

Watching, Kasumi winced. "That must hurt."

"Knowing him," Hikaru said, "his ego hurts more than the rib."

"For losing?" Kasumi asked.

"For not grasping the lesson," Hikau said.

"Lessons through duels?" Kasumi mused with a chuckle. "That sounds familiar."

"She used to train us like that," Gaby said. "You know, back when I... Fionn did the same with Alex and me at Ravenhall, among other occasions. Alex finds it annoying."

"And you?" Hikaru asked Gaby.

"I got used to it both times," Gaby shrugged.

"You say that you are not Izia, yet you act like her," Hikaru observed in a mild tone.

"I'm not her, but she is part of me. And I *do* recall every lesson you gave us," Gaby said, pointed. "Including the ones when you said you wouldn't train Izia."

"Until you... she forced the issue," Hikaru acknowledged.

Fionn refilled the cup and tried a second time. He took a deep breath, twirled Black Fang, and his irises glowed with an intense green light.

Narukami smiled as he held his *bokken* in front of him, waiting.

Fionn lunged, releasing a downward strike over Narukami's head. The Storm God blocked the attack with an audible thud of the Fang on his *bokken*, and this time Fionn—to no avail—rained down fruitless blows upon his rival, despite each attack inching closer on his rival. The difference was minuscule.

Narukami swung at Fionn's neck twice. The first time Fionn managed to block and parry, but the second one, the counterattack, came too fast even with the Gift at full power. Narukami stopped the *bokken* just on Fionn's skin, in an impossible feat for any other than the first demonhunter. Narukami then gave a step forward and flicked the cup from Fionn's head.

"That was close," Kasumi said, disappointed.

"Closer than you think," Hikaru said. "I'm pleased to see how skilled my student has become. He is giving Father a real fight, the first in centuries. If he trained all of you with that level, no wonder the one hundred and eight have not been a problem for you."

"I think the only ones that can beat Fionn are Gaby, and my boyfriend Alex."

"Yeah," Gaby said. "He told me about the fight he and Alex had at Saint Lucy. While I'm not happy why it took place, I kinda wish to have seen it."

Hiraku interrupted with a polite clearing of her throat. "Father will speak now," she said. "You will be interested in hearing as well."

"Why are you failing?" Narukami asked Fionn.

"You are too fast for me," Fionn said ruefully with a half-smile. In truth, the speed difference wasn't too much between them. But even with the Gift at full power, Fionn was still a second behind every movement by the Storm God. Alex had once told him, as Fionn prepared for the battle against the Golden King, that he had found, after fighting two godly avatars, that the difference between winning and losing were mere seconds and millimeters, and that he had been lucky to have Sam and Yoko on his side to help to make up for the difference. But unlike Alex, Fionn had long since decided to not put others in harm's way unless there was no other choice. Hence why he had taken on battling the pseudo-Golden King on his own.

"You know that's not entirely right. You are a bit slower due to all the weight you are carrying here," Narukami touched his chest above his heart, "which the water in the cup on your head symbolizes. Otherwise, I must admit that we are equally matched, and this will keep going till both become even and then end exhausted. Hence your dilemma. In other words..."

"When an immovable object clashes with an unstoppable object, they destroy each other," Fionn mused.

"So, how would the immovable object defeat the unstoppable without giving the latter what it wants?" Narukami asked.

"The former would have to leave behind all it had been so far."

The Storm God nodded. "Asherah, the Prophet, and the Iskandar didn't realize this option until after the battle with Abaddon. By then they hoped that their option of splitting his essence into the Creeping Chaos, the Golden King, and the scions that would eventually corrupt the titans or become the tovainar you have faced so far. With the hope that existence bound to the mortal realm would erode Abaddon's essence with time. And it did to a point. Proof of that exists in your friend who tamed the scion and became the new titan of fire, redeeming himself. But it was not enough, mostly because when one side enacts a plan, it often assumes that..."

"The other side won't act," Fionn continued as his eyes widened. "Which clearly wasn't the case."

"Thus, you have a dilemma, and a decision."

"Which is exemplified by this lesson."

"To win this duel you need to spill the water in the cup on my head, correct?" Fionn went over the rules once more. "And if I want to win, I need to bring you down while stopping you from spilling the water, right?"

Narukami nodded.

Fionn bowed deeply. "I need to meditate on this for a brief moment, master."

Fionn walked to the lake's shore and examined the bamboo cup in his hand. He'd realized the core of the lesson, but it was one thing to be doing it here, and another during an eventual, and ultimately unavoidable, confrontation with Abaddon.

†††

Fionn placed the cup on his head once more, tied the cords under his chin, and got ready for his final bout against the Storm God. Both stood in front of each other. Fionn shifted into a defensive posture with Black Fang in front of him, taking a deep breath to calm his mind, to quiet his heart. There was no need for thought at the moment, just awareness. He lowered the tip of his sword to the ground, as Narukami flexed his fingers to improve his grasp of the bokken.

Fionn opened his eyes and readied Black Fang, with Narukami imitating the same ready stance. They were mirror images.

Fionn lashed out, striking Narukami's mid-section, who deftly parried the attack, turning the defense into an attack aimed at the cup. Fionn in turn blocked the attack with an upward swing, pushing the *bokken* aside and spinning on his heel, ending up back-to-back with Narukami. Both turned to face each other, trading blows. Narukami ducked to dodge a blow and lifted his *bokken*, striking the cup at the top of Fionn's head, at the same time Fionn stopped Black Fang's blade from hitting the Storm God's neck just above the skin.

"He failed again," Kasumi whispered, somewhat disheartened. "And it was so close."

The cup fell to the ground, bouncing around, a dry sound coming from it, echoing inside the walls of the volcano's crater.

Narukami stared at the cup for a long moment before he raised his face to meet Fionn's eyes and released a short, thunderous laugh.

The cup was empty. It had been before the bout between Narukami and Fionn had even begun.

"Well played, student," Narukami said, extending his hand to Fionn. "You won."

"Isn't that cheating? Kasumi whispered to Hikaru.

"The lesson was never about winning the duel per se," Gaby said ruefully. "It was about allowing yourself to let go."

Kasumi's eyes opened wide as the implication of Gaby's words, coupled with the welling up of her eyes, dawned on her.

"I'm sorry," Kasumi whispered, looking sad as well.

"Seems that you have, too, grasped the real lesson," Hikaru said to Gaby, cryptically smiling.

"Comes with the territory of having lived two lives with him already, and neither were long enough if you ask me," Gaby muttered.

"Now you understand," Narukami said to Fionn, placing his bokken to the side and bowed from the hips.

A soft sigh escaped Fionn as he bowed in turn. "I don't like it," Fionn said, "but I accept it." If he got the lesson right, and all seemed to indicate that was the case, he was afraid. His heart was as heavy as a rock the moment he looked at Gaby's eyes. Those eyes were now filled with a deep, yearning. She hadn't missed a beat. The silence between them said everything.

Narukami stared at both and with a frown, placed a hand on Fionn's shoulder, offering an understanding nod. "You don't have to, my friend," Narukami said, his voice grave. He took the tablet from his yukata and offered it to Fionn. "The universal truth of all masters: our journey might end, but theirs continue. We become the empty cup once we pour everything into our students, successes as well as failures, strength as well as weakness. Once they grow beyond us, their success is our reward. The question you are pondering right now is not if you are ready to fight this last enemy, which you are, but whether you are ready to let go of everything so others can grow upon what you have built. And that my friend, is not a question with an easy answer. But when you do, everything shall become clear, for illumination is within your grasp. When you reach the Tree, sit down and commune with it for as long as you can. Then maybe the answer you seek will appear."

Hiraku hugged Gaby to her chest and then took Fionn's face in her hands. "Time to go, my beloved students," Hikaru said softly. "I'm proud of you, my son. Dawnstar and Fraog would be proud of you, too."

"Thank you, master." Fionn eyes welled up as he felt once more the warmth of his surrogate mother. It made him feel like a child once more, careless, free, and secure, without the heavy burden in his grown-up heart.

Kasumi took out the stone with the teleportation spell, and set up everything to return to Husvika as the sun sank on the horizon. Gaby joined her, shivering. The air in the mountains grew cooler and winds howled. The creatures below, in the forest at the skirts of the volcano were growing restless.

"We need to leave!" Kasumi exclaimed.

Fionn started towards them, only to pause as something else dawned on him. "Hey, one more question," he said. "Will I see you again..." Fionn trailed off when he realized that Hikaru and Narukami had vanished into thin the air, their mission probably fulfilled. "I guess no."

"I hate these vision quests," Gaby said, ruefully.

"But at least we got what we came for," Fionn said, staring forlornly at the tablet.

Chapter 8
Honorbound

"*SO, WHAT'S THE PLAN?*" **ALEX** asked from the copilot chair. Yoko stood behind him and Sid, as they reached Ouslis, the southern continent the samoharo had claimed for themselves thousands of years ago. So far, they had been able to evade the orionian dart ships and were about to enter Samoharo airspace. Ouslis, as seen from the air, was a large land mass with a few rivers feeding lakes, a massive desert and even more massive rainforest. All filled with dangerous fauna and flora both original to Theia and from Ka'ab, the samoharo homeworld. It was a common joke to say that the samoharo themselves were the least dangerous thing on Ouslis, and that was only because they haven't been proven to be venomous... yet. Most people from the Straits that visited limited themselves to the coast.

"What's the plan, hmm?" Sid smiled as he corrected their course and entered Chichen Itza's airspace. Alex was probably the first human in centuries to have seen the actual samoharo capital instead of Tulum, the city where they received foreign dignitaries. That Sid and Yoko were willing to take Harland's message strain to the heart of the Samoharo Hegemony rather than using the traditional—and slower—diplomatic routes reinforced the direness of the situation, as well as how much his two friends were willing to break every rule from their culture in order to save it from itself.

"We'll cause a distraction. You will take the Figaro to this location and pick up the asset who must already have the tablet. Then you will pick us up before we get executed due to the distraction, with one of your superhero landing entrances for maximum confusion."

There was a beat before Alex responded, visibly distressed. "Who and how in the Pits are you planning to distract that will get us executed?"

Sid grinned. "The *K'uhul Ajaw*, the Samoharo paramount ruling council, and in particular the *nacom*, which is more or less the equivalent to the admiral in human ranks."

"And the how," Yokoyawa said, "is that he is planning to shame them to death for cutting communications and trying to leave the planet without at least taking refugees from the other species, while delivering Harlan's message."

"Aw, crap," Alex replied, almost banging his head on the yoke. "Aren't those the guys that banished you?"

"Under threat of execution if I returned, yes," Sid confirmed.

"I can't believe I'm saying this, but that's a lousy plan."

"Wello, it's a plan. And if the public shaming works, we might be able to save more people, isn't that worth the risk?"

"Since when are you the selfless hero risking his life... wait a minute. You know something they don't. That's why you're so confident."

Sid and Yoko exchanged knowing looks.

"Your covenant thingie!" Alex exclaimed. There was a reason why Sid had been able to keep with the rest of the Band, something Alex had gotten so used to that it had slipped his mind for more than a decade, until now. "The blood ritual you once told me about, the one allowed you to keep pace with Gaby and me while smelling of cacao and dark chocolate when fighting?"

"I thought you had forgotten that," Sid laughed. The Covenant was a ritual that select samoharo warriors, such as the guards of K'uhul Ajaw, underwent to receive the blood of the Prophet by eating sacred cacao seeds from his Grove. Once ingested, the seed became part of them, and its power could be summoned when required, enhancing a samoharo's physical, mental, and mystical skills. "Yes, that 'thingie' as you said. Only works if you follow the honor rules that bind them, and guess whose is still working, unlike theirs?"

"So, if you never lost it, that means all the samoharo lost it and thus you can beat them easily?" If Sid had kept it since the day they met, when he had already been banished, it was logical to assume that for the past decade and a half, no other samoharo had a working Covenant. Because if they had expelled Sid, and only him, for refusing to follow orders, it meant that the rest had turned their backs on honor unlike Sid. "What about Yokoyawa?"

"I got it reactivated during the fight with Shemazay," Yoko said.

"So, you could have beaten him without my intervention," Alex mused.

"I got it back while he broke my ribs," Yokoyawa said as he rubbed his now healed ribs. "I did need your help. But that's why I could throw the scimitar that way. That's when I found out."

"And you're absolutely positive that the rest of the samoharo warriors lost it?" Alex clarified. In theory, it sounded good for the plan, but bad for the long-term survival of the samoharo. Now he understood why Sid intended to shame the leaders of his people. It was not just a distraction, but aiming to make them see sense and perhaps recover something that could help them to survive.

"Leaving behind half a planet to save only your own arses is not a very honorable thing to do. I mean, at least take the dogs. They are the best of us," Sid said.

"Point," Alex conceded. "But assuming you manage to convince them, where are the ships?"

"See all those ancient buildings over there?" Sid pointed at the ancient stone-like temples on the horizon of the city. "All of those are our arks, they were turned into temples to keep them maintained. And they are emitting a lot of energy signatures, which means they are readying the engines."

"Okay, we will jump from there and then you can pick up Dr. Tze Tze, it's already marked it down so you can't get lost," Yoko said as Sid transferred controls to Alex.

"Good, because all the buildings look the same to me," Alex admitted, red-faced. Samoharo architecture wasn't widely studied, outside certain degrees such as Alex's. Despite that, he never managed to discern between a temple, an observatory, and a pyramid. "And who is Dr. Tze Tze, the asset? Can he pilot the Figaro while I make my entrance?"

"One, shame on you for flunking architecture," Sid replied as he stood up. "Two, the good doctor is the one that taught me all I know. He can pilot the Figaro."

"Just be aware, he taught him *all*," Yoko added, putting an emphasis on the word. "Including the sense of humor."

"Aw, crap," Alex muttered. "There are *two* of him?"

† † †

"I guess I'll have to eyeball it and probably create a distraction by landing somewhere... prohibited," Alex muttered as he got closer to the avenue Sid had called the Avenue of the Dead. "Lovely name." The area—smack in the middle of a rainforest with massive trees and near a large river—was surrounded by what seemed to be temples of some sort. Samoharo structures were peculiar in themselves: they were stepped pyramids with energy lines running across their brightly colored painted walls, generating luminous signals—pictograms—that must be the names or indications of which building was which. Alex should have thought twice before saying he understood samoharo. People from the Straits learned the basics of their closest neighbors' languages, Samoharo and Kuni. On top of that, he had learned Core and Sign Language. He had tried to learn freefolk, or at least Sam's dialect, but he'd only managed to make a few words stick. His brain had been fried after cramming so much information inside. He had a problem now. It was one thing to be able to *speak* the languages, and another to read them. Core was easy, it shared the same alphabet as the Straits. Kuni used ideograms. Samoharo used pictograms, and as Sid put it once, humans lacked the tongue flexibility to enunciate it well—which also meant he couldn't stop and ask someone for directions.

Of course, that was assuming that he didn't stick out like a sore thumb. Humans never visited the samoharo capital. Sid had marked the Figaro's map databanks the position of the Calamuk library but considering that half the city was underground he lacked the street references.

A ping with a text message arrived on the Figaro's console, which read "Park here. DRTT."

"Uh, I guess I've arrived," Alex muttered to himself. Below, there was a group of samoharos waving at him. Alex docked the Figaro, not as smoothly as Sid did it, but close enough. He opened the rear hatch and exited the Figaro to meet the samoharo waiting for him.

"Dr. Tze Tze I presume," Alex said to the áak samoharo, extending a hand to salute the scientist. He was almost the same height as Sid, but sported his hair in a more conservative, long ponytail fashion. He was followed by a dozen samoharos of all kinds, their skin ranging across the entire spectrum of green hues. They carried at least four large crates and a small case. The other samoharos passing by gave them odd, confused looks at the procession.

"You prezume well, Dr. Leon," Dr. Tze Tze replied with a peculiar accent Alex had never heard. But it was illogical to expect that all samoharo would have the same accent, or even the same dialect for that matter.

Alex rubbed the back of his neck. "No one calls me that."

"But we are people of science," Dr. Tze Tze said. "I know of your projects, be proud of them."

"Yeah." Alex laughed nervously as he saw from the corner of his eye a couple of guards approaching. "Look, I would love to talk about this, but I think we are pressed on time. Who are all of them?"

"My rezearch team. We all decided to go with you and join the Foundation'z efforts to zave az many people. I have a question for you: if you knew Ziddharta and Yokoyawa will be taken to custody and then execution after they finizh talking with the Council, and that rezcuing them would be hard and time consuming, what would you do?"

"Leaving aside that I was well aware of the possibility, I would ask you if you have someone that can pilot the Figaro while I make my way into the Council chamber to break them out. I don't leave my own behind."

"Good. That's the anzwer I wanted to hear." Dr. Tze Tze punched Alex in the arm. "Now let'z go because that'z what'z gonna happen in a few minutez. Itzel will help you with the flight."

"Just get me closer to the Council," Alex smiled.

† † †

"Please, don't turn your back on us. You trusted me and the Greywolf after the Titan crisis, please trust us once more. We will make things better. We have a plan."

Harland's message echoed through the large hall of the *K'uhul Ajaw*. Energy lines ran across the amphitheater of grey stone, forming fretworks decorating the walls. It was round, with the twelve members of the council—samoharos of both types and different ages—seated on tall balcony-like cavities, two meters above the ground. Below each one was an armed guard. And in the middle of the space, with the spotlight on them, with their hands bound by orichalcum chains that were meant to stop a samoharo from breaking them, stood Sid and Yokoyawa.

"This is going well," Yokoyawa observed in a mild tone. "We're still alive."

"Your definition of 'well' needs some work," Sid said dryly.

"That you two are mocking this council in front of your betters shows how little regard you have for your people. We expected this from you, Siddhartha Itzmana. But not of you, Yokoyawa Quetzalcoatl," the eldest member of the council said gravely.

Yoko shrugged. "Times change. People change."

"Look, your opinion of me is well known, so can we skip that?" Sid asked. "I have to know, are you going to help the humans and the Freefolk? Our allies?" Rather than humble himself, make himself small to appease the council, Sid stood as tall before them. While he was addressing the council, his eyes focused on a tall, older meemech samoharo, the admiral Hunapuh.

"We are helping our neighbors from the Straits," another council member said flatly.

"I meant the message from my friend," Sid clarified. He was losing his patience. The problem with such a long-lived species as the samoharo, is that they were prone to get stuck with their old paradigms.

"We acknowledge the message," the council leader said.

"So, you are not going to help at the very least to evacuate as many as you can?" Sid asked, though he knew the answer already. The way the leader had replied to Sid's inquiry and Harland's message clued Sid in that the council had made their decision long ago and that the radio silence was them ignoring Harland's pleas. That really pissed off Sid.

So much for honor, Sid thought.

"You ask us to help them? The monsters you were trained to kill? *After* your ship brought the attention of the orionians?" a third council member exclaimed. "We have seen the videos of one of them stopping a warp train with his bare hands. Or the Greywolf fighting across a whole continent with a demon. What do they need our help for?"

"The orionians would have come here anyway," Yokoyawa countered, calmly. "Abaddon would have brought them." Although the calm, if Sid knew Yoko, was a thin coat covering his cousin's increasing annoyance. "The Gifted are not monsters, they are our friends. And the help, if not for them, is for the rest of the civilian population trying to survive the infection currently afflicting our shared planet."

"You are a bunch of cowards hiding behind rules and an honor you clearly lack," Sid said, raising his voice. There was no point in trying to convince them nicely as Yoko had asked him to try first. "I would have expected that you would recognize the efforts of those so-called 'monsters' to save all of us. I can't say I'm disappointed. But I nonetheless hoped that at least a few among you would still possess some empathy. Since that's not the case, we're out of here."

"You cannot leave," the council leader said. "You are to be judged."

"Yeah, right," Sid said, raising his hands and breaking the chains without effort. Yoko promptly did the same. "One last thing: how many among our people can still call upon the Covenant?"

The council members sat in a stunned silence. No one had managed to break those chains in decades.

"I thought so," Sid said, then he looked at Yoko, who was dusting his wrists from the orichalcum. "I guess it's only the two of us."

"That will have to be enough," Yoko shrugged.

"Time to go!" Sid said to the hidden nanoparticle comms he had been carrying concealed in a small sweatband on his wrist.

Nothing happened. The council members looked at each other confused.

"Have patience, Sid," Yoko admonished.

"That's your cue!" Sid exclaimed. But much to his chagrin nothing happened, besides a brief rumble echoing the walls. "Apologies, it takes him time to..."

The roof of the Council chamber exploded in tiny debris as lightning struck the ground next to Sid. "Good thing his aim is better than his timing," Yoko said, wry.

As the dust cloud cleared, the silhouette of a man with a glowing sword became clear. The sword had the now legendary six wings hilt and the man rose from the half-kneeling position with an amused smile.

"Happy with your dramatic entrance?" Sid shook his head.

"Sorry, the wall was thicker than I expected," Alex explained as he rubbed the back of his neck with his left hand, as he waved Yaha at the council, greeting them in samoharo. The specific greeting that Sid had told him would rile up the Council. "*Bix a beel!*"

"The iskandar!" the council leader exclaimed. By that point Hunapuh was already up from his seat and leaving the council chamber, sporting a smile on his face.

"I would love to talk with you guys, but we are in a hurry," Alex said, breathing heavily. Sid ran towards a corridor full of befuddled guards that Yoko pushed with ease into the walls, as if the larger samoharo was a warp train himself.

"Did you get them?" Yoko asked, looking at a new batch of guards who preferred to stay away from the champion of the samoharo.

"Ready and in the ship," Alex said, dodging the samoharo guards in the way. "Did you convince them?"

"By the looks on their faces and the cacao smell in the air, only one."

"Only one?" Alex asked with a mix of sadness and surprise.

"The one that matters," Sid replied.

Chapter 9
Fling a Light into the Dark

"HAVE YOU HEARD ANYTHING FROM the Figaro?"
Sam asked Hardland for a third time. He sat on a bench in the
hangar of the Geoda, next to the Mayor of Skarabear. Kasumi
paced nervously not far away.

The Geoda was a geodesic dome with an omnitriangu-
lated surface, built on top of the remains of an ancient castle
in Husvika. It was mostly automated by a new kind of A.I.
that the Foundation had developed, G.E.A.R.I., based on the
Figaro's, currently hosted—due to lack of materials—in a
toy robot. G.E.A.R.I. took charge of the hydroponic gardens
and climate control, as well as communications.

The Geoda had been Harland and Fionn's secret project
since the Chivalry Games, though most of the foundations
for the whole secret base had been set up by Dawnstar almost a century ago. The ruins of Husvika once belonged to
one of the first human-freefolk kingdoms, from which the
original inhabitants of Skarabear came. The region where
the castle was now, almost into the polar circle, was inhab-
ited by the Elder Ice People, an ancient fey race that never
spoke and weren't that friendly with any visitor who wasn't
from Skarabear. Both locations were connected through a
portal Dawnstar and her father Greygulch had created. She
had created this base hoping that her son and daughter-in-
law one day would return, and in case they needed to set up
a place to hide from Byron.

Harland looked between Fionn and Gaby, who likewise
expectantly awaited the arrival of the Figaro. In a way,
Dawnstar had gotten her last wish... a century late. Her son

was back, and her new daughter-in-law had ended being the reincarnation of the last.

"Not yet," Harland said to Sam. Vivi was approaching her former student. Unlike Sam, she was calm—or at least, was good at faking it. Harland had sworn off playing cards years ago, but he recognized a good player. Vivi was one of them. "Radio signals are down. You got here first because teleportation is faster. They have to cross half a planet while evading those aliens."

"They seem worried," the Mayor whispered to Harland in a deep baritone.

"It has been a tough year for them. Add to that, that their boyfriend," Harland nodded towards Sam and Kasumi, "needs to take a medication that has become extremely difficult to obtain. Then the Figaro has to deal with Orionians and..."

"And also the infected zones," the Major replied. "It will be a tough flight. Got it."

"I see something," Gaby exclaimed. Her sight was unparalleled.

The Figaro approached at speed, causing Harland to fear that they had been found. But the Figaro began to slow down and landed gracefully on the landing pad next to the X-23. The hull was covered in new scorch marks, but otherwise it seemed fine. The samoharo contingent descended first, carrying several crates and the last tablet. They were followed by Sid, Alex, and Yoko in a weary procession.

"Rough flight?" Harland asked.

"A few skirmished near Orca Bay," Sid replied.

"Portis is a mess," Alex added, looking miserable. He then headed for Sam and Kasumi.

"He took it bad, the state of the city," Yoko whispered. "Had to have an impromptu therapy session. Are Gaby's family alright?"

"We evacuated them. They're in the Kuni's outpost with Kasumi's. Couldn't find Alex's though. Given how rarely he talks about them, I had no way to find them," Harland explained.

"Most of the Strait's inhabitants were admitted into the Hegemony. At least they are being taken care of, if only due proximity," Sid said ruefully.

"I take it the Council didn't take my message well?" Harland asked.

"I don't think it was your message, but his." Yoko nodded towards Sid.

"That bad, uh?"

"Let's say he humiliated them," Yoko suggested.

Sid shrugged. "I just said a few harsh truths."

"Nothing they didn't need to hear," Dr. Tze Tze said with his peculiar accent. "Now, we will take the time to zolve this riddle and understand the information hidden in the tabletz. Do the other tabletz are here?"

"We have them here." Vivi pointed at a table where they had been placed. She had been studying the artifacts to occupy her time. "Why don't you put them on a disc, rotate them, scan the resulting image and project it in a hologram? Together they look like the blades of a windmill, worth trying that," Vivi suggested out of the blue, leaving everyone silent for a moment. "You know that I'm a researcher too, right? And I like adventure movies a little too much, according to some."

Joshua, who was entering the room, turned around at the sound of that and promptly returned to where he'd come from.

"That could work," Dr. Tze Tze said. "Thank you for the zuggeztion. It will zave time."

"Then it's settled," Harland declared. "Let's go to work."

The Major of Skarabear then approached Sam, who chatted animatedly with Alex and Kasumi. "Ahem," the Major said. "My apologies for interrupting your spirited talk, but you have a call, Ms. Ambers-Estel."

"A call?" Sam said, surprised.

"An emergency transmission from Mr. Stealth in the Mistlands, technically."

Sam's shoulders dropped.

† † †

"I thought this was a private call," Stealth complained through the screen. The whole band was behind Sam, whose grimace was a sign of her annoyance verging on seething rage by then. Her blood boiled. They were sitting in a small conference room Harland had set up to give them some privacy, while the rest of the Foundation and the samoharo deserters worked to find the Life Tree.

"They're here to keep me from cursing you all to the Infinity Pits." Sam shrugged. "Or at least to keep me from hanging up on you. What's the issue now?"

"I would expect more respect for the new Librarian, and in honor of who Mother was... is."

Sam raised an eyebrow.

"Right, I forgot with whom I'm talking to, not even Mother got that much respect from you." Stealth chuckled. Then his voice filled with sadness as his expression changed. "When I visited the lake where Mother's new avatar was incubating, the place had been obliterated, and the body was destroyed. Mother won't be back, at least to the mortal realm. And the shamans can't commune with her. It seems she and her siblings are doing their own battle in the upper levels of reality."

"Aw, crap," Alex muttered behind Sam, summarizing the feelings of everyone.

"It means we are alone," Sam replied.

"It is worse. The Elders want you to take the DragonQueen title."

"They can want the ice cream lemon flavored, as Alex says," Sam retorted. She was sick of the matter, of the constant asking.

"You have made your feelings about the matter perfectly clear before, but there is a problem," Stealth continued with forced patience.

"What now?"

"Most of the elders—and their tribes as whole, really—won't evacuate further north to the ARK as Harland is proposing, without the express order of the DragonQueen, since the shamans can't commute with the Trickster Goddess. Some are even thinking of journeying to the depths of the World's Scar. We don't know what the situation is there, but it's safe to assume it's not good."

"So, the fate of our whole species lies on me renouncing my life and the ones I love? That's blackmail," Sam complained. She had done more than enough for her people. But she wasn't willing to sacrifice her personal life, which was precisely what happened to anyone who accepted the title. They became more of a symbol, an object, than a person. And Sam had been struggling for quite a long time to find out who she was as a person, to throw it away. Especially now that she was in a stable relationship with two people who not only understood her, but complemented and supported her all the time.

"They look after you because of what you did to give us magick back. For many here, you are now on par with Queen Kary, even Asherah. And they are afraid of what to do next. I'm sorry to sound harsh," Stealth said, "but it is time for you to step up to the plate. This is not a normal situation. I wish I could change things, but my vote doesn't carry the same weight as Mother's for obvious reasons. In times of war the DragonQueen or King has always led our people, since Asherah's time. That's the tradition."

"Tradition you say? Uh?" Sam muttered as the gears in her head turned at full speed, her belly feeling full of butterflies as a plan came to mind.

It was Stealth's turn to raise a brow. "What are you thinking?"

"Something I need to do before accepting the title and order them to move their legs to the agreed rendezvous point," Sam said. "Tradition says that the Elders can't break a formalized relationship without consent of those involved. Dad, can you officiate a quick heartjoining ceremony?"

Stealth and Vivi laughed at the way Sam twisted the rules in her favor. If she pulled this one off successfully, then she could set a precedent for her to break with other annoying customs she would have to follow. It was a simple, yet groundbreaking plan. What was surprising was no one had tried it before. Then again, Sam had never been the usual freefolk magus.

"What's that?" Alex asked.

"Sam is proposing to marry both of you, bedhair," Gaby explained, amused.

"I thought we would elope like Fionn and you did?" Kasumi mused.

"Not in this case," Sam said. "By doing it this way, the elders can't order me to do anything to change it."

"I can't, I don't know all the words, but as head of the tribe I can designate a member to help me as I preside." Fionn turned to Vivi." "Would you do the honors?"

Sid gave her a slight nudge.

"Of course. But while you are head of the tribe, and obviously Sam's dad who supports her request, who supports their request? I mean we need to be sticklers since the elders will throw a fit after this, assuming we survive the week. This has to be impeachable," Vivi said firmly. Leave it to the teacher to point out the potential blindsides of Sam's impromptu wedding.

"Given that I'm his wife and also an elder of the tribe, despite being only thirty," Gaby said with a laugh, "I support both their requests. After all, you, Alex, are my best friend. And Kasumi, you're like my sister. Should that be enough for the elders?"

"It's fine by me," Stealth said on the screen.

"Then it's settled," Vivi replied. "And after our mission, they'll owe us their lives so... Are you ready?"

"I didn't bring my formal wear," Alex replied, looking at his worn gear. "And I mean, I thought that at some point I would get two rings and kneel in front of both of you..."

"I don't care about that," Sam replied. She turned to Kasumi. "You?"

"Not really." Kasumi was smiling. "And we can always do it again, with fancier trappings. But it doesn't matter to me, I want to be with both of you."

"Then let's proceed!" Sam gushed.

"Sam, as the oldest member of the tribe, which under freefolk law makes you the head of the future household, your hand goes first, for you are the foundation. Who wants to go next?" Vivi asked Alex and Kasumi, who exchanged a glance.

"Alex, you are next," Kasumi said as she pushed his hand over Sam's.

"As I place your hand over the foundation, you become the walls that will protect the members of this family," Vivi recited.

Sam and Alex took Kasumi's right hand with their free hands and placed it over theirs.

"This is where the tradition changes slightly when it comes to throuples, for there is a different line to recite in the ceremony. As Asherah's taught us that where two hearts live, a third can do as well, you will become the balance that will keep this family's equilibrium."

Vivi grabbed the three hands and with a white ribbon Gaby loaned from a nearby desk, Vivi began to wrap their wrists, tying them together, as she recited the rest of the blessing ceremony:

"Our stories tell us that when we are born, there is a heart destined to be our mate. Sometimes that heart comes in the shape of one being, sometimes in the shape of two. Sometimes they look like us, sometimes they are our opposites, and sometimes they walk in the middle. It matters not, for when we found each other, we understand a fundamental truth that the Great Spirit, Kaan'a, gifts us with: when we, after many trials, find those with whom our hearts beat in synch, matters not who we are, or how many we are in this new family, love is love, and there is only one life before you now. You will be shelter for the other. You will be the warmth in the coldness of the winter, the starlight that will guide you in the dark of the night.

"As I tie these binds around your wrists, your three paths become one, your three hearts beat as one. As I tie these binds around your wrists, remember to treat yourselves and each other with respect, treasure what brought you together. Give the highest priority to the tenderness, gentleness and kindness that your connection deserves. As I make the final knot on the binds joining your lives I ask you once: do you want to be each other's heartmates till the last star in the universe shines a light?" Vivi asked.

"Yes," Sam said first, with an assurance Fionn had never seen before. Her smile was beaming.

"Yes," Alex replied, without hesitation but in a lower tone, as he was clearly too nervous to even remember to breathe and his hand shook. But he never broke eye contact with Sam or Kasumi.

"Always," Kasumi said, unwavering, smiling at both her new life partners.

"Then by blessing of the tribe's leaders," Vivi said as she looked at Fionn and Gaby, who nodded in assent, "and the blessing of the Great Spirit, Kaan'a herself; your paths are one. And no one but you or Kaan'a can split it again, for their blessing is everlasting."

"Should we kiss?" Kasumi asked, her voice filled with both excitement and nervousness. Sam found that endearing and cute. On the other hand, Alex was sweating profusely and trying to contain his anxiety, though his face beamed with happiness.

Sam laughed affectionately. "I think Alex is about to suffer a nervous breakdown, so yes."

Sam and Kasumi both kissed Alex on one cheek, and then they kissed each other. Sam then took a deep breath, closing her eyes for a second. Alex grabbed her left hand and Kasumi the right, and she tightened her grip on them. She opened her eyes, let go all the air and turned to the screen.

"Stealth, please tell them that yes, I will become the new DragonQueen, if that helps you convince them to evacuate. But one thing: make it clear to the elders that they should stay the fuck away from my personal life and that of my husband and wife from now on or they will find out if I *can* breathe fire. I have heard the whispers."

"Thank you, my champion," Stealth said with a chuckle. No one doubted that Sam could pull that off. "Now I need to get thousands of freefolk moving to the North Pole. I will see you at the agreed upon point, Harland."

"Safe journey," Harland replied.

"You, too. And to the rest of us. I have faith in you. Be careful," Stealth said, before cutting the transmission.

† † †

An Elder Ice People approached the three of them and offered Sam an ice dagger, Alex an ice sai, and to Kasumi, an ice pendant in the shape of a snowflake.

"It's their way to express congratulations," Fionn explained, beaming with pride at his daughter. She had upended centuries of tradition by the simple yet nigh-impossible task of standing her ground against age-old tradition—a momentous achievement. And yet, he could feel tension that lingered in his shoulders. He traded a knowing look with Gaby, who averted his gaze.

"So, does that make you my stepmom in law?" Alex asked Gaby. "That feels... weird."

"It will be painful if you ever call me that, understood?" Gaby muttered.

"Yes, ma'am," Alex replied, offering a martial salute to Gaby, who could only counter with her crooked smile as she hugged her best friend.

Fionn could only shake his head. Leave it to Alex to break the tension of a situation with a bad joke.

I hope that never changes, Fionn thought as the words of the Storm God echoed again in his head. To stop an unstoppable object, you must leave everything behind. He looked at Sam and how happy she was with her new wife and husband, despite knowing what might be expecting them in a few hours. She had a family of her own now, a very peculiar one.

The rest of the afternoon was spent in a small celebration. It was the first that any of them had had in a year, and even then, under the looming shadow of what they awaited them the next morning. Close to midnight, when most had settled in for a nap, Sid crept over to where Fionn was resting, if spending time in the dark with his eyes open, as the glow in the irises was now becoming painful, could be called resting.

"Can't sleep?" Sid whispered.

"No," Fionn replied in hushed tones. "The Gift isn't letting me."

"I don't think it's just the Gift," Sid said. "It's how comfortable the pillow feels."

"So, you get it."

"I was special ops. I always got like that before a mission. Especially in my last one, when I wasn't sure what I wanted to do."

Fionn was at a loss for words. Not many—Fionn included, most of the time—gave Sid the credit he deserved. He might be the cynic, the one complaining or doling out sarcastic remarks. But he was also the most observant and full of empathy, beneath a solid veneer of crankiness.

"Look, I can't tell you what to do or what to expect tomorrow. You have more experience than anyone here dealing with these," Sid made the air quotes gesture, "'climatic battles.' I guess that you felt the same before your first fight against Byron. What I can tell you is whatever you decide, you know we have your back. Just ponder which will be the course of action that will give your family," Sid nodded towards where Sam, Alex, and Kasumi were resting together, and Gaby was trying to fake being sleep but was clearly listening the conversation, "the best odds for their futures."

"How did you choose to disobey orders? Knowing what that would entail for you; banishment, not seeing your family again?"

"I followed my consciousness. And it was as if I lit a match in the dark. I let go and all the weight on my shoulders disappeared and I felt empty."

Again, that word, empty.

"Thank you." Fionn smiled at Sid, who put his hand on the former's shoulder.

"That's what I do, I build things and dispense wisdom. Anyway, it is ready," Sid added to Fionn. "The tablets have been deciphered and we're building a tracker for the coordinates. I need to go back and supervise the modifications on the Figaro. It'll be a tough ride."

Fionn suppressed a halfhearted chuckle. He regretted not learning to pilot the Figaro.

I wonder if I will get the chance to fly again.

† † †

At the hangar, amidst a rain of sparks and the noise of power tools working non-stop, Andrea waved Alex over to the Figaro, which was undergoing emergency refurbishments. "Alex, come take a look."

Andrea was one of Alex's friends from university and had been one of the Foundation's top researchers alongside her husband Birm, another of Alex's friends.

"What have you been doing to my ship?" Alex asked.

"Better not let Sid hear you call the Figaro *your* ship," Andrea teased. "Sid's got us working on every possible situation you may encounter on this jaunt."

"Such as?"

"A new electrostatic shield to improve the stealth. Water shielding between panels for any radiation you might encounter. Improved oxygen recyclers and solar panels." She pointed at several places on the Figaro as she spoke.

Alex noticed several samoharo working on the engine. "What are they doing?"

"Installing three regenerating dragon cores and new reinforced relays. Dr. Tze Tze also installed an emergency 'kick starter' in case you need to use your Gift to recharge the cores, and a heat converter in case Joshua needs to do it."

Alex gave an approving nod. "Wow, he and Sid have thought of everything."

"Dr. Tze Tze's staff has been a big help," Andrea said. "Everyone is working well together."

"How does this work?" Alex pointed at the contraption in front of him. It was waiting to be loaded into the Figaro.

"By using Yaha and the pendant that Sam wears in tandem as the 'needle' for the compass, or rather tracker," Andrea said. "I've been helping Dr. Tze Tze create this tracker for the Life Tree's position based on the tablets' instructions. The projection says that the pendant fits a cavity on the bottom of the pommel. Together they are a sort of tuning fork that needs a bit of energy to operate. But since you will be copiloting and Sam needs to save all her energy for the fight, I added one of your old armor batteries as a power source.

It's made from orichalcum."

Alex marveled at his friend, grinning. It was no wonder why Harland had hired her and Birm right after graduating. Together they were two of the most capable engineers he knew. And now that they were parents, they had extra motivation to aid in the crazy efforts to save the planet. For them it was very personal. "I knew you would come up with something brilliant."

"Of course," Andrea said with a smug smile. "I'm learning a lot from Dr. Tze Tze."

"Should we start?" Sam asked as she approached the ship. Dr. Tze Tze was with her.

"Yes!" Andrea replied. "It will be ready once we calibrate it, you can load it into the Figaro, and once you get there, you can unplug Yaha and your dragon pendant."

Alex unsheathed Yaha as Sam offered her dragon pendant. Alex grabbed it and made a reverse grip flip on Yaha. As he moved the pendant closer to the bottom of the pommel, he could feel both pulling to each other, not unlike playing with magnets. The pommel opened, revealing a receptacle into which the pendant fit perfectly. Heat emanated from Yaha's blade, so Alex placed it into the orichalcum structure, the only thing that could endure for a time the energy being released by the combined weapons. As soon as he released Yaha, the battery turned on and the electronics displays powered on. Dr. Tze Tze tinkered with a dial, trying to find the appropriate tuning frequency. In a short time, the display indicated a series of coordinates.

"Take it to the Figaro," the doctor said. Two of his assistants carried the device up the loading ramp.

"Then it is time to say goodbye," Alex replied with a forlorn look at Andrea. Birm, alongside Quentin and Professor Hunt had walked over to see the device being activated. Alex and Sam hugged their friends.

"You two take care," Quentin said, "so you can tell me the whole story later."

Sam laughed. "Another case study for you research?"

"Obviously!"

† † †

The band gathered beside the Figaro. Everyone had left the hangar of the Geoda to give them some privacy. The tension was palpable in the air. Each knew the stakes of the dangerous journey they were about to embark on. They all wore their new tactical armor and looked serious and composed until Fionn gave in and fidgeted, pulling at the armor.

"It keeps wedging," Fionn muttered as Gaby helped him fix the back of the armor.

"Maybe if you stop moving," Gaby replied.

"Family," Kasumi interrupted. "There is something I want to tell you."

"Oh, no," Alex said, earning an elbow in the ribs by Sam. "Sorry."

"Joshua and I have decided to stay behind."

"Why?" Gaby asked, confused, for Kasumi had been married for only a few hours and she was normally inseparable from her wife and husband.

"Are you sure you want to stay?" Sam asked, hugging Kasumi.

"Of course not!" Kasumi said, faintly incredulous. "Especially not now. But of all of us, Joshua and I have the best chance to keep all of the people here alive, both from the cold and the incursions. You know that the few titanfighters who remain will give a good fight, but these new incursions are too powerful. We have an advantage. That doesn't mean I won't worry about you two in that place."

"Why are you looking at me when you say that?" Alex asked.

"Because of the two, *you* are the one that does the craziest things to save everyone. At least Sam thinks things through. I can trust she won't do anything insane," Kasumi said.

Alex sighed. "Fair point."

Sam pulled Kasumi into a kiss. "Please, please promise me you will be safe, snow princess."

"I can ask the same from you," Kasumi said, then pulled Alex over to kiss him too. "My knights in shining tactical nanoarmor."

"We need to workshop that," Alex said, smiling at her. "We love you."

"I love you both," Kasumi whispered with tears in her eyes.

† † †

"This is not a goodbye, lizard." Joshua fist-bumped Sid. "Just a see ya later."

"Aww, are you getting all sentimental on me, leech?" Sid said with a coy smile.

"I'm gonna miss you guys," Joshua said. He hugged Vivi, who was clearly nervous. "And I'm sorry for making fun of your fondness for adventure movies."

"It's okay. I should have been more empathic, as well."

"We *are* coming back, you sad sack." Sid rolled his eyes. "I'm not planning to die."

"He is being polite!" Vivi admonished Sid.

"Take care of them. As of now, they rely on the titan of fire to survive the apocalypse," Yokoyawa said.

"I will," Joshua promised. "And one last thing: thank you for being my friends."

"Anytime," Sid replied with a sincere smile.

† † †

"I wanted to say that I'm sorry for getting you into this mess. If I hadn't asked you for help with Hunt and..." Harland said to Fionn and Gaby. The whole accumulation of events since that fateful day weighed heavy on his shoulders. He couldn't help but to feel as if he was the cause for everything bad that had happened to the two people he cared for the most.

Gaby knelt in front of him and pulled him into a strong hug. "Nonsense," Gaby said, trying to not cry. "*You* are the reason Fionn and I found each other again in this century, in this life. You have taken care of my friends. You are the true heart of this group. You don't owe us an apology."

"You are my best friend." Fionn joined the hug. "You gave me a second chance; you took care of Sam as if she was yours. You took us in without knowing us. You don't have to apologize for anything. It's us who owes you all. And I feel I will never be able to repay you in full."

"You can repay me by making it back alive," Harland said, breaking the hug, his lower lip trembling a bit.

"We'll try." Fionn winked, as Gaby gave a kiss on Harland's forehead.

"See you on the other side," Gaby said to him.

"See you on the other side," Harland repeated, almost as if it were a promise. His usual parting words with Fionn and Gaby, unlike previous times, felt loaded with an ominous weight this time.

†††

As everyone was about to enter the Figaro, Fionn raised his voice.

"Listen. For some reason you chose me as the leader of this family, and I ran with it without much thought. But in the past years I realized something: I have never thought that being a leader is about giving orders. It's about making sure that once everyone knows their part and executes it, they return home safe and sound. So, I promise you this: regardless of what it takes, all of you are coming back home. I will make sure of it. You are my family, and I will take care of you."

†††

"Are you okay, wifey?" Alex asked as he and Sam entered the cockpit and took their respective seats. They were so used to each other and Kasumi by now that Alex knew when Sam was feeling trouble by the subtle cues in her body language.

"I already miss our wifey, hon," Sam said as she looked at Kasumi through the window and returned her wave. "But for the first time in my life, I'm actually scared. I think I know how Dad feels every time. The whole Greywolf title, my own new title, and all else."

"Expectations that make you feel like you're on a wire above a bottomless pit?"

"Yes, that."

"As you told me once when I was feeling down, you're not alone. We are one in this together." Alex grabbed her hand as Sid took his seat and flipped the switches to start the Figaro's engines.

"If any of you want to go to the bathroom, this is the last chance," Sid announced through the comms. "I don't think we'll find a charging station where we are going."

Everybody laughed at the lame joke.

"That said," Sid added, glancing at Gaby, "do you mind if I play *The Wrong End of the Sword* album as music for the flight?"

"Only if everyone agrees," Gaby muttered, turning red as a tomato. Everyone promptly raised their hands.

"It's unanimous," Sid said. He made a hand gesture, a silent prayer, and the Figaro started to move. "Here we go."

†††

It was an uneventful, if tense, flight. Sid had flown the Figaro close to the ground, using the stealth system to pass undetected in case the orionians lingered, but they hadn't encountered any. Perhaps the samoharo had finally gotten rid of them.

The Figaro arrived at the coordinates that the improvised turning fork had led them too. Sid landed the Figaro gracefully as they hadn't seen anything or anyone around the frozen landscape. The ground was covered in ice and the mountains could be seen in the distance. The sky was clear, but with a blue-grey tonality. Everyone descended from the ship and looked around.

Fionn looked around. "Are we sure the coordinates are correct?" There was nothing resembling a tree for kilometers around.

"Yes, they are correct," Sid said, visibly frustrated. "There's just nothing here."

"There is a big crater, surrounded by smaller ones. That's not nothing," Yoko pointed out.

Sid rolled his eyes. "I meant the Tree."

"These craters don't seem caused by the crash of something. Rather, they seem carved by something that ripped the rocky grounds from the continent by force. The cracks, they are consistent with cooling lava," Alex said as he kneeled to examine the ground.

"There is no volcano around," Fionn replied. "Since when did you became an expert on soil damage?"

"Months studying the explosion site," Alex muttered. He stood up and looked towards the sky. "Maybe we are not accounting for some variable, like stellar drift. Or... hmm," Alex muttered. In the precise spot he was focusing on, there was a cumulus of clouds, pink in color like those of a sunset. But they seemed to be deformed, as if seen through a lenticular lens of a drop of water. "That's odd."

"What's odd? Those pink clouds?" Sam asked him as she looked at the spot he was staring at in the sky. "They look... weird."

"And there are no more clouds in the sky, just in that space. Does it look familiar to you?" Alex pointed to the otherwise clear blue-grey sky. "Or at least feel familiar?"

"Like the rip into the Tempest after the Bestial was summoned?" Sam acknowledged. "Or when we were inside it? Because I can sense a lot of magick energy coming from it."

"Yeah, or maybe the entrance to the..." Alex began before an excited Sid interrupted.

"No frikking way!" the samoharo exclaimed raising his pilot shades.

"What's that?" Gaby asked, staring at what seemed to be a giant, crystal clear sphere made of water, floating above the craters. Of course it wasn't made of water.

"Something impossible inside a planet, I thought. A seemingly stable wormhole," Sid gushed.

"That sphere is a wormhole? Why is it not a hole?" Fionn asked.

"A hole is a circle in two-dimensional space. In tridimensional space, a hole is a sphere," Alex explained. "I saw something similar at Sandtown, except that it seemed to end in outer space. This one was pink clouds. Which means an atmosphere and that might mean..."

"Which means that the Life Tree is inside. Makes sense, the best place to hide it without disconnecting it from the planet would be inside the Tempest, as there are no fixed locations nor coordinates inside there, just the place where your mind wants to be," Sam added.

"When you entered the Tempest, how did you do it?" Fionn asked Sam.

"Dunno, I used the teleporting spell Mekiri left prepared inside my head," Sam explained.

Alex shrugged as he looked at Yokoyawa, who did the same. "She took us through a portal."

"Excuse me, but why is a wormhole hanging out in the sky that strange in a world where we can do magick?" Gaby asked, confused.

"Because they don't happen in nature, not like that," Alex said. "They are usually microscopic and super instable. If they did happen like that, traveling faster than light would be easier. There are many proposed methods to traverse space: speeds nearing lightspeed, quantum space bubbles, generation arks, a portal network of mass-energy conversion relays, and the theoretical stringspeed. All of them have severe downsides. That's why none of our species used those. Mekiri and her siblings basically teleported our respective species here once we left our planets. There was simply no way three separate species from three different planets in the cosmos would reach the same planet, all at the same time, without akeleth intervention. The ships were the easiest way to teleport massive amounts of people."

"And that's why while there might be teleportation spells to move around the planet, we lack the understanding and power to use them for more than reaching the Long Moon and back," Sid added, rubbing his hands with glee. "A wormhole like that, if we can measure it, would give us a chance to understand how to reach other planets once more."

"Ahem, we have to save this one first," Gaby pointed out.

"Of course, of course. Planet saving, that's important too... but if we fly the Figaro through that, I can set the A.I. to record everything while we find that Tree," Sid said, not willing to let the matter die. The others rolled their eyes.

"Given that I don't see another course of action, and the coordinates brought us here. We might as well enter that hole that looks like a sphere," Fionn relented.

"I'll get things ready!" Alex and Sid replied in unison and ran to the ship.

"I'm starting to wonder with whom I just got married," Sam shook her head.

"The loves of your life?" Gaby suggested with a smile as she slipped her arm over Sam's shoulders. "One of them a single lab accident away from becoming a super villain?"

Fionn laughed. "Stop scaring her."

† † †

"Okay, Dr. Alex," Sid said as he flew the Figaro into the sky. "Are you certain this is what we need to enter the wormhole in a safe way?"

"It's just a theory," Alex said as he flipped some switches on the console. "You are the one that studied with an astrophysicist. Hull is being electromagnetically charged."

"Wello," Sid called out, looking at the rest of the band sitting in the cockpit. "Everyone sit tight, things might be rougher than reaching outer space."

"Why are we doing as descending barrel and circling the wormhole?" Yoko asked.

"I'm trying to match its rotation speed while the hull of the Figaro is being electrically charged so we can enter the wormhole without it popping like a bubble and collapsing on us," Sid explained. "Think of it as entering a wave without the feeling of being hit with a brick wall."

Yoko nodded at the simple explanation.

The Figaro flew around the sphere several times, slowly increasing their speed, as the hull became so electrostatically charged that the hair of most began to rise from their heads. As the Figaro matched the speed, Sid turned it on its side, aligning the heat shields with the surface of the sphere

"Speed and charge matched," Alex whispered. "How do you think it looks on the inside?"

"No one knows, but we're about find out," Sid sighed. "One way or another." He pushed the yoke and slowly submerged the Figaro into the sphere. The ship disappeared in midair without a trace.

Some say the Tempest is a space between spaces, a realm compressed between the dimensions that make the universe, a sort of hyperspace.

Some say the Tempest is a quantum state at macroscale, brought forth by the interactions of the thaum particles that are generated by stars and that fuel the fifth force of nature known as magick, serving as a sort of reality underpinning.

Some say the Tempest is a liminal realm created by the collective unconscious of every dreaming being in the universe, where the core concept of what magick is resides.

Some say the Tempest is the manifestation created by the souls of living beings that it is in constant friction with the material world and hence it's inherent volatility, a spiritual space.

Some say the Tempest is the subconscious of the universal mind, a place of dreams and nightmares where the universe finds a sort of resting place.

A few know that the Tempest is all of the above and none of it at the same time.

The only thing that is certain is that when one enters the Tempest, assuming that is possible in a living, corporeal state, at the end of a proverbial dark tunnel, one might find a light.

Only a handful of living beings had been there. Most of them were currently on board the Figaro right now, and all they saw was a brilliant light.

Chapter 10
The Tree at the Root of Creation

As THE LIGHT SUBDUED AND they opened their eyes, through the window of the Figaro's cockpit, they saw what few had witnessed before.

In an open space, against a background of cerulean and pink cumulonimbus, illuminated by an unknown source of light akin to a setting sun, and the occasional lightning in the farthest reaches, there was an archipelago of several islands floating in the air. Some of those islands had stone arches and ruins from an ancient civilization on their surfaces. Some had lush foliage or bare ground. But the entire archipelago, independent of the altitude at which they floated, surrounded a larger island, which became larger as the Figaro slowly approached. In the middle of the central island, surrounded by more ruins, stood a colossal, leafy tree. It looked like a mix between an ash, a fig, and a humbagoo tree. Its roots went clean through the island, with some disappearing in the darkness below. The canopy was lush, dense and broad, with the branches reaching for the heavens. The trunk of the tree had branches and quartz-like crystals sprouting from it, and across the surface of both, energy lines ran, emitting a soothing blue-white light. Flocks of birds that looked like pure energy flew between the islands and when they reached the tree, they disappeared among its leaves.

"Is that... is that the Life Tree?" Sam asked softly, awed, as she stood up from her seat and looked through the cockpit windows.

"It is beautiful," Gaby added.

"And huge," Vivi murmured. "It must be easily as tall as a mountain."

"I better find somewhere around the Tree to land. Maybe on the other side of the roots where the ruins are sparse. For some reason," Sid said matter-of-factly, "the cores of the Figaro are drained." He flew the Figaro around the Life Tree.

"It doesn't make any sense," Yokoyawa said.

"It does if you look at the distance we travelled according to the indicators," Sid pointed out as he began the landing procedures in a clearing at the base of the Tree.

"You can't travel infinity," Alex mused in delight as he stared at the indicator of distance. "Unless we went into some sort of hyperspace, or stringspeed."

"And yet, here we are. At the Root of Creation, it seems," Sid said. Even he seemed to be awed by the beauty of the sight. "We better land and let the cores regenerate again so we can go back."

† † †

"How does it not collapse under its own weight?" Vivi wondered as they walked around the Tree towards the ruins. There was a faint whisper in the air, one that filled them all with peace.

"Better question, how do you forge a sword out of a tree branch?" Alex added. He took the pendant from Yaha's hilt and returned it to Sam.

"Because the branch used changed into a forgeable crystal," Fionn said. "And due to the dying wish of a mother to give the father something to protect their children from the Demon. Through that, it was transformed into a sentient sword that carries the hopes of that wish. For Yaha means 'hope.'" He nodded at the sword in Alex's hand.

"The Life Tree is the embodiment of the Kaan'a's consciousness. It is as much a tree, as a giant crystal is a mountain. A spirit unto itself. It is said that the tree bears fruits that become our very souls. It's the way we see the Universe trying to understand itself, by giving birth to itself. The Tree is not grounded; it creates the terra firma around it. Its roots can go as far as the deepest of the Pits, touching every living world in the universe. It floats inside the farther reaches of the Tempest for the Tempest is impossibility made reality by the existence of spirit. In these holy lands, the Tree just is, and around it exists all else. It exists across all time, from beginning to end and then again anew. We come from it, and we will return from it. The Tree at the center of creation. For Theia was the First Garden from where life came from before Time and the Tree was brought to Real Space after the Fall," Fionn concluded, looking up towards the canopy, which seemed far removed into the sky.

"How do you know that, Dad?" Sam asked, holding hands with Alex as they walked.

"I'm not sure," Fionn mused absently. "The words just came to my mind, as if I had always known them. I'm pretty sure my father told me that a vagrant who stumbled upon this place during a night when magick went bonkers, saw them carved somewhere in the ruins."

"That gives me an idea, like in the Tower of Salt," Gaby said. "Can I borrow your pendant?"

"Sure," Sam replied, handing it to Gaby.

"And now for my next trick," Gaby joked. "Sorry, I know that's your line for your show. In all seriousness. Sam, grab my hand. Everyone, grab each other's hand until we are all connected in line. And no matter what you see, don't move, don't panic. It's only visions from the past."

"What are you planning to do?" Vivi asked, ever so faintly suspicious.

"Using the psychometry that the queen passed to me to see if we can learn a bit on the story of this place. It will be a bit painful."

The last to join their human chain, Sid said, "Define painful."

"A slight migraine," Gaby smiled with her crooked smile.

Sid rolled his eyes. "Great," he said, and winced.

Gaby closed her eyes briefly before reopening them, her irises glowing blue, as the island changed before their eyes in a white blur. The whole island became full blurred images for Gaby and the rest. They were unable to move, as if their bodies were stuck in a cataleptic state. She had learned to surf through the memories of a given place. And the pendant that was made of a part of the Tree would be a better conduit to share them without the painful feedback. Or at least, that was her hope.

The shock into her brain didn't take long to hit. But the migraine, mercifully, was lessened from being shared among many.

The ruins disappeared from sight, the Life Tree was still on Theia when there was nothing but small animals. Winged people appeared, the Akeleth, and prayed below the Life Tree. The First Days of Creation.

It became night. The Life Tree was surrounded by campfires of what seemed a brief respite in a battle. They saw a dying woman in the arms of a man. The man was crying in her chest as the woman, who stroked his hair, as her breathing became weaker, had been stabbed by a sharp crystal from the tree. As she passed away, her soul was absorbed by the crystal. The man yelled at the sky and lightning struck the ground, his irises glowing gold and electricity crackling across his arms. He stood up, fury in his eyes and walked towards the edge of the vision, only to be stopped by a tall memech samoharo who had on his back the Stellar Ehécatl, and a young woman, almost a girl, with big turquoise eyes and olive skin that had grey patches along it.

"That must be Asherah," Sam whispered. "And the man is Iskandar."

"That's the Prophet," Yoko said.

The girl hugged the man as the samoharo spoke, seemingly convincing him to plan something better. The samoharo approached the woman and closed her eyes, before carrying her away.

The image changed. A young Forge, a preteen at the oldest, was in front of an improvised forge as another man, tall, with fiery red hair and who had a passing resemblance to Joshua of all people, brought the crystal, still stained with blood. The samoharo explained something intelligible about the Stellar Ehécatl. Forge grabbed the crystal and introduced it into the fire, then took it out with a pair of long tongs and began molding it with a hammer, as Asherah cast a spell on the crystal. The man with the golden eyes stared from a distance. The image continued for a while until it jumped to Forge delivering a newly forged Yaha to the man, who examined the sword. Its blade immediately turned into pure light, as the ground shook and people hurried.

"I guess the tests to determine the age of Yaha were wrong as they didn't account on the age of the crystal used for it," Alex mumbled. "Who knows how long ago this was."

The images jumped once more. It was day, the ruins rebuilt back to the memory of what they were. There were children running around, couples sharing happiness and laughter, while an old man kneeled in front of a tombstone. He stood up with the help of another person, and the old man gave away Yaha. The old man walked into a house and took a black box from the surface of a table and placed it inside a small metal chest, which he proceeded to bury under a stone in the cobbled ground. The man lay in bed and closed his eyes. As he took his final breath, his body shook as if jolted by an electrical current. Then the corpse opened his eyes and mouth wide as beams of light shot out from them. The light condensed above the bed, forming a silhouette of a young man, made of pure light. The silhouette floated toward the Tree. The soul kept ascending to the ceiling, as the body of the man dissolved into thin air, leaving nothing but his clothes behind.

The image jumped again, with more people living under the Tree. All of them had golden irises.

"I wonder when the Gift began to use other elements aside lightning," Gaby wondered.

"Probably when freefolk blood entered the human bloodlines, which might explain why humans began to be able to use magick," Vivi proposed.

The inhabitants of the small town gathered around the Tree, as the ground shook with a massive earthquake that sundered the land. As the Life Tree began to fly towards a portal in the sky, the land below became covered with lava. Dragons flew in the distance, turning into ashes an army on horseback.

Angry, Fionn murmured, "The Wyld Hunt."

The image changed one final time. The town was almost deserted. The few people around lay on the ground, dying for an unknown reason.

"A sickness, perhaps?" Alex wondered with sadness.

A young boy, no older than fourteen, appearing to be of Kuni descent, tied Yaha to his back with a string, and then grabbed a baby, with a tuff of messy brown hair peeking out from the blankets. The baby had a familiar face. Both the baby and the boy had glowing golden irises and crackling energy across their arms. The baby didn't stop crying. The boy stopped at the edge of the island, as if he was hearing a voice, a black and red raven flying near him.

"Narukami. Ywain," Fionn whispered, his eyes widening in recognition as he glanced towards Alex.

The young boy leapt from the island, trying to escape

something. Below the island there were several portals, with the boy falling into one, the baby into another, and Yaha into a third. The passage of images broke, the feedback forcing everyone to release their hands.

"That was quite a trip," Sid said, shaking his head.

"Sam," Fionn said, "with the time flow being different inside the Tempest, what are the odds of those portals leading to different points in time?"

"I couldn't say for certain," Sam replied. "But it's possible. Why?"

"The young boy is Narukami Ishiguro, who would become the Storm God after defeating the Cursed Titans millennia ago. But the baby... the baby I'm pretty sure it was Ywain. And between our generation and Narukami's, there are several centuries."

"Whatever happened here would explain why Ywain had the Gift since the beginning," Gaby consoled Fionn. Anything related to Ywain was still an open wound for her husband. "But we know he lived a full life, otherwise Alex wouldn't be here rambling about science and comic stuff and... where is Alex?"

Alex was not there. Sam strode towards one of the ruins, following her new husband. If anyone could find where he went after the psychometry broke, it was her or Kasumi.

† † †

"What are you doing?" Sam asked when she found Alex inside the ruins of a house, examining the cobbled floor covered by dirt and grass. He stopped at a particular rock embedded in the ground and began digging around it. It was an endearing sight for her, which made her smile. Her boyfriend... no, her husband—a word that brought a smile to her face—was quirky, but usually came up with interesting surprises. Their life together wouldn't be boring, if they managed to make it out alive.

"During the vision I thought I saw something like the datacube I borrowed from Ravenhall. I just hope it's still here and works," Alex explained as he pulled from the ground a metal box. He opened it to reveal a black, long rectangle made of some unfamiliar material.

"What is this?" Sam asked, kneeling next to him as Sid and the others followed.

"My best guess is that it is a data storage unit of some

sort," Alex said.

"Do you think it still works? After all that time?" Gaby asked.

"Who knows? Data might be corrupted; the programming language might operate under a different mathematical base. But we are inside the Tempest and time flows differently here. These ruins shouldn't be that preserved. So, I say it's worth a shot. As long as we don't move it much, so it doesn't fall apart," Alex said as he carefully placed the box on a slab of stone.

"I could link this to the pad and to the Figaro, so Wanderer can try to decipher it," Sid offered. "And then project the images on that wall."

It ultimately took Sid and Alex a couple of hours to hook up the box to the pad, for they were taking their time and taking extra care. While they were doing that, Fionn stood outside, with Sam.

"I'm sorry for being a lousy father," Fionn said, breaking the silence. "You deserved better growing up."

"Yes, I deserved better, but you are not a lousy father. You are just a mortal who went through a rough emotional patch," Sam hugged her dad's arm and leaned her head on it. "You did your best, took care of me, patched my knees when I fell from my first trike ride, helped me with my homework, took me on holidays, and above all, cared for me as if I had been your own daughter and not a distant descendant. And since that day at the Bestial, you *have* done your best to reconnect. Thanks to you I met my new husband and wife, and my best friend-slash-stepmom-slash-reincarnated great-great-grandmother or something. You were there for my impromptu wedding. All I am now; it was in good part thanks to you. I'm lucky to have you in my life and I love you with all my heart, Dad. I can't possibly thank you enough."

Fionn's eyes welled. "Thank you, Flammie."

"You haven't called me that in ages, Dad," Sam said, blushing. "Remember when you gave me that nickname? It was around the time of the infamous 'Murder on Canvas,' as the media called it, that you worked on... if I recall correctly."

"Yes, funny that you recall that and not that you had set on fire the homework of one of your classmates."

"Homework she stole from a friend she was bullying," Sam shrugged.

"Always breaking or twisting the rules, aren't you?"

Fionn laughed.

"The applelime doesn't fall far from the tree," Vivi interrupted. "They are ready."

† † †

"Okay, here we go," Alex said as Sid turned on the pad and an image projected onto the wall. Alex was holding his breath, as a chirping sound came from the black box, a sign that there was some sort of mechanism inside. The light on the wall became a holographic image of random signs.

"Drats. Most of the data is corrupted, sans a few files," Sid said. "Tze Tze's algorithm is trying to translate them."

A ping soon came from the pad.

"The first of the recovered files is ready," Sid announced, sighing in relief. This was, by far, one of the most important discoveries of the century. He and Alex felt bad because Harland wasn't there with them. But they had made sure the Wanderer made a copy of any recovered file to share it with him.

"The first one, is a scientific paper from Old Earth," Alex read. "It says *On the configuration of quantumorphologically beings appearing on Earth*, by... names are intelligible, but mention *Berkley, UNAM, CERN, and Tokyo*. No idea what those are. Maybe schools?"

"That's not important now," Sam rsaid, placing her hand on his shoulder. "What does it say? In laypeople terms, hon."

"It says that the creatures appearing in the last thirty years on the surface of the planet present quantum properties at a macroscopic level—basically, they are matter and energy at the same time—which explained why their weapons were unable to damage them," Alex said.

"And why ours can?" Fionn asked. "And I'm not talking just about the Tempest Blades, but samoharo weapons, demonhunter fangswords, titanarmors."

"The difference is magick, I guess," Sid pointed out. "Arcanotech. And Stellar Ehecatl. The Tempest Blades are sentient wave-particle dualities with their own observer, powered by the entity that gives life, put together through freefolk magick, samoharo tech, human imagination, with a dash of divinity."

"So basically magick, quantum physics, and probably time travel," Gaby listed with her fingers.

"It's a shame. The authors of this text didn't have the whole picture, but they were on the right track. They even had a scale similar to the one used by the demonhunters to classify incursions. But it looks like they never got the chance to go further," Alex said.

"Why?" Vivi asked.

"The first problem they found was that one particular creature, that had been seen all over human history, was the macroscopic version of the Observer effect, which I suspect is what they called what we know as Witness Effect. By the year this paper was written, there were reports of said creature that everyone, including an event where tens of thousands in a stadium... thousands?" Alex said, confused.

Gaby raised an eyebrow. "What was the population back then?"

"Nine billion humans," Sid replied after browsing through the data.

"Wow!" Alex exclaimed. "The maximum population in Theia doesn't reach a billion. All species included. Anyway, that creature was seen by everyone as a different creature at the same time, and all got transformed into incursions by witnessing the event. Thousands of humans morphed in one go, and that can take any shape or form at any time. Abaddon the first demon uses the observer effect at macro scale to be impossible to kill by the usual methods."

Alex made a gesture of cutting the throat and stabbing the heart, all while making cartoonish dying noises and showing his tongue.

"If that creature was Abaddon, makes you wonder how the Founders and their allies, managed to survive the fight to seal him into two bodies and several shards," Vivi observed.

"You mention a first problem, which means there was another one," Fionn observed.

"The second problem is that there was no more time for research as everything came to a screeching halt that year. It says that it was published in 2065. Here is another file, a newspaper article by its appearance. Total environmental collapse. They destroyed their planet biosphere before they even got a chance to fix it, thanks to the incursions. It blames the political elite and names several billionaires," Sid continued as he browsed through another file.

Sam interrupted. "What's a billionaire?"

"Apparently the one percent of the population that had

all the resources of the planet under their control," Alex shrugged. "I get people having money, like Gaby's family, or Harland's, but hoarding all the resources like that seems insane and dangerous."

"Sounds like a crapshow. Our ancestors were a mess," Gaby noted. "But then, how did they get the ARK?"

"The last readable file," Sid said. "It says that there were groups of people that did work to try to save things, and there is a picture of their patron. Do you recognize that face?"

"Mekiri." Sam smiled at the image of her mentor. "And is *that* a samoharo... in a badly executed disguise charm?"

Yokoyawa nodded. "With the crest of our StarCommand around the time our conflict with the orionians began in earnest."

"Basically, thousands of years ago everyone was dealing with the same crap we're dealing with right now, but without the Freefolk and their magick. Which makes all the difference then," Alex said.

"Why do you say that?" Fionn asked.

"Think about it. There are five basic forces that make the Universe, magick being one of them. But humans and samoharo, either, they didn't know about it or didn't have access to it till their arrival here. And even then, access was restricted to all but the Freefolk, who had no technology to speak of, but had a greater connection to their world and as former shapeshifters could withstand the thaums running through their body. Magick, the thaums, with that, faster than light travel without needing a deity, artificial gravity, teleportation, alchemy, worldforming, you name it. Everything explained with a theory. We had everything as separate entities, but Magick connected everything," Alex explained.

"And Magick comes from thaums, thaums come from stars. Magick works only if there is an observer, like the freefolk, forcing it. Humans acquired the ability after both species began to mix. Magick creates its own dimension, the Tempest, that reacts from the subconscious of every living being working as a universal observer," Sam concluded.

"This... this is too much to make sense of." Vivi shook her head. "And will no doubt cause a massive religious crisis all over the planet. It's like saying the Universe is dreaming us, while we observe it back to make it real."

"All of this is giving me a headache," Sid said. "And, frankly, making me hungry. We should take a break."

"I'm surprised to say that I agree with him," Fionn said.

† † †

It was Vivi who broke the silence that had descended on their camp. "In hindsight, that was a huge, sobering, even nightmarish amount of information we found. I'm not sure it's even wise for others outside our circle to know about this. I'm not sure we are ready yet."

"It certainly puts things into perspective," Alex agreed, staring at Yaha in his hands. Fireflies flew around the blade. "Can't avoid being afraid."

Sam hugged him. "We will find a way to manage. We always do," she said.

"What now?" Sid asked from in front of the magick fire Sam had created. She didn't want to burn anything from the Tree when they made their camp. They had left the Figaro on the other side of the Tree, where there weren't ruins or roots to impede a landing. They'd set up camp in the ruins, for there the climate was temperate on the strange night that had fallen on the place, stars and moons visible in the distance. It was its own pocket dimension within the Tempest.

Sid finished wrapping the piece of Life Tree Root in his tomahawk handles, as Forge had suggested. He passed them to Sam, who sealed the union with a spell, as she'd done with her quarterstaff and a whip Vivi had taken from the armory. While they didn't glow like a Tempest Blade, they emitted a faint blue-green light. It was anybody's guess what abilities they would obtain.

"We take turns to keep watch while others rest, for we don't know when the assault on this place will begin," Yoko suggested. The samoharo stared at Alex, who was downing one of his last three pills.

"I agree," Fionn said, staring at the Tree. He was about to suggest he take the first guard, as he was too unsettled to be able to get some sleep.

"I will do it," Sid offered, looking at Fionn. "I'm used to light dozes. I will wake up or break from mediation or whatever the next one in turn."

† † †

Fionn stared at the Life Tree while everyone prepared to

take turns keeping watch. He could swear that the Tree, through the rustling of its leaves and the chirping of the birds, was talking to him, as if a song was being sung by all the souls inside it. Between the light from the magick fire, reflecting on the crystals growing on the Tree's trunk, the shadows cast by the ruins, and the fireflies flying towards the canopy, there was a mystic air of connection to something bigger. This Tree was the source of souls. Instead of mere sap, it was the souls of all living beings that flowed inside. Every planet with life out there in the vast cosmos had a seedling from this Tree, all of them connected through the roots deep into the Tempest. No wonder why his ancestors had chosen to bury their dead under the roots of the humbagoo trees to honor this entity that was beyond any description made in ancient myths.

And here he was, Fionn—the son of a humble vagrant, a medicine woman, and a surrogate mother fleeing an uncomfortable future—a man whose dreams of adventure while training to be a carpenter, became a nightmarish reality. Now he was the last line of defense for the Life Tree against an ancient, terrible, unstoppable enemy. He looked at the camp behind him. Fionn was sure he wouldn't be able to be there, to go through this, if it weren't for them. And that made him ponder just how far would he be willing to go to keep all of them alive.

"I know what you are thinking," Gaby said, startling him. Fionn had to give it to her. When Gaby wanted to sneak up on someone, she wouldn't be detected by anyone. "The lesson from Narukami, the nightmares you occasionally have and kept from everyone since the day we met."

"How did you?"

"I'm your wife. And I'm not the only one that speaks while asleep, so after years sleeping together, I have heard a lot. I have one question, though."

"Which one?"

"Why does it have to be you?"

"Because you made the call last time and I have never forgiven myself for that!" Fionn snapped, before he could catch himself. If the others in the camp heard anything, they were doing their best to fake that they hadn't. "Sorry. I didn't want to yell at you, or to imply that you are Izia or..."

"No, you are right, I did indeed choose last time. And you shouldn't castigate yourself for that. It was my choice,"

Gaby said, placing her hand on Fionn's arm. He raised an eyebrow at hearing her reply. "Yes, my choice. We have known the whole thing about Izia for quite some time. Since... my stay at the hospital... One day I woke up next to you and all of Izia's memories, my memories came back in a rush. Perfectly clear in my mind. They don't feel like watching someone from afar anymore. They feel mine. And I've come to terms with that. I'm Gaby now, and I was Izia. This is my second chance as well, which is why I don't like the idea of you playing the martyr. We've sacrificed enough already."

Fionn sighed. "Are you willing to let any one of them," he said, waving his hand at the camp, "do it if it comes to it? Alex? Sam? They just got married. I know Yoko would do it in a heartbeat, and I suspect Sid would as well. But would you let them? Because you know as well as I that there is a possibility that we might have to make that decision, and we won't have time to debate it."

"I would prefer it if none of us had to make that call," she said. "And you don't get to decide for the others. You have that bad habit, and it has bitten you in the ass more times than you'd care to admit."

"I *know* I don't get to do that. But I'm not pondering this decision out of a martyr or a hero complex. I don't want to make anyone, much less you, go through what I did. I don't want to die, nor do I want anyone else to do so on my behalf. But..." he trailed off and sighed. "I'm willing, if it comes to that. Not as team leader, which to be honest I never understood, but as a parent, as head of a family. My daughter is over there, and even if I wasn't the best adoptive father years ago, we've rebuilt our relationship. Alex is like my little brother, and your best friend. Vivi, Sid, Yoko... they're my friends, they are part of our tribe. If Harland, Kasumi, or even Joshua were here I would say the same about them.

"Look, years ago, when I was a child, and my father had died protecting us from the Silver Tribe raiders, I was angry at what had happened, and I was acting out, like any grieving child does. My mother took me on a gathering trip to the woods where we saw a grey wolf dying to protect its pack from a massive, enchanted wild boar. We helped its puppies to escape, healed the mother from its injuries, but couldn't help the grey wolf, their dad, like mine. When I asked my mother why things had to be that way, she hugged me and told me '*Your father, like that old wolf, gave his life to protect his family. That is what matters most to our tribe, to the Grey-wolf, the family.*' Might sound dumb, old fashioned or whatever, but that lesson has stuck with me all my life. Now I see why."

Gaby considered him in silence for several long minutes, making him nervous and self-conscious. Even after all this time, she had a knack for making him feel like an awkward teenager. Gaby finally smiled, her crooked smile flashing before him, which made Fionn recover the breath he didn't know he was holding. Gaby hugged and kissed him.

"It's not dumb, you silly," Gaby replied, as tears ran down her cheeks, breaking the embrace. "But you are not making the decision alone. I am also head of this family. It's *our* choice to make. I don't like it, but you're unfortunately right. If it comes to it, whoever has the best shot to take him down for good has to take it."

Finn nodded. "We will do what we must to keep them safe," he said, tears rolling down his face as well.

"Geez," Gaby said with a wet laugh. "We sound like we're ancient elders." She wiped at her tears, and then Fionn's.

"Technically I'm one hundred and forty. And if we add both your past and current lives..." Fionn mused, calculating their ages.

"I'm almost a century and half old. Funny how it works." Gaby chuckled. "I'm going to meditate with you. Maybe that will help me to understand what you are thinking."

Fionn hugged her. "I don't know what I would do without you."

"Let's hope we don't have to find out," Gaby kissed Fionn.

Both climbed over one of the largest roots of the tree, finding a spot large enough for both to sit side by side and meditate. The Tree seemed to have understood their intentions, for vines and smaller branches surged from its trunk to keep them from falling, while one of the birds—seemingly living in symbiosis with the Tree itself—soothed their minds with a sweet tune.

The image of a glowing green root in the middle of darkness wouldn't leave their minds for a long while.

† † †

'Hours' later, so to speak, as time inside the Tempest had a different meaning of itself and thus went with whatever it preferred, Sam and Alex stared at the 'sunrise' over the floating island. There was no sun of course, but something was doing the equivalent job. They were ending their guard shift and had decided to walk around the tree, while Fionn, who seemed to need sleep no more, was meditating, sitting under the shadow of the tree. The trunk of the tree was so thick that they hadn't reached a fourth of the whole grass-covered stone pathway built around it.

"I'm still trying to wrap my mind around it," Alex mused.

"Around what, hon?" Sam asked, resting her head on his shoulder in spite of the height difference.

"Nine billion humans on a single planet," Alex said. "When now, thousands of years later the whole population of Theia was barely eight hundred million before this year, all species included."

"That's a lot of people," Sam admitted. "Their cities, they must have covered all the surface of the planet. No forests, no trees. And what they did to their planet..."

"They made our job easier." A young man appeared, turning around an invisible corner. He was sporting short blond hair and a pearly smile, decked out all in black. "The boss did a lot of nudging, whispering here and there. But the damage, that was on them. Willingly."

Alex pressed the comms in his ear to call for the others, to warn them, but only got static. The Gift hadn't alerted them of incursions appearing here. This guy was different to the other demons. He had no presence at all, like a walking void.

"Don't bother, I'm blocking the signal. Have you wondered why in horror movies the signal always gets lost when the monster appears? It's no coincidence." The young man smiled, as he played with a couple of daggers.

"Sam, warn the others," Alex whispered to Sam as his Gift activated.

"I'm not going to leave you alone with Abaddon," Sam replied, activating her own.

"I don't think that one is Abaddon." Alex observed. "And you're faster than me."

Sam sighed and ran, enhanced by a haste spell.

"Yes, run to daddy, maybe you'll see him before the boss cuts him down."

"You were the one at the mall." Alex cut the man's mocking words. "The same sensation of vacuum around you."

"Good memory."

"I won't forget that day."

"Me, neither," the Deacon laughed. "That explosion was beautiful."

"You are not human," Alex concluded. "A demon?"

"Partial credit. I'm something else. A devil of sorts. You might have heard of me. My monicker at least..."

"You are the Deacon. I did find out who blew up everything."

"You did what not even your mentor could. And he tried to catch me."

"The legendary serial killer."

"Wrong. You see, I'm not *just* a serial killer. I'm not just the mentor of serial killers. I'm the God of Serial Killers. I'm the Ragnarok. Old Earth's gods? I killed them all. But I can't allow you, filthy human, to do the same. The two on your account are enough. This is when you die," the Deacon declared as he showed his grin. His teeth shifted shark-like, a feral grin. If they had faced this kind of demon around the time they faced Byron, none of them would have had a chance. But now? The Band had found them difficult, but not impossible, to beat. "And to be clear, it's really personal."

"You talk too much." Alex didn't intend to waste time enduring a long speech from the guy. He didn't care. As soon as Sam was out of range, Alex summoned his bow and shot three arrows, aiming for the head or the chest. But the arrows deviated from their trajectory by some sort of invisible shield.

"No, no, no," the Deacon said. "I see you're in no mood for my story. And I'm in no mood to allow you to shoot me. Close combat is better. And you can't avoid it, I assure you any energy arrow you shoot my way won't hit at that distance. I've studied you. You can't use that silly bow in close quarters."

The Deacon summoned the black armor he'd worn at the mall from that fateful day in Saint Lucy. It was made of material that absorbed light, like a living shadow. It was like Joshua's beast, at least in composition, but instinct told Alex that if it was a living creature, it had been subjugated or even brain killed to be a simple adaptable armor. From his wrists, two dark energy blades protruded.

Demons have caught up with modern technology. What fun, Alex thought ruefully. He clashed his wrists together to summon his own prototype armor. It had taken him a year to polish it, with the limited resources available. And the durability was questionable. But if that dark energy was of the same kind that he had encountered at the Star Mall, the one that gave his arm frostbite for a few days, then prototype or not, it would be his best chance at facing this demon.

The question on Alex's mind wasn't if he could beat the guy. It was if the Deacon's presence meant that Abaddon was there and had caught them with their guard down.

That was concerning.

† † †

Fionn had spent all night—if it could even be called a night—meditating under the Life Tree, reflecting upon all the events that had taken him to this place. It had been a restful action, for at least this time he didn't endure nightmares.

Empty.

That was the word that kept bouncing inside his head. Fionn kinda understood the actual meaning, but there was a part of him, the one that was still human—he had to admit to himself, he hadn't felt human since the day at the hospital—that didn't want to admit what could happen. He had spent most of his time meditating, pondering on diverse scenarios, but few, if any, came with positive outcomes. The upside was that as he had meditated a strange bond between him and the Life Tree had formed, as if his Gift, or at least part of it, had resonated with the Tree and they were now in synchronicity. And through that, his consciousness had reached a new level he had never experienced while learning to control his Gift. It was as if he had spent not one night, but forty-nine days sitting there, in contemplation. It had been enlightening.

But the smell of food had brought him back to reality. And right now, 'empty' referred to his stomach. Evolution of his Gift not, he was still more or less human.

At one point, Gaby had joined him in the meditation, but she had finished earlier, to make a campfire to eat something. Said breakfast would never come.

Sam then arrived, dashing his plans of something delicious. "Dad, they're here!"

Gaby stopped short and summoned Heartguard and Soulkeeper to her hands, as Fionn opened his eyes. His hand went instinctively for Black Fang, but he'd left it below the root. Sam noticed the sword and went for it when a wave of energy hit her, sending her and Black Fang flying away into the deepest reaches of the Tempest. Gaby turned around and was about to get into attack position when a cloud of mist enveloped her, making her disappear.

"I never expected to get all of you caught by surprise. I also never expected that you would find this place so quickly," Abaddon said. He appeared from behind one of the ruins' walls. A man taller than Fionn, with grey skin and white, long hair, his face a mix of lupine features with human and freefolk ones: long ears, dog like nose, large eyes, one green, one blue—the same colors as Fionn's and Gaby's— slender but with defined muscles. He was wearing a red velvet robe and underneath some sort of garment that ended with a top that looked like a turtleneck. He carried a heavy blade, a mix between an axe and a sword, made of some dark matter.

Fionn descended from the giant root, his Gift activated, his irises glowing green and the wind picking up. There was a tightness to his expression. There was no thought in his mind, but rather a strange sense of balance from the meditation, which helped to rein in his rage, to the point he appeared calm and collected. Even if his blood boiled.

"Oh, I get you are angry," Abaddon said with a sharp-toothed. "This display of power should be enough to cower other mortals. But we know that you are not mortal anymore. And this won't work on me. Be assured, I didn't kill your wife, nor your friends. Not yet anyway. They are busy with some friends of mine, extensions of sorts. I did, however, make two exceptions: your favorite student and your daughter. They are gone or soon to be dead. I won't risk those two shooting me with another of those arrows."

"I never pegged someone who wore a turtleneck and a pimp bathrobe as being afraid of a simple arrow," Fionn replied, toneless. His knuckles were white. The only reason he didn't throw himself into a frenzied attack was that he could still sense Gaby on a nearby floating island, and Alex on the other side of the Tree. Sam was another matter. But inside the Tempest she had more experience than him about how to get out of there. He had to keep his faith in them. That didn't mean he wasn't furious.

"Ah, yes, some genetic memories I got from certain sample I took from a hospital, told me you tend to mock your opponent's wardrobe and/or lair. Pretty childish if you know what I mean. Oh, right, sorry," Abaddon added mockingly.

Fionn flinched momentarily at the comment but managed to keep himself in check. He wasn't going to give the demon the satisfaction of getting under his skin even if he was about to flay the demon barehanded.

"So, that did get a more emotional reaction. See? You flinched slightly; your left eye betrayed you. I bet it was mention of the *sample.*"

Fionn's breathing became more pronounced, as the wind increased in strength, enough to make Abaddon's robe fly away.

"My bad. I suppose I shouldn't press the button of you being a lousy father to, well, all your children, and an even worse teacher to your students. Plus, a lousy leader, because here you are. You have no weapon, no friends, no distractions. Just your pure rage. Your undiluted pain. You and I are not that different, deep down."

"Either way I will beat you," Fionn said as the ground cracked under his tennis shoes.

Abaddon raised his hands. "We will see, but first, I want something from you."

"What?"

"I want to talk."

The wind currents disappeared as those words hit Fionn, taking him by surprise. "Wait, what?"

Chapter 11
Belief

A PROXIMITY ALARM BLARED AT the small office where Harland was trying to sleep. It was a small space, the opposite of what one would expect for the unofficial leader of what was left of the Free Alliance. No more than a hundred souls survived. Most of them were employees of the Foundation: his assistant Amy, Alex's friends—Quentin, and Birm and Andrea and their kids—the samoharo research team that the Figaro brought with them, Scud, the two surviving solarian knights, Salvador and Chakumuy, and a couple of titanfighters like Bev Johnson. Most freefolk had left to join the massive migration group led by Stealth, whose plan was to set a trail into the freezing north for Harland's group to follow. The Freefolk were more likely to survive the bad weather currently hitting the North Pole of Theia. A few had remained with Harland's group to serve as guides when he decided to pull the plug and evacuate Husvika' Geoda.

And of course, the main protectors of the group of survivors: Kasumi and Joshua. The Champion and the Titan of Fire, lifelong friends. The latter had even brought a small group of humanoid creatures, 'monsters' as they called themselves, that were living hidden in Carpadocci. In exchange for joining the group, they offered their unique skills to aid the survival efforts.

Harland couldn't be more thankful that they had elected to stay behind to protect the survivors that had decided to follow Harland instead of returning to their camps after he refused to comply with Abaddon's bounty. They gave the gathered people a feeling that their trust had been rewarded with a sense of security, while the rest of the Band went into what many had whispered was a suicide mission. Harland knew this weighed heavy in Kasumi's heart most of all.

Harland took a moment to rub his eyes, while G.E.A.R.I, in its silly toy body, kept sending a signal to... someone, whoever could listen. There was no reply, of course. Harland walked across the long corridor that led to the northern side of the Geode. His pace was hurried. He was exhausted. How long had he been without a proper rest? He couldn't remember. Unlike his friends that could push their mortal limits, he needed a hearty dinner, a long, relaxing bath, and an even long rest. Preferably a whole month, if such a luxury was even feasible or ever would be again in his lifetime. But, given how things looked at the moment, even getting a few hours to breathe in peace would be too much to ask. He passed by the hangar, where most of the adults were currently packing as many provisions as possible into the vehicles they had left. Children and the infirm would take precedence and take the X-23, piloted by Scud, while the rest would take the snow trucks towards a location. If Harland was entirely honest with himself—and at that particular moment, he didn't relish the reality of it—he wasn't sure where it was, or if it was a good idea. He was acting on strong coffee, a hunch, and a poem as guides. His hope was that Stealth's group would have arrived first, and that the place was real and still standing. He wondered if Old Earth's engineering would have been strong enough to last that long.

Then again, the Ark had endured travelling across intergalactic space to reach Theia, although aided by the powers of the Trickster Goddess—who was also unable to help them. All of his allies fell one by one, Hardland had noticed. They left what remained of humanity to die a slow and agonizing death even after barely surviving a first extinction event millennia ago on a distant planet that no one even remembered anymore.

But it wasn't as if he had the luxury of too many options. Once the Figaro had left, the Infection and the incursions and the creatures that came with it were detected in the Geode's sensors. Which meant that the World's Scar, as last their defensive measure, had fallen.

A part of him wished that Fionn had stayed, to have someone to bounce ideas off during this new emergency. Someone with a clearer head. But it had fallen to Harland to lead the survivors' next move and be sure they held on until the Band managed, somehow, to fix everything. That was his sole source of hope. Because somehow, they always delivered no matter how impossible the odds.

He couldn't be less. Even if he felt now as small as others saw him.

Keep it together, he thought. *They don't have anyone else to look up to.*

He looked at the people gathered in the hangars as the blizzard shook the walls.

A freefolk girl did a few small tricks to keep the children distracted while their parents worked around the clock. Birm and Andrea were checking that the trucks' energy cells were up to the task of hauling close to one hundred people as fast as possible. Dr. Tze Tze and Scud were finishing the adjustments on the X-23. The 'monster' people Joshua had brought with him from Carpadocci were helping pack everything, shoulder to shoulder with the people that had received them with suspicion, but not a word of thanks despite Sam's stern look when they arrived. Meanwhile Quentin, Professor Hunt, and the Major of Skarabear were comparing notes to pinpoint the exact location where Harland had decided to move the operation and the best route to reach it, as he only had his notes from a previous recon flight. They did so without questioning him once the Infection was detected and he proposed his plan. But his deepest fears were that he was leading all these people to their deaths.

So that's how it truly feels, uh? Harland thought as he entered the security office. *How did Fionn put it once? Like walking on a tight rope above a dark, endless chasm, not knowing if the next step will end everything? That's how you felt, old friend, when I roped you years ago into looking for Hunt when he was kidnapped.*

"Are you okay, boss?" Kasumi's question broke him out of his reverie. Her voice was sweet but firm, as usual, and she offered him a warm smile. She had changed into her tactical gear. The nanoarmor with its clean running energy lines over part of her demonhunter outfit made her look like a futuristic warrior.

It must be weird and sad to be recently married and separated from Sam and Alex, not knowing if they will see each other again.

Harland pondered his reply, taking her hand, he led her

towards the stairwell, far from the ears of the others.

"To be honest? No. I'm freaking out."

"Wondering if your plan is the right one?" a deep voice asked behind Harland. He turned his head and saw Joshua, sitting on the steps, smoking an herbal cigarette, which he proceeded to offer. Harland wondered if the herbal mixture Joshua used to keep the Beast relaxed would be what he needed right now to calm himself. Joshua seemed as sharp as always, but then again, his biology was different from a human.

"No, but thank you for the offer," Harland said. "I need to keep a clear head."

"I guess that's the question we all ask ourselves at some point in our lives," Joshua continued.

"Let me ask you something," Harland replied. "Have you ever second guessed yourself in... how old are you... a millennium?

"I can't talk about my life before Shimizu sensei found me during the times of the Great War, because to be entirely honest, it's all a blur. And I'm pretty sure I spent a good chunk trapped in that buried city," Joshua said with a half-smile. "But since I joined Kasumi's family, well, plenty of times. Then again, I haven't been in a position of leadership before, like you right now."

"Are you second guessing your orders to evacuate this place?" Kasumi asked. "Because of the risk for the people you are trying to protect?"

"Yes!" Harland replied.

"Then I would say that you made the right decision," Kasumi said.

"What?"

"You are not worried because of optics. You are not a politician. But leadership, true leadership, asks us to make tough choices. Now is no time for caution."

"Where did you learn that?"

"From watching you at work during the past few years. When you second guess yourself, it's because you are seeing all angles of the situation with one concern, how it might affect those following your orders. Any other boss, or politician, would bark orders, confident of themselves," Kasumi replied. "Confidence is good, it's great once you are in combat, so to speak. But when it comes to decision making, overconfidence can blind you to the risks. Fionn sensei used to be anxious before an important fight. Gaby sings to herself. Sam still gets anxious. And Alex has to go to the bathroom every five minutes."

Used to? So it wasn't just me who noticed the change in Fionn? Harland thought.

"For the record, I don't think your plan is stupid," Joshua added. "As you said earlier, we don't necessarily have the means to defend this place. I mean, Kasumi and I can deal with several, but many will slip through." Joshua indicated the survivors who would then be targeted. "And at some point, we'll be overrun. I'm pretty sure you already did the calculus in your head of that scenario, so I don't think you took the choice of enacting this plan lightly. It is risky though. But survival always is."

"I know, that's why I'm anxious."

The artificial voice of G.E.A.R.I. called through the comns: "Signals received. Freefolk contingent up north has found what seems to be part of the hull. They have been joined by most of their population above the Mistlands. They believe they have found a path and are sending the coordinates."

"What about the Kuni?" Kasumi asked, and concern belied her outward calm. Not that Harland could fault her. She was worried about her family.

"No information received. However, before going offline, sensors detected movement towards the north of the Auris continent before the latest storm began."

"We can assume they mobilized their people when they got the encrypted message. Good, time to go then."

"What about the samoharo?" Scud joined the conversation, followed by Dr. Tze Tze. "Sorry for interrupting, Boss, we came to tell you we are ready to depart."

"If the Leaderzhip waz zmart," Dr. Tze Tze added, "they are probably moving towardz the zouth pole of the planet, until the reactorz of the fleet are warm enough to enact their zelfish plan. One can hope they took the people from the Ztraits with them at the very leazt."

"That leaves the Desert and the Grassland, and my other regions in the dark," Joshua pointed out, dejected, allowing himself to exhale a long sigh.

Harland couldn't blame Joshua's forlorn mood. All he could see was people divided, trying to save themselves from the evil unleashed by the greed of a few, instead of keeping a united front. Even he was trying to save what he could of people that still believed his Foundation was the best option. But Harland couldn't help but wonder, if Humankind, joined by the Freefolk, and any other creature with them would have a shot a surviving an inhospitable universe in case they had to leave a home planet for a second time in the existence of their species.

Is this the best choice? Running away from a dying planet instead of trying to save it by any means?

Harland had discussed it with Fionn before he left on what he called 'mostly a suicide mission,' and they had reached the same conclusion, even if they talked about it obliquely as 'Plan A' & 'Plan B.' Protecting the Life Tree was of course the best option, for it meant the planet would remain alive and at least somewhat inhabitable, and their souls would remain intact. But even if they succeeded in that, who knew how extensive Abaddon's damage to the whole biosphere was? The infection zones were, for all intents and purposes, dead. Reforming them would take a miracle akin to healing the planet itself, and even if that were possible for the newly found world forming alchemy used in some survivors' encampments, the process would take more than a generation. Fionn and Harland weren't sure the next generation would have enough time for that. Hence Plan B, the one both had discussed for years since Byron warned Fionn about his master's during their fateful duel abroad the Bestial: get as many survivors as possible inside the fabled ARKs that were buried somewhere in the North Pole, and off planet entirely if needed. Originally, they had no idea where, but with the revelation of what the Long Moon was, Harland had ordered to get everything ready to reach it and hole up there till some other option appeared. But first they had to reach those ARKs. Their existence was more than just a poem he had recited once to Skarabear's mayor, about the frozen halls of the human kings, for those halls were the ARKs. Harland knew they still existed due to the reports from freefolk travelers informing about the ancient giant structures. He and Sid had even once made a reconnaissance flight to check the sites, though they couldn't land to explore them due a sudden blizzard.

However, one thing was knowing they still existed after millennia and another was to be sure they were even intact, even less in any condition for orbital flight. And that was not counting the strange aliens Fionn had told him about, the ones that had sent the samoharo into a frenzy, locking every survivor on the planet. What was already a battle for survival had become a knock-down and drag-out fight, with the last one standing yet undetermined.

Sid had always been right, Harland was forced to admit. Since the first day they met, Sid always talked about how their collective destiny was not about being hidden on a planet with a thick enough ionosphere to disguise it from outsiders by cloaking most, if not all, signals of technology coming from its surface. A rogue asteroid, Tawa Seridia going supernova, a blast of gamma rays, a spell out of control, a new virus, anything could erase every trace of the species on Theia ever existing in the universe. This time it had been an actual demon, feeding from their own worst instincts.

"We might have been born on a planet, but if the legends are true, we are not meant to stay there forever," Sid had told him once. "The cosmos is the actual home we need to tame."

And yet, Harland knew they had to fight to save the planet from being destroyed. Hence, years ago Fionn and Harland had decided to split efforts on their respective projects: Fionn would do everything possible to save the planet, and Harland would fund all research needed to create a space program. Of course, it would have been faster and easier to have the samoharo on their side from day one. But that wasn't the case, and why there was only the Figaro and the X-23. Harland *wanted* to find the ARKs earlier, before all the apocalypses began.

But we ran out of time before we even knew, and now all rests on Fionn and the others pulling a miracle while we scatter away like ash in the wind.

"G.E.A.R.I., broadcast the encoded signal again, this time with the coordinates," Harland ordered.

"Still hoping they'll listen and help?" Scud asked.

"Pretty dumb, isn't it?" Harland assented.

"I can think on worze thingz than hoping otherz to change their mindz," Tze Tze said.

"The creatures are approaching fast," Joshua pointed out. "If we are gonna leave it's now or never, even with the blizzard outside."

"Fionn reached an agreement with the Elder Ice People. They will come with us and will keep the blizzard at bay from us but still as cover for our tracks. They are at risk as well so, as of now, they are part of our group," Harland said. "But you're right. Time to leave. I wish I had more time to see that the signal made it out."

"One of the creatures has breached the Geoda," Joshua told them, flicking his cigarette and summoning Fury. Kasumi promptly summoned Breaker.

"Leave, boss. We will give you some cover," Kasumi offered.

"But..."

"Alex theorized that Gifted are resistant to the decay, because we have our own source of cosmic energy that kinda violates the laws of thermodynamics, remember? And the titans were Gifted people once, so Joshua will be fine." Kasumi smiled at Harland. It was clear to him from her forlorn expression that she wasn't even sure of that herself.

"We will reach you as soon as it is safe," Joshua said. "Leave us two snowtrikes. We will make sure the signal is out before leaving."

"Be careful," Harland said. "Please."

"Signal uploaded eighty percent," G.E.A.R.I chimed.

"Go!" Kasumi pushed Harland away, as Scud picked him up and took him to the hangar, where everyone was ready to leave.

† † †

"I think the last time we fought together," Joshua said, as the lights flickered around them, with the few plants decaying fast as the air filled with the smell of decaying matter, "was when we punched that robotic creature on the top of the train."

"Ah, yes!" Kasumi smiled. She was thankful for Joshua's banter. To say she never felt fear or anxiety before a fight would be a bald-faced lie. But this time, the knot at the bottom of her stomach felt as heavy as a mountain. The odds of both making it alive out of here, of her seeing her new wife and husband again were slim. "We never saw more of them. I wonder what happened to them."

"Probably discarded by the Dark Father. Afterall," Joshua said, and nodded towards the three incoming incursions. "Those are more cost effective."

They looked like three mutated versions of hippopotamus, drooling black ichor from their jaws. The few remaining plants withered away. Everything around them became dull and grey. It was as if these new incursions were draining even the color out of things.

"These are new," Kasumi said.

"They feel the same as the one that hit Alex in the back," Joshua explained.

"Then this is personal," Kasumi said, twirling Breaker and sending a slash at an incursion that came close to her, slicing its jaw off.

The remaining incursions, on their limited intelligence, attacked as one.

"Montoneros," Kasumi whispered in Alex's native tongue.

Kasumi and Joshua fought as a well-oiled machine. If he went up, she attacked down. If Joshua used a feint and took a defensive stance, Kasumi took the offensive. Fury was a column of fire on Joshua's hands, while Breaker hit every target with the force of a tsunami, breaking the floor tiles with every hit. The incursions attacked Joshua with more frequency, attracted no doubt by the heat emanating from his Tempest Blades, which left the incursions open to Kasumi's retaliation.

The incursions were finished in no time.

"I don't want to say it," Kasumi muttered under her breath, as vapor formed with every word.

"Then don't, or you'll jinx it," Joshua whispered.

More incursions broke through the Geoda's windows, filling the place with twenty more of them.

"Jinx!" both exclaimed at the same time.

"They are too many!" Kasumi yelled.

"I can try to take them out with me," Joshua offered, as he was about to set his body on phoenix mode.

"The refugees need us," Kasumi stopped him, freezing his left arm. "And G.E.A.R.I. is not finished yet."

"Then I will make just a small explosion. Go to the hangar, I will be right behind you." Joshua smiled. "I promise. I know how to do it."

Kasumi nodded and ran towards the security office near the hangar, as flames erupted from Joshua's body. He concentrated, slowing his breathing. Small tongues of flame escaped his lips with every exhalation. The Beast went to sleep as he woke the Titan of Fire core inside him. He had to do it with precision, enough to burn the incursion but not the whole place. Joshua let go, causing a controlled wave of fire that consumed the visible incursions. Kasumi reached the security office in time to raise a wall of ice to protect herself and G.E.A.R.I. from the fire.

Small explosion, yeah right, Kasumi thought.

"G.E.A.R.I. come with us!" Kasumi said, kneeling next to the small toy robot that hosted the A.I.

"Can't move until mission is complete or upload will be corrupted. Ninety-seven percent uploaded. Two more minutes," the A.I said to Kasumi with what seemed to be resignation to its fate. "Farewell."

"We don't have two minutes. Let's go." Joshua grabbed Kasumi by the arm and pulled her to the hangar where two snowtrikes were waiting for them.

"Godspeed, boss," G.E.A.R.I said with its childlike, toy voice before ceasing to exist as the last incursion on the Geoda finished absorbing the final remnants of energy from the place.

† † †

Joshua and Kasumi raced through the blizzard following the radio tracking signal from the X-23, several kilometers ahead. The blizzard had died down where they were, but in front of them there was a wall of white. The Elder Ice People were doing a good job concealing the refugees from the incursions that were tracking them by something as simple as body heat. Any source of energy seemed to be food for this new type of incursion. Even the blizzard itself.

As they drove into the storm, jumping up and down through the ice mounds, barely able to see a thing, Kasumi crashed onto something.

Or rather, something crashed onto her.

An incursion had caught up with her and jumped at her. Kasumi barely got out of the crash, rolling to her left. Summoning Breaker once more, she used the naginata to catch the incursion's jaws and avoid being bitten by it. With a powerful double kick, Kasumi pushed away the incursion, which charged her once more. Annoyed, Kasumi readied Breaker and ran towards the incursion, sliding next to it as Breaker cut it lengthwise on the right side, destroying it.

Kasumi stood up from the fight, no worse for wear. She advanced a few steps as the rest of the incursions raced towards her. She lifted Breaker over her head as the blade trembled in her hands, glowing with white light. Putting all her weight and strength, all her Gift into the slash, Breaker descended on an arc that hit the ground with terrible force, cracking it and creating a chasm that grew to reach at least a kilometer in length and fifty meters wide. The forerunners among the incursions couldn't stop in time and plunged into the frozen void.

Kasumi dropped to her knees, with an exhausted wheeze. The ground cracked around her, threatening to send her tumbling into the same chasm along with the incursions. But Joshua grabbed her by the arm and pulled her onto his snowtrike, accelerating as the chasm increased in width.

"What was that?" Joshua asked her, incredulous.

"I had a plan," Kasumi replied, recovering her breath.

"Your boyfriend is rubbing off too much on you."

"Husband," Kasumi observed, as she realized what she had done. "I almost killed myself."

"Yes, and you promised to make it back to Sam and Alex alive," Joshua said. "So, I intend to make you keep that promise."

† † †

An hour later they arrived at the source of the radio signal. Kasumi and Joshua found themselves in the eye of a storm, the night sky yawning an inky black above them. The entire place was dark aside a few lights casting shadows on the broken walls of an artificial structure that resembled a large cruiser like those that sail through the Lirian Ocean. Except this one was all black and grey, with few windows in the hull.

As they approached, they saw a small man making motions with a torch, calling them. Joshua deaccelerated the snowtrike and turned it off away from the camp, as Kasumi cooled it down by placing snow on top of it. Both walked towards Harland, who beamed at seeing them.

"I'm so glad that you made it here in one piece," Harland said as Kasumi knelt to hug him. "Stealth and his freefolk contingent are already inside setting up camps on all the levels not covered by ice."

"Barely," Joshua replied. "There are too many of those things around. They're hunting us."

"I think we lost the incursions, but they will soon track us down. So, this is the ARK?" Kasumi asked as she looked at the imposing artificial structure.

"The last standing one, of those that brought humankind to Theia," Harland confirmed.

Joshua pointed at a considerable breach on one side of the ship. "That's a large rip in the hull, it won't help if we want to reach the Long Moon."

"We need to seal it, that's true," Harland acknowledged. "But first we need to turn on the engines so we can activate its systems and then seal it internally without freezing."

"And you think you will know how to use something that was built who knows when with who knows what language interface?" Joshua raised an eyebrow.

"Tze Tze believes it. He's using his translation algorithm to work things out. Birm and Andrea are working on the energy system," Harland added. "Quentin and Professor Hunt are helping with all the notes they have from ancient texts."

"I'll go and help them," Joshua said. "No good if they freeze while working on it."

"I will keep guard outside." Kasumi smiled reassuringly at her old friend. "Just in case."

"Call me if you need help," Joshua warned her. "No need for more of Alex's plans."

Confused and concerned, both, Harland turned to Kasumi. "What happened?"

Kasumi rubbed the back of her neck. "Well..."

† † †

"What is this place?" Joshua asked, his voice echoing on the metallic walls. It was a large engine room, containing three huge reactors of some kind, still intact, with a fourth damaged.

"Looks like they were some kind of nuclear fusion reactors," Birm said. "But they were drained millennia ago. The trip to Theia must have exhausted them completely. The counter is not registering any kind of activity."

"At leatz they are zealed," added Dr. Tze Tze. "Who knowz what ancient humanz used as fuel for theze reactorz. Though the dezing has zimilitudez to the onez we used once."

"Maybe there is a way to start them," Andrea suggested. "Might not get off the ground right away, but at least it will keep us from freezing. And if we seal that section with the gap, then we would have a shelter until we repair it to function.

"We would need a powerful zource of energy," Dr. Tze Tze declared as he looked at Joshua.

He nodded and grabbed the power conductors that were still attached to one of the reactors. "I'll do it."

"I will jury rig something for you to channel the energy," Birm promised.

† † †

Joshua, who was now wearing some weird pair of metal mittens that captured the heat he could generate through his titan powers, poured all the energy he could muster from the Titan of Fire core inside him, trying to reactivate the strange reactor that once powered up the human ARK. But as soon as the material inside it began to glow and emit a blue light and heat, it died.

"What the Pitts?" Birm muttered. "There was a spike of energy and radiation coming through the counters, but it died right away."

"They're here," Joshua said. "Those new incursions are sucking it dry. Get everyone inside, I will try a second time, maybe from inside the reactor."

"If our notez are correct," Dr. Tze Tze admonished. "You will be exposed to an unhealthy dose of radiation. You could die attempting something that might be impossible."

"Not impossible," Joshua said matter-of-factly. "It's necessary."

† † †

"Joshua, now it would be a good time to turn the lights on," Harland said through the comms.

"I'm trying!" Joshua yelled back. "But I can't make the reactor work! Those things are too close!"

"Energy is being drained as Joshua pours it in," Birm added.

"The creatures," Kasumi said, pointing out the incursions that had chased them down. They were surrounding the camp. "Boss, get everyone inside. I'll deal with them."

Kasumi knew it could be a losing battle, fighting on her own while Joshua tried to power up the ARK, but if she could offer the refugees a bit more time, maybe the others would stop Abaddon in time. It was worth a shot.

Stealth joined Kasmumi and Harland at her side. "I'm here with you," he said, as Scud grabbed a large ice axe from the crates and joined her.

"I always wanted to fight alongside one of you," the samoharo smiled at Kasumi. A few of the Elder Ice people joined them as well.

BOOM!

A red light flashed across the snowy field as one of the incursions was blasted out of existence.

That light seems familiar, Kasumi thought, recalling when she saw Sid activating the Figaro's weapons at the park to deal with the biomechanical critters from the Dark Father. A second blast came. It was a welcome distraction to get Harland inside. Whatever was attacking the incursions was giving her a chance to get him inside and fulfill her duty as bodyguard.

"What are we waiting for, boss?" Kasumi asked Harland as she tugged him along by the hand. But he remained unmoving amidst the wind and the snow, staring at the approaching lights, as the creatures either disappeared or were blasted away by something coming from the lights.

"The creatures. They're retreating," Harland replied. "Either they are scared, or something is calling them."

"Our energy seems to be coming back," Kasumi observed as the torches they had with them were recovering their power.

"Is that a samoharo metal bird?" Stealth asked from behind. More and more of the refugees were coming out of the ARK, to witness what was arriving.

"The flag ship of the old fleet," Scud replied. "That thing is really ancient for it to still fly."

"So, there is still hope," Harland whispered.

† † †

Lights in the sky broke through the blizzard casting light on the remains of the ARK. As more lights joined to illuminate the people below, Harland, slightly blinded by the glare off the snow, saw the silhouette of a giant flying ship, at least twice the size of the Bestial. It was probably the largest flying machine Harland had seen in his life. The markings of the underbelly were familiar. They were samoharo iconographs.

"It's the Admiral's flagship," Scud said.

"Seems they *did* get my messages," Harland laughed. "And that Sid managed to convince at least one of them."

From the underbelly of the ancient ship, a small pod descended, carrying a large meemech samoharo with greying hair, accompanied by two large samoharo warriors, all decked out in their combat armors. They painted an intimidating figure compared to Yokoyawa's gentler one.

"Who's the guy?" Joshua asked, as he approached the main group, coming out of the ARK with Dr. Tze Tze and Birm.

"Admiral Hunapuh." Scud turned to answer Joshua who was staring at his hands as he and Kasumi were vanishing, followed by an explosion of dark smoke, taking everyone but Harland and Stealth by surprise.

"Where did they go?" Scud asked, confused at the sudden disappearance of Kasumi and Joshua.

"Judging by the whiff of brimstone," Harland replied with a smile as he pointed out to the sky. "And that passing dark eagle, Joshua's boss is sending them as reinforcements."

"If the others need help, he could take us all with them," Scud said.

"I'm surprised he's helping at all. Or maybe he is testing us to judge if we deserve his aid."

"I see the Ah Puch is still acting on whims," Hunapuh said as he descended from the pod, then addressed Harland. "And you are President Harland."

"Interim President," Harland corrected. "Thank you for answering our call for help, Admiral."

"Ha!" Hunapuh laughed, startling everyone as freefolk and humans approached the area under the light. More pods began to descend from the ship. "You humans and your minutiae. I like you!" He then studied the ARK. "I take you didn't manage to make it work. These old things can withstand the rigors of space only if they are properly maintained. And even then. Matters not! We are here to pick up all of you and take you to off planet with us."

"What changed?" Dr. Tze Tze asked.

"Your former protégé Siddhartha was pretty eloquent in reminding us who we are. The others in the council didn't like to be embarrassed that way, but I care not. This time the samoharo have allies to face the darkness of the cosmos, unlike last time!"

"If I may," Harland interjected. "You know some of our allies are at the moment risking their lives to protect the Life Tree."

"They found the Life Tree? I thought it was a legend?" one of the samoharo soldiers whispered.

"Yes," Harland continued. "We found it and the Greywolf took his group to defend it from Abaddon. And if the Judge—or Ah Puch as you know him—took my two friends, it means things are not going well. If we are going to do something more than survive and expect the end of days, we need to help them. If you agree, of course."

"Ha! I knew I liked you," Hunapuh reiterated, already texting on his armpad. "You know the feelings of your people. There is another ship almost here, with Kuni refugees. I will ask if any of their demonhunters want to join, while that ship takes this group of refugees. I have a squadron of warriors ready to fight. It seems they admire Siddhartha, Yokoyawa, and Xcub too much."

"Me?" Scud asked with the equivalent of embarrassment on a samoharo's face after hearing his real name.

"Stealth, I know I have no right to ask more than what I already have but..." Harland turned to Stealth, who walked promptly away. Stealth said nothing, but simply climbed over a crate. He placed his left hand on his throat and his voice was enhanced as if it were being emitted from a speaker. Thunder arced through the sky as the northern light fluctuated.

Like mother, like son, Harland chuckled.

"Freefolk! What I am about to ask may represent great sacrifice. I will only take a few volunteers with me in this deadly mission while the rest protect our people. Let me ask you: Who amongst us is willing to join me and fight the ancient enemy alongside The Greywolf, The DragonQueen, and their tribe?" Stealth yelled at the freefolk.

There were several seconds of silence, enough to make Harland's heart sink.

Then one hand rose. And another. And a third one. Soon more than a dozen hands were raised. Old and young, from all the freefolk tribes, volunteers said their farewells to their families and walked towards Harland. Unsurprisingly, most of Ravenstone's faculty volunteered. They had known Sam since she was a teenager. They had taught alongside Vivi. Many owed their lives to Fionn and his Band of heroes.

Salvador approached Harland, followed by Chakumuy and the surviving titanfighters of the group.

"We will go as well. They are our friends," Salvador said.

"And this is our planet, too."

Dr. Tze Tze approached as well.

"I will go with you, with some of my engineerz," the good doctor said. "Knowing Ziddhartha, his zhip will need repairz and a crew to aid him."

"I will go with you, Doctor," Birm offered. "I know that ship as well. And I know how to use a bow if needed."

"What about your family?" Harland asked, taken aback.

"We will be fine," Andrea exclaimed from the back with their kids. "We don't leave our own behind, right?"

"That's right!" the titanfighters replied.

"You have your volunteers," Stealth said. "Now they need a leader. You."

"I... I... I don't fight. I... can't," Harland sighed, looking and his body, his short stature.

"Mother didn't like you because you were a fighter. She liked you because you were a good man, above all else. The real stature of a person is not measured by their height, but by the reach of their actions towards others. In that regard you are a human that walks tall alongside true titans, un-flinchingly, remember?" Stealth winked at Harland, who opened his eyes wide at hearing those words. "Just lead us like you have done till now. We will do the rest.

"It wasn't a dream," Harland murmured.

"It never is," Stealth replied.

Hardland turned to Dr. Tze Tze. "Can you track the Figaro's location?"

"Of courze I can!" Dr. Tze Tze replied, half-amused, half-offended by the question.

"Good. Let's go, then," Harland replied.

We're coming Fionn, just hold on.

Chapter 12
The Blades of the Tempest

MOST PEOPLE THOUGHT THAT WHAT gave power to the Band of the Greywolf was that they are owners of all the known Tempest Blades. On the surface, they were right. By their very nature, the Tempest Blades were the fusion of the cumulative knowledge and prowess of four species. They were nigh indestructible weapons with the power of nova bombs. Thus, why most people would think that they gave that power to their owners. And that's where their arguments begin to go awry.

The Tempest Blades don't have owners; they have wielders, partners, friends—and they cannot lend their power. They have what they have, no more, no less. In the hands of someone with a strong will, they can do the impossible. In the hands of those with the Gift—only obtained by choosing to put your life on the line for others, honoring their Covenant bonds to do the right thing, wield magick to reshape reality through great pain, or learn to become one with their inner beast and rise phoenix-like from their darkest places—the Tempest Blades perform miracles.

To begin with, the title of the Tempest Blades never belonged to the weapons themselves. That misunderstanding grew with time. Their actual title was Blades of the Tempest, and it refers to those that, with or without the weapons, chose to do the right thing despite the risk or their fears. It refers to the heroes that wield them.

And those heroes, right now, are the last hope of people, fighting the battle of their lives, despite the million odds against them. Because they chose to. Because every choice they made took them to this place.

Because they used every second chance they encountered to make amends.

Because they know they are not alone.

Because they chose who they want to be.

Because the journey ends here.

And they will make sure one way or another, it ends, one way or another, here, on their own terms.

† † †

What did Fionn say? Take one day, one fight at a time? Focus on this one and you can help him later.

The Deacon jumped and punched the air, which filled with fractured images from Alex's past, rendered as if a comic, but depicting the events in a somber, more tragic way. The same way Alex's depression usually made things look in his head. Like breaking the fourth wall. The sensory attack confused him, to the point that he barely managed to sidestep to avoid a descending attack. The Deacon didn't stop. He moved inhumanly fast, and the onslaught continued, the armor taking the brunt of the attacks as he tried to bring Yaha around and get on an even footing. With every punch, more images appeared in the air, illustrating all of Alex's life, especially the past year as a failure, putting emphasis on every mistake he made.

Yaha surged from his hand to block the attack aimed at his heart, the energy released causing a shockwave that sent both opponents in opposite directions.

Before you fight, use your head, Alex recalled and took a defensive stance, half his armor broken. *A bit late for that. But if that paper bit was right, this guy is using Abaddon's technique of shaping himself into your worst fear. I didn't expect them to look like comic pages.*

"Nice trick," Alex said. "But it won't work on me. My therapist is excellent."

"Maybe this will work on you then!" the Deacon quipped, and he punched Alex all over the body, demolishing the nanoarmor with each rapid-fire strike while Alex's attacks with Yaha were deflected or caused little cracks in the Deacon's armor. This was like his final test to get his degree. But instead of debating, he was being pounded to death as memories rushed in.

Fionn had pulled him aside before they'd boarded the

Figaro at the Geoda. "Alex, we are about to embark on a journey that for all of us, but specially you, is the final test."

"Why?" Alex asked, confused.

"Because I want you to take my place after all is done," Fionn said simply, taking Alex aback. "To protect the others."

"What about you?" Alex asked, his eyes widened in realization. "Unless..."

Fionn nodded. "I might have to make a difficult decision if it comes to it to stop Abaddon once and for all. That's why I ask you two things: if the moment comes, you will do as I say without hesitating. And that you will take care of Gaby and Sam, who have their own challenges ahead."

"Always," Alex had replied.

† † †

"Hmmm." The Deacon stopped his attacks suddenly and looked at the Life Tree. "My master just disposed of your partner, your friends, and the Black Fang itself. It seems your master will die alone, right after you."

Alex used the distraction to shift into the same stance that Fionn taught him, and he had used to cut the Beast Shaliem momentarily from Joshua years ago, holding Yaha with both hands, hilt over his head, the point of the sword aimed at the floor, the blade guarding his left shoulder and flank. Focusing through the Gift, the connections between the armor and the Deacon became crystal clear, and Alex aimed at one of them in the chest, hitting with all his strength. But unlike that time with Joshua, the clash rebounded on him, sending Yaha flying from his hands and destroying the remaining nanoarmor. Alex only had on his original combat gear now. Yaha, being almost an entity of pure energy, was repelled by the Deacon's armor as the arrows had been, but not before leaving a breach in the breastplate.

"All that power in your attack to create a meager breach in my armor?" the Deacon observed. It wasn't larger than a human fist. "And losing your sword in the process, because I got distracted? You pathetic loser!"

The Deacon headbutted Alex, breaking his nose with a rush of blood and leaving him dazed. The Deacon forced him into a kneeling position. Alex's irises faded to normal as he tried to focus his breath and redirect all his energy somewhere else. He only had one shot to make this work, one shot at something he had never managed to do. Then again, he had only one shot with Shemazay and he'd made that count. Like he'd done during his last hoops game, and during his last attack against the Dark Father.

"You will die a failure, as I showed you. But at least I'll execute you in the comic book style that you clearly want," the Deacon said. He lifted one arm. But Alex, as a thread of blood came from the corner of his right lip, smiled.

"What are you smiling for?"

The Deacon was slow to notice how Alex's irises flared with power. That glow distracted the Deacon for a split second and he failed to notice the specks of light amassing on Alex's palms, forming two crackling orbs of energy. The crackling extended to all of Alex's body.

"This!" Alex snapped. He thrust his hands forward and into the breach in the Deacon's armor. An explosion of light and thunder filled the place.

CRAKOOOM!

The Deacon stared blankly down at the massive smoking hole in his chest, where his core used to be. He staggered back, attempting in vain to close the charred pit with his hands. Not about to allow him the opportunity, Alex extended his left hand, summoning Yaha back. But instead of his hand, the sword traced an arc in the air, cutting the Deacon's head with ease, before Alex caught it in his right hand.

"This time, I didn't forget the head," Alex said as he stared at the dissolving body of the Deacon, his last declarations echoing in Alex's head. He stared at the Life Tree, where on the other side was Fionn, alone, weaponless, facing Abaddon.

"Go and help him, please," Alex murmured to Yaha, and he used all his strength to fling his blade at the Tree. The sword dissolved into a beam of light.

I'm not feeling so well, Alex thought before collapsing to the ground, exhausted. In the distance he heard a roar and smiled. *She's tougher than they give her credit for.*

† † †

"So much for a quiet breakfast," Sid muttered as he ran along the trunk of the tree. He grabbed a vine and swung around the giant incursion attacking him. It was a serpent made seemingly of solid black smoke with a jaguar's head. Its visage brought to mind a dark deity from the samoharo pantheon.

"I haven't even had my first coffee," Sid complained as the serpent followed him. Of course, that left Yoko and Vivi free for the counterattack. Sid passed through one of the stone window frames of the ruins, the serpent hot on his heels. It got stuck, as Sid had hoped it would. While it struggled to free itself, Vivi blinded it with a mist spell as Yokoyawa cleaved the Stellar Ehécatl through the body. It fell to the ground with a thud and practically a small earthquake.

"Did we cut its head? "Sid asked.

"Yes," Yokoyawa said. "Let's find the heart core before it regens."

"That would have been cool, 'cept for one thing. Didn't the myth said that it could regrow more heads if you cut one?"

"Oh," Yokoyawa muttered as three heads regrew from the neck of the serpent. One of the heads went after Vivi, the other after Yokoyawa.

Sid jumped in front of Yoko and pushed Vivi away. One of the heads caught his right arm in its maw, a flash of pain shooting all the way up into his spine when Sid realized that about halfway down his arm no longer worked. Or moved at all. It was gone. With a pained grimace, Sid used his free hand with the remaining tomahawk and slashed savagely at the beast's eyes. Finally, its jaws opened. He dropped to the ground, staring in shock at his wound as Vivi stood and cast every defensive spell she knew to keep the monster at bay, avoiding looking at the carnage that was once attached to him.

"Go back to the Figaro," Yoko said, helping Sid up. "I will take it from here."

"If you are planning to do what I think you are planning to do; you're an idiot. No one has tried that in millennia. You barely got the Covenant back."

"As you once told me, hooman habits rub on you, like doing crazy things to save their friends. And I want us to make it out alive. Go now and heal yourself."

"Please, save Vivi," Sid urged, and he began to run.

Yoko strode towards the black serpent currently overwhelming Vivi's defensive spells. The large samoharo unleashed a guttural scream as he dropped the Stellar Ehécatl to the ground and stripped off his armor. Beating his chest and thighs to attract the attention of the black serpent, Yoko scratched his chest drawing blood. He smeared the greenish blood on his face, chest, arms, and thighs.

"Ka ke ka ke! Au'la ka ke, chen kai!" Yoko chanted as he approached the three headed serpent, all its heads focused on him. "By the blood of the Prophet that runs in my arteries, I honor thy covenant by unleashing the God of the Winds to lend me his shape!"

The air filled with the sweet fragrance of cocoa as Yokoyawa began to grow and accelerated his pace towards the black serpent. His limbs shifted to claws and his hair turned into multicolored feathers. When the transformation finished, Yoko had changed into a giant feathered serpent, the representation of the God of Winds and Father of the Prophet, his namesake Quetzalcoatl. With a bestial growl, Yoko and the black serpent locked themselves into furious combat around the roots of the Life Tree, as samoharo beliefs indicated would happen at the End of Days.

† † †

Sid ran as fast as he could to reach the Figaro, but the effort and the blood loss exhausted him. He soon dropped to the ground, almost passing out. But someone picked him up into a strong set of arms and carried him back to the Figaro. As his eyesight refocused, he saw Joshua carrying him, while the Beast was serving as tourniquet around his stump. That even the Beast had proved to have enough self-control to not suck Sid dry proved how the creature had become one of them.

"How?" Sid asked between hard breathing, wondering how Joshua, and probably Kasumi, had arrived there.

"My boss thought you might need extra help and got us here... somehow," Joshua replied reaching the underbelly of the Figaro. "I will leave you in the med bay and then I'll return back there to burn that thing down."

"Thank you for not going with a hand joke," Sid said as Joshua took him into the med bay and took out the first aid kit to stop the bleeding.

"Not the time," Joshua replied. "I might have to cauterize the injury to stop the bleeding. Not sure if that will stop you from regrowing the limb."

"Do it, but before that I have something to do," Sid said through gritted teeth as he lifted the bloodied stump and recited. "Blood of the ancestors that runs through my veins, lead me to the correct path, keep me from going astray."

Droplets of the greenish blood floated in the air and glowed forming the constellation of the Serpent, to then evaporate in the air.

"Do it now," Sid told him. Joshua applied the strongest anaesthetic spray onboard on Sid's wound and then placed his right hand over the stump and emitted enough heat to sear the tissues and cauterize the wound. Sid almost passed out from shock, but to his credit he pushed through. The air filled with the aroma of cacao.

"What was that?" Joshua asked confused.

"A wayfinding blood incantation to track the heart and brain cores of that demonic serpent. You might go back there and burn the serpent away, but you might damage the Tree as well. And kill Yoko. And Vivi. If a head survives... I have a plan, though. The Figaro's weapons were based on mining ships designed to extract ore while minimizing the risk of exploding a gas bag. They just need extra power, as the trip discharged a lot of the Figaro's energy."

"I see." Joshua smiled at the irony, or the coincidence, as he helped Sid to stand up and walk toward the engine core. "Plug me in. The Figaro should be easier than turning on the ARK."

† † †

With Joshua standing by and ready to feed his own power into the energy core, Sid reached the Figaro's cockpit. It was a jury-rigged solution and he hoped Dr. Tze Tze's reinforced relays held. It would've been easier with Alex, but Sid had to make do without him this time. He took his seat in the pilot's chair and through the window saw both the black demonic serpent and Yoko entangled, moving far too fast. At least the incantation had worked. There were six green dots glowing inside the serpent's body and three heads.

"Vivi, if you hear me, try to keep the black serpent pinned with some spell!" Sid gasped through the comms, wincing with the pain. Then he pushed another button. "Wanderer, activate Fire Blossom Protocol. Surgical Strike Mode."

Outside, Vivi stood and began to cast. She may not have been on par with Sam's raw power, but she would be damned if she couldn't pull her weight in the fight. Gusts of wind entrapped the black serpent while a web of fine threads restricted its movement to help Yoko pull their target into position.

"Activating Fire Blossom Protocol. Energy core for the weapons not on full charge, needs external output," the AI replied with its newly installed artificial voice.

"Accept external output at relays thirty-seven and thirty-nine. Ready, Joshua?"

"Here I go!" Joshua shouted, and he grabbed two charge outlets connected to the energy core and unleashed all the power of the Titan of Fire. Sid saw the energy bar for each cannon filling up, getting ready to shoot. He only had to aim six shots at different parts at the same time.

"Energy core for weapons systems online," the A.I. replied. "Fire Blossom Protocol Activated. Surgical Strike Mode selected. Please state targets."

"Aim for the six cores detected on the smoke serpent," Sid replied as the targeting visor descended on his head. The magnifying lenses put the image of both serpents battling and biting each other.

"Cores detected, with a twenty percent margin of error. Quantum Witness Effect in play."

Wanderer calculated the location where the points would be. It would take a split second to shoot when it was locked in. Wanderer was having difficulty tracking the cores due to the roiling movement between the creature and Yokoyawa's feathered serpent form. The only thing that remained constant was the blood spell that Sid had cast to make the cores glow.

"I hate myself," Sid mumbled. It was a risky order, and there was the slight chance that it could be misinterpreted. And if that were the case, only the Figaro's shielding would protect him.

"Wanderer, switch targets, aim for DNA traces of Pilot zero-zero-one on the field attached to the smoke serpent core, except inside the ship itself. Discard similitude traces from Pilot Zero-Zero-Four."

"There is risk for Pilot Zero-Zero-One as weapons systems can't separate targets, with the required precision," the A.I. replied in what Sid assumed was a disappointed tone.

"Just do it!" Sid exclaimed as he punched the button.

The Figaro fired.

It took less than a second between Sid pushing the button and the cannons unleashing the energy beams into each target. The black serpent wiggled around, trying to free itself. One of the lasers grazed Yoko's side, who fell to the ground and returned to his normal shape.

One of the weapons shifted its position and began to heat the Figaro's shield over the cockpit.

For the first time in his life, Sid prayed to the Prophet. *I hope the heat shield withstands that.*

Joshua poured more energy into the core, which in turn increased the output of the weapons to the point they melted. But the black serpent was well and fully carbonized, the heads falling to the ground with a series of deep thuds. Two of them fell near Yoko, the third about to crush him, but Vivi created a strong wind to send it flying over the tree.

The Figaro's systems died, half of them marking errors from burned relays. Sid knew he'd have his work cut out to repair it. There would be delays getting home.

But first we need to survive what follows, Sid thought. He exited the Figaro as fast as he could, followed by Joshua, who looked spent.

"Are you okay?" Sid asked him.

"Will take me moment to get my second wind. Maybe I need to drink someone's blood," Joshua joked.

"There must be a couple of blood packs in the med bay. Think of them as a smoothie," Sid quipped.

Vivi was kneeling next to Yokoyawa, tending his wounds. She had summoned a loincloth made of vines and leaves to protect his dignity. There was a large burn wound on his right side.

"Is he okay?" Sid asked nervously. Despite how often he was at odds with the big guy, they were family.

"Your hand!" Vivi exclaimed, grabbing Sid's stump. "Where is your hand? Maybe I can find a way to reattach it."

"It is inside that thing, carbonized probably," Sid replied, wincing through the pain, trying to reassure Vivi with a half-smile. "It will grow back... eventually, hopefully... with the right treatment. How is he?"

"I will live," Yoko said, trying to stand up with Joshua's help. "I don't know what hurts more, the transformation or the burn."

Sid sighed in relief. "At least you didn't die. I would hate for you to become a martyr on my watch."

"We need to go back to where the others are," Joshua interjected.

BOOM!

"Now what?" Sid groaned, looking up at the sky.

A meteor raced through the air, leaving behind a trail of fire and smoke.

†††

Gaby found herself transported to one of the smaller islands floating alongside the big one. It was covered with a heavy mist, where shadows moving in the background could barely be seen. She wandered with care, for she didn't know where the edge of the island was and falling into the Tempest would be an extraordinarily bad idea. She wondered if Sam would be all right after Abaddon sent her flying into the Tempest. Her... it was hard to describe their complicated kind of relationship now, best friend, adoptive daughter, great-granddaughter of a previous life. Point was that Sam was precious to Gaby, her first female friend ever. The one she shared her deepest secrets with and had spent many a night talking and laughing, up to and including planning a shared musical magical show where Gaby's band would play their music while Sam performed illusions with Kasumi. Even Gaby would assist in some illusions powered by real magick.

She will be fine, Gaby assured herself. Sam knows the inside of the Tempest, she even rewrote some of the rules of magick, for Heaven's sake. If someone could thrive here during a crisis it would be Sam.

It didn't mean that she didn't worry. But at least she could focus on returning as soon as possible, because she knew the two dunderheads currently facing a serial killer and the God of Evil were liable to get themselves killed in some heroic stunt if she wasn't there to bang some sense in their heads.

Or at least, that's what she kept telling herself to keep calm. Deep down, she feared losing her husband and his best friend. Of losing her planet.

Gaby summoned her Gift, attempting to use her psychometry to find a path. But the mist blocked it. There was no sound. All her senses seemed to be neutered by the mist.

"So, this mist is the actual challenge, huh?" she muttered. "Taking the shape of our fears."

"You are right," a familiar, hated, voice said. From the mist a shadow approached, soon resolving into a man dressed in a custom fitted business suit. He had the same bright blue eyes that Gaby had. She tapped the ground with her left foot and rolled her eyes. Exasperated, she sighed.

"Really? This trick of trying to trap me inside my head? Trying to talk me to death? Don't you get tired of it? The ice state is gone, along with Gavito. I'm not confused about who I am. Knock it off," Gaby scoffed at the approaching being, bracing herself for the reveal beneath the eyes.

"Who are you then?" Girolamo asked.

"Father?" Gaby said, not out of surprise, but to confirm what she had suspected since she saw Abaddon's first transmission, the mocking blue and green eyes. One for her, one for Fionn, both for their unborn child. Only one person had that shade of blue eyes. The same person she always remembered when staring at herself in the mirror, for she had inherited most of her looks from the man that had made her life a living hell. The same man that had surrendered his body to become the avatar of the God of Evil.

"Yes," Girolamo said. "If you are so sure of who you are, why do I sense hesitation in your heart? Afraid of having to choose now between your love and your duty? Of the consequences you suffered by playing hero?"

"I know who I am. I can choose whatever I want to be."

"You are not a mother. You never will be," Girolamo said with a cruel smile.

"I know," Gaby replied with a pang in her heart. "The medics told me as much, thanks to your associate's experiments. That red fern almost killed me. But you know what? I still have my family with me and that will help me heal, one way or another. There is always a way."

"You are confused. They are not your family. I am," Girolamo rebuked, offering her his right hand. "Come with me, daughter, so you are not confused between who you are and who you want to be."

"Seriously, this whole shtick of trying to mess with my head is only working to make me furious," Gaby said, right hand reaching for the handle of Heartguard. "No, Girolamo. There is no confusion. I'm certainly not your daughter."

"Who are you then?"

"Okay, you want to do this again, fine," Gaby spat. "I'm Gabriella Galfano-Estel. *And* I'm Izia Estel. I'm a hero. A musician. And the heart of my family and tribe."

"So many roles, just one tiny person."

"I'm not tiny. You can't make me feel small. You know why? Because I don't give you that power over me. I can balance them all because there's more than enough of me. And when I falter, I know they will have my back. You on the other hand, are a pathetic excuse of a father, to begin with."

"You never understood what I had to do to reach my dreams," Girolamo lamented. And for the first time, Gaby was unsure if it was Abaddon speaking or her father, slipping through the cracks of the consuming black hole that was the demon.

But Gaby was not the same small child that justified her dad's actions anymore. Being sent to that awful assassin school was a *reward* that she'd never forget.

"Enough with the tired 'woe is me,'" Gaby scoffed, seething with contempt and years of anger pent up anger. Her hand changed trajectory, instead reaching for the object on her back. "Dreams of absolute power? Over who? For *what*? People like you who covet power are the least fit to have it. And you. How many friends and family did you sacrifice? Like my mom? Like me? Did offering your body and soul to that creature help you to achieve your dream? Did murdering your wife help you?"

Girolamo was taken aback. It was him, manifesting through Abaddon's quantum-psychic attack.

"What?" Gaby smiled. She couldn't deny finally enjoying calling out her old man. Or what was left of him. "Did you think I didn't know? Took me years to put it all together. But I did it. Funny, I got the final proof the day you appeared in my apartment. The day that Alex did me the favor of punching you out, because he knew that if I put a hand on you first, I would have killed you, and you would have gotten at last your little assassin. So, tell me, was it worth it? Destroying the world, your world, for profit?"

"If your mother had understood. If you had. There wouldn't have been need of hurting you."

"Talking like a textbook abuser, blaming the victim for *your* actions. But you know what? I was done being your victim years ago. When I took the reins of my life, I cut out the most toxic family member ever. And it was the right choice, for I have a new family. A found one. And I will fight for them against anyone that dares to hurt them."

"I will be your worst nightmare then, your fears made flesh!" Girolamo writhed in pain as he took a monstrous shape, his voice dropping several octaves.

"Alex was right," Gaby observed as she pulled Golden-hart Special, the guitar strapped across her back, around and with a swift motion, inserted Heartguard and Soulkeeper into the instrument. She found herself unfazed by the monstrous form of her father, an amalgamation of the childhood creatures she imagined hiding inside her closet and her own father. She was frightened no more of the bully that had haunted her youth.

"By now you should have learned that Alex will find the weaknesses, Fionn will make the plan. Sam, Sid, and I will kick your ass. And then there is Kasumi, Joshua, Yoko, Vivi—even Harland the pacifist—to close the deal. Really, you never stood a chance."

"You won't be so confident once after I obliterate Fionn and the Tree. Once you're dying."

"For that, daddy dearest," Gaby said as she finished tuning a string and adjusted the guitar over her left shoulder, "you will have to deal with me first.

"A guitar? What? Your blades are broken still? You can't wield them while playing that thing."

"A guitar forged by the maker of the Tempest Blades and powered by them," Gaby smiled her crooked smile.

"It won't stop me."

"On that, we will have to disagree!" Gaby shouted, her voice rising to a sonic scream, and at the same time she strummed a single note on Goldenhart Special. The sonic boom dispelled the mist, her father—everything. She could see the Tree, a tiny Fionn facing off with a giant demon, and a rain of necrotic meteors on fire descended upon the Life Tree.

I hope the profits were worth more than the memory you became, father.

Gaby played a second riff, and the sonic boom coming from her mouth destroyed a couple of meteors, echoing across all the Tempest, but it wasn't enough. As the first meteor hit the Tree, she doubled over in pain.

She gritted her teeth and strummed a third rift as life slipped from her body.

† † †

Kasumi appeared in front of Alex, who was lying on his back, breathing heavily, spasms wracking his body. Yaha was nowhere to be found, the only traces of a fight were the dissolving remains of a guy in armor with a gaping hole in the chest.

Alex managed a smile for her. "Hello, Snow Princess."

"Hello, Kareshi," Kasumi said softly. She knelt next to Alex and placed her finger on his neck. He was arrhythmic, bound to go into cardiac arrest, again. She bent his knees and placed her demonhunter overcoat below his head. There was nothing to stop a cardiac arrest. Not when he needed to be hit by lightning to fix his cardiac rhythm, and Sam was not around for that. The only source of energy was Alex himself.

There was a pause, and Kasumi had a eureka moment. She opened his vest, exposing his bare chest. There were new cuts that would leave scars. She bent to place her ear on his chest and locate his heart.

"Not sure this is the moment for this, Princess."

"Shut up, Alex," Kasumi scolded him with a chuckle. "I'm about to try something really crazy. You've rubbed off on me too much."

"Double entendre aside," Alex said, wincing, and forced his next breath to come slow. He was trying to calm himself as Kasumi manipulated his body to put him in the position she needed. "I *am* glad to see you."

"Me, too. You tried the kaminariken, right? You know you can't use that technique at will. You barely made it out alive the last time you did."

"Didn't have a choice. Can you tell me again what kareshi means?"

"Boyfriend in Kuni."

"We are married now."

"Not the time for this, *anta*. Do you trust me?"

"With my life."

"Good, because this is going to hurt and I'm not sure if it's gonna work."

"We can go a little crazy."

Kasumi's plan was simple. Use the finger pressure point technique she had taught Alex to bind Joshua's Beast when it was out of control. The side effect of that had been sealing or rerouting energy paths on Joshua's body, which resulted in him able to control the Beast long enough to absorb all the power of the Titan of Fire and become one with it. So, logic dictated that she could reroute Alex's life energy paths the same way, and his own Gifted body would shock his heart till it beat regularly again.

It was a long shot, but it could work—and that made it worth trying.

Kasumi was about to hit the first pressure point, above the liver, when a myriad of voices invaded her head: calling her worthless, weak, a burden to others. Then flying signs appeared in Kuni writing, insulting her more, trying to make her doubt. Usually, she would ignore those like she had done all her life. But this time the voices sounded like Alex's and Sam's, even if Alex was quiet.

And that made her tear up.

Alex noticed the change in her expression.

"He is attacking you with your worst fear," Alex said. "Abaddon. That's how he killed Old Earth. Whatever it is, you are stronger than that. And I need you to be because I think my heart is about to stop."

Kasumi looked at Alex and only saw love in his eyes, his Gift fading away.

"Do you mind my being deaf?"

"No," he said, and took her hand. "I love all of you, ever since the day I met you on that beach. And I'm sure wifey does the same. You are my princess, and the strongest human in the world."

"Thank you," Kasumi said as she turned off her hearing aids, called forth her Gift and used superhuman speed to hit every one of the eleven pressure points on Alex's body. They followed the path of the Dragon Constellation—liver, heart, lungs, plexus, even the forehead—as the voices and words kept assaulting her mind. But she never hesitated.

Kasumi struck each point with such force that she left bruises in Alex's body, the impacts even making him bounce from the ground. When she finished, those bruises glowed with golden light and electrical currents came from them, electrocuting Alex with his own power, restarting his heart as it should have been from the beginning. As the energy subsided, his breathing became regular.

"That hurts," Alex signed to Kasumi. "But if I can do this, I think I'm fine."

Kasumi hugged him with such force she broke a rib.

"Ouch!"

"Sorry," Kasumi said as she turned on her hearing aids. "Can you walk?"

"With help, yes," Alex said as Kasumi helped him to get up and zipped his vest.

They saw a meteor hitting the Tree.

"Aw, crap," both exclaimed in unison. Pain invaded their bodies and a guitar riff echoed through the air.

† † †

Sam found herself floating away in an unknown region of the Tempest, surrounded by dark clouds and shivering in the frigid atmosphere. Most magi that physically enter the Tempest die within minutes because they forgot that the Tempest itself lacked breathable air, unless one arrives ready with an elemental spell to make the Tempest create it. By the time they realized their mistake, they had died of suffocation.

The floating archipelago where the Life Tree resided had its own atmosphere, due magick.

The only reason she remained breathing now, and relatively unhurt, albeit in pain, was that her True Spell, the Bubble Shield accounted for breathable air. Mekiri had made sure of that when she bestowed the Gift upon her favorite magus. And given that it was a True Spell, Sam had cast it subconsciously when she'd been struck by the attack.

Thus, she was inside the bubble, floating away, and pissed off.

At least I managed to warn Dad and Gaby, she thought. *Now I need to find a way to get back there to help.*

A green light caught her attention. She turned her head to her left, wincing in pain. If it weren't for the Gift, she might have ended up with a broken neck. Floating inside the bubble, next to her, was Black Fang. Since she was nine years old, when Fionn rescued and adopted her, Sam had wondered how it would feel to hold it in her hands. But the sword became nothing but dead weight, for it only allowed Fionn to lift it—and, occasionally, Harland, if it was an emergency. Then a few years ago, when Alex told her of his insane plan to stop the Dark Father, he had asked Yaha to bestow the same rights he had to Sam, allowing her to wield it during the fight. At first Yaha had refused, and kept sending electrical discharges across her hands, burning them raw. Sam suspected that was because of how contentious her relationship with Alex was at the time. But once Yaha realized that Sam would give her life to save Alex, even from himself, the mythical Tempest Blade accepted her as its wielder. And since Alex and Sam began their relationship, Sam had used Yaha in missions when Alex was not in the right frame of mind to wield it. It had become *their* Tempest Blade. Even Breaker had allowed her to lift it occasionally without the nipping frostbite, once Kasumi joined their relationship.

But Black Fang was another matter. While the other Tempest Blades had experienced different wielders over the ages, Black Fang had accepted only one person in its long and storied history.

"Look," Sam said tentatively, and extended a hand to grasp at the pommel. "I know I'm not Dad, and you don't like me much, but you *have* known me all my life. And we both are stuck here. I have to grab you to take you with me back to Dad."

She grabbed it and pulled it towards her with haste, hoping that by doing it quickly, the sword wouldn't oppose her. But Black Fang remained as light as a feather in her hands and was in the contrary, glowing as much as it ever did with Fionn.

"Thank you," Sam said to the sword. She knew that to an onlooker it might seem ridiculous, but Sam knew they took things personally. Fury, Joshua's blade, was still pissed off about the death of its original wielder several centuries ago. It didn't help that the current soul inside Fury *was* said wielder. Being polite and asking for consent were the basics if you hoped to wield a Tempest Blade, as was learning to deal with the extra voice in your head when they inevitably responded.

"Now, I need to figure out how to get us back there. Yes, I could fly with a spell, but this is the Tempest. Even if I knew the right direction, it could take us a second or a century to get there and the oxygen in here won't last more than a couple of hours..."

Black Fang vibrated in her hand, like a cellphone with an incoming call. The sheath slid a little, revealing the greyish steel beneath, glowing green. A beam of light pointed towards the darkest of the clouds.

"Are you sure that's the way?"

Black Fang vibrated once more.

"Okay, I trust you. Let's go there. But first a slight tweak."

Sam's irises glowed lilac from her Gift. The bubble reshaped itself, becoming closer to her body, but creating two spheres, one over her head, and another on her back, to contain the remaining oxygen. Her body changed as well, with lilac hair and fox tail. This time, however, a pair of wings made from pure light grew on her back and with a strong flap, sent her and the sword towards the direction Black Fang had indicated.

"I hope we don't encounter one of those ethereal krakens."

Sam arrived at the point the sword had indicated. There was nothing there looking remotely like the Tree archipelago, or even a shortcut. Just dark clouds and a floating iceberg, as large as the Bestial. For a second, in the back of her mind, Sam feared they had travelled back in time and found where the Bestial's corpse had been trapped before being summoned by Byron. But then she reminded herself that time travel didn't work that way, at least according to Alex.

"Are you sure?" Sam muttered. Her stomach was a knot. There was no way to know how much time had transpired, given that time was relative, if it existed in the Tempest at all. "What can be inside this piece of ice that can aid us?"

Lightning cracked in the clouds, illuminating for a moment the shape inside the ice. It was a corpse with milky white eyes, leathery dark skin, and some missing sections of skin and muscle, like something had taken bites from it. It had two horns, broken wings, a row of sharp teeth with one large right black fang and an even larger gap where the left fang should have been. The light released by the sword pointed to that precise gap.

"No way," Sam whispered. A chain of lighting broke the darkness as it arced across the sky and Sam found herself face to face with the corpse of the last dragon: the Montoc Dragon that had helped Asherah in her pilgrimage, the same dragon that had sacrificed himself to destroy the Bestial and save the Freefolk, his body rumored to have become stardust except for his enlarged left fang that held all his powerful magick. The same dragon whose soul now resided in the sword she was holding in her hand.

The Dragon of Myth.

Black Fang.

Sam approached the frozen corpse. While time flow inside the Tempest was, uneven at best, to find the corpse floating, preserved in a decent state was nothing short of miraculous. Then again, Montoc Dragons were rumored to be born out of dying stars and thus, beings of pure magic. As she approached, the ice cover began to crack and disperse, allowing her to touch a spot on his head. It felt cold.

The body is mostly intact, but I would have to use my Gift to repair the wings... what are you thinking? Sam berated herself. But her inner voice, perhaps the part that came from her Gift was having none of that. What am I thinking? That I need to get where my dad and my newly minted husband are before they manage to get themselves killed. That's what I'm thinking. And I have the spell I found at Carpadocci.

Yes, necromancy to enslave a corpse to do your bidding was a taboo. And the Carpadoccian spell had been created for that by human wizards with their rituals. Freefolk eschewed the practice, banishing anyone that tried it, because it meant violating the free will of the soul. Plus, being returned into a rotting, broke corpse. At most, the freefolk allowed summoning the souls of the dead to talk with them. Dawnstar, her ancestor and Fionn's mom, had been an expert on that, and she had taught Gaby... Izia to do it.

So, in a way, I would be following family tradition but with a few tweaks, she thought. *No, it's wrong, that spell is coercive. And Black Fang trusts me, we have the same goal... that's it.*

Sam approached the colossal head and allowed the sword to rest against it.

"Listen. I know that what I'm about to ask you will be painful," Sam said to Black Fang. "But I'm never gonna survive unless I get a little crazy here. And I know you want to help Dad. This is the only way to get there in time. I promise I will share my Gift with you to ease the pain from the broken parts. Do you agree?"

The sword shook on its own volition, glowing with intensity.

"I take that as a yes," Sam said and then looked upwards, more out of custom than because there was an up in the Tempest. "Now, forgive me, Goddess Ishtaru, The Trickster, for abusing your blessing bestowed on me, for I'm about to cast my own created spell, breaking with centuries of tradition."

Sam took a deep breath, her heart beating like a war drum and entering arrhythmia. It was the downside of her Gift. She considered the words she wanted to say, for her spell was more a request than an order. Then she thought in the ancient freefolk language to choose the right words. But her memory wasn't as good, she couldn't translate the last sentence. That one would have to be in Core, in fact, she'd use a line from one of Gaby's new songs.

"Isoide kohl it all San bajbel helgdnl elabora her kendoh. Black Fang Derk! Kitka Yo! Miracles will happen as *I* speak!" she intonated.

The sword vibrated as a green energy engulfed both it and the corpse. Sam had her hopes renewed for a moment, but they amounted to nothing. Total silence. And the sword felt empty, dead. Like a regular sword.

Did I blow it up? Sam thought, frantically trying to find out where she made a mistake. No freefolk since Queen Kary, more than five centuries ago, had dared to create their own spell from scratch, not without extensive research and testing. Only Asherah had been able to create spells on the fly. But Samantha was neither Kary nor Asherah. She felt small.

"C'mon, Dad needs our help!" Sam pleaded, hot tears tightening her throat. "My husband needs my help! My wife might be in danger as well. I don't want them to die! Mekiri please!"

You were allowed to fix Magick, what else do you want? A voice whispered in the air. Sam couldn't be sure who it was. For Mekiri hadn't replied to her prayers since all hell broke loose. Regardless, she took the words as a challenge.

What I want? I want to save my family.

Silence again. Not even thunder in the distance.

"Fine!" She wiped her tears, then screamed into the void. "Damn right I rewrote the rules. This is gonna work because I say so!"

Breathing the last of her oxygen, Sam's eyes became pure light as she merged her Gift with her Freefolk side once more, this time permanently. Resolute, she raised her voice so it could be heard from there to the Heavens, both as a prayer and a challenge of her own. Her words etched themselves in the fabric of the core concept Magick once more. Circles made of light, with runes on them, orbited around her. Her oxygen replenished, while the circles grew to engulf the dragon and sword.

She could hear in the distance a familiar guitar riff. If Gaby was fighting back something with her music, Sam could do the same with her magick.

"Isoide kohl it all San bajbel helgdnl elabora hêr kendoh. Black Fang Derk! Kitka Yo! Miracles will happen as *we* speak!"

Her voice reverberated in the air, as if it had been multiplied by hundreds, and one of the voices sounded inhuman, but equally forceful. As if it had been spoken by a dragon.

A green thunder broke the darkness. The whole place basked in light.

Then she heard something synching with the guitar riff.

A distant roar echoed. The roar of a dragon not heard in centuries. The roar of a dragon as ancient as the stars. The roar of a dragon as powerful as the wielder of his fang, as indomitable as the magus attempting to raise him from the dead by breaking every rule.

The energy circles exploded as green light infused the corpse. As the rest of the ice exploded, the giant eyelid closed and opened three times. By the third blink, it opened, and instead of a milky white dead eye, there was a glowing green eye, staring at her.

† † †

The Tempest Blades tolerated no owners; they had chosen wielders, partners, friends. And like the Blades themselves, their wielders had been forged by the difficulties in their lives. All the fights they prevailed upon. Just for a moment like this. For they were the true Blades of the Tempest.

Chapter 13
Hope

"TALK?" FIONN ECHOED, SURPRISED. HE hadn't seen that coming. He jumped down from the colossal root where he had been meditating but kept close to the Tree. There was a knot in the bottom of his stomach and worry gnawed at him for the others.

But he knew better. They were more than capable of handling themselves after all they had gone through. He had to face his real fear, for this was the only real chance they had to end this.

Fionn's pulse raced.

I can do this, he thought. *I have to do this.*

He steeled himself. His role was to protect the Life Tree from Abaddon, no matter what. This was going to be one shot in a million. The proverbial Call of Destiny. All or nothing.

It all came down to him and his choices from this point on.

"Well, beat the crap out of you for fun, too, but mostly talk. I can multitask," Abaddon said, running for the Tree, forcing Fionn to come out into the open and intercept him.

"I have an offer for you: Join me!" Abaddon said as he threw the first punch, forcing Fionn to block with his forearms. It healed so fast he didn't even realize it had been broken.

"Wait, what?" Fionn replied, surprised.

"There might be an opening in army quite soon, depending on how the Deacon does against your student." Abaddon threw a kick.

"The Deacon? The serial killer?" Fionn asked, deflecting the kick. The density of the demon's body made each hit feel was being caused by a block of tungsten.

"Correction, the god of serial killers. The one you never caught," Abaddon countered, referring to the only open cold case Fionn couldn't solve as Justicar.

"You know he's gonna lose," Fionn said. He trusted Alex to take care of that fight on his own. After the Dark Father and Shemazay, The Deacon wouldn't be much of an issue.

"I don't care about the result." Abaddon threw a haymaker. "All is the same for me."

"Then why offer me his spot if it's all the same for you? Oblivion," Fionn replied with a jab to the plexus, the force enough to stop Abaddon in his tracks.

"I have found it useful to recruit certain beings. Most demons from the Pits are too unreliable, too savage, to serve as anything more than as cannon fodder." Abaddon continued to throw punches, which Fionn blocked, as he talked. "Corrupting the other inhabitants, and making them devils has a downside, for they are bound by nature to follow a single goal. Mabuse, the Deacon is like that—solely focused on killing sentient beings. He did it here, he did it on old Earth, and while that created fear, it didn't help to advance the cause." Abaddon swept at Fionn's legs, but Fionn jumped and somersaulted over the attack.

"Orionians, they are useful, but cowardly. I could have asked the samoharo, finest warriors in the universe. But they are too honor bound. Eldara, your ancestors, pitiful beings were happy to let themselves be eaten by a black hole of my creation, if Ishtaru hadn't found them first. Humans, they are easy to sway, but too unpredictable and weak." He threw several rapid jabs that Fionn was scarcely able to block.

"But you, the Gifted that Ishtaru created, you are another thing entirely. Your kind has proven capable of killing your superiors. And of all the Gifted, you have the best qualities of the three pest species. You have war skills unlike anyone else. I will need those qualities and skills when I raze Last Heaven." Abaddon threw a punch that slipped past Fionn's defense, and it struck his jaw with a crunch of bone.

Fionn staggered back. The pain was there for the briefest of moments before his jaw pulled itself back into shape, healing. "I thought you only needed to destroy the Tree to unravel the Universe," Fionn pointed out.

"Unravel, yes, but the silly beings you called gods will oppose me. This battle is being fought in different realms and times as we speak." Abaddon this time aimed to break Fionn's knee, but he managed to evade the attack by millimeters.

A point of light appeared in the distance floating beyond the edge of the island. The point grew into a tiny disc, a portal. Fionn could have sworn he saw a red and black raven and dark eagle flying nearby. A slashing strike whipped by his ear in a near miss.

"You want me to kill the gods for you? You got the wrong guy for the job." Fionn punched Abaddon dead in the face. He was satisfied to see it whip backwards.

"If you mean your student or your daughter, no. They have to die. They're too hopeful, too spirited. I might even let your wife live, unlike last time I made this offer. And only because the human that offered his existence for me to take it had a certain fondness for her." Abaddon shrugged and smiled, baring a row of shark-like teeth.

"If you have the memories of her father, you know she won't accept. What makes you think I will?"

"Because—aside from my generous payment in sparing her—I know you, better than you yourself do. You are jaded. Since the day you lost your father, you've become disappointed in the world. You did what you did, becoming this sort of *hero* because you were fooled by your education. The Great War certainly did a number on you. It was splendid entertainment for those of us trapped in the Pits. And when Luykerion trapped you there for what must have been years for your soul, just to prove a point to Ishtaru, I could smell the growing despair inside of you. The realization that nothing really mattered. I laughed got a good long laugh out of it all, and I wasn't the only one."

The memories came to Fionn's mind like a rushing river during monsoon. The laugh. He'd heard that laugh. This time, the memories were more than mere nightmares. It had been real, not something his delirious mind had created to deal with the searing pain of his body undergoing complete regeneration. Knowing that such a harrowing experience, now vivid resurfacing memories, was a result of Ben Erra, the Judge of the Freefolk pantheon, sent his blood to the boiling point. He wanted to cave the Judge's face in. But given that Ben Erra was nowhere near, Abaddon had to suffice.

Instead of punching Abaddon, Fionn summoned all the energy around him, and pushed it in a single beam by extending his hands, unleashing a kaminariken at point blank on Abaddon's face, caving it in as desired. The demon now had a donut for a head: no eyes, no nose, no mouth. But he remained standing as if had been a mere slap in the wrist. A mosquito bite.

And yet he laughed with that terrible, inhuman, eldritch laugh that was impossible to replicate by any organ from a being evolved under the usual rules of nature. It was the laugh of something that was begotten in the indescribable realms that existed before the Known Universe. And for the first time it dawned, it truly dawned, on Fionn what kind of monster he was facing. For Abaddon kept laughing while his head regenerated. And while he did that, he grabbed Fionn's right hand, and with a swift movement, broke it. This left Fionn open to another attack, which Abaddon took advantage of by punching Fionn so hard in the chest that it felt as though the First Demon's hand had gone through to the other side.

If it weren't for his Gift working overtime, Fionn would have died then and there. Now, he was only in pain.

"Yarghhh!" Fionn cried.

Abaddon's mouth recreated itself as he spoke. "You of all people must have come to the same conclusion as me. The Universe doesn't care about you. After I finish here, no one will care. Humans had more than one thousand genres of music. All gone and no one cared. Old Earth had more than eight million species. Only a few hundred survive here. And no one cared. Despite what your Trickster Goddess must have told you to keep you under her thumb as a pet, a mere pawn, there is no great destiny, no mysterious plan, no universal mind wanting to know itself. There is no reason for any of this to exist. This is not even a random occurrence that means that life is a miracle. There is nothing at the beginning, and there will be nothing at the end. Just painful failure after failure. Nothing you accomplish will matter. So why not end all of this once and for all? Instead of helping to prolong suffering with every universal cycle, rebooting itself in an eternal recurrence that will amount to nothing but the same oblivion. You of all people should see the futility of trying to save a world that will disappoint you with the horrors that you sentient beings inflict upon each other. All your sacrifices just stalled the inevitable."

"I'm not buying your sales pitch," Fionn ground out between clenched teeth.

"If you join me in destroying everything, including the gods that toyed with your soul, I will allow your consciousness to exist in the entropy where we reside, were nothing will disappoint you. Eternal bliss, because there it won't matter anymore. This is an Eternal Recurrence Cycle, repeating over and over. In a multiverse of possibilities every story ends the same: with us winning, for we represent the fundamental concept of the end of all things. Including death. Nothing will die because nothing will exist but us, as befitting an uncaring random probabilistic event of particles acting in a particular way. Even the being you call Kaan'a is nothing but a random occurrence from a previous universe, taking its place now. Nothing you do has or will matter. So why fight me? Why cling to hope? Be a good random piece of matter, either join me or sit down and let me finish this. You earned that rest. Why keep fighting when all you have been fed is a lie?"

Fionn remained silent for a long time, breathing heavily through his mouth and nose. He was tired, exhausted. And even in spite of his healing factor, bleeding internally. There was a certain degree of truth to Abaddon's words: he had sacrificed his family for the sake of the Alliance, only for it to break at the first opportunity, forgoing any long-lasting peace. He had sacrificed his mental health to keep others afloat. For what?

For what? I will always love you, in this life or another, Izia told him once. And when he married Gaby, she had said exactly the same thing. And that had given him the meaning. Love. He loved his wife in this life and in a past one. He loved his daughters, both the first and the adoptive. He loved his students-turned-friends. He loved when Gaby smiled at him while composing a new song. He loved when Sam challenged authority to do the right thing for a cause she believed in. He loved when Alex talked endlessly about his latest geeky subject with a wide grin, even if Fionn could barely follow half of it. He loved how Kasumi took every opportunity to defy expectations. How Joshua worked so hard to improve himself, even if he didn't recall what he'd done wrong. How Yokoyawa saw everything with exasperating philosophy. How Sid pushed to reach the stars. How Vivi had decided to jump in with them instead of living a calm life, and did so with glee. How Harland poured heart and soul to lead and lift others up, even if he doubted himself. He loved the laughter, the music, even the sad moments; because they meant something happy took place as well before or after. Past or future, didn't matter. Not even the present. The answer to the question, the things that truly mattered at the end, which would allow him to do what he knew he had to do, despite the fear that gnawed his heart.

It's not the journey that matters; it's with whom you shared it.

For the first time in his life, he was at total peace.

He spat the blood clot in his mouth, molar included, and smiled at Abaddon the wolf's smile.

"You know what?" Fionn said as he blocked every single punch and kick from Abaddon. "You might be right, the world sucks. And maybe nothing we do matters. Which is why everything we chose to do matters. And right now, I chose to stand up to you. So, you can shove your offer where the sun doesn't shine."

"I knew that would be your answer. The previous guy said something similar. And in the previous universe I heard the same from Kaan'a. The result is always the same: nothing you do will matter. Not now, not in a million years."

"If nothing I do will matter, why not try everything and anything? Because all that matters is what we do with the time we have, with the people we love. Our choices. And I choose to fight. You will have to go through me to touch that Tree."

"Talk like a real fool. Enough of this."

"You didn't want to talk. You were just stalling. Until your forces could get here."

"Something I learned from you humans. I also wanted to see something."

"What?"

"Existence is painful for me. I wanted to share that pain with you and see if you would break like the human that fought me right here ages ago. When I gave him the same offer. After I killed his wife and his newborn child. After I took his allies and world from him. Like I'm doing with you. Even with his pithy, momentary victory, grief consumed him the rest of his days. But I give you this, the other guy fought while broken. You haven't. If I cared, I would respect that. It doesn't matter anyway."

CRAKOOM!

BOOM!

"You heard that? It's the sound of inevitability."

"I'm so gonna kill you," Fionn growled.

"I think not," Abaddon snatched Fionn's left leg with such speed that he had no time to react. The Demon crushed his femur like a dry log and threw Fionn against the tree as if he were a ragdoll, the force of the impact knocking all the air out of his lungs. He lands next to smaller roots near a human ruin.

He hit the ground with a muffled grunt, Fionn's healing factor already hard at work. His body emitted green speckles of light like erratic, dancing fireflies. Any other person would have fallen unconscious. Instead, he willed himself to his feet. As he did so, something heavy fell from the top of the tree and landed between him and Abaddon.

It was a giant head that resembled a jaguar and a serpent. And the way it had been separated from its body, indicated the use of a high-powered laser. Only one thing had that kind of weapon. Fionn smiled, as the First Demon let out a startled, "What?"

Fionn smiled. "I think my family wants to have a say."

"Enough," Abaddon said. He raised his hand and in the sky several portals opened, unleashing a rain of meteors against the tree. Fionn saw the first one hit a branch, which rotted and became dust in what seemed like milliseconds. Those were not regular meteors. These accelerated the decomposition of regular matter, like a fungal rot.

The Life Tree shook in pain, and Fionn swore he heard it scream.

It would take a miracle, or a crazy plan, for Fionn to save the Tree now. But something caught his eye, an obsidian arrow tip. The kind of tips that never lost their keen edge.

Whatever Fionn did would end in a lot of pain.

The whole island became full of fire and smoke.

And everything, everywhere stopped, as all life could feel their souls were being ripped from their bodies.

† † †

His existence was painful. It was an inalienable fact. But Fionn knew one thing: no one would survive if he didn't do something. Meditating under the Tree hadn't been only to assuage his fears of dying now that he had a lot to live for. It had been to commune with the Tree, much like the Freefolk did with the Ancestors' trees in the Mistlands. To be part of the greater network of lives that made the universe. And that had given him an idea.

Alex, after their fight at Saint Lucy, had asked him in private if he thought less of him because of his mental health problems. That maybe it wasn't a good idea to have a student so crazy. At first Fionn was about to reply with a standard comforting reply, an empty one. But instead, Fionn had hugged him and told him that he wished he were as half as 'crazy' as Alex was, because it meant he could see the world in a different manner, and that he was proud of him for achieving what he had while having dealt with his illness. And that he knew Alex would care for Samantha always. Because 'crazy' people could be heroes too.

It had changed their relationship, from mentor and student to brothers.

Time to be the crazy hero, little brother, Fionn thought as he dragged himself toward the nearest root. It was a small, blue, energy like tendril, wriggling around as the Tree received impact after impact from Abaddon's meteor necrotic attacks. It was a long shot, a one in a billion shot, but it was the only idea he had left. Because the crazy makes their own miracles. Fionn grabbed the obsidian arrow tip, sharp as any scalpel, and cut deep into his right arm. Before his healing factor kicked in, Fionn pushed the root deep inside his arm with a muffled groan of pain. Forge had mentioned that the roots of the Tree had the ability to copy or learn from the Gift. Maybe it would learn from his. The injury sealed around the root, and he lost the strength in his legs. He looked up as the last and biggest meteor was about to hit the Tree and closed his eyes, focusing all of his Gift, burning the core to the maximum, not to heal his arm, but in sending its healing energy to the tree.

While Fionn didn't believe in fate, destiny, or even coincidences, he believed that everything was connected one way or another. And if his nightmares had been right, if his soul had climbed out from Hell through a glowing green root of the Tree, there was a chance that event had changed his Gift to what it was now. And if that was correct, it was time to return the favor.

The world shook around him, and clouds of dust covered the place. His heart stopped beating.

† † †

"The Life Tree is gone and with it, the last barrier before the universe is undone. Now, time to destroy—" Abaddon said. But he was cut off as a shadow emerged from the dust cloud. A gentle breeze cleared the air, showing that the Life Tree was still alive and standing. The damage from the meteors was healing.

"It can't be," Abaddon hissed.

Fionn stood between the Demon and the Tree, alone, dizzy, weakened, with the root inserted into his arm serving as some sort of IV. He looked haggard and tired, bleeding from different parts of his body that couldn't heal properly, but he started at the Demon in defiance.

Fionn laughed, raw and ragged. "Yes, it can." He could feel every hit on the Tree as if it were in his own body, the most excruciating pain any living being could suffer. A thousand deaths per second. Not like Fionn cared anymore, as he stood defiantly. "I told you I would keep fighting."

"...You're crazy," Abaddon gasped, shocked for the first time in his unfathomably long existence.

Fionn smiled through gritted teeth, tasting blood. "And proudly so."

"Clever idea," Abaddon said slowly as he approached Fionn. His right hand shifted into a large axe. "But you only gave it a few moments of respite, because once I kill you for good, it won't heal anymore." He raised the blade above their heads.

Fionn braced for impact, all his focus on healing the Tree. If he managed to endure a few more seconds for someone else to arrive with help, all would have been worth it.

No, that will take too long. I need to move without dislodging the root.

Abaddon swung the unforgiving axe in a downward arc.

Sparks appeared in Fionn's left hand, and a beam of light appeared there, taking a familiar shape.

Abaddon's axe bounced with a resounding clang, deflected, while at the same moment there was a brilliant flash of light and the boom of thunder that blinded and deafened Fionn and Abaddon for a second. As Fionn recovered he saw Yaha, tightly grasped in his left hand unleashing a storm of electrical currents that pushed Abaddon back.

The Sword of Hope had arrived.

Fionn could feel his second wind. The Tree was not only absorbing his healing factor but was sending him—for lack of a better word—vitality in exchange. Abaddon unleashed a barrage of attacks at Fionn, which he parried with Yaha with an economy of movement despite the fact that each impact rattled his bones. Fionn ignored it, he was going to stand his ground as long as he could. His Gift exploded with a level of energy he never had, greater than what he used to defeat the alien ships. And with each explosion, green wings flashed on his back.

"Fine," Abaddon said. "I will remove your arm and that dammed root before killing you and the tree. As the prophecy said, you will die alone."

A sonic boom hit Abaddon with all its strength, peeling away a layer of leathery skin. As he tried to regain his footing, a kick to the head sent him reeling back several meters. In front of Fionn, Gaby stood holding two Tempest Blades glowing red and blue. Her irises were pure light. Energy crackled around her. And she was pissed off. Not even the Infinity Pits would ever witness such fury as a woman protecting her family.

"Leave my husband alone," Gaby said, as the ground beneath her began to crack. She took a deep breath, and she unleashed a second sonic scream on Abaddon, damaging what was left of his humanoid shape.

Abaddon was left with only wet muscular tissue and sinew. He leaned into the continuous sonic, shark-like teeth bared in a lipless grin fit for the undead. He sprinted at Gaby, axe arm raised.

BOOM!

Abaddon stopped. His arm was gone at the elbow. The stump iced over, the tissue scared with electrical burns. He turned to his left and growled. Fionn looked over and smiled.

"I was aiming for his head," Alex complained as he drew another energy arrow. Electricity crackled across his body. Kasumi was next to him, the ground freezing around her feet. Her left hand was on Alex's shoulder, which would explain the freezing damage on Abaddon's arm. She was sharing her Gift with Alex, who looked beaten up and exhausted, but kept shooting arrows to keep Abaddon at bay.

She finally learned to control her Gift, Fionn thought.

"He has a big one, you will hit the next one, anta," Kasumi said as Breaker, in her right hand, glowed eager to score the Demon's flesh.

"Pathetic mortals!" Abaddon declared. "You think this silly performance scares me? I command all the mewling beings of the Pits. I am Oblivion made..."

A ball of fire sucker punched him in what would be the stomach, and Abaddon's hulking frame landed in a heap. The ball of fire turned into a shadow that retracted to reveal Joshua, holding the ever-burning Fury.

"The mewling beings from the Pits say hi, we want our dimension back," Joshua said, as the Beast growled and floated as a tattered cape made of shadows behind him.

"You traitor. I will cut..."

Two hydra heads struck Abaddon in the face like great serpents. Even as he tried to stand, two vines broke from the ground and whipped around him.

"Nah nah," Sid said, sitting on the shoulders of Yokoyawa, with Vivi walking along. He showed his bandaged stump. "If anyone is gonna cut something, it's me. You owe me one hand. I want all of yours in payment."

"And with interest," Vivi added.

"You think I feel fear?" Abaddon scoffed. "With all of you here, there is no way you can stop this!"

Abaddon ripped what remained of his right arm off and flung it into the air. That arm bled into two large birdlike creatures, flying straight at the Tree. "I need only to win once."

A blast of green-lilac fire hit both demonic birds, sending their smoldering remains crashing into the ground.

Abaddon positively seethed as he conjured forth ten demons from his flesh. "Attack!"

The ten demons raced towards the Band, who defiantly braced for them. But those demons stopped in their tracks as a roar echoed through the Tempest, followed by gusts of wind. A roar not heard in centuries. A large shadow approached the ruins beneath the Tree.

"Is that a dragon roar?" Gaby asked Fionn.

"She did it!" Vivi exclaimed, delighted.

"I owe her a pizza," Alex muttered to Kasumi, who chuckled good-naturedly.

A second fireball hit the demons, reducing them to ash. From the sky, a dragon descended at full speed and landed in front of the Tree. It perched on a wall of the ruins. It was larger than the Figaro. Parts of it had been replaced with energy constructs made of pure magick. Its eyes were glowing with a bright green energy. A familiar sword was embedded in its neck, also glowing brightly.

"You'll need more than that," Sam declared triumphantly. "My friend here wants in, and he's every bit as pissed as I am."

"How?" Fionn asked, taken aback. As a child he'd always dreamed of seeing a dragon. And now, after a lifetime, here one was: The legendary dragon that had befriended Asherah. The protector of the Freefolk. The one whose soul powered his fangsword. Black Fang the dragon, looked at Fionn, who could have sworn that the dragon winked at him before staring at Abaddon and roaring once more, the deep sound reverberating in their very bones. It was good to have his longtime friend back, even if it was in a new shape.

"Black Fang decided to help you, but thought that being a fangsword was not enough, so we reached consent," Sam said as she caught her quarterstaff, which Gaby tossed at her. "And I'm the DragonQueen now. I get to rewrite the rules!"

"It doesn't matter!" Abaddon retorted, having freed himself from the vines, his body growing in size with each step, his muscles releasing heat and vapor with every movement. "Even with that zombie, you can't fight all my army!"

Thousands of portals opened behind him, including the first one Fionn hadn't lost track of. But while the others closed as soon as an army of ground and flying demons, led by the remaining members of Abaddon's one hundred and eight demons, appeared, the first one only grew. And its edges were white, instead of the orange demonic ones.

"And I assure you Greywolf, when I'm done here, I will make sure that you die last, in abyssal darkness. Alone."

As one of the flying incursions went for the Tree, an energy beam hit it from behind the tree. It was an energy beam like the ones the Figaro shot.

"He is not alone. None of them are while I'm here," Harland's voice could be heard through the air, coming from the massive samoharo iron bird war cruiser. "This is Harland Rickman, commander of the Theian Alliance. This will be your only warning: go into that portal and never return, or you will know true reckoning."

"Never!"

The ship fired on a fifth of the demonic army, obliterating it. A demon broke ranks and ran towards the Tree, with an axe made of dark matter ready to hit the nearest root. But the demon found himself crashing against an invisible shield, to be decapitated by the Solarian Knight Drakarolov. From the war cruiser a large group of people descended. Freefolk led by Stealth, surrounded the Life Tree on the blind side of the Band, casting in unison the largest defensive magick shield in history. A small group of titan fighters, those saved by Alex and Kasumi months before, and led by Simon Belerofont and Bev Johnson. Bev gave a thumbs up to Alex. And next to them, a group of demonhunter led by Hiroyuki Kuromatsu, the rival that Kasumi had defeated at the Games. The man bowed to her and ordered his people around.

"Demonhunters! This is what we trained all our lives for! The Great Hunt is here! Commander Harland gave us our orders," Hiroyuki yelled. "Nothing touches the Tree. Not while we breathe!"

Lastly, a final group of soldiers descended from the ship. It was the samoharo tactical squad to which Sid had belonged at one time. With them was Scud, Dr. Tze Tze and his team, all making a mad dash towards the Figaro, carrying a hodgepodge of equipment to repair it and get it back into battle.

"Eagle Warriors, Jaguar Warriors," the samoharo commanding the ship said through the comms. "Earn back your honor. Defend this place. Follow the path set by our siblings!"

"I can't believe it," Sid whispered as he jumped to the ground.

"You convinced them, cousin," Yoko said simply. "Or shamed them, either way it worked."

Fionn's eyes welled up as Alex and Gaby stood next to him. Sam took to the skies again with Black Fang. He was lost for words. He knew his family would come through, but he'd never expected to get reinforcements like this. As small an army as it was, it was more than he'd ever dreamed possible. Fionn offered Yaha back to Alex, for he was its actual wielder, after all.

Alex shook his head. "Keep it for now." He pushed his sword back to Fionn. "You need a sword while yours is powering a dragon body. I still have my bow."

"You will need your arm free and healed," Vivi said, as she extracted the root with care and began healing Fionn's arm. "The rest of our people will take on healing the Tree. I, on the other hand, will heal you."

"Call it, Fionn," Gaby said, grabbing his right hand as it was being healed. "We are here, ride or die, with you. Always."

Fionn looked at Gaby for a second and saw the same defiant look in her eyes and Izia had when they fought Byron together a century ago. He took a deep breath and moved in front of the group. He raised Yaha, whose blade exploded into pure light. This was it. All or nothing. The Journeys' End.

"Protect the Tree," Fionn screamed as he aimed Yaha at Abaddon, then growled at the demon. "But he is ours!"

Fionn's irises glowed with an intensity never seen. His Gift, free from healing the Tree, was burning at full power with one goal.

It would be the fight of a lifetime.

† † †

"This little show of grandstanding doesn't impress me. While my lesser demons destroy your lesser allies and gnaw the Tree. I and my One Hundred Eight demons will..."

"Eleven," Alex interrupted as he created a new arrow in his Thunderbow. "You only have eleven. We have destroyed ninety-seven since you destroyed Saint Lucy. I personally ripped the arms off a few of them. That felt nice."

Black Fang unleashed a stream of fire so hot the flame was blue verging on white, disintegrating three more of the demons."

"Make that a hundred gone," Sam added. "Nice round number."

"We will destroy you all!" one of the remaining demons snarled.

"I don't think so," Fionn said as Yaha glowed in his hand and that demon's head fell from its body. It was a strange feeling to use another sword instead of Black Fang. Nonetheless, he felt at ease, looking at the people standing next to him, who had endured so much and yet prevailed at every time by never giving up.

Never had a more capable Band of Heroes existed, a familiar voice said inside his head, as a red and black raven flew over their heads. *I'm proud.* Even Mekiri, in her diminished state kept fighting. It made Fionn smile, because it meant that Abaddon was shaken as well.

Abaddon pointed his right arm at Fionn. It transformed into a dark energy blade. His surviving demons ran to meet the Band of the Greywolf, who met their charge without hesitation.

Yokoyawa ran at a heavily armored demon, scimitar ready to strike when a teleporting tomahawk appeared in front of him, flying straight at the demon's eyes. Sid slid under the demon's legs, punching it in a weak spot with his left hand. As he passed below, he caught his teleporting tomahawk. The demon stopped for a second, barely blocking Yoko's big swing at its head.

"I had him," Yokoyawa said.

"So did I," Sid countered with a grin.

A female demon-witch cast a spell made of black arrows at Vivi, who countered with a levitation spell. She dodged the arrows as they exploded around her. Vivi countered with her own spell, returning the favor with a rain of thorns that shredded one arm of the witch. The demon-witch, annoyed, supercharged a magick spell aimed at Vivi, who stood her ground by summoning an energy shield composed of green winds.

A second demon-witch joined the first, her twin, and both prepared a second blast, joining their spells together into a massive energy ball. Their attack never came to fruition, as both were in turn blasted clean out of existence by a stream of dragon breath as Sam flew by on Black Fang.

As the battle brewed around them, Fionn and Abaddon clashed. Incessant, they leapt from one floating stone or small island to another, equally matched. Abaddon cut in half the stone on which they were standing. As Fionn evaded the cut, Yaha fell to the ground below. Alex ran over and threw it back to Fionn. It teleported back into Fionn's hand.

"Don't lose my stuff!" Alex shouted at him.

Fionn didn't see a long-haired demon about to slash his back. But its attack was deflected by a whirlwind in the shape of two twin blades joined as one, Heartguard and Soulkeeper, followed by a sonic scream that sent the demon crashing into a wall.

"Thank you!" Fionn called out, Gaby at his back.

Gaby grinned as she caught her Tempest Blades and split them once more. "I said in my wedding vows that I will always have your back." Gaby ran at the long-haired demon. It pulled a guitar axe out of thin air to face her.

A demon dressed like a haunted house worker floated in the air, throwing energy spheres at Joshua and Kasumi, who ran in a zig-zag to evade them. Joshua made a couple of hand signals, to which Kasumi replied, splitting up. Joshua then created a ball of fire in his hands as the Beast shielded him from the explosions. He threw the ball at the demon's head, who tilted its head to the right to let the ball pass. But Kasumi had jumped behind the demon, using the Tree's branches as springboards and, with the aid of Breaker, volleyed the energy ball back at the demon like a game of demented tennis. It struck the demon square in the back, setting it ablaze.

Another demon, wearing robes and large pauldrons, resembling a sculpture of the Dark Father, targeted Alex mercilessly, be it by an edged weapon or with purple magick spheres that crackled with electricity. Alex dodged every attack and pulled the sai he had been gifted by the Elder Ice People from his bracer to deflect the few ones too close to comfort. It had been engraved with runes by the Elder Ice People to make it sturdy as an iceberg. For someone that had been on the verge of another cardiac arrest, he felt reinvigorated, no doubt in part to Gaby's song echoing through the sound system of the grounded Figaro, as it underwent repairs, and in part because the Life Tree itself was lending them the same vitality it had bestowed on Fionn.

"Who do you think you are, Godkiller?" the demon challenged Alex, who jumped onto the lower branches of the Tree. "A weapons master? An artificer?"

Alex swung from a vine that Vivi grew in his path to launch himself into the air, as he charged an energy arrow with the Thunderbow, unleashing it at the demon's head.

"You know?" Alex exclaimed with a laugh. "I like that one better!"

Fionn and Abaddon kept clashing swords, each blow stronger than the previous one, sending shockwaves everywhere.

If we keep this pace, Abaddon won't have to touch the Tree to kill it—our battle will do it for him, Fionn thought, narrowly evading a stream of acid spewed by a flying demon. Black Fang and Sam raced through the sky to get it away from Fionn. Black Fang used what remained of his sharp teeth to rip the head off the demon, while Sam jumped off Black Fang and cast an ice dagger the size of trike to pierce its heart.

Sam landed next to her dad, as Gaby, with a kick, buried the long-haired demon into the ground and unleashed a sonic scream point blank to obliterate its head.

The Band of the Greywolf surrounded Abaddon.

Abaddon, enraged, crossed his arms in front of his chest as the remains of his special demons, defeated by the Band, flew across the battlefield to enter his body. Abaddon screeched at the sky, unleashing a column of dark energy that summoned dark stormy clouds. He opened his arms, unleashing a blast of necrotic energy and heat that knocked everyone away, even taking down Black Fang from the skies. Sam's True Spell barely managed to contain the blast and keep everyone alive, but the necro energy sapped most of her energy.

Abaddon's body grew into the shape of a flayed giant, and he grabbed Fionn by the leg. Upon smashing him several times into the ground, he flung the unconscious man at Gaby, sending both flying backwards. Only Sam's timely intervention saved them from further injury. She ran to her dad and Gaby. Sam looked for Vivi, but she was lying unconscious not far from away, next to Sid. Exhausted, Sam used the last of her magick reserves to heal them.

Abaddon approached her, raising his fist which transformed into a meteor attached to an arm.

† † †

"You won't let me get closer to that tree? Fine. I will instead destroy the island itself while you float away in the Tempest!" Abaddon said as he aimed to crush Sam under his fist.

"Oh no you won't," Alex whispered as he ran, his arms extended, and fists closing as he approached the point of impact. "Sam, shield to the ground!"

His movements grew slower with each step, as if he were dragging a granite obelisk. Sam knew very well what he was doing. He never shut up about that.

Sam cast her Bubble Shield, but instead of a sphere, she shaped it as a disk covering a large area on the ground.

Abaddon's fist dropped. When it hit, its pressure would crush everyone below. But it never reached them. The asteroid-like fist stopped less than two meters from the ground. Abaddon pushed down to no avail. There was someone pushing against him.

Below his fist, using all the electromagnetic field from the Tempest itself that he could gather during his run, his arm bracers crackling with the resulting electricity, stood Alex, lifting an amount of weight that he never could have dreamt of.

"My back is going to kill me after this," Alex muttered through gritted teeth.

"Lift with your legs!" Kasumi yelled running towards the battle, while Gaby dragged a concussed Fionn from under the fist.

"How?" Gaby asked.

"Warptrain, remember?" Alex said. "But unlike then, I don't have a broken arm."

Alex shoved upwards and sent Abaddon reeling back. He then extended his right arm and Yaha rematerialized there.

"I'm gonna take her back if you don't mind, Fionn."

"What are you doing?" Gaby asked.

"Being the walls, like the vows said, so you three can come back here with a better plan, compared to what I'm about to do,"

"Alex..." Sam called him.

He winked at both of them. "Not planning to die, today of all days," he said, then turned to face Abaddon, who was recovering from being pushed back, never taking his eyes from the Demon.

Alex stood in the middle of the battlefield, Yaha in hand, as Abaddon approached. They stood face to face. If Alex had learned anything from dealing with these so-called deities, it was that they had gigantic egos. Abaddon was not an exception. If anything, the Founders' plan became clearer: by trapping him in different—relatively—mortal avatars, they forced him to go native to further his plans. He had done it when slowly corrupting Old Earth's inhabitants. He had done it here. Despite its horrific, maddening visage, that barely registered for Alex at that point and being made of strange matter that had to adapt to the world's rules. Abaddon was still stuck following the same rules of materialization in the real world, which meant he could be harmed in a significant way, regardless that he was more powerful than any of the other divine avatars Alex had encountered. Alex couldn't avoid musing if somehow the Trickster Goddess had set him onto this path for this precise day. But that would require believing in fate and Alex—like Fionn—didn't entertain those ideas.

Then again, none of the minor demons dared to get closer. Rather, they were encircling them.

The breathing of the demon was heavy, but calm. More to impress than to bring air to his lungs, if he had them. The body was emitting too much steam, which meant that he was using more energy than any other avatar.

Perhaps he is still unstable from joining all his parts? Alex thought, as he glanced at movement to his left, a shadow jumping from branch to branch to reach altitude.

"Ah, now I get a one on one with the so-called 'God-killer,'" Abaddon said. "When I saw you alive after your encounter with the Deacon, I was hoping for this."

"I hate that nickname," Alex scoffed.

"Are you not a killer of gods?"

"I can't deny, since I just added a third one." Alex showed a third mark in his left bracer. "I don't mind adding a fourth."

"How dare a worthless human defy a deity! Don't you fear gods? Your superiors?"

"You just bought your own publicity, didn't you? And, no, for the record, I don't believe in gods. But I believed in the one that was my friend!"

Alex jumped and punched Abaddon, taking the First Demon by surprise.

"That one and the following are for Mekiri, you sonuva—" Alex said, while he waited for the demon to get up. He was being realistic. His odds of defeating Abaddon on his own were lower than in any other fight. But that was not Alex's goal, he had enough experience by now to know he didn't have to do everything. He needed to keep Abaddon busy long enough until the person that could beat him was ready to do so.

"You know you will fail, right? You are a disgrace to—" Abaddon pontificated.

"Yeah, yeah, keep yapping. It doesn't matter. You won't get inside my head ever again," Alex rebuked him.

"And you think you can kill me?"

"I will do what I must," Alex said as Yaha glowed with the same pure energy when they'd faced the Dark Father.

"You will die, braver than most, but like all do," Abaddon

growled, transforming his regenerated arm into an energy blade of dark light.

Both weapons clashed in an exchange of vicious slashes and parries. In a way, challenging Fionn to a duel some months ago had allowed Alex to see if he was up to the task of wielding a sword. He had never been the best sword-fighter, but after the Games he'd worked hard to become better.

And right now, he only needed to be marginally better than Abaddon for enough time for Fionn and the rest to recover from the demon's massive shockwave.

The duel continued, moving around the ruins, Alex using the walls to compensate for the height difference, leading the demon as far as he could from the Tree, towards the edge of the island. Abaddon was even stronger than Shemazay. Each strike cracked the ground beneath them.

"I see you improved since you fought one of my other selves," Abaddon said. "But that only means that you will lose later than expected!"

The demon cleaved his sword on the cobbled floor of the ruins, breaking the ground under Alex. Alex fell. Abaddon looked from above and tried to crush him with the debris.

"Or maybe not," Abaddon laughed, turning his back to the crater. A piece of wall hit him on the back of the head. The crater exploded in debris as Alex pushed them around using his Gift to get free.

Abaddon barely had time to react as Alex unleashed a series of attacks with Yaha, leaving cuts all over the demon's body. Abaddon aimed at Alex's chest, but he ducked to avoid the slash, taking advantage of being shorter, and then made a vertical strike, slicing off the demon's hand for a second time. Abaddon jumped back onto the island, while Alex chased him to push the advantage. Several smaller demons joined in to come between Alex and Abaddon, but Alex closed his free hand and a rain of debris from the ruins flew at his command, hitting them like shrapnel.

"Impressive," Abaddon admitted. "Quite impressive. Not even the original Iskandar fought like that. And he saw those moves in a movie from Old Earth. But the only thing you have achieved are some small irritations and cutting off an arm that can regenerate. None of that matters. You can't defeat me on your own."

"I know," Alex said, lowering his head and Yaha, seemingly defeated. He then looked up, grinning. He had learned his lesson. "But I don't have to."

Abaddon saw two blades, one made of fire, the other as dark as the night sky, falling upon him. The First Demon had to jump back, almost falling from the island, and received two deep gashes in his chest.

"Took you long enough to get here," Alex chided as he readied Yaha once more. To his left, was Joshua, with Fury all in flames. To his right, was Yokoyawa holding the Stellar Ehécatl, with Sid still riding on his shoulder, tomahawk in hand.

"He knocked me farther than I thought," Joshua said. "Ready?"

"Thank you for inviting us to the fun," Sid replied.

"The more the merrier," Alex said, and they ran towards Abaddon to attack him at the same time.

Chapter 14
Dragonwolf

"*THEY'RE NOT GOING TO LAST* long," a voice said next to Fionn, dizzy and confused. The voice was filled with concern.

"If Alex falls, Joshua and the others will follow," a second familiar voice said. "I have to go."

With his brain healing from the trauma and destroyed leg working at rebuilding itself, Fionn tried to take in all the cacophony of words around him and make sense of them. He closed his eyes to allow himself to refocus and finish healing.

The battlefield was chaos after that last shockwave.

"We need a plan... Dad, wake up!" Sam said. "Enough, I'm going back, or that thing will kill Alex."

Fionn grabbed Sam's hand, stopping her from running towards Abaddon. He sat up.

Alex, Joshua, Sid, and Yoko held Abaddon at bay as much as they could, fighting with a coordination born of a year from hell. Yaha in Alex's hands was nothing but a solid beam of light, and the Fury's flame roared. Fionn saw Alex fighting and realized why his former student had been capable of killing three gods—with assistance—and survive to tell the tale. Alex wasn't thinking about anything, other than keeping his family safe. It was as if his mind was empty and focused only in the moment. The others were the same.

Empty.

But they looked exhausted. Haggard. The previous battles, heck, the previous *year* was showing its toll. That was why Abaddon took his time searching for the Tree. He knew that the odds of facing resistance were high. At least this way, after a protracted year-long battle, he could make sure his rivals were too weary to endure a long fight. For a demon that claimed to hate existence and all the living beings in it, he had learned a lot from them.

Fionn looked around.

Kasumi seemed dazed, yet still managed to deal with several incursions on her own, with Breaker converting them to mincemeat. She was looking around trying to find where Sam was and crossed sights with Fionn. She touched her aids. They weren't working.

"Where are Alex and Sam?" she signed.

"Sam is here," Fionn replied, then pointed to where Alex was, fighting against Abaddon.

In the distance, Fionn could see the samoharo metal bird battleship with Harland aboard taking severe damage. The Freefolk led by Stealth were barely keeping the defensive shield around the tree standing against the barrage of necro-meteors that Abaddon had summoned. Vivi split her focus between aiding the shield and aiding Alex, Joshua, and Sid to remain alive. She looked about ready to collapse.

And at the edge of the island, behind the First Demon, the first portal that had opened from thin air, without anyone summoning it, tracked every movement from Abaddon.

Alex hit Abaddon square in the face with a leaping punch, making him stumble to his right.

The portal moved to a new position.

It was not a random occurrence.

That's Mekiri's and Ben Erra's doing, Fionn thought. It was the way they were trying to help while dealing with their own battle, who knows where and when.

That portal might have been their last apparition in the real world, sacrificing what they had left in their avatars for this.

It then dawned on Fionn the meaning about the empty cup lesson.

There it was. The only opportunity to finally end this, to get rid of Abaddon for good. Abaddon was the unstoppable object.

The only way to destroy him once and for all was to not fight him with equal force, but take him somewhere where he would be empty, where he wouldn't be unstoppable. That meant in his own realm, the Infinity Pits, where his avatar body would be forced to collapse unto itself because that place was so dark that there would not be another observer, other than perhaps the person taking him there. But if that person became the empty cup as well, instead of the unmovable object, Abaddon wouldn't have something to oppose. And if a third party managed to attack him from distance, while moored in the Pits... it was a risky, complicated plan. But it made sense. Every single decision in Fionn's life had taken him to this point, to teach the tools to do it, to this choice. And he knew it.

He sighed, took a deep breath, and smiled. Oddly enough, it was as if a heavy weight had been suddenly lifted from his shoulders by accepting what he was about to do. He turned to Gaby and Sam, with an all-knowing look.

"I have an idea," Fionn said, chuckling at having stolen Alex's trademark phrase. He then hands signaled to Kasumi, "Get Alex back here! We need his arrows!"

Kasumi made a mad dash to reach Alex, who parried attack after attack, slowly buckling under the pressure. While Joshua and Yokoyawa tried to get Abaddon off from him to no avail.

Staggering, crippled by the pain that his slowly returning healing ability was causing by mending his multiple fractures, Fionn grabbed his fangsword Black Fang, which let loose a mournful growl as it glowed green. He then stared at the portal, calculating how much speed he would need to push Abaddon into it. It would be a one-way trip. Sam and Gaby turned to look at the portal as well.

"It is the only choice, isn't?" Gaby asked mournfully.

"I know what to do. But I won't if neither of you are on board," Fionn said.

"Why, Dad?" Sam asked, realization dawning in her eyes. She knew him all too well. "You can push him into the portal and then jump."

"You know he will climb back again. This has to end now, with him destroyed in the only place where he can't respawn. I know you don't like it, Sam. Neither do I. But sometimes being a father means doing what's best for your kids," Fionn said, and kissed his daughter goodbye on her forehead. "I need to borrow your ride while you aid Alex in casting the largest Atomic Thunder and shoot it towards the portal at my signal."

To Sam's credit, she didn't argue against the plan. She would do the same if the roles were reversed.

She's grown so much, Fionn thought. *And she has a family of her own to worry about now.*

"I love you, Dad," Sam said, unshed tears brimming in her eyes. "You will have to share your Gift with him to simulate the missing parts like his wings. My magick won't reach that far."

"I love you, Fionn. Do it before I regret agreeing to this." Gaby kissed him goodbye, as she laughed and cried at the same time.

Fionn smiled. "I love you both."

A wordless cry of pain cut through their goodbyes. The sound of a broken bone echoed through the air, and they looked up in time to see Alex fall. His left leg had a new bend where it shouldn't.

"My love, they need all the inspiration in the world, for their heart," Fionn whispered to his wife. *They are in your hands, the best place to be*, Fionn thought, looking into Gaby's eyes. He then began his last ever dash to save the day.

Gaby sheathed her twin blades inside Goldenhart. She began to play a riff that echoed across the Tempest. Taking a second to look at the sky, she licked her lips and improvised the lyrics, using her heart as a guide.

And here we are
Miracles by the universe
This is where we belong
Flying through the darkness,
Towards our chosen destiny

As Fionn ran, he could feel the Gift's core inside him changing into something else, larger than what could ever be contained inside his own body. In less than a thought, he found himself crossing the battlefield at an impressive speed. His body wasn't healing anymore. It didn't need it.

Empty cup, he reminded himself and smiled as he cleared his mind and soul of everything he had been till then: soldier, son, father, husband, mentor, and friend. He was all of those things and none of them. He just was.

Only lighting breaking the sky guides us
Through pain and sadness
Through gritted teeth
We won't falter

The spark of my hope will not be extinguished.
Tearing through the darkness

Fionn ran towards the waiting Black Fang, passing in front of Abaddon who attempted to intercept him, but instead was stopped by Yokoyawa and Joshua, each one grabbing the demon by a leg. The temperature difference scalded their skin, until Kasumi arrived to freeze the legs by cleaving Breaker into the ground. She then grabbed Alex's prone form and carried him away over her shoulder.

Strongest person in the world indeed, Fionn thought with a smile.

Sid threw his small axe towards the demon's eye, destroying it. As Fionn reached the dragon Black Fang.

† † †

"I will hold him steady, you two work your magick," Kasumi said as she froze the air around Alex's leg creating an improvised ice cast. She then grabbed Alex by the waist and hugged him tight from behind, allowing him to stand without losing his balance or putting weight on the broken leg.

"What's going on?" Alex asked.

"Dad had an idea," Sam said, now openly crying and pointing at the portal behind Abaddon. "Your kind of idea, so we better make it count with the biggest motherfrikking Atomic Thunder ever."

"Aw, crap!" Alex replied. "Is it the only way? I can't handle all the energy we'll need."

"You tell me," Sam said as she took her position next to Alex. "We are in the Tempest, hon, and have all the energy we need. Just make the shot count." They summoned the Thunderbow, which changed into a weapon of pure energy, charging the arrow, by drawing energy from the Tree itself, as the ground shook.

Sam's eyes glowed with energy as her fox tail split into nine identical appendages. Her Bubble Shield surrounded the three of them, ripping a chunk of ground and taking them into the air.

"I'm gonna hate myself for this," Alex muttered as he gritted his teeth, summoning all that was left of his Gift. "Just don't let me die from a heart attack."

"Not in this life hon," Sam promised as her irises and hair shifted color. Kasumi followed and joined her own Gift to the special attack.

"I will share the energy load with you," Kasumi told them.

Alex took a deep breath, focusing on drawing energy from everywhere and everyone, all at once, aided by Sam using her body as a conduit and Kasumi working as a fuse to keep him from dying. Alex saw through his Gift, from all over the Tempest and the Tree itself, rivers of energy flowing towards him. He braced for the impact and the searing pain he was about to endure. But that pain barely came. Behind him, Kasumi's eyes glowed as the influx of energy passed through her, her Gift at last reacting as she wanted, cooling down Alex.

At that moment in time, the three of them became one, and together they held all the power of the universe at their fingertips.

The spark of our hope will not be extinguished.
Tearing through the darkness
To change the world's destiny
To force a new dawn
We won't quit even if it hurts
The stars burst from our chest
Until we can love again

† † †

Fionn jumped onto the dragon's back. Black Fang roared. "Ready for one last fight, buddy?"

The dragon roared once more as the green glow of the fangsword enveloped them. He poured his gift into Black Fang to replace the missing parts, as Sam's magick had done. Black Fang took to the skies and flew as far as at it could go from the battle.

"What are you doing?" Harland asked him through the comms.

"What we always knew I would have to do," Fionn replied. "Give cover to that floating magick bubble over there. We only have one shot."

"Admiral, focus all defensive measures on protecting that bubble from flyers," Fionn heard Harland say through the comms. "See you on the other side, Fionn."

"See you on the other side, but not too soon, Harland."

† † †

"What the Pits is he doing?" Joshua grunted as Abaddon broke his arm. The Beast appeared to surround it with a cast of deepest shadow.

"Something really stupid, I'm sure," Sid said as he glanced at what Alex, Sam, and Kasumi were doing. He kept throwing his newly improved teleporting axe again and again at Abaddon to keep him distracted from Fionn. "Let's keep this motherfrikker busy until then!"

Yokoyawa said nothing; he simply sliced a leg from beneath Abaddon while Vivi summoned once more thick vines ground to tie Abaddon in place when he hit the ground. Sid jumped onto the vines to keep blinding the demon and give Fionn cover.

We will fight, make our stand
Because the bonds that tie us
The love that guide us
We are people with a mission

† † †

Black Fang stopped and Fionn took a second to survey the scene, and then urged the dragon to fly at full speed. Alex and Sam were drawing energy from everyone around, and a good portion donated by the Tree itself, as the circles of light that had formed in front of the bow, grew into an arrow and a ring of bright energy half the height of the tree itself. It left scorch marks in the ground and sliced any incursion fool enough to get close. Inside the ring were nine rings rotating at furious speed, forming a bizarre mandala of sorts.

Gaby's soundwaves from her song wove themselves into the mandala. As Gaby's song hit his ears, time slowed for him as he allowed the core of his Gift to explode.

"Let go of everything." Fionn allowed himself to breathe deeper than he had in years. "Including myself."

With each exhalation, his mind became an empty space and his senses became drunk with all the inputs from the world around. He could hear the heartbeats of everyone. The faint noise from all the energy flowing towards the arrow Alex was creating, the ice in his leg cast cracking under the pressure while Kasumi hugged him, the whisper of fur that a fox tail made as it flicked the air, the strain in the muscle fibers of Yokoyawa and Joshua.

The epic rock song being sung by Gaby, the music waves empowered by her own Gift energizing everyone.

And here we are
Miracles by the universe
This is where we belong
Flying through the darkness
To bring a new dawn

No more thoughts, yearnings, or regrets. The only thing in his mind was everything and anything that gave meaning to all of this. He felt goosebumps flush his skin as he smiled. The only thing now inside him was happiness. Hope.

Green flames erupted from him body as his eyes became pure light. The Gift was no longer a sphere of energy inside of him, rotating to produce energy. The Gift was him, and he was becoming the energy as every cell in his body exploded. At the very same second the descending dragon picked up speed and strength. Thought and action became one as he became one with the universe. It was a sensation that words could do no justice. It simply was.

As Black Fang flew by the tree, the green flames engulfed him as well, and Black Fang, too, became one with Fionn. A true dragonwolf, made of pure energy and willpower. Winds picked up around the floating island, allowing the dragonwolf to accelerate beyond what should have been possible.

The dragonwolf roared.

"I think that's the signal to get out of here!" Sid yelled as he, Yoko, and Joshua disengaged Abaddon. Yoko cleaved his sword into the ground, grabbing it with his right hand. Joshua hugged Sid with one arm and grabbed Yoko's free arm as the winds threatened to blow them away. Vivi's vines grew in a hurry anchor them to the ground.

The dragonwolf swooped over their heads. It impacted Abaddon with such force that the energy lifted him from the ground, as if the First Demon were a mere ragdoll, and took it along for a ride towards the portal.

As they approached the portal, Fionn's voice echoed across the air. It sounded unearthly.

"Now!"

Alex and Sam released the arrow. The aftershock almost

knocked them clean over, if it hadn't been for Kasumi holding them steady. The arrow caught up with the dragonwolf in a blink, drawing energy from everything in its wake. The demon, the dragonwolf, and the arrow entered the portal.

Fionn looked back at his family and smiled. His heart was content.

Time slowed for everyone as they realized what was about to happen, the proximity to the portal creating a gravity lensing effect.

After the arrow passed through, the portal began to close.

The last thing heard was Sid asking, "Why didn't he jump?"

† † †

As they fell through the portal, Fionn saw the silhouette of the Infinity Pits closing in, as best as he could understand the alien geometries that he was seeing. Fionn braced for the impact. The force of their crash created a cavernous crater and sent them barreling into one of the largest and darkest Pits.

The alien composition of the Pit burned Black Fang. The dragon tried to use Abaddon as a heat shield, but it was not possible to keep the body intact. Black Fang's soul returned to the fangsword as the rest of the corpse crumbled to ash. Fionn gripped the Sword and cleaved into Abaddon's chest, blade glowing with the only source of light in the murky Pit. Fionn focused his Gift into pushing the blade forward, with the rest healing the burns as they appeared in an endless cycle of pain. Fionn gritted his teeth, blood pouring freely from his mouth.

Abaddon hit the ground of the Pit, as meaningless as the term was in the eternal darkness. The brimstone smell hit Fionn's nose, nearly gagging him, but he pushed through, staking Abaddon to the ground. The demon struggled to rise, but the blade holding him weighed the same as the largest of the Montoc Dragons. And Fionn wasn't budging despite the brimstone that seared his skin.

"What are you doing?" Abaddon screamed as he realized where they were: the Pit where he had been begotten and trapped at the start of the universe. The only place where he was truly vulnerable to final death. "Release me!"

A source of light approached. It was the energy arrow,

pushing through the gravity well of the Pit.

Fionn's smile was red with blood. "I'm going to give you what you really need: freedom from your painful existence through a quick death." He glanced back and managed a pained shrug, for the energy arrow moved as if through treacle. "Well, almost quick. This place is super dense."

Abaddon saw the energy arrow closing in.

"You will die with me! If you let me go, I will help you to get out of here. You will get a second chance. My offer still stands!"

"No thanks. Some journeys have to end," Fionn said as the back of his t-shirt burned away from the radiation emitted by the arrow beam. The skin on his back was next.

Abaddon tried to free himself. He pushed up against the pit. He tried to shapeshift into different forms. But he couldn't free himself. He ended up being nothing but a pair of frightened eyes, a gaping maw, and tentacles lashing at everything.

"Nooooo!" Abaddon shrieked as the beam hit them, burning them inside a massive explosion that dispelled the darkness of the Infinity Pits for a brief second, as if a supernova had exploded.

As the familiar feeling of having his body disintegrated, Fionn's consciousness raced through all the memories of his long life in femtoseconds. Memories from his birth, growing up, meeting Izia, the Great War, marrying Izia, the death of Izia, reawakening a century later, taking care of Sam, meeting Gaby, Alex and the rest, reconnecting with Sam, saving the world, enjoying holidays, marrying Gaby, having adventures, saving the world many more times. The failures, the tragedies, the triumphs, seeing Theia from outer space, seeing the Life Tree, riding a dragon. All his choices taking him to this exact moment. While there were sad parts, he would have made the same decisions if given the chance to do it all over again. It had been a good life, even if he would miss his soulmate. His consciousness smiled as it faded away from existence. Fionn had finally let go of everything and was at peace for the brief moments this state of enlightenment lasted.

All turned white, then dark, then... nothing but a void. Nonexistence.

"It was a good life, wasn't it?" A new, comforting voice said, from nowhere and all around at the same time. *"Still..."*

And realization came. It was the voice from when he got the Gift. And it hadn't been Mekiri's doing like with everyone else.

† † †

Silence filled the air around the Life Tree. All the incursions had disintegrated. The samoharo ship had taken everyone back to Theia, leaving only Harland and Dr. Tze Tze's crew still working on the Figaro. Everyone had left them to mourn Fionn's loss.

Soon, the news about Fionn's sacrifice would spread all over the world.

And that's how one of the greatest heroes gave his life to destroy the ancient enemy that had taken so many lives, plagued so many planets. Sometimes the greatest achievements require the greatest sacrifice...

"Fuck that!" Alex exclaimed to the air, as if he were speaking to someone else. He tried to stand up, but putting any weight on his broken leg made him wince in pain. "There must be a way to save him."

"Alex..." Sam said, grabbing his hand and making him take a seat. Her eyes welled up. "He's gone. It was his choice."

Alex hugged Sam as she cried on his chest. Kasumi joined the hug.

"It's not fair for you. Or Gaby," Alex whispered. "There must be a way... I'm sorry."

"It's not your fault," Sid said, his voice breaking as the samoharo and Vivi approached. Vivi kneeled next to Alex.

"I need to set the bone in your leg so I can heal it properly," Vivi interrupted. "It will be painful. Once I finish with you, I will begin regrowing Sid's hand. I hope Sam can lend me a bit of her power."

Alex nodded, allowing himself to be guided to the ground. Kasumi offered him a piece of root to bite as Vivi set the bone. He almost lost consciousness from the pain. Vivi then began the healing spell.

"But once my leg is fine," Alex mumbled through the root, "I will break this place if I need to, to get him back."

Sam hugged him.

As Vivi continued healing Alex, Gaby walked towards the edge of the floating island.

Alex is right, it's not fair. You, and I, she thought as she placed a hand over her abdomen, *have sacrificed so much in this and past lives. Can't we get one last miracle, please?*

Sing, was the only reply she heard in her head.

Gaby looked around. She wasn't sure who'd said that, her own mind looking for a way to grieve the loss of her husband, the Life Tree trying to communicate, or someone else. Maybe there was room for a last miracle, and it was her subconscious prodding her to try it. She closed her eyes, took a deep breath, and let her heart pour out all it had inside as her voice drew from her Gift to send her song to the distant reaches of reality.

Ah, ah, ah
Ah, ah, ah

Yaha's blade emitted a faint glow and Alex tried to reach it but found himself unable to move.

Ah, ah, ah
Ah, ah, ah

"Stay put," Vivi admonished him. "Or not even the Gift will make your leg heal properly."

"Won't be the first time," Alex replied, staring at his left wrist, still stiff from breaking it years ago. Kasumi stood up, grabbed Yaha, and handed it to Alex, who smiled at the fact that the sword didn't even protest beyond a zap of static.

"It's heavier than it looks," Kasumi smiled. "It tingles."

"You get used to it," Sam replied.

"Sam, can you lend me your pendant again?" Alex asked as the pain in his leg subsided at last. Sam handed it over, exchanging a quizzical look that Alex replied to with a nod towards Gaby. He inserted the pendant once more into the bottom of Yaha's pommel and whispered to the blade. "Yaha, please help my friend when I can't."

Oh my Angel
Come back to me
You can survive
Home is not that far
I will send my love to you
So you can kiss me again under the stars

Yaha began to glow, the light increasing in strength, emanating heat. The sword blinked out and reappeared in front of Gaby, floating under its own volition.

Gaby continued to sing and as she did, Yaha vibrated and emitted light.

Ah, ah, ah
We have a tempest in our souls
You and me
Me and you
Ah, ah, ah
If I'd make a deal
I'd change our places
But I can't
So I will send my love to you
So you can kiss me again under the stars

"Yaha has become a microphone and antenna," Alex told Sam and Kasumi. "Transmitting Gaby's song somewhere else."

Reality was reacting to the song, or rather, the energy that Gaby projected into Yaha. This was her own version of the energy technique. To become a guiding light.

Ah, ah, ah
You and me won't fail
We are one, destiny we will defy
It's our one desire
For our love grows higher

Gaby raised her voice, her song echoing through the ruins, as a chorus coming from the Life Tree itself joined her. Bird-like wings of pure warmth and energy grew from her back as she sang.

Ah, ah, ah
We have a tempest in our souls
You and me
Me and you
Ah, ah, ah
If I could make a deal
I'd change our places
But I can't
So I will send my love to you

So you can kiss me again under the stars

"Do you see?" Yokoyawa whispered to Sid.

"That's the third time I have seen those wings coming from one of them," Sid replied in a whisper. "And if that happens when one of them stops a warp train barehanded while sporting those wings, Gaby then can pull this off."

Focus love on my song
Come back to me
For what do we have wings for if not to fly back home?
You and me
Me and you
Always
I promise

† † †

"I knew she would come up with something beautiful. She was my failsafe as much you were Mekiri's. I'm a sucker for these stories. And yet even I have limits. Your body is gone. It's the second time it got destroyed that way, and inside the Pits, unlike last time. Creating a new one will be tough."

"I will figure it out. I have a guiding light."

"That's why I will give you a reward, which you earned, but with one condition."

"What's the condition?"

"Nothing bad, I swear by me. You will see, my Guardian Spirit."

† † †

A portal opened once more in front of the island. It steadily increased in size as the energy emitted by Yaha, amplifying Gaby's song, connected. It quickly reached a size large enough for a human to cross through it. As Gaby flowed into an encore, a silhouette approached the portal and crossed through it with such force that it pushed Gaby and Yaha onto the ground. As dust settled, a large green skull made of energy cackled and laughed as it floated above Gaby. Sam's first reaction was to cast a bubble shield in front of Gaby, as Alex's summoned the bow by instinct and Joshua set Fury ablaze.

"At last, I'm free from the darkest prison, I shall explore

the pleasures of flesh as I carve my bloody path through this..."

"Not on my watch," a voice said behind it, destroying the skull spirit with a single slash. The skull's essence was reabsorbed by the portal as it closed. "Sorry," the familiar voice said. "That thing must have seen the portal and jumped into it as I was about to cross, taking a bit of the glow I was emitting with it."

"Dad?" Sam whispered, the bubble shield flickering out of existence. Alex stood up, his leg healed at last.

"Fionn?" Gaby said, with a heavy feeling in her stomach. She stood up and stared at her husband.

He was scratching his neck, embarrassed for allowing that damned spirit to get ahead of him. In his left hand there was a newly reforged Black Fang. Fionn was completely healed. Perhaps the strangest part of all of this was the massive pair of greyish wings sprouting from Fionn's back. Wings that emitted a faint green glow, reminiscent of his Gift. But other than that, he sounded the same. He looked the same.

Gaby ran to Fionn, who cleaved Black Fang into the ground and ran as well. Both met in an embrace... but Gaby passed right through Fionn, leaving everyone in shock.

Fionn and Gaby turned at the same time to face each other.

"What... what is happening?" Gaby asked, trying to touch Fionn's cheeks. It was like trying to touch warm air. It was there, but at the same time not solid enough to caress it.

"I'm not sure," Fionn said. "I... I... I don't recall much. I know I died, for good."

"Abaddon?" Joshua asked.

"Gone, of that, I'm one hundred percent sure. As I said, I died with him as the arrow impacted us," Fionn replied as he looked at Sam, Alex, and Kasumi with a faint smile. Alex's shoulders slumped. Knowing his best friend, Gaby knew Alex was feeling not just exhausted, but guilty. "But it's okay. I'm fine I think, just not sure what's going on."

"You don't remember anything at all?" Harland said as he approached.

"A voice, gentle. It wasn't Mekiri, but someone else. They proposed something to me... and it was the only way for me to come back, given that my body... It was an eternity."

"And only an hour here," Alex added. He was examining

the energy emitted by Fionn, with the perception the Gift granted him. "You don't seem to be particularly fleshy at the moment."

"A spirit," Yoko said.

"A what?" Sid asked.

"I knew it," Kasumi interjected. "The legend of the Storm God said something like this."

Fionn was about to reply, when he tilted his head as if he'd heard something in the distance.

"What's happening?" Gaby asked him, holding his gaze. She wanted to kiss him, to hug him, to go home at last. But it seemed that it wasn't to be. Not a miracle, but a seemingly cruel joke.

"I have this deal. And I have to go where I'm needed. Right now, a girl on the other side of the planet, across the Grasslands is fending off an incursion on her own and she is only ten. She needs help. And then I need to help the Tree to heal the rest of the damage."

"So, you are a guardian spirit," Yokoyawa said with a faint smile. "Now it makes sense."

"Will we see you again, Dad?" Sam asked Fionn. Gaby waited for the answer with bated breath. She didn't care about deals, guardian spirits or stuff like that. She only wanted them to be together.

"Of course, I wouldn't have made a deal if it didn't allow me to be with you. With Gaby. It will take time until I figure out some things, like how to get a body," Fionn added with a shrug.

"You are back, but why is this hole still in my heart?" Gaby asked as tears flowed down her cheek. "Why can't we get a break? Always apart, different times, and different generations?" Gaby muttered.

Fionn turned to Gaby and put his hands near her face, an ethereal embrace as best as he could manage. "No matter where or what I am, no matter how much time passes, I will always love you. And I will always return to you." He leaned forward and placed his lips over her mouth, and she felt the kiss of a warm summer breeze. "You are my universe. You are why I was allowed to return." He stepped back then dissolved into the air, leaving Gaby standing alone, clutching her chest.

Alex approached slowly, still not placing much weight on his leg, and offered her a hug. Gaby accepted. The best friends stood there, as Kasumi hugged Sam. There was a sense of loss in the air, but at the same time one of hopefulness. If Fionn had managed to pull out one last miracle, even if it didn't work as expected, then things could be fixed. Starting with a good part of the planet that would have to regenerate from the damage caused by Abaddon.

"What now?" Sid asked as Alex let go of Gaby.

"Why are you looking at me? Gaby is now head of the clan, she's the boss," Alex said. "Or Sam, the Dragonqueen?"

"Oh, heavens please no," Sam rolled her eyes. "I don't want that responsibility. I already have enough with you and Kasumi."

"Says the only one of us that actually knows how to cook," Kasumi said as she shook her head.

"Because Fionn trusted you enough to ask you shoot that arrow," Gaby explained, wiping the tears from her eyes. She smiled at Alex. "And if I'm now the head of the family, I say that it's your call. It's time for you to step up."

Alex called Yaha to his hand. The sword disappeared from its spot in the ground and rematerialized in his hands. He took out the pendant and gave it back to Sam. He stared at the sword, reflecting on its meaning: Hope. But Alex wasn't particularly hopeful now.

"Let's go home," Alex said, exhausted.

† † †

Inside the Figaro, Sid tried to take his rightful place as pilot, but missing a hand would make that difficult. He looked on with sadness when Alex replaced him as pilot and Harland as copilot. Vivi took Sid to the med bay where Dr. Tze Tze's crew would aid her in healing Sid's injury. Alex turned on the engines of the Figaro and the ship began to lift as Yoko summoned a path to get them out of there and back home.

None of them was sure if they would even see the Life Tree again, but it wasn't as if Alex cared much. In silence, he piloted the Figaro following the path into a portal that took them into the orbit of the Long Moon. It made sense, since there was no home to go back to for now.

The Figaro landed inside the landing bay of the Long Moon, where Forge and the people from the Foundation were waiting for them. No one said a word, for there were no words left that could help them. Except Forge, who like Alex, had trouble reading the room.

"You need to see this."

He led the surviving members of the Band of the Grey-wolf—a name that might need to be retired—to the observation deck where they'd rested a few days ago, even if it felt like it had been a year. They stared at Theia, with its orbiting rings. The planet's surface was crisscrossed by traces of green light, as if someone circled it at blinding speeds. Theia was healing itself.

Gaby stared at the planet and cried, for she knew that while the mission had been accomplished, the cost for her had been so high. Alex limped his way over to her and looked at Sam, who nodded. Alex opened his arms and let his best friend cry her heart out, while Kasumi did the same for Sam.

In the landing bay Joshua was recounting the abridged version of what had transpired to anyone who would listen. Yoko and Dr. Tze Tze discussed building a new ship using the Figaro's merging of human, samoharo, and freefolk knowledge. Vivi healed Sid guided by the samoharo researchers while Forge offered to make a cybernetic skeleton for Sid's hand so the tissue could grow around it.

And back on the observation deck, Gaby finally fell asleep in the arms of her best friend as Sam cried and laughed next to them, telling Kasumi stories of growing up with her dad. Alex sat, full of contentment, and watched the planet below, wondering about the next day.

Below them was a planet grateful to have survived to see a new day.

Quite a journey, huh?

Chapter 15
Journey's End

THE SUN WAS HIGH IN the sky, casting its warm light on Theia. In the town of Skarabear, right in the center, a ceremony in honor of Fionn Estel, the Greywolf, the hero who'd sacrificed himself to save the world for the nth time, was taking place. Harland had given a eulogy in front of the bronze statue that his adoptive town had made decades ago as family, close friends, and those who'd fought alongside him paid tribute to the deceased hero. It was a more intimate, smaller ceremony than the official one that the now disbanded Band of the Greywolf had to endure two weeks before. And as on that occasion, one person had refused to attend.

Alex sat on the lakeshore not far from the town. Here, years ago, Fionn had trained him for the Chivalry Games. The same place where Alex had discovered in the old diaries of Ywain the basis for the spiritual energy technique that Fionn refined, and which had proven key to defeating Abaddon. A technique that was the result of centuries of testing the limits of the human spirit.

"I wish I had never discovered that stupid technique," Alex muttered as he skipped a stone on the lake's surface. It bounced for more than half the distance of the large lake before it sunk into its crystal-clear waters, where once the legendary fangsword—Black Fang, another casualty of the fight —had waited for a wielder of its choosing. As he observed the stone sinking into the deceptively deep waters, Alex wondered if he would be able to dive towards the bottom of the lake and back the same way Fionn had done when he was sixteen. Probably not, which meant he would have drowned. A part of Alex spurred him to do it anyway, the part that made him feel severe guilt for firing the energy arrow that helped beat Abaddon, at Fionn's expense. But he was trying to keep it quiet.

A gust of wind hit him in the back and Alex couldn't avoid rolling his eyes as the shadow of a pair of wings fully opened obscured the sun for a second.

"Well, for starters, I was almost half your current age," a familiar voice said behind Alex as Fionn took a seat next to him, becoming less spectral by the second until he resembled an almost solid being again. It was an improvement since the last time they'd seen each other at the Life Tree. "Why are you not at the funeral?"

Alex wasn't in the mood to deal with the apologetic spirit form of Fionn, or whatever his former mentor and friend was now. It was already hard enough dealing with the guilt, even if it had been the right choice in the moment. But Alex felt it added insult to the injury of having to deal with some sort of annoying ghost bugging him for the past month.

"It was a nice eulogy," Alex replied. He grabbed another stone and sent it skipping with enough force to make it cross the halfway mark. Alex made a small celebratory gesture. "I'm getting closer to make it reach the other side in one throw."

"I guess, I never expected to hear my own," Fionn replied, grabbing a stone and making it skip till it reached the other shore. Alex rolled his eyes.

"Show off." Alex turned to face Fionn. There were so many questions ricocheting around his head. And the other person who could answer them wasn't in the right mindset to do so. After all, Gaby was now a grieving widow before her mid-thirties, and on top of that, she had been left as leader of the Wind Tribe that Fionn had reformed. And truth be told, Alex had been helping her as much as he could but at the same time avoiding her, as he was ashamed. "How does it work now? Now you can grab a stone, when the first time you returned, Gaby literally went through you. I know you are dead, and this is a spiritual manifestation of some sort. And your senses. How do you perceive the world with you being you know..."

"A spirit? I'm not sure either, it is becoming something progressive. I'm discovering new things every day."

"What's next? Enough power to create a second World's

Scar, but this one with better interior design than the one that Mekiri created millennia ago? What with how picky you are with those things and all."

"If you are implying that I'm some sort of god... no, I'm not. I think. I'm still not sure who brought my soul back, or if I can pull a Mekiri and create an avatar in a few decades. Look, Alex, you're always searching for an explanation for everything. For once wonder at how things are in the world and let it be."

"Easy for you to say," Alex muttered. "You're some sort of guardian spirit, and I'm the one that killed you to become that. There have been sightings of you, like those of that dead musician, all over the Core Regions at the same time. And to be blunt, you owe me as much, probably more. So, an explanation shouldn't be an issue. You owe me that for leaving me with this guilt."

† † †

Fionn remained silent for some time. If he was honest with himself, and at this point there was nothing else to do, he wasn't sure what was going on, or who had brought his soul back and had transformed him into a spirit. He had recently discovered that he was on par with the power that Mekiri herself had showed when she had an avatar. He knew that being hadn't been Mekiri, and certainly not Ben Erra. Fionn had his suspicions of that being's identity, for only one had that kind of power, but he hadn't dared to say it aloud, partly out of fear, partly for guilt, and because he never felt worthy of such honor.

"You don't want to mention me, because you don't feel you earned it, even in spite of me saying that you did, but fine. You at very least owe them some sort of explanation; you have to help them heal. That's one of the reasons I granted you this boon. The other is because I like Gaby too much to let her live heartbroken. That might be good inspiration for music, but she deserves better," the new voice said. There was no clear source of origin, nor name, it only was. The universe itself. Kaan'a.

"Then why not bring my body back, too?"

"There was nothing left, even for me to save, but you can always create your own avatar with practice and time. This was bound to happen sooner or later. It's one of the possible evolution pathways of the Gift. Not everyone takes it. But as usual, you had to rush things."

"Sorry."

"Don't be sorry. Instead, talk to him."

"I know," Fionn replied.

† † †

Fionn pinched the bridge of his nose. "I can sense things. I guess the closest thing as reference for you would be like watching a movie in one of those holographic rooms, or like the storytelling technique I showed you years ago. And you haven't answered my question about why you missed the funerals."

"For starters, it's weird to be at your funeral when I'm still talking to you. And I'm not good at funerals, never have been," Alex said, staring at the lake once more, before throwing another stone. "They mess with my head, and I don't want to go there again. I don't want to make Sam or Gaby sadder than they are now. And with everything going on, I haven't been able to go to therapy. Heck, I can't even get my meds as supplies are barely restarting after all that happened. So, call my absence a crude attempt at self-care till I can get help instead of you know, listening to that voice inside my head that is making me feel like a murderer."

"Okay, let's clear up some things," Fionn said to his former student. It would be probably one of his last lessons to Alex. "One, it wasn't your fault, you didn't kill me. So please, *please* stop thinking that. You are not a murderer. I asked you to help me because I trust you. We did what we had to do. Was a great plan? No. Not my best work. But it was my choice. The alternative was losing. And two? Don't allow your martyr complex and out of control guilt to push away the people you love. They're hurting too, you know? I know it's my fault. They need you in their lives right now as much as you need them. They can help you to process things as much as you can help them if you let them instead of secluding yourself in a proverbial mountain."

"Talking from experience?" Alex asked, with a raised eyebrow.

"It took me a long time, and Gaby knocking some sense in me to realize that. It cost me time that I could have used better. But unlike me, you don't need a second chance to make amends, you have your first right here, right now. Don't waste it."

Fionn smiled and placed his hand on Alex's shoulder.

He was quiet for a second or two before he spoke. "It is a strange sensation," Alex said. "It feels like some sort of air pressure, like the wind from a blow-dryer on your skin."

"It's even weirder for me," Fionn said, looking down. "And I don't know how to begin to describe it. I'm not sure how I'm going to make this work with Gaby."

"You know, you are even worse than those ghosts from that old winter solstice story." Alex sighed heavily. "At least they gave more advice before getting all mopey."

"As short as his advice was, it is right," another familiar voice said behind him. Alex and Fionn turned their heads and saw Gaby walking alone, and a few meters behind, Sam and Kasumi holding hands. "As much as this situation hurts right now."

Alex stood up and gave Gaby a hug so strong that she gasped for air.

"I'm so sorry for not being there for you. I'm sorry for making this about me and not considering..." Alex began, but Gaby pushed him away, both to break the hug and recover her breath.

"Just stop, okay?" Gaby replied. "I want my best friend at my side right now. I'm still trying to make sense of all of this."

"Yeah Alex," Sam added. "We're all in the same boat thanks to Dad's friendly ghost here."

"I'm not a ghost... I'm... some sort of guardian spirit, okay? And as I told Alex, I'm sorry for having put you all in this position. If I could have come with a better idea at the time or..." Fionn said, rolling his eyes, before Gaby put her finger on his lips. Or tried to.

"We knew that any one of us dying was a real possibility. We knew what we were getting in to," Gaby said as her eyes welled up. "It's too much to process in such a short time. And with you being this..."

"See?" Alex added. "I was asking him what's going on."

"I guess," Kasumi interjected, "that we're seeing the process of becoming a deity like the Storm God in real time. Maybe you'll get a statue in the Seven Fortune's Temple."

"Process?" Harland echoed as he joined the group. He was with Sid, Vivi, Yokoyawa, and Joshua.

"Yes," Kasumi said. "Think about it. We are merged with akeleths, of which Mekiri was a member, and she is the Trickster Goddess; thus, a logical conclusion is that Fionn is now like them."

"If you *are* on your way to becoming a god, Dad, are you planning to make another World's Scar with better decor?" Sam asked Fionn with a cheeky smile. Fionn in turn looked at Alex, who only shrugged. "Does that mean I have to pray to you now instead of to the Trickster Goddess? That is going to be so weird to explain to my future kids, like, no, you can't pray to your grandpa to pass your exam, you have to study."

"If I had known that was a possibility, I would've delayed my postgrad exam till now," Alex added thoughtfully, scratching his chin.

"I wonder if I need to pray to him during a demonhunter mission," Kasumi added.

Fionn was finding the exchange of those three, whose relationship had evolved to this point where all were in synch, funny. And would have laughed if it weren't for the expression in Gaby's eyes. As much as she was trying to stifle a laugh, inside she must've been filled with grief. If spirits could feel guilt, Fionn would be proof of the concept. The friendly banter could only lessen the somberness of the occasion to a point. And he could tell that his time here for now, was running out.

"Look, I'm not sure what's happening to me, who's doing it, or where Mekiri is. But no prayers, please. It's awkward."

"Drats!" Sid exclaimed. He wore a strange case of metal and clear freefolk crystals over his stump where the soft tissue of his hand was growing on the cybernetic hand Forge had made. For now, the progress was slow and consisted of Sid complaining about it being itchy. "And here I was planning to build a temple for Saint Fionn, patron spirit of those that always get themselves into problems."

Fionn couldn't help himself and laughed. "Too long." His laugh though, had an unearthly, reverberating quality that reminded everyone that he wasn't alive—for lack of a better word. "Doesn't roll off the tongue."

"Don't worry, Sid," Alex nodded. "We'll workshop it."

"Sorry to interrupt your stand-up show, but would all of you mind if *oh angel* here and I have a moment of privacy, please? I'll catch up with you," Gaby said, her voice betraying a melancholic mood.

"We better go back to the town and have something to eat," Sid said, offering a faint smile and an exit to the conversation. He gave Fionn what was possibly the most serious, gloomy look he had ever seen in the samoharo. "See you around, pal."

"See you around," Fionn replied with a heavy heart.

"You owe me a talk," Gaby said to him. He knew her well. In that regard, Gaby shared more personality ticks with her past life as Izia than she liked or wanted to admit.

Unfortunately, dying and then somehow returning as a spirit surely counted as the biggest mess he had ever created. It ruined all the plans they once had, and now? They had to figure out how to move forward. Such a simple yet impossible task.

"I know. And I'm going to start by saying that I will be with you..."

† † †

"Always," Alex said playfully to Sid, "thinking with your stomach."

"Regenerating a hand from scratch consumes a lot of calories," Sid complained.

"I told you I can try to make it grow with magick," Vivi said. "But you won't let me."

"It's a cultural thing," Yokoyawa replied. "I will explain at lunch."

"It'll be a long lunch then," Vivi said. "I believe this is the first time in almost a year we can actually sit to talk about plans that don't involve any of you fighting for dear life."

"Yeah. We have plans," Sam said, quickly glancing at her belly and then to Kasumi's.

"Starting with getting regular jobs and finding a place to live," Alex sighed.

"And in which region," Kasumi added. "I still think the three of us should move to Kyôkatô."

"It feels like the end of an era," Joshua interrupted.

"It is," Alex replied. "But there's always the next page."

"That actually sounded wise," Sam said, smiling. "I'm proud of you."

"Thanks, I try," Alex said, reddening. "I had an excellent teacher, but I'll never be half as good."

"I'm not so sure about that," Kasumi said, resting her head on Sam's shoulder and winking at Alex.

Sam turned to look at Harland, who was walking near them. "By the way, Harland, which were the last words of your eulogy speech? You never read them in either event.

And I'm sure I saw one more page in your hand."

"I thought of keeping them only for us," Harland said, still somewhat lost in his thoughts. "And, given that only us are here..." He cleared his throat and said,

"As for Fionn, only those close to him know what truly became of him, but they won't say a word. Some people say that he sacrificed himself to save the world and his remains are buried at the roots of the mythical Life Tree. Others whisper that he became some sort of guardian spirit, and if you are in need, if the dark is coming for you, and you hear the howl of a dragonwolf, and are hit by a sudden gust of wind, he will come to your aid. Myself? I hope that either way, he may have found, always in the heart of his soulmate, at least some small measure of peace, the kind we all seek and yearn, but few of us will ever find.

"With time, heroes become legends. Legends grow into myths. And those myths became the stories we tell each other to give us hope as we walk toward the future. That's the power of storytelling."

"That's beautiful," Sam replied as she stopped, turned back towards Gaby and Fionn and shouted, "Hey, Dad, did you hear that?"

But Fionn was gone, with only a cloud of feathers flowing around. Gaby was standing alone, wiping the tears from her eyes with her right hand, while in the left, she was holding one of the feathers close to her chest.

Sam wistfully smiled.

Thank you for everything, Dad, she thought, remembering the words he told them while at the Long Moon.

"It's not the journey that matters; it's with whom you shared it."

Epilogue
Voices Heard Across the Universe

SOME DECADES LATER... GIVE OR take.

"And that was the whole, actual, real story. Sans a few mistakes with dates, to be honest. Neither your dad nor I have been good with them in any recount," Gaby said with a crooked smile to the young man seating across the tea table in her dressing room. It was a large room full of clothes racks, a vanity mirror, shoe boxes and three different guitars. She was getting ready for her final concert, the dedication to celebrate the launch of the FireRaven, Theia's first exploration spaceship. Sid's dream was finally realized after decades of hard work. Gaby had agreed to take a break from the endless days of preparations when Scud, her former bandmate and now one of the pilots for the mission, had asked her to talk—and perhaps knock some sense into—one of his fellow pilots. One Gaby was well acquainted with.

That talk ended up being a complete recounting of everything that related to their family and tribe.

She looked at her godson, how much he had grown. He was almost the spitting image of his father, but had the green, large freefolk eyes of Sam and the nose of Kasumi. How Sam had managed to mix the features of all three parents so their children looked like them, Gaby could never wrap her mind around. She knew it had been tough, painful, and only worked twice. Gaby smiled at the young man. It was as if she was looking at old friends—family—back then when they were younger.

"I..." Michael, the young man—her godson—replied. He was tall, almost as tall as Fionn had been. His hair was shoulder-length and a bit unkempt, which Gaby assumed was not exactly per regulation. "You never told me you knew how to use the freefolk storytelling technique that way, and with your psychometry in the mix. It was like..."

"Watching a holographic movie? Yeah, I've heard that before. It's a bit exhausting to do so, though," Gaby said with a sigh, feeling a bit lightheaded. While she looked almost as young as she had been when the story took place, with only a few barely noticeable wrinkles—a side effect of the Gift slowing her aging process—using her psychometric visions was still draining. "Which, well, maybe wasn't a good idea before a big concert."

"I'm sorry, godmother," Michael said. "You shouldn't have to do this before your final performance. If Scud wasn't such a meddling samoharo..."

"Trust me," Scud interjected. Gaby looked at her formed bandmate with fondness. While not as musclebound as Yoko, he had grown from the scrawny samoharo he was during his drummer time with Hildebrandtia into quite a hill of muscles. "This talk was important, and who better to knock sense in you that the tribe head?"

"It's family matters, Scud," Michael replied ruefully.

"Good, then, that he asked me," Gaby admonished her godson. "Because last time I checked, Scud is part of the tribe. I inducted him myself. He is family. And he is only looking out for you."

"Since when is the slacker the responsible one in this friendship?" Michael asked.

"Since the responsible one is acting all anxious, bordering on collapse," Scud replied. "And I have been around these blocks and with your folks long enough to know when to ask for help. Besides, your mom asked me to look after you. And your other mom. And your dad. And your sister. And Sid. And the Captain. And I'm sure they asked you to do the same for me, brother, so get used to it."

"I'm not getting used to you being the responsible one."

"Good, because it's exhausting." Scud looked at Gaby. "Seriously, I'm not sure how you managed to do so for so many years. Even after we disbanded Hildebrandtia, you keep making music, while taking over the Wind Tribe and the Greywolf family after, y'know."

"I had help, from you, from this dunderhead's parents..." Gaby nodded towards Michael.

"Dunderhead?" Michael interjected, about to say something, but Gaby gestured for silence.

"I'm your elder on top of being your godmother. I get to say it," Gaby chided him. "What I don't get is why you asked me to tell you all of this. Your parents always told you everything, and it's not like it's much of a secret in your family."

Michael looked down, avoiding Gaby's gaze.

"I will give you two a bit of privacy," Scud said, reading the room. "Gaby, thank you. It was an honor."

"Thank you, Scud. For everything. And please take care of this bedhair, okay?"

"I can try. Michael, don't be late or the Captain will have both our heads," Scud said as he left the room.

"I won't," Michael said, watching the door close behind him.

Gaby laughed. "He is so funny when he tries to be all formal and serious." For her, even after all these years, and accounting for the fact that samoharo aged slower than humans and even freefolk, Scud was still a teenage drummer. Sid and Yoko must have been rubbing off on him during training.

"He is a slacker, but he's a good friend."

"Take it from me: if a samoharo has your back, they will be your ride or die best friend till the end of times," Gaby said sagely.

"I know."

"So, are you going to tell me the real reason why you asked me to tell you everything you should already know when you should be focusing on your big assignment?"

"No one can lie to you, can they?"

Gaby offered Michael her trademark crooked smile as reply. "They have tried. Only your granddad managed to do so, once."

"I admit I have always wondered about him," Michael explained. "He was gone by the time me and my sister were born. You never remarried. And I know about the sightings. All the tribe knows. But those are usually short, so it's not like I have been able to talk to him to ask longer questions when he visited me. Mom gets all teary eyed, my other mom focuses on training and teaching her demonhunters, and Dad..."

"Doesn't like to talk much about the topic? Yeah, your dad has some problems expressing what he is feeling. And your grandad's 'death' is a sore topic. I think he still feels a bit guilty, deep down."

"And he wasn't around much when I was a kid."

"Oh, that's not his fault, and on this I will always defend your dad, who did the best he could. That one is totally the fault of a certain spirit that asked him to take his place. And I have taken him to task for that."

"Which leads me to my actual question. Why Dad? The story you just told me tells me you or my mom—Sam— would have been better suited for that."

"Don't be so harsh with your dad, Michael," Gaby's voice took on a serious undertone. "He didn't ask for it. But your mom was busy dealing with the whole DragonQueen thing, and to be honest my heart wasn't on having adventures and hunting incursions anymore. So, it fell to the only remaining students of Fionn to take his place. And Kasumi did it until your sister was born, which meant your dad had to do it all on his own. Like tracking down those minor rebel gods. Everyone had gone their separate ways. And as I told you, it was a struggle to keep it together. Unlike your mothers or I, the Gift wasn't kind to him. Or, look it at this way. This was not the story of a retired hero getting a second chance. It was a 'passing the torch' kind of story where your dad got said torch pushed on him by circumstances and admittedly, our own selfishness. But that's not what's bothering you, is it? It's your recent promotion ahead your mission."

"Being chosen as second in command is pushing me into a position I'm not comfortable with. I don't like giving orders to people I trained with at the space flight program. And I don't even know if I'm the right person for it. I mean, Yaha didn't choose me, it chose my sister, who also hasn't struggled as much with the Gift, unlike me."

"Wielding Yaha doesn't mean you are the leader. Fionn only wielded it for less than ten minutes, and that was an emergency thing. Samantha wielded it longer. Yaha has an already complicated legacy as it is, but it's mostly perception. You have to understand, the Tempest Blades have a mind of their own. They choose their wielder based on compatibility, among other things. Yaha tends to pick those that need the most help. And mine... well, yours now, choose their wielder based on their own perception on how much you care. You might have the iron will of Kasumi, the fearlessness of Sam, but you got the soft heart from your dad.

That's why you struggle with your Gift. Because you wear your emotions in your sleeve, but you're not as explosive in temperament. Yaha would have been a poor fit for you, given how much Alex had to train to use it properly. Heartguard and Soulkeeper chose you because they want to protect you, while you protect others. That's why you got promoted, too, because I'm sure in your training you proved the right person to take care of a whole crew if, heavens forbid, something happens to Yoko. As for the Gift and your struggles."

"Yeah?"

"Look," Gaby said. "No one as young as you or your sister should have gotten the Gift at that age. Not your dad, not me, not even your mothers. Ywain got it as a newborn. Now that's awful. No one should get it—not that way, at least—period. To get it means tragedy. But if you do get it, the best thing you can do is to learn to use it to aid others. Your parents were lucky to not have lost either of you. That day was probably the angriest I've seen your dad and Kasumi. I could swear either of them were about to break the world, beating that sorcerer with their fists, and the whole Wyld Hunt, for hurting your mom. If not for Fionn's spirit calming them down, I'm not sure how far things would have gone. Probably an altered landscape. Can you imagine a blizzard-electric storm ravaged valley?"

"Really? I don't remember that."

"Maybe that's for the best. It was scary," Gaby said. "Bottom line with the Gift: it never gets easy to use it, you only grow accustomed to it. You should ask your dad, in earnest, before you leave, how to do it. That said, no matter where you are, be assured that Fionn and I will be always watching you and if possible, will advise you."

"That sounds ominous." Michael stared at Gaby, suspicious. She looked more tired than ever, for he had seen her after her tours, and she had never looked this exhausted. "What's going on, godmother?"

"There are reasons why this is my last concert ever. I can feel it," Gaby said, offering him a sad smile.

"Oh," Michael said, quiet. "Can I do something?"

"See? Too caring for others. That's the kind of question your dad used to ask when we were teenagers. You have so much of both your parents and your grandfather. And no, you can't do anything, but thanks for asking. Knowing how kind you are is more than enough. It makes me feel at ease."

Michael was about to reply when his communicator beeped. He took it out and looked at the screen.

"Apologies, the Captain is calling me," Michael replied as his shoulders slumped.

"Tell him I say goodbye and thank you," Gaby said, her cheerful demeanor returning. "Be careful outside, the universe is big and still full of good and bad in all stripes."

"I will," Michael replied as he hugged his godmother. "I'm gonna miss you so much."

"And I will miss you, too, bedhair," Gaby said, mussing his already messy hair even more. "Seriously, call your dad."

As Michael left the room, Gaby gathered her bearings. She heard her godson making a call. The advantages of the Gift having enhanced her senses tenfold.

"Dad, I just wanted to talk quickly before I depart. I need your advice..."

At least he is not as stubborn as everyone else in this family, Gaby thought with a stifled laugh.

† † †

The concert was to take place in a large park in Saint Lucy. The park had been built on the spot where the explosion that had destroyed part of the city took place. Harland had decided to make it a commemorative park to honor all the lives lost that day, while the city had expanded once more in the other direction. Across the river, near the bay, an artificial structure had been designed and built to host the launch of the FireRaven. It was a platform with a ramp like the barn ramp Sid and Alex had built to test launch the original Figaro—by now it and all the following models were at the Technology Museum of the Foundation—but larger. The ramp also had more technology in it than the Figaro had back then, to keep the FireRaven safe from intrusions, as well as to keep the audience safe during the launch. On the platform, resting while its cores began to gather energy for the upcoming launch, sat the FireRaven.

"Impressive, huh?" Joshua asked Gaby. He stood next to her backstage, still adjusting his guitar. They hadn't played together in a concert for a while, not since Gaby had retired from public view. But Joshua had made a point to visit her now and then to jam at her house, in between his journeys to other regions of Theia. He hadn't grown old. Gaby wondered if he ever would. But the companionship of her bandmate and friend made her smile. "I have to give it to Sid, that's one of a hell of a design. The kid will have fun flying it."

Gaby couldn't avoid admiring the sheer scale of the ship. It was at least five times larger than the old dreadnoughts from the Great War, meant to hold a large crew composed mostly of humans, samoharo, freefolk—the few that didn't get sick at being in outer space—and a few fey and felp orcs. The crew even consisted of a couple of the so-called 'monsters' from the Deseret. All Theia was represented by the crew of the ship, whose nose resembled a raven's beak. Plastered on the fins of the ship, there was the new Theia flag: a circle resembling a planet, surrounded by twelve stars. And inside the circle, a tree. The Tree.

Gaby felt as if a thousand butterflies flapped around her stomach, a lightness invading her chest as she fed from the energy of the crowded open-air auditorium. The ceremony was about to start. Leaving aside the fact that this was a momentous, historic moment for all of Theia, and even after years of playing music in concerts and touring, she still got nervous about being in front of an audience. This being her last concert only made things more complicated. Officially she was retiring to go back to Skarabear, a well-earned rest after a life of adventures, of saving others, of sharing her many gifts with the world. Most people said that they were sad to hear the announcement, but everyone understood the reasons. Which, ultimately, had made this possibly her most well-attended concert ever. One last hurrah for her and the public, or so the train of thought went.

But the truth was, and she was already feeling it in her bones and every cell of her body, that something was about to happen. And only three living people knew or suspected what she was about to do. What she had been training for since that fateful day at the lake in Skarabear. She wouldn't have it done without their blessings, without spending time with them, and one of them was about to take the stage.

Harland reached the podium aided by Amy, his trusty former aide, who later had become the Alliance's Secretary of Education. Harland, by virtue of having already been older when all these adventures began more than three decades ago, was now an elderly gentleman, and a life of adventuring and later ushering the Alliance as its first president had taken a toll on his body. Gaby was happy for Harland. Her friend had managed so many things by sheer force of will and wise words that having an adoptive family now to take care of him was a just reward. Maybe Mekiri never returned in the physical sense, but surely she guarded him.

That red and black raven resting on the lights above the podium was too much of a coincidence.

"We are here reunited," Harland began his speech. "Not just to listen to Hildebrantia's concert, although that's always a plus. We are here to celebrate how far we have come after so many hardships. To say farewell into the stars to our siblings aboard the FireRaven, the first of many to come, exploration and defense spaceships built by the Theian Alliance, with resources and expertise and aid from all the people of the planet. From the Core Regions, to the Grasslands, to the Hegemony, to the Deseret. We are here, together, not only as survivors from worlds lost in the distant past, but as a single family looking towards the future. The road has not been an easy one. There are still many challenges, many hardships to face here on our planet. But as before, we will stand together to solve them, because we know that cooperation and kindness are the way forward. And now, the FireRaven will extend this to every other species we can find still hanging on among the stars. We will explore, we will try to make friends, and we will defend those that need it. For the universe is ours and it is time we take it back from the nightmares that so long have kept us cornered. Thus, I ask you all to join me and wish a safe trip to our brethren inside the FireRaven, and that they return at the end of their mission, with many new stories to tell."

† † †

The FireRaven raced across the launching ramp. Three hundred souls made its crew. With a roaring boom the massive ship defied the augmented Theia gravity, passing with ease the previously impregnatable ionosphere and reached outer space within minutes, to the cheers of those on the ground and stationed at the refitted Long Moon.

As the noise from the launch subsided, Harland retired from the podium and offered a smiled to Gaby, who grabbed the microphone and asked:

"Are you ready to rock?" Gaby asked.

Joshua played a long guitar riff to set on metaphorical fire the audience.

"Are you ready to rock?" Gaby asked a second time, raising her voice.

† † †

At the end of the concert, Gaby began singing what in the past decades had become her most popular song but was also considered by many as an unofficial hymn for Theia, as cheesy as it sounded in her own words: Voices Heard Across the Universe. As the violin and guitar section of the chorus approached and the audience clapped, Gaby's body was overcome by an excess of energy. The process, her process to reach the next stage, had begun. She danced on the stage with a huge smile in her face, as she gave a long look to all her friends, mentally waving good-bye once more.

There are days when I dream to fly.
Flying free as a comet across the sky.
Sometimes it takes a leap of faith,
To even try.

Let us be guided by the stars.
Let us shine like a star.
Let our voices be heard,
Across the universe.
Let us fly!

There are days when it's hard to hope.
When you're almost out of breath.
Sometimes all it takes is a tiny spark,
To let our hearts burn fire!
To let our voices be heard!
Millions of voices together as one.
Sing all!

Harland and his adopted family watched from their VIP seats. Yokoyawa wasn't there, obviously, but Vivi—sporting green scales that ran down her neck—and Sid sat alongside Harland to Gaby's surprise. Sid's biomechanical hand was tapping along to the beat of her song. They had been gone for years on a strange adventure and had only recently returned. With hatchlings, which did explain why they weren't on the FireRaven mission.

Alex, Sam, and Kasumi stood off to the side. Alex hugged Sam from behind as her long red, lilac, and now a bit of grey, hair swayed to the music. Kasumi was on Sam's left, her eyes closed, and Gaby knew she was focused on the vibrations of the song. Kyoko, their daughter, was on Sam's right, with Yaha in its sheath on her back. They all held hands with Sam. The soon to be retired Dragonqueen was teary eyed as she continued to stare after the FireRaven. She no doubt prayed for Michael, who much to her chagrin took after her side of the family in terms of adventuring, but with the stubbornness of his dad. Alex smiled at Gaby, knowing what was coming, the change that only those with the Gift and the years of knowing each other could notice. He was holding back tears, for in a few hours there wouldn't be a way back.

But Gaby was fine with all of that. She had come to terms with everything and could admit, at least to herself and Alex in private, that she'd had a happy life. And whatever would happen in a few hours, she would always be there for her friends. Her heart beat hard when Alex's smile grew while he looked around. Beneath the weary eyes, the injuries that made it difficult for him to use Yaha anymore, and the faded scars from countless battles after taking Fionn's place as the 'go-to-hero'—along with Kasumi—Gaby's best friend could smile in true peace. Alex nodded towards the other side of the ampitheater, pointing at something. As she was about to look that way, the riff of the chorus hit and she tightened her grasp on the microphone, as the world became less tangible to her for a moment. She belted out with all her strength the lyrics, harmonizing perfectly with the choir singers. Her voice, after many years, echoed through the air with such force that even inside the FireRaven, halfway through the solar system, her words were heard.

> *C'mon, C'mon, C'mon.*
> *Let us break free from our chains.*
> *C'mon, C'mon, C'mon.*
> *Let us show others the way.*
> *C'mon, C'mon, C'mon.*
> *We're all it takes.*
> *Together we can change,*
> *All the universe.*
> *Let's teach them to fly.*
> *Let our voices be heard.*
> *Across the Universe!*

Gaby looked to where Alex had indicated as the instrumental part of the song gave her a brief break. She saw the familiar green glow coming from beneath a grey hoodie. The man wearing it stood near one of the columns. He raised his head and smiled at her, then winked. Fionn looked exactly the same as the day of their first date at that karaoke bar. And she felt that young again, as her heart almost jumped out of her chest and time slowed for both of them.

Gaby smiled at Fionn, and saw him singing one single word, that made her heart bounce with happiness each time he said that to her, for it meant the time had come.

The same word they said to each other when they began their journey.

The same word that ended the song.

"Always."

About the Author

Ricardo Victoria Uribe (pen name Ricardo Victoria) lives in Toluca, Mexico. He holds a Ph.D. in Design from Loughborough University. Currently he teaches sustainable design at his hometown university. He is a founding member of Inklings Press. He was nominated for the 2016 Sidewise Awards for Alternate History. He has co-authored a book on sustainability explained through science fiction and fantasy, published in 2024 by Luna Press Publishing. He's the author of the science fantasy series "Tempest Blades" composed of 4 books: "The Withered King", "The Cursed Titans", "The Magick of Chaos" and "The Root of Hope".

Ricardo is a fan of anime, 80s' cartoons, Japanese RPG videogames, toys, and mythology. He also likes dogs.